T0078414

The Klingon™

Hamlet

The Restored Klingon Version

Klingon Language Institute
Flourtown, Pennsylvania
1996
www.kli.org

POCKET BOOKS

New York   London   Toronto   Sydney

Hamlet

Prince of Denmark

by

William Shakespeare

restored to the original Klingon™ by
Nick Nicholas and Andrew Strader

edited by Mark Shoulson
with assistance from
Will Martin and d'Armond Speers

layout and design by Lawrence M. Schoen
with assistance from Sarah Ekstrom

A part of the Klingon Shakespeare Restoration Project.
A sponsored project of the Klingon Language Institute

This book is a work of fiction. Names, characters, places and incidents are products of the author's imagination or are used fictitiously. Any resemblance to actual events or locales or persons, living or dead, is entirely coincidental.

The Klingon Language Institute is a nonprofit 501(c)(3) corporation and exists to facilitate the scholarly exploration of the Klingon language and culture. *Klingon*, *Star Trek*, and all related marks are Copyrights and Trademarks of Paramount Pictures. All Rights Reserved. Klingon Language Institute Authorized User.

POCKET BOOKS, a division of Simon & Schuster Inc.
1230 Avenue of the Americas, New York, NY 10020

Originally published in 1996 by the Klingon Language Institute
Illustration copyright © 1995 by Gennie Summers
Klingon translation copyright © 2000 by Paramount Pictures.
All rights reserved.

An earlier edition of this book was published in 1996
by the Klingon Language Institute.

STAR TREK is a registered Trademark of
Paramount Pictures.

A VIACOM COMPANY

This book is published by Pocket Books, a division of
Simon & Schuster Inc., under exclusive license from
Paramount Pictures.

All rights reserved, including the right to reproduce
this book or portions thereof in any form whatsoever.
For information address Pocket Books, 1230 Avenue
of the Americas, New York, NY 10020

ISBN-13: 978-0-671-03578-5
ISBN-10:   0-671-03578-9

First Pocket Books paperback printing February 2000

10 9 8 7 6 5 4 3 2

POCKET and colophon are registered trademarks of Simon & Schuster Inc.

Cover design by Matt Galemmo
Front cover illustration by Phil Foglio

Printed in the U.S.A.

The translators, editors, and officers
of the Klingon Language Institute
wish to thank Paramount Pictures
for boldly going where none had gone
in commissioning the creation of the Klingon language;
thereby setting in motion something truly extraordinary
and quite in keeping with the *Star Trek* legacy.

This volume is dedicated to the memory of Gene Roddenberry.
He may or may not have approved of what we've done,
but we hope he'd have liked it in either case.

Gennie Summers—1994

laDwI'vaD:

naDev qonwI' qab'e' Dalegh:
SeQpIr qab 'IHmoH QuchDaj ghegh.
wIDeltaHvIS nuqaD Qu' Qatlh
'IHmo' 'ej Dojqu'mo' chovnatlh.
vaj navDaq 'ang'eghlaHchu' qab,
'ach Qu'vam ta'laHbe'bej yab.
toH, yabvam Dun wIDelchu'chugh
tugh naDmey maqmo' QopchoH Hugh.
'ach yab potlh law', qabHey potlh puS:
qab yIqImHa', paq neH yIbuS.

To the Reader.

This Figure, that thou seest here put,
  It was for gentle Shakespeare cut;
Wherein the Grauer had a strife
  with Nature, to out-doo the life:
O, could he but haue drawne his wit
  As well in brasse, as he hath hit
His face, the Print would then surpasse
  All, that was ever writ in brasse.
But, since he cannot, Reader, looke
  Not on his Picture, but his Booke.

PREFACE

From its founding in 1992, the Klingon Language Institute has grappled with the warrior's tongue, embracing the willful suspension of disbelief necessary to study an artificial language originally created as little more than a prop. The volume you hold should be ample evidence of Klingon's evolution, from the sound stage to popular culture, from a back lot at Paramount Pictures to Klingon and *Star Trek* fans throughout the world. Working with only a thin grammar and a glossary of some two thousand words the membership of the KLI has studied the language, taught the language, engaged in word play from puns to palindromes, composed original poetry and fiction, translated books of the Bible, and now perhaps the most well known of Shakespeare's plays, *Hamlet*.

I ask that you join us in our suspended disbelief; accept for a moment that this is the original version of the play. Don't concern yourself with temporal anomalies of how you can be reading this play from the future (it never concerned you before, whether in front of the television or at the theatre). A wondrous thing has been created here, a translation (or restoration, as we prefer) that has been labored over, argued about, and finally put before you. Take the time to read it, not just the English text but the corresponding Klingon as well, one never knows when a bit of classical Klingon might not come in handy. And speak it, I pray you, trippingly on the tongue. Surely that's how the Klingons do it.

Lawrence M. Schoen, Ph.D.
KLI Director

FOREWORD

"You have not experienced Shakespeare, until you have read him in the original Klingon." Thus speaks Chancellor Gorkon, in the film *Star Trek VI: The Undiscovered Country*. For some viewers the line produced hearty chuckles and knowing nods. Among others it served as inspiration. This volume is the finished product crafted by just a few from among the inspired. Since its initial penning in 1600, *Hamlet* has earned the distinction of being one of the most often quoted works in the English language, second only to the Bible, and has been translated into spoken and written languages worldwide. Still a matter of much debate among Shakespearean scholars, we have taken the study of the melancholy Dane and his words one step more. One step in a different direction, at the very least.

It is our hope that this volume of *Hamlet* will be but the first in a growing collection of Shakespeare's works, returned to their "original" state. Be it a showpiece on a mantle, a bookend, or a well and often read volume, it is our wish that it brings you and yours enjoyment.

Sarah Ekstrom
KSRP Coordinator

INTRODUCTION

It is with great pride that we bring to the peoples of the Federation this edition of the works of the great Klingon dramatist, Wil'yam Shex'pir. It is with particular pride that we start this series with one of the cornerstones of Shex'pir's achievement, a play that both questions and encapsulates the very essence of being Klingon: the Tragedy of Khamlet, Son of the Emperor of Kronos.

Wil'yam Shex'pir is a figure of vital importance in Klingon culture. He was an astute observer of both Klingon character and Klingon politics. It has rightly been said that it is impossible for an alien to appreciate who Klingons really are, unless they have come to understand Shex'pir. At a time when relations between the Federation and the Empire have reached a certain degree of normalization, and when citizens of the Federation are increasingly seeking to know more about Klingons and their way of life (a need regrettably responded to by much misinformation from certain quarters), we are satisfied to present this work as a contribution towards better understanding and respect between our two races.

Wil'yam Shex'pir's biographical details are not important; what matters is that he lived at a time of crisis for the Klingon Empire; a crisis which has continued and escalated up to the present day. Almost all the problems confronting Klingons today have their origin in the time when Shex'pir lived. Shex'pir was aware of these problems, often long before most others, and he addressed them in his plays. These were acclaimed from the beginning, in the mess-halls and actor-bars of the Empire: these plays struck a responsive chord in the hearts of many Klingons. Given the subsequent political troubles in the Empire, these plays are read and heard by Klingons today all the more keenly.

It is regrettable that, during the years when the Empire and Federation were at war—a war the Federation fought on the propaganda front even more keenly than on the battlefield—certain individuals resorted to crude forgeries of Shex'pir, claiming him as a conveniently remote mediaeval Terran, a certain Willem Shekispeore, and hoping by this falsification of history to discredit the achievements of Klingon culture. We will not dwell on this unfortunate episode, although we are dismayed that this belief continues and persists amongst many in the Federation to this day. In this edition, we juxtapose the Klingon original with the most prevalent of the versions of "Amlet" purported to have been written by "Shekispeore." We think that the quality of the two plays—on the one hand, the spontaneous, direct, vibrant verse of Khamlet, and on the other, the flaccid, ponderous, convoluted meanderings of "Amlet"—speak for themselves. Those who persist in being Doubting Thomazeds would do well to consult the Central Federation Mediaeval Archival Database on the meagre, unconvincing amount of information extant on the existence of this Shekispeore, and compare it to the testimonials of the Declassified Approved-For-Aliens pre-Khitomer Personnel Rolls on Wil'yam Shex'pir.

It remains a fact, though, that these forgeries were as thorough as they were malicious: gigabytes of allegedly Industrial Age back-dated so-called Shekispeorian Criticism were fabricated, and the works disseminated as part of a well-organized campaign. This campaign appears to have succeeded far beyond its initiators' anticipations. For better or for worse, works like Amlet, for all their crudity, have acquired a certain resonance amongst citizens of the Federation, and Terrans in particular. This is no doubt due to their pseudo-mediaevalist parochial appeal, which has rendered these incisive masterpieces of sociopolitical analysis into innocuous picturesque period pieces—a genre favored on Terra (and Betazed) much more than on planets like Vulcan and the Human colonies.

This has had the interesting side-effect that passages in the two plays, pretty much identical textually, are interpreted in wildly differing ways by the two cultures. The differences between how Khamlet is read on Earth and Kronos are an excellent illustration of the different values of Klingon and Federation society; and a careful examination of this should prove rewarding to anyone interested in understanding Klingons better. To assist the novice reader whose Klingon is still not up to scratch for such a challenging text, or who is not as familiar with Klingon ethos as he might be, we have provided endnotes detailing the major discrepancies between the two texts. In this introduction we will refer to the cultural differences on a more general level.

Shex'pir wrote two major types of plays. His Classical plays follow the norms of traditional Klingon comedy (**lut tlhaQ**) and history (**qun lut**). The characters by and large follow the cultural norms of the old warrior society, and are usually intended as straightforward entertainment, although Shex'pir's character portrayal and command of verse are unequalled by other dramatists. These plays include *K'oryolakhnesh* (Coriolanus), *Khenriy Vagh* (Henry V), *Yulyush K'ayshar* (Julius Caesar), *The Confusion Is Great Because of Nothing* (Much Ado About Nothing), and what is frequently regarded as Shex'pir's greatest achievement, *Tityush Ardronik'ush* (Titus Andronicus).

In his 'Problem Plays,' on the other hand, Shex'pir departs from the conventions of the Klingon stage, and casts a critical eye on Klingon society, at both the individual level and in its relations with other civilizations. The Problem Plays enjoy a less wide audience; they are, as Khamlet himself would say, "stuffed to'baj legs to the general." Many Klingons find these plays confusing, wordy, and irritating; they also believe the plays spend too much time discussing aliens. But these same plays enjoy high repute amongst the upper classes of Klingon society, and the diplomatic corps. They include *Romyo and Djulyet* (Romeo and Juliet), *The Trader from Delviy Adu* (The Merchant of Venice), *Lir the King* (King Lear), *One Dreams in the Middle of the Hot Season* (Midsummer Night's Dream), and the play the reader currently has on his viewscreen.

To come to this particular play: *Khamlet* is widely regarded amongst Klingons as a problematic play. This is because of the daring innovations by Shex'pir on the conventions of the genre of the revenge play (**bortaS lut**). In the Klingon tradition of the revenge play, *Khamlet* would have been a simple affair: Klaw'diyush should have been dispatched with little ceremony ten minutes into the play. This does not occur. Instead, Khamlet spends a positively un-Klingon amount of time talking about what he should do, rather than getting anything done. Most Klingons cannot make head or tail of this; in some parts of the hinterlands of the Empire, *Khamlet* has even been banned from performance, as liable to corrupt the youth.

It is only the more perceptive Klingons who, like General Chang (may the Black Fleet commend him!) realize that the play is not about revenge at all. It certainly is not about the ghost of Khamlet Senior, who becomes almost an incidental figure. What the play deals with, rather, and what draws real feelings of dread from its audience, is the threat of the Empire becoming 'soft' and ineffectual, and the Klingon people becoming alienated from their traditional warlike virtues.

In effect, *Khamlet*, with its fawning courtiers, its insistence on ceremony, its healthy *Realpolitik*, and its underhand dealing (a world where Klaw'diyush survives a direct challenge from Layertesh by flattery rather than ritually disemboweling the offender; where the opinion of someone as garrulous as Polonyush can be taken seriously; and where Houses like that of Duras can pretty much ignore Imperial authority) is nothing less than a nightmare scenario, a chilling portrayal of a malaise and decay so pervasive that it infects the hero himself. And this is the crux of the play. Even the ending, where the slaughter of the dishonorable is supposed to signal the restoration of Klingon order, leaves a bitter after-taste: Khamlet exacts his revenge almost by accident, and Vortibrash Junior is as much an advocate of *Realpolitik* as Klaw'diyush before him. The restoration of order calls for a king like Khamlet Senior, or Vortibrash Senior, who followed the old ways and believed in honor. No such salvation is forthcoming for Khamlet's Kronos, a planet left to an uncertain future; and many Klingons, from Chang onwards, have feared that Khamlet's Kronos is too close to our own contemporary Kronos for comfort.

In a real sense, with its oppressive and relentless atmosphere, *Khamlet* is more akin to *The Trial* or *1984* in Terran literature than to "Amlet." And significantly, the problems addressed in *Khamlet* are still foremost in the minds of the honorable in the Empire. It is a topic which Shex'pir frequently returns to in his plays—even his putatively 'Problem-free' plays. There can be no better summary of his thinking than that in *The Confusion is Great because of Nothing*: "But manhood is melted into curtsies, valor into compliment, and men are only turned into tongue, and trim ones too." (IV 1.317-319)

The malaise in Klingon society depicted in *Khamlet* pervades all levels of society; from the artful Klaw'diyush and the tedious anagram-puns of Polonyush, through to even the lowest commoners, the equivocating gravediggers. With this in mind, the gravedigger scene is much different from the 'light relief' expected in traditional tragedies. It is no longer funny, but almost absurdist—and deeply disconcerting, as the audience realizes that, if not even a "dirter" can speak with the directness required of honor, Khamlet's world is in deep turmoil. The real light relief in the play comes with Oshrik in V 2; his idiom, drenched with faddish loans from Federation Standard, can be safely held up to ridicule, since one would well expect a courtier to be corrupted. (Some scholars would contend Oshrik's language can still be heard in the Officer's Mess of the Klingon Military Academy!)

Khamlet is set in the 23rd century, although the fine details of the technologies and aliens mentioned are not always consistent. All the aliens figuring in the play are now familiar to members of the Federation, although the Ferengi, long familiar to the Klingons whose space they border, were only encountered by the Federation as recently as 2364. It would have been unwise for Shex'pir, however, to allow the political situation in *Khamlet* to reflect that of the contemporary Empire too closely. (The House of Duras was rather insignificant in the 22nd century; its place in the play acquired political poignancy only fairly recently, during the Klingon Civil War.) For this reason, the political situation in *Khamlet* is actually that of pre-Kahless Kronos, with rival houses able to effectively threaten a king who was more a *primus inter pares* than an absolute leader. The parallels to the Interregnum Empire are obvious, but clearly could not have been stated openly. Note that the pre-Kahless politics of the play does not prevent the characters from invoking the name of Kahless frequently, just as the recent restoration of Kahless The Unforgettable to the throne as a ceremonial figure has not yet had a significant effect on Klingon politics.

Relations between the Empire and the Romulans have always fluctuated wildly, from the 2268 detente to the Khitomer massacre of 2346, and the recent involvement of the Romulans in the Klingon Civil Wars. In the unspecified time-frame of *Khamlet*, the Klingons and the Romulans are on amicable terms, and Khamlet appears to have studied at Vulcan as part of a cultural exchange. (This drags the figure of Khamlet down into the 'malaise' of the play from its very onset.) There are in fact several parallels between *Khamlet* and *Yulyush K'ayshar*, which was written by Shex'pir during the detente as a tribute to the Romulan Ambassador. The areas of the Klingon hinterlands who object to the play's morals also cite its shows of amity with the Romulans as reason to distrust the play.

The disparities between Klingon and Federation culture are such that it is usually when Federation audiences think "Amlet" is mad that Klingon audiences think he has momentarily come to his senses. Such instances include the murder of Polonyush, Khamlet's overt flirting with Ovelya, and—as instances of "madness with method in 't"—some of his soliloquies. A good illustration of these cultural disparities lies in Act III Scene 1. For both Klingon and Federation audiences, something about the scene does not make sense; Khamlet/Amlet starts acting in an inexplicable manner, and to explain this it is usually assumed that he has caught a glimpse of the King and Polonyush spying on him, and he changes his behaviour to play up to them accordingly. In the Terran version, this turn in his actions comes right after his soliloquy, when he coldly dismisses Ofelea. To Klingons, his behaviour against the suddenly meek, apologetic Ovelya makes all the sense in the world. What doesn't make sense is the preceding soliloquy, which is explained by Klingon scholars as Khamlet giving the King and Polonyush what they want—a 'mad' Khamlet—although there is enough meaning and honor left in the speech that the King and Polonyush are not fooled.

It has caused Klingon social analysts no end of mirth to realize how highly Terrans prize the "To be or not to be" soliloquy; if Klingons had to single out one soliloquy above all others, it would be "'Tis now the very witching time of night," at the end of III 2, a speech which expresses the Klingon drive towards revenge masterfully. It is widely believed that this very cultural incongruity is what made General Chang (may he gain many victories in Krit'u!) quote the "To be or not to be" soliloquy so frequently; and which has succeeded in throwing Terrans 'off the track' in their attempt to understand Klingon culture for decades.

But it is important to bear in mind that *Khamlet*'s soliloquies are not intended as tomfoolery or slapstick—though the Act III Scene 1 soliloquy in particular is often performed as such. Their premise is sound enough that they won't be instantly rejected by a Klingon audience; it is their tendency to belabor the point, and to go on just a bit too long, that succeed in causing a deep feeling of unease.

There are many other illuminating parts of the play which we will let the Federation reader uncover himself. Read this work, Human, and learn.

Bureau of External Relations, Kronos—as translated by Nick Nicholas

Hamlet
Prince of Denmark

HAMLET,
Prince of Denmark

DRAMATIS PERSONAE

CLAUDIUS, *King of Denmark*
HAMLET, *son to the late, and nephew to the present King*
POLONIUS, *Lord Chamberlain*
HORATIO, *friend to Hamlet*
LAERTES, *son to Polonius*
VOLTIMAND
CORNELIUS
ROSENCRANTZ
GUILDENSTERN
OSRIC
A Gentleman
A Priest
MARCELLUS
BERNARDO
FRANCISCO, *a soldier*
REYNALDO, *servant to Polonius*
Five Players
Two Clowns, *grave-diggers*
FORTINBRAS, *prince of Norway*
A Captain
English Ambassadors
A Lord
A Soldier
Two Messengers
A Servant *to Horatio*
Danes
Ghost *of Hamlet's Father*

GERTRUDE, *queen of Denmark, and mother to Hamlet*
OPHELIA, *daughter to Polonius*
Non-Speaking: *Lords, Ladies, Officers, Soldiers, Sailors, and other Attendants*
SCENE: *Denmark.*

ACT I
SCENE I *Elsinore. A platform before the castle.*
[*FRANCISCO at his post. Enter to him BERNARDO*]

Bernardo	Who's there?
Francisco	Nay, answer me: stand, and unfold yourself.
Bernardo	Long live the king!
Francisco	Bernardo?
Bernardo	He.
Francisco	You come most carefully upon your hour.
Bernardo	'Tis now struck twelve; get thee to bed, Francisco.
Francisco	For this relief much thanks: 'tis bitter cold, And I am sick at heart.

Qo'noS ta'puq,
Hamlet lotlut.

LUTVAD GHOTVAM LUDALU'

TLHAW'DIYUS, *Qo'noS ta' ghaH*
HAMLET, *ben ta' puqloD; DaHjaj ta' loDnI'puqloD je ghaH*
POLONYUS, *Qang ghaH*
HOREY'SO, *Hamlet jup ghaH*
LAYERTES, *polonyuS puqloD ghaH*
VOLTIMAD
QORNELYUS
ROSENQATLH
GHILDESTEN
'OSRIQ
wa' 'utlh
wa' lalDanyaS
MARSE'LUS
BERNARDO
VERANCHISQO, *mang ghaH*
REYNALDO, *polonyuS toy'wI' ghaH*
vagh DawI'pu'
cha' tlhaQwI'; *molwI' Da*
VORTIBRAS, *DuraS tuq pIn be'nI'puqloD ghaH*
wa' HoD
tera' Duypu'
wa' yaS
wa' mang
cha' QumwI'
Horey'So wa' toy'wI'
QonoSnganpu'
Hamlet vav lomqa'

GHERTLHUD, *Qo'noS ta'be', Hamlet SoS je ghaH*
'OVELYA, *polonyuS puqbe' ghaH*
jawloDpu', jawbe'pu', yaSpu', mangpu', yo'mangpu', latlh toy'wI'pu' je; jatlhbe' chaH
LUT DAQ: Qo'noS

LUT 'AY' WA'

LUT 'AY'HOM WA' *tlhIn. ta'qach'a' tlhop 'avwI'Daq jen.*
['avtaH VERANCHISQO. ghaHDaq 'el BERNARDO]

bernarDo	chol 'Iv?
veranchISqo	Qo', jIH HIjang. yItaDchoH 'ej yIngu'egh.
bernarDo	taHjaj wo'!
veranchISqo	bernarDo?
bernarDo	jIHbej.
veranchISqo	bImatlhba', qarqu'mo' bIcholmeH poHlIj.
bernarDo	qaSpu' ramjep. QongDaq yIghoS, veranchISqo.
veranchISqo	qatlho'bej, Qu'wIjvo' choSonmo'. bIrqu'. 'ej roplaw' tIqwIj.

Bernardo	Have you had quiet guard?
Francisco	Not a mouse stirring.
Bernardo	Well, good night. If you do meet Horatio and Marcellus, The rivals of my watch, bid them make haste.
Francisco	I think I hear them. Stand, ho! Who is there?

[*Enter HORATIO and MARCELLUS*]

Horatio	Friends to this ground.
Marcellus	And liegemen to the Dane.
Francisco	Give you good night.
Marcellus	O, farewell, honest soldier: Who hath reliev'd you?
Francisco	Bernardo has my place. Give you good night. [*Exit*]
Marcellus	Holla! Bernardo!
Bernardo	Say, What, is Horatio there?
Horatio	A piece of him.
Bernardo	Welcome, Horatio—welcome, good Marcellus.
Marcellus	What, has this thing appear'd again to-night?
Bernardo	I have seen nothing.
Marcellus	Horatio says 'tis but our fantasy, And will not let belief take hold of him Touching this dreaded sight, twice seen of us: Therefore I have entreated him along With us to watch the minutes of this night; That if again this apparition come, He may approve our eyes and speak to it.
Horatio	Tush, tush, 'twill not appear.
Bernardo	Sit down awhile; And let us once again assail your ears, That are so fortified against our story What we have two nights seen.
Horatio	Well, sit we down, And let us hear Bernardo speak of this.
Bernardo	Last night of all, When yon same star that's westward from the pole Had made his course to illume that part of heaven Where now it burns, Marcellus and myself, The bell then beating one,—

[*Enter Ghost*]

Marcellus	Peace, break thee off; look, where it comes again!
Bernardo	In the same figure, like the king that's dead.

bernarDo	bI'avtaHvIS jot'a'?
veranchISqo	vIHbe' je ghew.
bernarDo	vaj maj. Qapla'.
	Horey'So quv, marSe'luS je Daghomchugh—
	jI'avtaHvIS qochma' chaH—vaj tImoDmoH.
veranchISqo	SuH, chaH vIQoylaw'. 'eH, yItaD! chol 'Iv?
	['el HOREY'SO, MARSE'LUS je]
Horey'So	qo'vam juppu'.
marSe'luS	Qo'noS pIn'a' lobwI' je.
veranchISqo	tlhIHvaD Qapla'.
marSe'luS	Qapla', SuvwI' yuDHa'.
	DuSonta' 'Iv?
veranchISqo	Qu'vaD mucho' bernarDo.
	Qapla'.
	[mej]
marSe'luS	SuH! SuH! bernarDo!
bernarDo	toH, yIja':
	SaH'a' Horey'So?
Horey'So	SaHlaw' 'ay'Daj neH.
bernarDo	nuqneH, Horey'So QaQ. nuqneH, marSe'luS.
Horey'So	qaStaHvIS ramvam, narghqa"a' HoSDo'Hey?
bernarDo	paghna' vIleghpu'.
marSe'luS	Sunaj neH ja' Horey'So. ghaH jon qechvetlh
	'e' botqu' je ghaH, qa'Hey Dojqu"e'
	cha'logh wIleghpu'bogh Harbe'taHvIS.
	vaj naDev ramvam tupmey 'avlI'meH,
	vItlhejmoHpu'. vaj cholqa'chugh HoSDo'Hey,
	mInDu'maj 'ollaH ghaH, 'ej qa'vaD jatlhlaH.
Horey'So	wejpuH. narghbe'ba' bIH.
bernarDo	toH, loQ yIba'.
	'elbe'meH lutmaj, teS Surchem DarIHlaw'.
	vaj bIH DIHIvqa'meH, wanI' wIleghbogh,
	qaStaHvIS cha' ramjep, wIja'.
Horey'So	maba'.
	'ej maHvaD ghu'vam ja'choHchu' bernarDo.
bernarDo	qaStaHvIS wa'Hu' ram,
	lengDI' QuvHov poS yuQvetlh, 'ej, DaH SepDaq
	wovmoHbogh, bochmeH ghoSpu'DI' lengwI';
	naDev ma'avtaHvIS marSe'luS jIH je,
	'ej wa'logh Qoy'lu'DI'—
	['el lomqa']
marSe'luS	bIjatlh 'e' mev! peqIm! DaH cholqa' bIH!
bernarDo	Heghpu'bogh ta'ma' rurmeH chenta' bIH.

Marcellus	Thou art a scholar; speak to it, Horatio.
Bernardo	Looks it not like the king? mark it, Horatio.
Horatio	Most like—it harrows me with fear and wonder.
Bernardo	It would be spoke to.
Marcellus	Question it, Horatio.

Horatio	What art thou, that usurp'st this time of night,
	Together with that fair and warlike form
	In which the majesty of buried Denmark
	Did sometimes march? by heaven I charge thee, speak!
Marcellus	It is offended.
Bernardo	See, it stalks away!
Horatio	Stay! speak, speak! I charge thee, speak!

[*Exit Ghost*]

Marcellus	'Tis gone, and will not answer.
Bernardo	How now, Horatio! you tremble and look pale:
	Is not this something more than fantasy?
	What think you on't?
Horatio	Before my God, I might not this believe
	Without the sensible and true avouch
	Of mine own eyes.
Marcellus	Is it not like the king?
Horatio	As thou art to thyself:
	Such was the very armour he had on
	When he the ambitious Norway combated;
	So frown'd he once when, in an angry parle,
	He smote the sledded Polacks on the ice.
	'Tis strange.
Marcellus	Thus twice before, and just at this dead hour,
	With martial stalk hath he gone by our watch.
Horatio	In what particular thought to work I know not;
	But in the gross and scope of my opinion,
	This bodes some strange eruption to our state.
Marcellus	Good now, sit down, and tell me, he that knows,
	Why this same strict and most observant watch
	So nightly toils the subject of the land;
	And why such daily cast of brazen cannon,
	And foreign mart for implements of war;
	Why such impress of shipwrights, whose sore task
	Does not divide the Sunday from the week;
	What might be toward, that this sweaty haste
	Doth make the night joint-labourer with the day:
	Who is't that can inform me?
Horatio	That can I;
	At least, the whisper goes so. Our last king,
	Whose image even but now appear'd to us,

marSe'luS	HaDwI' SoH. bIHvaD vay' yIjatlh, Horey'So.
bernarDo	ta' rurqu' bIH, qar'a'? yIqIm, Horey'So.
Horey'So	rurqu'bej bIH. mumerqu' 'ej mubItmoH.
bernarDo	bIHvaD jatlh vay' DaH neHlaw'.
marSe'luS	'eH, Horey'So. bIHvaD yIjatlh.
Horey'So	ram repvam, vIDbogh porghvetlh 'IH'e' je, ben yItmeH lo'bogh Qo'noS ta' webHa' wImolpu'bogh, boDoQta', HattaHvIS. vaj nuq tlhIH jay'? ghuy'cha' Sara: pejatlh!
marSe'luS	bIH mawlu'law'.
bernarDo	SuH! Haw'meH moDchoH bIH.
Horey'So	peloS! pejatlh! pejatlh! Sara: pejatlh!
	[*mej lomqa'*]
marSe'luS	DaH Haw'ta', 'ej jangQo'.
bernarDo	nuqneH, Horey'So? DaH bIchIS. bIQomlaw'. wa'Hu' manaj neH DaH 'e' DaHar'a'? toH, vuDlIj nuq?
Horey'So	jI'Iprup jay': wanI'vam vIHarQo', 'olbe'chugh tu'chu'bogh 'ej vItbogh mInwIj.
marSe'luS	ta'ma' lurur, qar'a'?
Horey'So	bIrur'egh je! DuraS pIn tlhIvqu' Hay'taHvIS je ghaH, yoDSutvetlh'e' tuQ. qejmeH qabvetlh 'ang ghaH, chuchDaq yoDDuj qInSaya qIpDI' je, QeHtaHvIS ja'chuq. Hujqu'.
marSe'luS	qaStaHvIS ramjepna' tup qar, DaH wejlogh vID 'ej nujuSpu' ghaH, ma'avtaHvIS.
Horey'So	qechwIj vIchavnISbogh vIwIvlaHbe'. 'ach nom jIwuqnISchugh jIqelchu'pa', vaj wo'vaD qaS Qugh taQ 'e' pIHmoHlaw'.
marSe'luS	toH, DaH peba', 'ej ja'choH Sovbogh vay': qatlh wo' rewbe'pu', negh je vumnISmoH yepbogh 'ej SaHnISqu'moHbogh ram Qu'vam, qaSDI' Hoch ram? 'ej qaStaHvIS Hoch pem, qatlh, chenmeH may'morgh, baS lutetmoHlu'? qatlh, veS mIqta'mey je'meH, novvaD mechlu'? 'ej qatlh Duj chenmoHwI' lumuvmoHqu'lu'? pavqu'mo' Qu'chaj, chaHvaD Hatlaw' len. DaH vummeH pemvaD jIjnIS je ramjep, moDmo' Doy'wI'pu'. Hochvam chavnISlu', qaSbeHmo' nuq? 'oH QIjlaH 'Iv?
Horey'So	SuH, jIH. toH, joS lutlhuplu'bogh vIja'qa'laH. wanI' DaSov: DaH maHvaD narghlaw'pu'bogh

Was, as you know, by Fortinbras of Norway,
Thereto prick'd on by a most emulate pride,
Dar'd to the combat; in which our valiant Hamlet—
For so this side of our known world esteem'd him—
Did slay this Fortinbras; who, by a seal'd compact,
Well ratified by law and heraldry,
Did forfeit, with his life, all those his lands,
Which he stood seiz'd of, to the conqueror:
Against the which, a moiety competent
Was gaged by our king; which had return'd
To the inheritance of Fortinbras,
Had he been vanquisher; as, by the same cov'nant,
And carriage of the article design'd,
His fell to Hamlet. Now, sir, young Fortinbras,
Of unimproved mettle hot and full,
Hath in the skirts of Norway, here and there,
Shark'd up a list of lawless resolutes,
For food and diet, to some enterprise
That hath a stomach in't: which is no other—
As it doth well appear unto our state—
But to recover of us, by strong hand,
And terms compulsative, those foresaid lands
So by his father lost: and this, I take it,
Is the main motive of our preparations,
The source of this our watch, and the chief head
Of this post-haste and romage in the land.

Bernardo	I think it be no other, but e'en so:

Well may it sort, that this portentous figure
Comes armed through our watch; so like the king
That was and is the question of these wars.

Horatio	A mote it is to trouble the mind's eye.

In the most high and palmy state of Rome,
A little ere the mightiest Julius fell,
The graves stood tenantless, and the sheeted dead
Did squeak and gibber in the Roman streets:
As, stars with trains of fire and dews of blood,
Disasters in the sun; and the moist star,
Upon whose influence Neptune's empire stands,
Was sick almost to doomsday with eclipse:
And even the like precurse of fierce events,—
As harbingers preceding still the fates
And prologue to the omen coming on,—
Have heaven and earth together demonstrated
Unto our climatures and countrymen.—
But soft, behold! lo, where it comes again!

[Re-enter Ghost]

I'll cross it, though it blast me—Stay, illusion!
If thou hast any sound, or use of voice,
Speak to me:
If there be any good thing to be done,
That may to thee do ease and grace to me,
Speak to me:
If thou art privy to thy country's fate,
Which, happily, foreknowing may avoid,

ben ta'ma' Hay'meH qaDta' DuraS pIn,
vortIbraS, ghaH tungHa'mo' Hembogh DujDaj.
'ej Hay'DI', vortIbraSvetlh tlhIvqu' HoH
ta' Hamlet yoHqu'—yoHqu' ghaH, 'e' noH
mIchvam Hoch ngan. vaj ra'mo' may' mab'e'
lu'olchu'pu'bogh chutmey, batlh lurDech je,
yInDaj ghajHa'pu'DI', Hoch SepDaj'e'
nIteb ben charghbogh ghaH, ghajHa'nIS je,
'ej SuqnIS may' QapwI"e'. mabchajvaD
rapbogh Sep yoSmey SuDruplI' je ta'ma'.
'ej SuqmeH vortIbraSvaD yaHnIS bIH,
chaq lujchugh ta'. vaj ra'mo' may'chaj mab,
'ej poQmo' ghItlhvetlh chut lulajpu'bogh,
HamletvaD yaHnIS SepDaj'e'. toH, qaH:
vortIbraS Qup'e' tujmoHmo' 'ej tebmo'
lagh toDuj'e' wej qeqmoHchu'bogh poH,
yoSvamDaq yoSvetlhDaq je, Sepchaj veHDaq,
chutmey pabbe'taHbogh vIDwI' tlhoQ'e'
nom boSta'. Soj, jajHuch je SuqmeH chaH,
HuH Qu'vaD HuHchaj qu'moHta' QupwI'.
'ej Qu'chaj ra'bogh ghovchu' wo'maj qum:
raDmo' rojmabDaj, HoSmo' je mangghomDaj,
Sep'e' ghajHa'bogh vavDaj Suqqa' neHba'.
'ej qeqmeymaj meq potlh, ram Qu'maj mung je,
wo'majDaq moDbogh mISHey Hal je 'oHlaw'
wanI'vam'e'.

bernarDo

toH 'oHba'. 'a ghaytan taQbe' wanI',
ma'avtaHvIS nucholDI' San HoSDo'Hey,
nuH qengtaHvIS. ta' rur, 'ej ben, DaHjaj je,
veS qeqvam meq ghaH ta'vetlh'e', qar'a'?

Horey'So

lam 'ay'Hom neH bIH. 'a yab mIn lunuQlaH.
tIQtaHvIS, chepbogh romuluS wo' quvDaq
poSchoH Hoch mol, loQ pumpa' yulyuS Dunqu'.
'ej chImchu'. romuluS vengHeDaq jawchoH
'ej jach lom'e' wej luqatHa'lu'bogh.
lIy tlha' chal qulmey tIqqu', SISbogh 'Iw je.
pemHovDaq qIj maQmIgh. 'ej Hov QIbmo'
ropmo' bIQ'a'mey wuvmoHbogh maS'e',
Hargh maQmIgh maqlaw' 'oH. ben mIchmajvaD,
wo'maj nganpu'vaD je, wanI'mey qu'
nungwI'mey rap, San QeH pIHmoHtaHwI' je,
wa'leS lotna' lIHwI' je 'angpu' je
jIjrupbogh chal, ngeHbej je—
'a SuH! peqIm! DaH cholqa'!

['elqa' lomqa']

yIt 'e' vInISrup, tugh muSangchugh je.
loS, Dolqoq! QIch, ghoghlaH joq DaHutlhbe'chugh,
HIjatlh!
bIjotmeH SoH, 'ej naD vISuqmeH jIH,
vay' QaQ vIchav DaH 'e' DapoQqangchugh,
HIjatlh!
wo'maj nem Qugh DaSovchugh, vaj, SoHvo'
leSSov wISuqDI', Do' wIbotlaHchugh,

O, speak!
Or if thou hast uphoarded in thy life
Extorted treasure in the womb of earth,
For which, they say, you spirits oft walk in death,
Speak of it: [*Cock crows*]—stay, and speak!—Stop it, Marcellus.

Marcellus	Shall I strike at it with my partisan?
Horatio	Do, if it will not stand.
Bernardo	'Tis here!
Horatio	'Tis here!

Marcellus   'Tis gone!   [*Exit Ghost*]
We do it wrong, being so majestical,
To offer it the show of violence;
For it is, as the air, invulnerable,
And our vain blows malicious mockery.

Bernardo   It was about to speak, when the cock crew.

Horatio   And then it started like a guilty thing
Upon a fearful summons. I have heard,
The cock, that is the trumpet to the morn,
Doth with his lofty and shrill-sounding throat
Awake the god of day; and at his warning,
Whether in sea or fire, in earth or air,
The extravagant and erring spirit hies
To his confine: and of the truth herein
This present object made probation.

Marcellus   It faded on the crowing of the cock.
Some say that ever 'gainst that season comes
Wherein our Saviour's birth is celebrated,
The bird of dawning singeth all night long:
And then, they say, no spirit dares stir abroad;
The nights are wholesome; then no planets strike,
No fairy takes, nor witch hath power to charm;
So hallow'd and so gracious is the time.

Horatio   So have I heard,and do in part believe it.
But, look, the morn, in russet mantle clad,
Walks o'er the dew of yon high eastern hill:
Break we our watch up: and, by my advice,
Let us impart what we have seen to-night
Unto young Hamlet; for, upon my life,
This spirit, dumb to us, will speak to him:
Do you consent we shall acquaint him with it,
As needful in our loves, fitting our duty?

Marcellus   Let's do't, I pray; and I this morning know
Where we shall find him most conveniently.

[*Exeunt*]

SCENE II   *A room of state in the castle.*
[*Enter KING CLAUDIUS, QUEEN GERTRUDE, HAMLET,
POLONIUS, LAERTES, VOLTIMAND, CORNELIUS, Lords,
and Attendants*]

HIjatlh!
pagh, yavmaj chorDaq mIp DanIHta'bogh
DaSo'moHchugh DaboSDI', HattaHvIS—
'ej pIj wanI'vetIhmo' SuyItnIS, qa'pu',
SuHeghpu'DI'—vaj HeS yIja'. [jach jajlo'ghogh Qa'] yIratlh!
yIja'! marSe'luS, yIt ghaH 'e' yImev!

marSe'luS	SuH, vIqIp'a'? betleHwIj vIlo''a'?
Horey'So	yevQo'chugh, vaj yIqIp.
bernarDo	naDev!
Horey'So	naDev!

marSe'luS

loj rIntaH! [mej lomqa']
nurna' Suvwl' ghall. vaj wImawpu'bej,
yolqoq wInIDmo': muD rur, rIQlaHbe'mo'.
wIqIpDI' 'ej malujDI', ghaH wIvaq. natlh.

bernarDo

jatlhrup ghaH, jachDI' Qa'.

Horey'So

'ej jachDI' 'oH,
DIvwI' Da, yay'mo'. ghIjlaw' pIch jabbI'ID.
HoSbogh ghogh jenqu' chu'DI' jajlo' Qa''e',
pomey chuS'ughHey'e', reH vem pem qa'.
'ej ghumDI' 'oH, bIQ'a'Daq, qulDaq joq,
chalDaq joq, ghorDaq joq lutu'lu'chugh je,
vaj tugh bIghHa'meychajDaq moDqu'nIS
lengbogh 'ej Hopbogh qa'pu'. 'e' vIQoy.
'ej DaH 'e' toblaw' Dolvetlh.

marSe'luS

ngab, jachDI' jajlo' Qa'. 'ej ngoDvam ja'lu':
qaSbeHDI' QI'lop poH, yo' qIj mangpu'
DIquvmoHrupDI', jach po Ha'DIbaHvetlh
qaStaHvIS rammey naQ. 'ej jachtaHvIS,
ghorDaq lengQo' Hoch qa' net Har: ngIlbe' chaH.
pIvmoH ram muD. 'ej SIghlaHbe'taH yuQmey.
jonbe'nIS Sor HoSDo'. luj qa' SeHwI'pu';
quvqu'mo' poHvetlh potlh, 'ej Dunqu'mo'.

Horey'So

vIQoypu' je 'ej loQ vIHar. 'a SuH:
nIH HuDvetlh jen rambIQDaq yItlaw'taHvIS,
ngup Doq tuQ po. ma'avtaH 'e' wImev.
SaqeS je: Hamlet QupvaD Hoch wIleghbogh,
qaStaHvIS ram, wItey'. jI'Iprupbej:
HamletvaD jatlhrup maHvaD tambogh qa'.
ghaHvaD wISovmoH, vangmoHmo' wo' Qu'maj,
'ej 'utmoHmo' parHa'ghachmaj. Qoch'a'?

marSe'luS

wIruch, Satlhob. 'ej ghaH wItu'meH DaqDaj,
qaStaHvIS po, vISov. SIbI' maghoS.

[mej chaH]

LUT 'AY'HOM CHA' ta'qach'a' qumpa'.
['el TLHAW'DIyuS TA', GHERTLHUD TA'BE', HAMLET, POLONYUS,
LAYERTES, VOLTIMAD, QORNELYUS, jawpu', toy'wI'pu' je]

Claudius	Though yet of Hamlet our dear brother's death

Though yet of Hamlet our dear brother's death
The memory be green; and that it us befitted
To bear our hearts in grief, and our whole kingdom
To be contracted in one brow of woe;
Yet so far hath discretion fought with nature
That we with wisest sorrow think on him,
Together with remembrance of ourselves.
Therefore our sometime sister, now our queen,
The imperial jointress to this warlike state,
Have we, as 'twere with a defeated joy,—
With an auspicious and a dropping eye,
With mirth in funeral, and with dirge in marriage,
In equal scale weighing delight and dole,—
Taken to wife: nor have we herein barr'd
Your better wisdoms,—which have freely gone
With this affair along: for all, our thanks.
Now follows that you know, young Fortinbras,
Holding a weak supposal of our worth,
Or thinking by our late dear brother's death
Our state to be disjoint and out of frame,
Colleagued with the dream of his advantage,
He hath not fail'd to pester us with message,
Importing the surrender of those lands
Lost by his father, with all bonds of law,
To our most valiant brother. So much for him.—
Now for ourself, and for this time of meeting:
Thus much the business is:—we have here writ
To Norway, uncle of young Fortinbras,—
Who, impotent and bed-rid, scarcely hears
Of this his nephew's purpose,—to suppress
His further gait herein; in that the levies,
The lists, and full proportions, are all made
Out of his subject:—and we here dispatch
You, good Cornelius, and you, Voltimand,
For bearers of this greeting to old Norway;
Giving to you no further personal power
To business with the king more than the scope
Of these delated articles allow.
Farewell; and let your haste commend your duty.

Cornelius &   In that and all things will we show our duty.
Voltimand

Claudius   We doubt it nothing: heartily farewell.

[*Exeunt VOLTIMAND and CORNELIUS*]

And now, Laertes, what's the news with you?
You told us of some suit; what is't, Laertes?
You cannot speak of reason to the Dane,
And lose your voice: what wouldst thou beg, Laertes,
That shall not be my offer, nor thy asking?
The head is not more native to the heart,
The hand more instrumental to the mouth,
Than is the throne of Denmark to thy father.
What wouldst thou have, Laertes?

tlhaw'DIyuS Heghpu' loDnI'wI' vIparHa'bogh. Hamlet.
wej 'e' wIIIjmeH, ghu rur De'vam: Qupchu'.
'ej 'It tIqDu'maj, bIH DIDamoHmo',
'e' ra' lurDech. 'IQwI' wa' Huy' lughajmeH
tay'nIS 'ej gheghnIS wo'wIj ngan QuchDu'.
'ach tIqwIj Suvmo' rIntaH noHbogh yabwIj,
ta' vIqelmeH jI'IQba' 'ej jIvalba',
Dotlhwlj vIqawmo' je. vaj ben be'nI'wI',
DaHjaj ta'be'nalwI' je, Qojbogh wo'vam
ta'cho'qoch je,—jIQuch net jeylaw'DI',
HaghtaHvIS wa' mIn, nIjtaHvIS je latlh,
nolDaq jIloppu'DI', tlhoghDaq jISaQDI',
Dotlh Quch, Dotlh 'IQ je 'ay'mey rap vIlelDI'—
vISawpu'. ghu'vamvaD SuqeSpu' je,
valwI'pu' quv, 'e' vIbotbe'. 'ej ghu'vaD
SughIbpu', SaraDbe'taHvIS. Satlho'.
DaH ghu' boSovchu'bogh wIqelnISchoH.
puj HoSmeywIj 'e' noHlaw' vortIbraS.
pagh, Heghpu'mo' loDnI'wI' vIparHa'bogh,
wo'Daq Dach Sun, matlhwI'pu' je 'e' Harlaw'.
'ej nIvchoH ghaH 'e' naj. ghaH DorDI' qechvam,
munuQbe'Qo' ghaH, jIHvaD QumtaHvIS.
loDnI'wI' yoHqu'vaD ben Hoch Sep'e'
jeghpu'bogh vavDaj, chaw'taHvIS Hoch chut—
vIjeghnIS 'e' Del Hoch muQumpu'bogh.
wejpuH ta'meyvam chav. DaH qepvamDaq,
jIvangmeH jIH malja' wIbuSchoHnIS.
be'nI'puqDaj ngoQna' Sovbe'law'taH
DuraS pln, vortIbraS Qup SoSloDnI',
reH ropmo' 'ej QongDaqDaq yIntaHmo'.
ghaHvaD jIQum. Sepmaj latlh 'ay' Dan nuvvetlh
'e' nISnIS ghaH. latlh SepDaq muvmoH nuv
net tuchnIS, SepDaj yoSmeyvo' ngaq chu',
ghuvpu' je, negh je muvmoHpu'mo'. Hat.
'eH, voltImaD, qornelyuS je, pln qanvaD
vanvam boQengmeH DaH SangeH. woQ'e'
lIchaw'laHbogh malja'vam neH Sanob.
Sumatlh—SumoDDI' 'e' yI'ang. Qapla'.

qornelyuS mamoDmeH, 'ej Hoch latlh wIchavmeH, ta',
voltImaD je SoHvaD mamatlh chIch 'e' wI'angrupbej.

tlhaw'DIyuS 'e' vIHonQo'. Qapla'! SIbI' pemej.

[*mej VOLTIMAD QORNELYUS je*]

toH, SuH! layerteS: De'IIj chu' yIDel.
"qatlhobqang" Hu' choja'. 'ut nuq, layerteS?
Qo'noS pln'a'vaD Qu' Datlhobpu'DI',
jochbe'chugh Qu', vaj temlaHbe' pln'a'.
toH, nuq DapoQqangchugh, layerteSoy,
'oH vIta'Qo' DapoQDI'? pagh, qar'a'?
wa' porgh lujeSchu'lI' qar'a' tIq, yab je.
'ej nujvaD toy'chu'lI' qar'a' ghop po'.
vaj Qo'noS ta'vaD toy'chu' je vavlI',
wo' qum wIjeStaHvIS. yIja', layerteS:
DaH nuq Daghajqang?

Laertes	Dread my lord, Your leave and favour to return to France; From whence though willingly I came to Denmark, To show my duty in your coronation, Yet now, I must confess, that duty done, My thoughts and wishes bend again toward France, And bow them to your gracious leave and pardon.
Claudius	Have you your father's leave? What says Polonius?
Polonius	He hath, my lord, wrung from me my slow leave By laboursome petition; and at last Upon his will I seal'd my hard consent: I do beseech you, give him leave to go.
Claudius	Take thy fair hour, Laertes; time be thine, And thy best graces spend it at thy will!— But now, my cousin Hamlet, and my son,—
Hamlet	[*Aside*] A little more than kin, and less than kind.
Claudius	How is it that the clouds still hang on you?
Hamlet	Not so, my lord; I am too much i' the sun.
Gertrude	Good Hamlet, cast thy nighted colour off, And let thine eye look like a friend on Denmark. Do not for ever with thy vailed lids Seek for thy noble father in the dust: Thou know'st 'tis common;—all that live must die, Passing through nature to eternity.
Hamlet	Ay, madam, it is common.
Gertrude	If it be, Why seems it so particular with thee?
Hamlet	Seems, madam! nay it is; I know not 'seems.' 'Tis not alone my inky cloak, good mother, Nor customary suits of solemn black, Nor windy suspiration of forc'd breath, No, nor the fruitful river in the eye, Nor the dejected 'havior of the visage, Together with all forms, moods, shows of grief, That can denote me truly: these, indeed, seem; For they are actions that a man might play; But I have that within which passeth show; These but the trappings and the suits of woe.
Claudius	'Tis sweet and commendable in your nature, Hamlet, To give these mourning duties to your father: But, you must know, your father lost a father; That father lost, lost his; and the survivor bound, In filial obligation, for some term To do obsequious sorrow: but to persevere In obstinate condolement is a course Of impious stubbornness; 'tis unmanly grief: It shows a will most incorrect to heaven;

layerteS   HajmoHbogh juHwI',
romuluSDaq jIchegh tugh 'e' yIchaw'neS.
SoHvaD jImatlh, bIche'choHDI' 'e' 'angmeH,
Hu' pa'vo' Qo'noSDaq vIghoSqangpu'.
'ach romuluS lubuSqa' yabwIj, tlq je,
rInpu'DI' Qu'wIj; SoHvaD 'e' vIchID.
'ej chaw'lIjvaD yab, tIqwIj je vIqoy'moH.

tlhaw'DIyuS   'ej vavDaj chaw' ghaj'a' ghaH? 'eH, polonyuS.

polonyuS   QIt jIHvo' chaw'wIj wItlhchoHta', joHwI',
mutlhobqu'lI'mo' ghaH 'ej nIDqu'mo'.
vaj rInDI' ghu'vam, mejmeH chaw' vInob
'e' chav 'ej naw'ta', QatlhtaHvIS je Qu'.
vaj joH, qatlhobqu'. mej ghaH 'e' yIchaw' je.

tlhaw'DIyuS   toH, poHlIj Qup yItlv, layerteSoy.
poHlIj yISeHtaH SoH. 'ej poH Dalo'meH
wIvlIj DaneHDI', Qochjaj pagh. DaH: Hamlet—
qorDu''a'ghotwI' quvqu', puqloDwI' je.

Hamlet   [*pegh'egh*] qorDu'Hom 'oH. 'ej puqvaD qorlu'law'.

tlhaw'DIyuS   qatlh qaStaHvIS poH'a', Sut qIj Dachoq?

Hamlet   ghobe'. quploD ghaHbe'law' puqloD'e'.
vaj pagh vIcho'laHlaw', joHwI'.

ghertlhuD   luSpetHey Sut yIwoDta', Hamlet QaQ.
'ej Qo'noSta'vaD jup mInDu' tl'ang.
lamDaq vavlI' quv lom yInejtaHQo',
yav bejtaHvIS mIn 'ugh. reH motlhqu' ghu',
reH 'e' DaSovbej. HeghnIS yInbogh Hoch.
'u'Daq ghomHa'nIS Hoch, 'ej 'u'vo' yaH.

Hamlet   HIja', joH. motlh.

ghertlhuD   toH, motlh 'oH 'e' Dalajchugh,
vaj qatlh DabuSlaw'taH? qatlh reH bI'Itlaw'?

Hamlet   jI'Itlaw''a'? Qo', joH. jI'Itbej jIH.
"'Itlaw'"'e' vISovQo'. muDelchu'be'
wovHa'bogh wepwIj neH, SoS QaQ. ghobe'.
muDelchu'be' 'ItmeH lurDech Sut qIj,
tlhuH joq vIraDnISbogh vItlhovchoHDI',
mInwIjDaq lIngtaHbogh bIQtIqHey joq.
jI'IQmeH chen, qoj nargh, qoj 'ang'egh Dotlhwlj,
'ach jIH muDelchu'be'. teH. 'Itlaw' Hochvam,
chIch tojmeH Hochvam DalaHlaw'mo' vay'.
'ach vay' vIngaS, 'ej 'Itlaw'wI'mey jey 'oH.
'ej 'oH lu'ang 'ej Dor neH DotlhHey Sey, joH.

tlhaw'DIyuS   qa'lI' vInaDnIS 'ej "bImatlh" jIjatlhnIS,
vavlI'vaD 'ItmeH Qu' Dapabmo', Hamlet.
'ach ben vavlI'vaD lojpu' vavDaj'e',
'ej lojbogh vavDajvaD loj vav. yItlhoj.
vaj 'ItmeH Qu''e' ra'bogh puq lurDech
lutoy'nIS yInmey, taHtaHvIS poH ngaj.
'ach mulbogh 'IQtaHghachvaD qaplu'chugh,
vaj multaHmo' quvHa'qanglu'law' neH.
qoHvam DaQo' Suvwl'. lalDanvaD tlhIvqu'

A heart unfortified, a mind impatient;
An understanding simple and unschool'd:
For what we know must be, and is as common
As any the most vulgar thing to sense,
Why should we, in our peevish opposition,
Take it to heart? Fie! 'tis a fault to heaven,
A fault against the dead, a fault to nature,
To reason most absurd; whose common theme
Is death of fathers, and who still hath cried,
From the first corse till he that died to-day,
'This must be so.' We pray you, throw to earth
This unprevailing woe; and think of us
As of a father: for let the world take note.
You are the most immediate to our throne;
And with no less nobility of love
Than that which dearest father bears his son
Do I impart toward you. For your intent
In going back to school in Wittenberg,
It is most retrograde to our desire:
And we beseech you bend you to remain
Here, in the cheer and comfort of our eye,
Our chiefest courtier, cousin, and our son.

Gertrude

Let not thy mother lose her prayers, Hamlet:
I pray thee, stay with us; go not to Wittenberg.

Hamlet

I shall in all my best obey you, madam.

Claudius

Why, 'tis a loving and a fair reply:
Be as ourself in Denmark.—Madam, come;
This gentle and unforc'd accord of Hamlet
Sits smiling to my heart: in grace whereof,
No jocund health that Denmark drinks to-day,
But the great cannon to the clouds shall tell;
And the king's rouse the heavens shall bruit again,
Re-speaking earthly thunder. Come away.

[Exeunt all but HAMLET]

Hamlet

O, that this too too solid flesh would melt,
Thaw, and resolve itself into a dew!
Or that the Everlasting had not fix'd
His canon 'gainst self-slaughter! O God! God!
How weary, stale, flat, and unprofitable
Seem to me all the uses of this world!
Fie on't! oh fie! 'tis an unweeded garden,
That grows to seed; things rank and gross in nature
Possess it merely. That it should come to this!
But two months dead:—nay, not so much, not two:
So excellent a king; that was, to this,
Hyperion to a satyr: so loving to my mother,
That he might not beteem the winds of heaven
Visit her face too roughly. Heaven and earth!
Must I remember? why, she would hang on him,
As if increase of appetite had grown
By what it fed on: and yet, within a month—
Let me not think on't—Frailty, thy name is woman!—

'e' 'ang. boH yabvetlh. Hub'eghbe'law' tlqvetlh.
Qlp Sovvetlh, 'ej DuSaQDaq Dub'eghQo'.
qaSnISbej ghu' wISovbogh. motlhqu'mo',
vay' qetlh'e' neH lutu'bogh nochmaj rur.
vaj qatlh, maDoghtaHvIS wIqeHtaHmo',
wISaHnIS maH? baQa'! lalDanvaD HeS 'oH.
Heghpu'wI'pu'vaD HeS 'oH. 'u'vaD HeS 'oH.
meqlaHvaD taQ 'oH. "HeghnIS vavpu'ra',"
reH maq meqlaH. 'ej Heghpu'DI' lom wa'DIch,
HeghDI' je wa'Hu' lom, reH jach meqlaH:
"qaSnISbej." 'IQtaHghach ll'be' ylwoD;
qatlhob. 'ej SoHvaD vav jIH 'e' ylHarchoH.
'eH, qImjaj qo'. ta'cho'vaD wa'DIch SoH.
puqvaD muSHa'ghach quvqu' 'angqang vav.
SoHvaD muSHa'ghachvam vI'ang je jIH.
toH vulqanDaq DuSaQ Da'elqangqa'law'.
'ach neHtaHghachwIj Qochqu' nab Daja'bogh.
qatlhob: naDev ylratlhqangchoH. naDev
Dubejjaj belmoHbogh 'ej Quchbogh mInwIj:
yaSghomwIj la', qorDu'ghotwI', puqwI'.

ghertlhuD	lujbe'jaj Qu"e' neHqu'bogh SoSII'. vulqanDaq ylghoSQo'. ylratlhneS, Hamlet.
Hamlet	SoSwI', jIloblaHtaHvIS, SoH qalobrup.
tlhaw'DIyuS	may 'ej muSHa'bej ghaH, nujangpu'mo'. toH Qo'noSDaq bIratlhtaHvIS, HIDa. reH 'e' vIchaw'. ta'be', yItlha'. jIQuchqu'. QochQo'mo' Hamlet, raDlu'be'taHvIS, batlh DataHvIS ghaH, jIHvaD monchoH tIqwIj. vIlopchu'meH, DaHjaj Hoch HIq vItlhutlhDI', jIQuchqu' 'engvaD 'e' luja' bach'a'. 'ej tlhutlhtaH ta' 'e' Qoyqa'moHbej chal, 'ej chuSlaw' ralbogh 'engmey. Ha'. maghoS.
	[ratlh HAMLET. mej latlh]
Hamlet	va, tetjaj porghwIj lamqu' lamqu' lamqu'! tugh ngoSjaj 'oH, 'ej ram SISwI' neH mojjaj! pagh, HoH'egh wej quvHa'choHbogh SuvwI' 'e' chaw'jaj neH chaw'Qo'bogh batlhmaj tIgh! QI'yaH! QI'yaH! va, jIHvaD Doy'law', raghlaw', qetlh 'ej lI'be'law' qo'vam Hoch malja'! baQa'! tI ghom neH ngejHa'be'lu'bogh 'oH. pa' boghpu'DI' tIghu, DaH 'oH luDanchu' pujchu'bogh neH 'ej moHbogh DochHommey. wejpuH qaS ghu'vam jay'! cha' jar neH lom ghaH! ghobe', jIlachbej, "cha'" jIjatlhDI' je. povpu' ben ta'. DaHjaj ta' qellu'chugh, vaj yIH neH ghaH, 'ej qeylIS ghaH ben ta"e'. SoSwI"e' ben muSHa'qu'mo', SoS qabDaq vaQchoH chal SuS 'e' botmeH, SuSmey ra' ghaH. Hu'tegh! jIqawnIS'a'? ghaH wuv SoSwI'. qaStaHvIS ben, pa' SopDI', ghungqa'law'taH. 'ach qaSpu'DI' wa' jar neH! vIQubQo'jaj.

A little month; or ere those shoes were old
With which she follow'd my poor father's body,
Like Niobe, all tears:—why she, even she—
O, God! a beast, that wants discourse of reason,
Would have mourn'd longer—married with mine uncle,
My father's brother; but no more like my father,
Than I to Hercules: within a month;
Ere yet the salt of most unrighteous tears
Had left the flushing in her galled eyes,
She married. O, most wicked speed, to post
With such dexterity to incestuous sheets!
It is not, nor it cannot come to good:
But break, my heart, for I must hold my tongue.

[Enter HORATIO, MARCELLUS, and BERNARDO]

Horatio	Hail to your lordship!
Hamlet	I am glad to see you well: Horatio,—or I do forget myself.
Horatio	The same, my lord, and your poor servant ever.
Hamlet	Sir, my good friend; I'll change that name with you: And what make you from Wittenberg, Horatio? Marcellus?
Marcellus	My good lord—
Hamlet	I am very glad to see you.—Good even, sir.— But what, in faith, make you from Wittenberg?
Horatio	A truant disposition, good my lord.
Hamlet	I would not hear your enemy say so; Nor shall you do mine ear that violence, To make it truster of your own report Against yourself: I know you are no truant. But what is your affair in Elsinore? We'll teach you to drink deep ere you depart.
Horatio	My lord, I came to see your father's funeral.
Hamlet	I pray thee, do not mock me, fellow-student; I think it was to see my mother's wedding.
Horatio	Indeed, my lord, it follow'd hard upon.
Hamlet	Thrift, thrift, Horatio! the funeral bak'd meats Did coldly furnish forth the marriage tables. Would I had met my dearest foe in heaven Ere I had seen that day, Horatio!— My father!—methinks I see my father.
Horatio	Where, my lord?
Hamlet	In my mind's eye, Horatio.
Horatio	I saw him once; he was a goodly king.
Hamlet	He was a man, take him for all in all, I shall not look upon his like again.

Qu'vatlh! pujchu'ghach: "be'" 'oH ponglIj'e'!
va, qaSpa' jarHom; Qoppa' waqvetlh'e',
vavwI' lom tlha'meH tuQpu'bogh ta'be'nal,
bIQHalHey DataHvIS, reH SaQtaHmo'—
tugh, tugh vaj—Qu'vatlh! 'ItmeH meqlaHbe'bogh
targh, poH nI' law', loSmeH ghaH poH nI' puS—
tugh vavloDnI'wI' nay. vav rurchugh ghaH,
vaj qeylIS lIjlu'be'taHbogh vIrur je.
rInpa' wa' jar, va, 'oy'choHmeH mInDu'Daj
DoqchoHmoHpa' mInbIQDaj qutmey yuDqu'—
naypu'. QI'yaH, qorDu'wem'a' QongDaqDaq
moDDI' chaH, chaHvaD ngeDqu'. mIghqu' Dochaj!
QaQbe'taH 'ej QaQchoHlaHbe'law' ghu'.
'ach tIq, yISIQ neH; tamnISII'mo' jatwIj.

[*'el* HOREY'SO, MARSE'LUS, BERNARDO *je*]

Horey'So	nuqneH, joH quv!
Hamlet	jIQuch bIcheplaw'mo'. Horey'So! toH, jlIlj'eghruplaw' je!
Horey'So	jIHbej, joH QaQ. 'ej reH toy'wI'lI' jIHrup.
Hamlet	jupna'wI' SoH, qaH. pongvetlh matlh qamechqang. qatlh vulqanvo' bIghIQchoHlaw', Horey'So? marSe'luS SoH, qar'a'?
marSe'luS	joH quv—
Hamlet	jIQuch qaleghmo' je. nuqneH, qaH yoH. 'a SuH! yIja': qatlh vulqanvo' bIchegh?
Horey'So	jIbuDqu'mo' jIHaDchoHQo', joH QaQ.
Hamlet	va, pumvetlh jatlhchugh je wa' gholna'lI', 'e' vIHarQo'. 'ej teSwIj yIngorQo', Dupumbogh mu'lIj ngeb DavoqmoHDI'. bIbuDlaHbe'ba'. Ha' qatlh tlhInInDaq SoH? bItlhutlhqu' 'e' pIghojmoHlaw' bItlheDpa'.
Horey'So	joH, vavlI' nol vIbejneSmeH jIcholpu'.
Hamlet	DuSaQ tlhejwI'wI', HIvaqQo'. qatlhob. va, SoSwI' tlhogh Dabejlaw'meH bIchol.
Horey'So	toH quqlaw' taymeyvetlh, joHwI'. jIchID.
Hamlet	vu'bejmeH! vu'bejmeH! yIqIm, Horey'So: bIrDI' nol chabmey, tlhoghDaj vaSDaq jablu'. QI'tu'Daq jIHtaHvIS, veqlargh vIleghchugh, vaj ghu' vImaSbej. tlhoghDaj jaj vIlegh, not 'e' vImaS, Horey'So. va, vavwI'— vavwI' vIleghlaw'.
Horey'So	nuqDaq?
Hamlet	va, yabwIj mInHeyDaq vIlegh, Horey'So.
Horey'So	wa'logh vIleghpu'. toH, ta' QaQqu' ghaHlaw'.
Hamlet	loDna' ghaH jay'. Hoch laHmeyDaj vIchovDI', vaj not ghaH rurbogh latlh vIleghqa'laH.

Horatio	My lord, I think I saw him yesternight.
Hamlet	Saw who?
Horatio	My lord, the king your father.
Hamlet	The king my father!
Horatio	Season your admiration for awhile With an attent ear, till I may deliver, Upon the witness of these gentlemen, This marvel to you.
Hamlet	For God's love, let me hear.
Horatio	Two nights together had these gentlemen, Marcellus and Bernardo, on their watch, In the dead vast and middle of the night, Been thus encounter'd. A figure like your father, Armed at all points exactly, cap-a-pe, Appears before them, and with solemn march Goes slow and stately by them: thrice he walk'd By their oppress'd and fear-surprised eyes, Within his truncheon's length; whilst they, distill'd Almost to jelly with the act of fear, Stand dumb, and speak not to him. This to me In dreadful secrecy impart they did; And I with them the third night kept the watch: Where, as they had deliver'd, both in time, Form of the thing, each word made true and good, The apparition comes: I knew your father; These hands are not more like.
Hamlet	But where was this?
Marcellus	My lord, upon the platform where we watch'd.
Hamlet	Did you not speak to it?
Horatio	My lord, I did; But answer made it none: yet once methought It lifted up its head, and did address Itself to motion, like as it would speak; But even then the morning cock crew loud, And at the sound it shrunk in haste away, And vanish'd from our sight.
Hamlet	'Tis very strange.
Horatio	As I do live, my honour'd lord, 'tis true; And we did think it writ down in our duty To let you know of it.
Hamlet	Indeed, indeed, sirs, but this troubles me. Hold you the watch to-night?
Marcellus & *Bernardo*	We do, my lord.
Hamlet	Arm'd, say you?
Marcellus & *Bernardo*	Arm'd, my lord.

Horey'So	joH, wa'Hu' ram vIleghlaw'.
Hamlet	'Iv legh'a'?
Horey'So	ta'. vavlI'.
Hamlet	ta'? vav? chay'!
Horey'So	bIyay' loQ 'e' yISeH, 'ej teS yItu'moH. nutu'taHvIS cha' mangvam, DaH nom SoHvaD wanI'vam taQ vIDel.

Hamlet   vIQoynIS jay'!

Horey'So   SuH: 'avmeH tay'taHvIS cha' mangvam yoH,
marSe'luS qu', bernarDo je, 'ej qaSDI'
cha' ram ramjep, rep chImqu' je, luqIHlu'.
chaH tlhopDaq nargh vavlI' quv rurbogh vay''e'.
'ej mIv je DaS yoD tuQmo', Suvruplaw' ghaH.
'ej QIt chaH juS ghaH, nurDaj leHtaHvIS,
'ej 'IQqu' gho'meH mIwDaj. wejlogh juSta',
bejtaHvIS mInchaj bItqu' merbogh ghaH.
'ej chuqchaj juv chanjaqDaj SaS. 'ach qaSDI',
yay' chaH. vaj pugh lumojlaw' tetlaw'mo'.
vaj tam, 'ej Qam, 'ej ghaHvaD jatlhchoHQo'.
jIHvaD ghu' naQ lutey' chaH, HojtaHvIS.
'ej qaStaHvIS ram wejDIch, 'avDI' chaH,
vItlhej. 'ej qaSbej ghu' luja'pu'bogh.
pay' mu'meychaj lu'ollu' 'ej lutoblu'.
Dochvetlh'e' Hu' luDelbogh rurtaHvIS,
nuchol narghwI'. vavlI' vIghov. 'ej chaH
nIb law', ghopDu' nIb puS.

Hamlet   'a nuqDaq qaS?

marSe'luS   joHwI', 'avwI'Daq jenDaq. pa' ma'avtaH.

Hamlet   'ej ghaHvaD Sujatlhbe''a'?

Horey'So   joH, jIjatlhpu'.
'ach jangmeH pagh mujatlh. toH wa'logh chaq
nach jenmoH. vIHchoHmo', ghaytan vay' jatlhrup.
'ach qaSDI', jachqu'choH jajlo'ghogh Qa'.
'ej chuSDI', Haw'meH moD ghaH. maHvo' ngab.

Hamlet   Hujqu'.

Horey'So   jI'IpmeH, yIn vISuDrupneS, joH quv:
teHqu'. 'ej ghu' pIja', 'e' poQ vajQu'maj,
mamatlhmo' 'e' wIHar.

Hamlet   maj, maj, qaHpu'. 'a jIHvaD nub wanI'vam.
DaHjaj ramjep Su'avqa''a'?

marSe'luS
bernarDo je   HIja'.

Hamlet   yoDSutmey tuQ, qar'a'?

marSe'luS
bernarDo je   yoDSutmey, joH.

Hamlet	From top to toe?
Marcellus & *Bernardo*	My lord, from head to foot.
Hamlet	Then saw you not his face?
Horatio	O, yes, my lord; he wore his beaver up.
Hamlet	What, look'd he frowningly?
Horatio	A countenance more in sorrow than in anger.
Hamlet	Pale or red?
Horatio	Nay, very pale.
Hamlet	And fix'd his eyes upon you?
Horatio	Most constantly.
Hamlet	I would I had been there.
Horatio	It would have much amaz'd you.
Hamlet	Very like, very like. Stay'd it long?
Horatio	While one with moderate haste might tell a hundred.
Marcellus & *Bernardo*	Longer, longer.
Horatio	Not when I saw't.
Hamlet	His beard was grizzled, no?
Horatio	It was, as I have seen it in his life, A sable silver'd.
Hamlet	I will watch to-night; Perchance 'twill walk again.
Horatio	I warrant it will.
Hamlet	If it assume my noble father's person I'll speak to it, though hell itself should gape And bid me hold my peace. I pray you all, If you have hitherto conceal'd this sight, Let it be tenable in your silence still; And whatsoever else shall hap to-night, Give it an understanding, but no tongue: I will requite your loves. So, fare you well: Upon the platform, 'twixt eleven and twelve, I'll visit you.
All	Our duty to your honour.
Hamlet	Your loves, as mine to you: farewell.

[*Exeunt all but HAMLET*]

My father's spirit in arms! all is not well;
I doubt some foul play: would the night were come!
Till then sit still, my soul: foul deeds will rise,

Hamlet	mIv je DaS?
marSe'luS bernarDo je	porgh naQ, joH.
Hamlet	vaj nach'e' boleghlaHbe'.
Horey'So	wIlegh. qabyoDDaj teqpu'.
Hamlet	qej'a' mInDu'Daj?
Horey'So	nachDaj 'IQlaw' law', joH, 'oH QeH puS.
Hamlet	chIS'a'? Doq'a'?
Horey'So	reH chISqu'.
Hamlet	'ej tlhIlHDaq mInDaj buSmoH'a'?
Horey'So	chIch buSqu'.
Hamlet	pa' jIHchugh neH!
Horey'So	bISaHchugh, vaj Dumerqu'.
Hamlet	ghaytan, ghaytan. nI''a' pa' ratlhmeH poHDaj?
Horey'So	QIt wa'vatlh toghlaH vay', pa' ratlhtaHvIS.
marSe'luS bernarDo je	nI'qu', nI'qu'.
Horey'So	vIleghDI', nI'qu'be'.
Hamlet	'ej chISchoH rolDaj, qar'a'?
Horey'So	yIntaHvIS rolDaj ghajbogh rurchu'. qIj 'oH, 'ej 'oHDaq DanchoH ghItlhmey chIS.
Hamlet	qaStaHvIS ram, jI'av. chaq yItqa'.
Horey'So	DIch.
Hamlet	vavwI' quv qab, mInDu' je ghajchugh ghaH, vaj poSchoHchugh je ghe''or, 'ej jItammeH mura'chugh je, ram Hoch: ghaHvaD jIjatlh. SuH, Hoch SatIhob. wanI'vam taQ bopeghchugh, qaSpa' DaHjaj, vaj wej 'oH lupeghHa'nIS ghoghmeyraj tam. DaHjaj ram qaSchugh latlh, vaj vumnIS yabraj, 'a vumbe'nIS jatraj. jupwI' boDataHmo', Savan. Qapla'. 'ej wa'maHcha'logh Qoy'lu'pa', Hur yaHDaq SaSuchbej.
Hoch	joH, mamatlhtaH 'ej pIvan.
Hamlet	Qo'. HIparHa'taH, SaparHa'mo' je. Qapla'.

[*ratlh* HAMLET. *mej latlh*]

yoDSutmey tuQ vavwI' lomqa'!
qay' vay'. Hu' qaS wemna', DaH 'e' vIpIHchoH.
tugh SaHjaj ram. yIloSII' SaHpa', tIqwIj.

Though all the earth o'erwhelm them, to men's eyes.

[*Exit*]

SCENE III *A room in Polonius' house.*
[*Enter LAERTES and OPHELIA*]

Laertes My necessaries are embark'd: farewell:
And, sister, as the winds give benefit,
And convoy is assistant, do not sleep,
But let me hear from you.

Ophelia   Do you doubt that?

Laertes For Hamlet, and the trifling of his favour,
Hold it a fashion and a toy in blood:
A violet in the youth of primy nature,
Forward, not permanent, sweet, not lasting,
The perfume and suppliance of a minute;
No more.

Ophelia   No more but so?

Laertes   Think it no more:
For nature, crescent, does not grow alone
In thews and bulk; but as this temple waxes,
The inward service of the mind and soul
Grows wide withal. Perhaps he loves you now;
And now no soil nor cautel doth besmirch
The virtue of his will: but you must fear,
His greatness weigh'd, his will is not his own;
For he himself is subject to his birth:
He may not, as unvalu'd persons do,
Carve for himself; for on his choice depends
The safety and health of this whole state;
And therefore must his choice be circumscrib'd
Unto the voice and yielding of that body
Whereof he is the head. Then if he says he loves you,
It fits your wisdom so far to believe it
As he in his particular act and place
May give his saying deed; which is no further
Than the main voice of Denmark goes withal.
Then weigh what loss your honour may sustain,
If with too credent ear you list his songs,
Or lose your heart, or your chaste treasure open
To his unmaster'd importunity.
Fear it, Ophelia, fear it, my dear sister;
And keep you in the rear of your affection,
Out of the shot and danger of desire.
The chariest maid is prodigal enough
If she unmask her beauty to the moon:
Virtue itself 'scapes not calumnious strokes:
The canker galls the infants of the spring.
Too oft before their buttons be disclos'd;
And in the morn and liquid dew of youth
Contagious blastments are most imminent.
Be wary, then; best safety lies in fear:
Youth to itself rebels, though none else near.

reH ghot mInDu'vaD narghnIS Haw'bogh HeS.
bIH DItu'be'meH So'chugh je qIbHeS.

[mej]

LUT 'AY'HOM WEJ *polonyuS juH pa'.*
['el *LAYERTES,* '*OVELYA je*]

layerteS   toH, DujDaq tepwIj lanlu'. vaj Qapla'.
be'nI'wI', chaw'DI' romuluS neHmaH,
'ej boQDI' lengbogh Duj, vaj yIbuDQo',
'ej De'meylIj HISovmoH.

'*ovelya*   DaHon'a'?

layerteS   Hamlet bangvI'Hey ram DaqeltaHvIS,
ngongna', 'IwQuj je neH 'oH 'e' yIHar.
DISbov Qup naH 'oH. 'eqqu' 'a taHQo'.
Doj 'a ratlhQo'. He' tup 'ej belmoH tup.
'a tugh loj Hoch.

'*ovelya*   loj'a' neH?

layerteS   'e' yIHar.
puqHom mojHa'lu'DI', HoSchoH Somraw,
'ej tInchoH porgh. 'ach 'ItlhDI' DojtaHghachmaj,
toy'chu' je yabmaj, qa' je Hoch laH'e'
ngaStaHbogh porgh. DaHjaj chaq DumuSHa'.
'ej HechtaHvIS yuDHa', DaH 'e' Sorghbe'
naDHa'ghach, tojrupghach je. 'ach yIyep:
patlh'a'Daj toy'nISmo' je toy'moHwI'vetlh,
vaj neHtaHghachDaj loblaHbe'bej ghaH.
ghot ram Dabe'nISmo', nay' pe'laHbe' ghaH.
pIvmeH 'ej taHmeH wo'maj, wIvDaj wuvtaH
wo' naQ. vaj wIvDaj vuSnIS wo'porgh vuD,
Qochbe'ghach je, porgh nachHey Damo' ghaH.
toH SoHvaD jatlhchugh je: "bangna'wI' SoH,"
vaj mu'Daj tob chav'e' neH ta'laHbogh
patlh DotlhDaj je wa' ghot. 'ej 'e' DapIHchugh,
vaj yonnIS yablIj. 'ej Do' mu'Daj tobmeH
lulajnIS Qo'noS che'bogh ghoghmey law''e'.
'ej bIquvHa'choHlaH, bomchaj Datu'chugh
bIvoqchu'taHvIS, pagh, ghaH toy'chugh tlqlIj,
pagh, boHmo' poQtaHvIS, SeH'eghtaHQo'vIS,
chIch ghaHvaD be'batlhlIj DapoSmoHchugh.
DuHvam yIqelchu'. 'ej yIyep, 'ovelya.
yIyep, be'nI'oy. 'ej DuDevqangchugh
parmaqIlj Duj, vaj 'o'DajDaq yIpol'egh.
neHtaHghach pu' chuqvo', Qobvo' je DoH!
'IHtaH be' yepqu', maSvaD neH 'e' 'angchugh,
vaj ngIlqu' be'vetlh. HIvrupchugh pumHa'ghach
vaj junlaHbe' je batlh. tIghumey chu''e'
plj ngejtaH gharghmey, narghpa' naHmeychaj.
'ej SISDI' QuptaHghach ramblQ, poblQ je,
nom charghnIS ngejbogh ropmey. vaj yIyep.
Qaghbe'meH vanglu'Qo'DI', HungDaj pol.
lotlh'egh QupwI', ghaH buQchoHpa' je ghol.

Ophelia   I shall the effect of this good lesson keep
                   As watchman to my heart. But, good my brother,
                   Do not, as some ungracious pastors do,
                   Show me the steep and thorny way to heaven;
                   Whilst, like a puff'd and reckless libertine,
                   Himself the primrose path of dalliance treads,
                   And recks not his own rede.

Laertes   O, fear me not.
                   I stay too long: but here my father comes.

                   [*Enter POLONIUS*]

                   A double blessing is a double grace;
                   Occasion smiles upon a second leave.

Polonius   Yet here, Laertes! aboard, aboard, for shame!
                   The wind sits in the shoulder of your sail,
                   And you are stay'd for. There; my blessing with thee!

                   [*Laying his hands on LAERTES' head*]

                   And these few precepts in thy memory
                   See thou character. Give thy thoughts no tongue,
                   Nor any unproportion'd thought his act.
                   Be thou familiar, but by no means vulgar.
                   Those friends thou hast, and their adoption tried,
                   Grapple them to thy soul with hoops of steel;
                   But do not dull thy palm with entertainment
                   Of each new-hatch'd, unfledg'd comrade. Beware
                   Of entrance to a quarrel; but, being in,
                   Bear't that the opposed may beware of thee.
                   Give every man thy ear, but few thy voice:
                   Take each man's censure, but reserve thy judgment.
                   Costly thy habit as thy purse can buy,
                   But not express'd in fancy; rich, not gaudy:
                   For the apparel oft proclaims the man;
                   And they in France of the best rank and station
                   Are of a most select and generous chief in that.
                   Neither a borrower nor a lender be:
                   For loan oft loses both itself and friend;
                   And borrowing dulls the edge of husbandry.
                   This above all: to thine ownself be true;
                   And it must follow, as the night the day,
                   Thou canst not then be false to any man.
                   Farewell: my blessing season this in thee!

Laertes   Most humbly do I take my leave, my lord.

Polonius   The time invites you; go, your servants tend.

Laertes   Farewell, Ophelia; and remember well
                   What I have said to you.

Ophelia   'Tis in my memory lock'd,
                   And you yourself shall keep the key of it.

Laertes   Farewell.

                   [*Exit*]

'ovelya   paQDI'norgh QaQ Damaqpu'bogh vI'uchbej.
                  'ej tIqwIj 'avjaj. 'ach, loDnI'wI' QaQ,
                  ghobyaS puS yIDaQo': QI'tu' He Qatlhqu'
                  lu'angtaH, ngIb He buD lughoStaHvIS.
                  HemwI' SuDwI''a', Duj ngaDHa' je Da chaH,
                  'ej qeSchaj pabrupbe'.

layerteS   toH, HIpIHQo'.
                  jIratlhtaHqu'. 'a SuH, DaH chol vavwI'.

                  ['el *POLONYUS*]

                  cha'logh chonaDmo', cha'logh vaj jIDo'.
                  cha'logh mavanchuqmo', vaj Quchbej ghu'.

polonyuS   layerteS, wej tlheD'a'? 'eH, tlj! tlj! wejpuH!
                  jonta'llj laQchoHlu', 'ej SoH nlloStaH.
                  SuH. naD yISuq.

                  [*LAYERTES nachDaq ghopDaj lan*]

                                      'ej yabDaq qeSvam puS
                  ylghItlhchu'. jatllj luchu'Qo'jaj qechllj.
                  'ej ghu'llj SujlaHlaw'chugh qechllj nglj,
                  vaj qechvam yIta'Qo' je. yIqejHa',
                  'a jup DawIvtaHvIS, batlh yIQutQo' je.
                  Hoch jup Daghajbogh tobchugh ghu'mey poH je,
                  vaj qa'll'Daq DabaghmeH mIr tllo'.
                  'ach tachllj SuchDI' SaSbogh mIywI' chu'
                  DatIvmoHmeH Qopbe'jaj vanbogh tochllj.
                  bISolnISbe'taHmeH ylyep. bISoIDI',
                  yISuvchu'; SoHmo' yepchoHjaj gholll'.
                  teSDu'llj lo'jaj Hoch. 'a chlch ghot puSvaD
                  vuDghogh yI'lo'. yIqImqu', noHDI' vay'—
                  yojllj DapeghtaHvIS. chlch waghjaj Sutllj,
                  yapchugh Huchjollj, 'ach taQQo'jaj bIH.
                  qutlhbe'jaj bIH, 'ach napjaj bIH: loD'e'
                  plj Del Sut tuQbogh. 'ej SutSarmey noHDI'
                  po'qu'bej romuluS patlh ghot, chuQun je.
                  nglpwI' nojwI' joq yIDaQo'. blnojDI',
                  plj tugh loj Doch Danojpu'bogh, jupll' je;
                  blnglptaHchugh, vaj vu'meH blpo'Ha'choH.
                  potlhqu' wa' Qu''e'. SoHvaD ylyuDQo'.
                  ram tlha'ba' pem, qar'a'. vaj tlha' je ghu'vam:
                  Hoch ghotvaD blyuDHa' je, 'ej blquvbej.
                  Qapla'. 'ej SoHvaD qeSwIj boQjaj naDwIj.

layerteS   jImejneS 'e' ylchaw'.

polonyuS   DupoQlI' poHllj.
                  vaj Ha' toy'wI'pu'lI' tlvu' ylghoS.

layerteS   Qapla', 'ovelya. qeSmeywlj qaja'bogh
                  tlqawchu'taH.

'ovelya   lu'. yabwljDaq ngaQ rIntaH.
                  'ej yabwlj poSmoHwI' DapoltaH SoH.

layerteS   Qapla'.

                  [*mej*]

Polonius	What is't, Ophelia, he hath said to you?
Ophelia	So please you, something touching the Lord Hamlet.
Polonius	Marry, well bethought:

'Tis told me he hath very oft of late
Given private time to you; and you yourself
Have of your audience been most free and bounteous:
If it be so,—as so 'tis put on me,
And that in way of caution,—I must tell you,
You do not understand yourself so clearly
As it behoves my daughter and your honour.
What is between you? give me up the truth.

Ophelia   He hath, my lord, of late made many tenders
Of his affection to me.

Polonius   Affection! pooh! you speak like a green girl,
Unsifted in such perilous circumstance.
Do you believe his tenders, as you call them?

Ophelia   I do not know, my lord, what I should think.

Polonius   Marry, I'll teach you: think yourself a baby;
That you have ta'en these tenders for true pay,
Which are not sterling. Tender yourself more dearly;
Or—not to crack the wind of the poor phrase,
Wronging it thus—you'll tender me a fool.

Ophelia   My lord, he hath importun'd me with love
In honourable fashion.

Polonius   Ay, fashion you may call it; go to, go to.

Ophelia   And hath given countenance to his speech, my lord,
With almost all the holy vows of heaven.

Polonius   Ay, springes to catch woodcocks. I do know,
When the blood burns, how prodigal the soul
Lends the tongue vows: these blazes, daughter,
Giving more light than heat,—extinct in both,
Even in their promise, as it is a-making,—
You must not take for fire. From this time
Be somewhat scanter of your maiden presence;
Set your entreatments at a higher rate
Than a command to parley. For Lord Hamlet,
Believe so much in him, that he is young;
And with a larger tether may he walk
Than may be given you: in few, Ophelia,
Do not believe his vows; for they are brokers,—
Not of that dye which their investments show,
But mere implorators of unholy suits,
Breathing like sanctified and pious bawds,
The better to beguile. This is for all:—
I would not, in plain terms, from this time forth,
Have you so slander any moment leisure
As to give words or talk with the Lord Hamlet.
Look to't, I charge you: come your ways.

polonyuS   Suja'chuqDI', nuq jatlhpu' ghaH, 'ovelya.

'ovelya   Hamlet joH buSneSbogh vay"e' muja'pu'.

polonyuS   majQa'. 'oH qawlu'chu'.
qen SoHvaD mobmeH poHDaj nobta' ghaH,
qaStaHvIS 'ebmey law'; jIHvaD net ja'.
'ej mu'meyDaj DaQoymeH nI'pu' poHllj,
'ej ghaHvaD ghlbqu'pu'. toH, teHchugh ghu'vam—
'ej teH, jIHvaD net HarmoHDI', chIch Hojlu'—
vaj bIyajHa"cghlaw'; qaja'nISba'.
'ej batlhvaD Qu'Daj yajnISchu' puqbe'wI'.
tlhIHvaD tlhetlh nuq? ylvIt.

'ovelya   bangDaj jIH, qen 'e' tobneSmeH, joHwI',
pljj SoQmey law' mujatlhpu'.

polonyuS   "bangDaj SoH"? Hu'tegh! be'Hom Soy' DaDa.
wej Dujmey law' DachIjmo', bI'ongHa'.
'ej bangqoq SoQmeyqoqDaj DaHar'a'?

'ovelya   joH, vuD vIHarnISbogh vISovchu'be'.

polonyuS   baQa', qaghojmoH. ghu SoH 'e' yIHar,
SoQvam Datu'lI'mo' DuSorghtaHvIS.
SoQmeyvaD qoghllj'e' yISoQmoHchu'.
'ej qogh DaSoQmoHbe'chugh—mu' vImawbej,
pe'vII vIQoDII'mo'—vaj pumDI' qoghllj,
qoHna' jIH 'e' vIpumlu'.

'ovelya   'a joH QaQ,
"bangwI' SoH" jatlhDI', nong 'ej quvqu' mIwDaj.

polonyuS   Ha', mIymeH mIwDaj neH 'oH. Hu'tegh! Ha'.

'ovelya   'ej SoQDaj tobchu'meH 'ej vItmoHmeH,
QI'tu' quv buSbogh Hoch 'Ip'e' mujatlh.

polonyuS   HIja', qoHQa'mey jonmeH janmey bIH.
pubtaHvIS 'Iwmaj, tIqvaD ngeDqu' chav,
jatvaD 'Ip nojDI' tIqmaj; 'e' vISovchu'.
qulqoqvetlh wovtaH law', 'oH tujtaH puS.
'ej qulqoqvetlh cha' Dotlhvam luchu'Ha'lu',
lay'taHvIS je chu'wI'—bIH tojmoHmo'.
vaj batlh qulna' 'oH qulqoq'e', puqbe',
'e' yIHarQo'. bIquvmeH, leS ghaH'e'
pljj yISuchQo'. 'ej ja'chuqmeH neH bang
tlhob, 'e' yIHon, "ghghgh" jatlhDI' Hamlet joH.
ngoDmeyvam neH tIHar: DaH Qupqu' ghaH.
'ej yItmeH, weghbogh tlheghDaj reH nI' law',
tlheghqoqllj chaw'lu'bogh nI' puS. nom jatlhmeH:
'ovelya, 'IpDaj tIHarQo'. SuyDuy bIH.
nur'e' lu'angbogh paHchaj lughajbe'.
'ach yonmeH Qu' quvHa'qu' qoy'lI' neH.
'ej tlhu'moHchu'meH chaH, Human 'oSwI' Da:
SoQ'a'mey, batlhqoq je lo'. pItlh jIjatlh:
'eH, Hamlet joHvaD QIch mu' joq DamechmeH
wa' lupllj lenHom Dalo'Ha'—baQa',
qaStaHvIS nemmey, pe'vII 'e' vIbotbej.
ylta'. qara'. mamej.

Ophelia	I shall obey, my lord.

[*Exeunt*]

SCENE IV   *The platform.*

[*Enter HAMLET, HORATIO, and MARCELLUS*]

Hamlet	The air bites shrewdly; it is very cold.
Horatio	It is a nipping and an eager air.
Hamlet	What hour now?
Horatio	I think it lacks of twelve.
Hamlet	No, it is struck.
Horatio	Indeed? I heard it not: then it draws near the season

Wherein the spirit held his wont to walk.

[*A flourish of trumpets, and ordnance shot off, within*]

What does this mean, my lord?

Hamlet	The king doth wake to-night, and takes his rouse,

Keeps wassail, and the swaggering up-spring reels;
And, as he drains his draughts of Rhenish down,
The kettle-drum and trumpet thus bray out
The triumph of his pledge.

Horatio	Is it a custom?
Hamlet	Ay, marry, is't:

But to my mind,—though I am native here,
And to the manner born,—it is a custom
More honour'd in the breach than the observance.
This heavy-headed revel east and west
Makes us traduc'd and tax'd of other nations:
They clepe us drunkards, and with swinish phrase
Soil our addition; and, indeed, it takes
From our achievements, though perform'd at height,
The pith and marrow of our attribute.
So oft it chances in particular men
That, for some vicious mole of nature in them,
As in their birth—wherein they are not guilty,
Since nature cannot choose his origin—
By the o'ergrowth of some complexion,
Oft breaking down the pales and forts of reason;
Or by some habit, that too much o'er-leavens
The form of plausive manners;—that these men,—
Carrying, I say, the stamp of one defect,
Being nature's livery or fortune's star,—
Their virtues else—be they as pure as grace,
As infinite as man may undergo—
Shall in the general censure take corruption
From that particular fault: the dram of eale
Doth all the noble substance of a doubt
To his own scandal.

Horatio	Look, my lord, it comes!

'ovelya   qalob, joHwI'.

[*mej chaH*]

LUT 'AY'HOM LOS *'avwI'Daq.*

[*'el HAMLET, HOREY'SO, MARSE'LUS je*]

Hamlet   choptaHvIS jejlaw' muDvam Ho'Hey. bIrqu'.

Horey'So   HIvruplaw' muDvam vID, 'ej chopDI' yoHbej.

Hamlet   DaH rep yIper.

Horey'So   wej qaS ramjep, qar'a'.

marSe'luS   ghobe'. DaH Qoy'lu'pu'.

Horey'So   qar'a'? vIQoypu'be'. vaj yItmeH qa'
tugh qaS poH motlh.

[*chuS lopmeH chuS'ughmey, 'ej 'emDaq baHlu'*]

                     nuq lopmeH baHlu', joH?

Hamlet   DaHjaj QongQo' 'ej lop 'ej tlhutlhqu' ta'.
chechqu' yupma'Daj. mu'qaD veSvaD SuvDI',
yoHqu' SuvwI''a'qoq, qochpu'Daj je.
'ej romuluS HIq HIvje''a' tlhutlhDI' ghaH,
Hugh yayDaj Dun lumaq chuS'ugh, DIr 'In je.

Horey'So   tlgh 'oH'a'?

Hamlet   tlgh 'oH jay'.
toH, wo'vam Sung jIH. jIHvaD motlhtaH tlghvam,
jIboghpu'DI'. 'ach vuDwIj tlhoblu'chugh,
vaj tlghvam'e' wIquvmoHqu' wIbIvDI'.
'ej tlgh wIpabtaHvIS, chIch maquvHa'.
neHmaH qIbHeS je DopmeyDaq nupumtaH,
'ej pIchmaj ja'choH latlh wo' ngan, 'e' qaSmoH
nach 'uHqu' chenmoHbogh yupma'vam'e'.
jatlh chaH: "chechwI'na' chaH". 'ej targh DIrur
pIj 'e' lumaqmo', lamchoH pongmaj QaQ.
DInIDDI', jenqu' chavmeymaj DIta'bogh;
nunoymoHmeH Hombotlh DujQuQ je bIH.
bIH jotlh je ghu'vetlh. toH, pIj ghotvaD qaS je:
Dotlhchaj Duy' naS lughaj chaH. chaq boghHa'pu'—
chuntaHvIS, mungDaj wIvlaHbe'mo' ghot.
chaq HoSqu' Dujchaj le', 'ej HoSqu'mo',
meqlaHchaj nuH, Surchem je pejchoH 'oH.
pagh, chaq latlhpu' belHa'moH DameH mIwchaj,
'oH QopmoHmo' wa' tlgh lupabtaHbogh.
wa' Duy'chaj DeghHom neH luqengtaH ghotvam,
Dotlhchaj lutoy'nISmo', pagh, puQmo' Sanchaj.
toH, qeyIlS Dunqu' rurmeH Dojchugh je
Hoch batlhmeychaj, 'ej batlhmey ghajbogh chaH
leHruplaHbe'chugh je latlh vay', vaj rambej.
ghotvam lunoHlu'DI', Sab batlhmeyvam,
SaHmo' neH Duy'chaj. webmeH batlh baSna',
naDHa'ghachvaD butlh mIghqu'—

Horey'So   'eH, joH! chol!

[Enter Ghost]

Hamlet Angels and ministers of grace defend us!
Be thou a spirit of health or goblin damn'd,
Bring with thee airs from heaven or blasts from hell,
Be thy intents wicked or charitable,
Thou com'st in such a questionable shape
That I will speak to thee: I'll call thee Hamlet,
King, father, royal Dane: O, answer me!
Let me not burst in ignorance; but tell
Why thy canoniz'd bones, hearsed in death,
Have burst their cerements; why the sepulchre,
Wherein we saw thee quietly inurn'd,
Hath op'd his ponderous and marble jaws
To cast thee up again! What may this mean,
That thou, dead corse, again in complete steel
Revisit'st thus the glimpses of the moon,
Making night hideous, and we fools of nature
So horridly to shake our disposition
With thoughts beyond the reaches of our souls?
Say, why is this? wherefore? what should we do?

[Ghost beckons HAMLET]

Horatio It beckons you to go away with it,
As if it some impartment did desire
To you alone.

Marcellus   Look, with what courteous action
It waves you to a more removed ground:
But do not go with it.

Horatio   No, by no means.

Hamlet It will not speak; then I will follow it.

Horatio Do not, my lord.

Hamlet   Why, what should be the fear?
I do not set my life in a pin's fee;
And for my soul, what can it do to that,
Being a thing immortal as itself?
It waves me forth again; I'll follow it.

Horatio What if it tempt you toward the flood, my lord,
Or to the dreadful summit of the cliff
That beetles o'er his base into the sea,
And there assume some other horrible form,
Which might deprive your sovereignty of reason,
And draw you into madness? think of it:
The very place puts toys of desperation,
Without more motive, into every brain
That looks so many fathoms to the sea
And hears it roar beneath.

Hamlet   It waves me still.
Go on; I'll follow thee.

Marcellus You shall not go, my lord.

['el lomqa']

Hamlet	nuQanjaj boQqangbogh 'ej Qumbogh qa'pu'!

qa' QaQ SoH'a'? veqlarghmang SoH'a'?
QI'tu' naD Daqem'a'? chaq ghe"orvo'
qulpummey Daqem'a'? bIHechtaHvIS
bIboQqang'a'? pagh bImIgh'a'? ram Hoch.
qayu'nISmeH bIchenpu'mo', qajatlh.
qapongmeH, Hamlet pong vIlo'rup. ta'!
Qo'noSngan'a'! vavwI'! SIbI' yIjang!
jIjIvmo' tugh jIlQay'rup 'e' yIbot.
yIja' neH. qatlh lomSut lughormoHlaw'pu'
HomDu'lIj'e' Hu' weghbogh Hegh bIghHa',
'ej naDpu'bogh SonchIy? 'ej qatlh DutlhISmeH
poSlaw'pu' naghmey mollIj nujHey 'ughqu'?
molDaq pIroQDI', bIvIHbe'chu'bej.
chay' ghu' vIyaj? yoDSutlIj naQ DatuQ,
lomna' neH SoHtaHvIS, 'ej maSwov DoS
DaSuchqa', ram DaghIjmoHtaHvIS jay'!
jotrupbogh 'u' qoH, maHbogh, tIq DaSujchu'.
'ej qechmey'e' SIchQo'bogh qa'pu'ma'
jubuSmoH. nuqvaD? qatlh? DaH nuq wIta'nIS?

[HAMLET cholmoHmeH ghop vIHmoH lomqa']

Horey'So	SuH, naDevvo' DatlhejmeH ghopDaj vIHmoH.

DaH SoHvaD tey'ruplaw'.

marSe'luS	Daq Hop DaghoSmeH

Ducholqangmo H, DochHa'qu'taHvIS mIwDaj.
'ach yItlhejQo'.

Horey'So	Qo', joH. yItlhejbejQo'.
Hamlet	chay'? jIHvaD jatlhlaw'Qo'. vaj ghaH vItlha'.
Horey'So	Qo', joH.
Hamlet	qatlh? Qob vIHajnISbogh yIngu' jay'!

jIHvaD mavjop potlh law', yInwIj potlh puS.
'ej qa'wI''e' not QIHlaHba' lomqa',
jubmo' Hoch qa'. mura'qa'law'. vItlha'.

Horey'So	'a joH, bIQ'a' DaghoS 'e' tlhu'moHneSchugh?

pagh, ghaH bIngvo' bIQ'a' botlh DungDaq HuSbogh
'ej ghIjqu'bogh qoj'a' DaghoSmoHchugh?
pa' pumbeHlaw' 'ej chong qoj'a'vetlh jej.
pa' chenqa'laH je qa'. 'ej qu'mo' qabDaj,
chaq SoHvo' che'bogh yablIj laHmey nge'laH.
bImaw'choHmeH DujotlhlaH. ghu' yIqel.
Hoch yabDaq 'Itchu'meH Qujqechmey lanlaH
Daqvetlh neH—'ItmeH DachtaHvIS latlh meq—
qelI'qam law' bIQ'a'vetlh ral lubejDI',
'ej bIngDaq jachqu' 'oH roD 'e' luQoyDI'.

Hamlet	DacholchoH neH ghaH. Ha' yIghoS. qatlha'.
marSe'luS	pa' bIcholbe'.

Hamlet	Hold off your hands.
Horatio	Be ruled; you shall not go.
Hamlet	My fate cries out,

And makes each petty artery in this body
As hardy as the Nemean lion's nerve.

[*Ghost beckons HAMLET*]

Still am I call'd; Unhand me, gentlemen;
By heaven, I'll make a ghost of him that lets me!
I say, away! Go on; I'll follow thee.

[*Exeunt Ghost and HAMLET*]

Horatio	He waxes desperate with imagination.
Marcellus	Let's follow; 'tis not fit thus to obey him.
Horatio	Have after. To what issue will this come?
Marcellus	Something is rotten in the state of Denmark.
Horatio	Heaven will direct it.
Marcellus	Nay, let's follow him.

[*Exeunt*]

SCENE V *Another part of the platform.*

[*Enter GHOST and HAMLET*]

Hamlet	Where wilt thou lead me? speak; I'll go no further.
Ghost	Mark me.
Hamlet	I will.
Ghost	My hour is almost come,

When I to sulphurous and tormenting flames
Must render up myself.

Hamlet	Alas, poor ghost!
Ghost	Pity me not, but lend thy serious hearing

To what I shall unfold.

Hamlet	Speak; I am bound to hear.
Ghost	So art thou to revenge, when thou shalt hear.
Hamlet	What?
Ghost	I am thy father's spirit;

Doom'd for a certain term to walk the night,
And, for the day, confin'd to waste in fires
Till the foul crimes done in my days of nature
Are burnt and purg'd away. But that I am forbid
To tell the secrets of my prison-house,
I could a tale unfold whose lightest word
Would harrow up thy soul; freeze thy young blood;
Make thy two eyes, like stars, start from their spheres;
Thy knotted and combined locks to part,
And each particular hair to stand on end,
Like quills upon the fretful porpentine:

Hamlet	jIHvo' ghopDu' tIteq.
Horey'So	yIra"eghchu'. pa' yIghoSQo'.
Hamlet	jach SanwIj.

'ej porghwIj Hoch 'aD machqu' IetmoHmo',
DaH bIH rotlh law', veqlargh Somraw rotlh puS.

[*HAMLET ra' Iomqaʼ*]

mura'II'. qaH, jIHvo' ghopDu' tIteq.
baQa', Iomqa'na' moj munISbogh ghot.
jIjatlh: peDoH. Ha', qa'! yIghoS. qatlha'II'.

[*mej Iomqa' HAMLET je*]

Horey'So	'Itqu'choH ghaH, qech jochqu' buStaHmo'.
marSe'IuS	wItlha'nIS. mujbej Qu'maj, ghaH wIIobchugh.
Horey'So	SIbI' vItlha'. wanI'vammo' tlha' nuq?
marSe'IuS	Hu'tegh, DaH Qo'noS wo'Daq nonlaw' vay'.
Horey'So	Do' ghu'Daj naQ che' San.
marSe'IuS	Qo'. SuH, wItlha'.

[*mej chaH*]

LUT 'AY'HOM VAGH. *'avwI'Daq Iatlh 'ay'*

[*'elqa' HAMLET Iomqa' je*]

Hamlet	nuqDaq choDev? yIjang! jIghoStaHQo'.
Iomqa'	yIqImchu'.
Hamlet	lu'.
Iomqa'	tugh qaSqa' bIjmeH repwIj.

'ej joy'bogh 'ej He'So'bogh qulmeyDaq
jIjegh'eghnIS.

Hamlet	va, bIDo'Ha'ba', qa'.
Iomqa'	Qo', HIvupQo'. 'a SoHvaD ngoD vIpeghbogh

tItu'chu', 'ej tIbuS.

Hamlet	yIja'. qa'IjrupMar.
Iomqa'	bortaS Data'rup je, choQoypu'DI'.
Hamlet	nuqjatlh?
Iomqa'	vavlI' Iomqa' jIH.

qaStaHvIS ram jIyItnISmeH vIqIchlu',
taHtaHvIS HupmeH bov. 'ej qaSDI' po,
jIpayII'meH bIjqulmeyDaq vIweghlu'—
webbogh Hoch HeSmeywIj vIta'pu'bogh,
qaStaHvIS yInwIj jaj, vISay'moHpa',
'ej bIH vIqIlpa'. toH bIghHa'wIj peghmey
vIja' net chaw'chugh, vaj lut Doj vIja'laH.
'ej qa'II' QommoHIaH lut mu'Hom neH.
ghoDaj bavHa'chugh yuQ, vaj mInlIj rurlaH,
lut mu' DaQoyDI'. taDlaH 'IwlIj Qup.
chevchuqlaH bagh'eghbogh 'ej jeDbogh jIblIj.

But this eternal blazon must not be
To ears of flesh and blood.—List, list, O, list!—
If thou didst ever thy dear father love—

Hamlet	O God!
Ghost	Revenge his foul and most unnatural murder.
Hamlet	Murder!
Ghost	Murder most foul, as in the best it is; But this most foul, strange, and unnatural.
Hamlet	Haste me to know't that I, with wings as swift As meditation or the thoughts of love, May sweep to my revenge.
Ghost	I find thee apt; And duller shouldst thou be than the fat weed That roots itself in ease on Lethe wharf, Wouldst thou not stir in this. Now, Hamlet, hear: 'Tis given out that, sleeping in my orchard, A serpent stung me; so the whole ear of Denmark Is by a forged process of my death Rankly abus'd: but know, thou noble youth, The serpent that did sting thy father's life Now wears his crown.
Hamlet	O my prophetic soul! Mine uncle!
Ghost	Ay, that incestuous, that adulterate beast, With witchcraft of his wit, with traitorous gifts,— O wicked wit and gifts, that have the power So to seduce!—won to his shameful lust The will of my most seeming-virtuous queen: O Hamlet, what a falling-off was there! From me, whose love was of that dignity That it went hand in hand even with the vow I made to her in marriage; and to decline Upon a wretch whose natural gifts were poor To those of mine! But virtue, as it never will be mov'd, Though lewdness court it in a shape of heaven; So lust, though to a radiant angel link'd, Will sate itself in a celestial bed, And prey on garbage. But, soft! methinks I scent the morning air; Brief let me be.—Sleeping within my orchard, My custom always of the afternoon, Upon my secure hour thy uncle stole, With juice of cursed hebenon in a vial, And in the porches of mine ears did pour The leperous distilment; whose effect Holds such an enmity with blood of man That, swift as quicksilver, it courses through The natural gates and alleys of the body; And with a sudden vigour doth posset

'ej QamchoHmo' jIbIIj Hoch tlhegh, bIyay'DI',
to'baj pachDu' rur bIH, pay' HajDI' 'oH.
'ach 'Iw neH ghajbogh teSvaD bov SanbIjvam
ja'be'nISlu'. yI'Ij! baQa', yI'Ij!
qaStaHvIS vay', vavlI' DavuvchoHchugh,—

Hamlet	QI'yaH!

| lomqa' | vaj vavvetlh chotlu'mo', quvHa'lu'taHvIS, |
| | qorDu'Daj wemlu'DI'—bortaS yIta'. |

| Hamlet | chot'a'? |

| lomqa' | quvHa'qu' chotDI'. reH quvHa' chotwI'. |
| | 'ach chotDI' Hujqu', wemqu', 'ej quvHa'qu'. |

Hamlet	SIbI' HISovmoH. vaj yabqech, bang choH joq
	vIDa jImoDchu'mo': SIbI' bortaSvaD
	jIHIv.

lomqa'	bIchavrupba'. bISuvnISDI',
	chaq vulqan tI DaDachugh je, bIbuDmo',
	vaj Qu' Dachavrupbej. yI'IjII', Hamlet.
	naHSormey ghomwIjDaq jIQongtaHvIS,
	mu'aw'pu' ghargh net maq. 'ej Qo'noS qoghHey
	lutojbejpu' webwI'pu', Hegh luja'DI',
	chIch ngebmoHmo'. SuvwI' quv, ngoD yISov:
	vavlI' mIv'e' DaH tuQ vav 'aw'pu'bogh
	Hu' gharghqoq'e'.

| Hamlet | tIqwIj: leSSov vIghajlaw'! vavloDnI'wI'! |

lomqa'	HIja'. tlhogh wembogh, 'ej qorDu'Daj ngaghbogh
	petaQ! DaH nga'chuq tuHnIStaHvIS chaH,
	'e' lajmeH quvlaw'qu'bogh be'nalwI',
	'urmangDaj nobmey much, 'ej 'ongchu' yabDaj.
	vaj Qapta' ghaH. Qu'vatlh, bImIghbej, yab!
	SumIghbej, nobmey, be' botojlaHchu'mo'!
	Sab be'nal Dotlh jay', Hamlet! jIHvo' pum.
	'ej reH nur leHtaHmo' muSHa'ghachwIj,
	vaj tlhoghvaD 'Ip vIlay'bogh DorbeHbej 'oH.
	'a DaH petaQDaq pum. 'ej SupHomwIj
	QaQ law', petaQvam jo QaQ puSqu' jay'!
	batlh'e' not ponlaH ngaghbogh wem, qar'a';
	ponmeH, QI'tu'ngan rurmeH chenchugh je.
	SuvwI'na' wovqu' muvchugh je wemDotlh,
	vaj DalchoH batlh QongDaq 'e' Har, 'ej tugh
	veQ Sopqang!
	QI'yaH! jajlo' vIlarghlaw'. nom jIja'nIS.
	qaStaHvIS pov, SorghomwIjDaq jIQong.
	reH tIghwIj 'oHtaH. pa' jIQongtaHvIS,
	taHtaHvIS jIHubbe''eghmeH len rep,
	mucholmeH pegh'egh vavloDnI'lI' 'ong.
	'ej He'benon vIychorgh HIvje' 'up qengDI',
	qoghDu'wIj 'ochDaq DIrroptaSvam qang.
	yoq 'IwvaD ghol luDamo' taSvam HoSmey,
	tugh porgh lojmItmeyDaq, porgh HemeyDaq je
	moDqu' bIH. moDDI', 'aj toQDuj lurur.
	jeDchoH 'ej SubchoH pIvtaHbogh 'Iw yIQ,

And curd, like eager droppings into milk,
The thin and wholesome blood: so did it mine;
And a most instant tetter bark'd about,
Most lazar-like, with vile and loathsome crust,
All my smooth body.
Thus was I, sleeping, by a brother's hand,
Of life, of crown, of queen, at once dispatch'd:
Cut off even in the blossoms of my sin,
Unhousel'd, unanointed, unanel'd;
No reckoning made, but sent to my account
With all my imperfections on my head:
O, horrible! O, horrible! most horrible!
If thou hast nature in thee, bear it not;
Let not the royal bed of Denmark be
A couch for luxury and damned incest.
But, howsoever thou pursu'st this act,
Taint not thy mind, nor let thy soul contrive
Against thy mother aught: leave her to heaven,
And to those thorns that in her bosom lodge,
To prick and sting her. Fare thee well at once!
The glow-worm shows the matin to be near,
And 'gins to pale his uneffectual fire:
Adieu, adieu! Hamlet, remember me.

[*Exit*]

Hamlet   O all you host of heaven! O earth! what else?
And shall I couple hell?—O, fie! Hold, my heart;
And you, my sinews, grow not instant old,
But bear me stiffly up.—Remember thee!
Ay, thou poor ghost, while memory holds a seat
In this distracted globe. Remember thee!
Yea, from the table of my memory
I'll wipe away all trivial fond records,
All saws of books, all forms, all pressures past,
That youth and observation copied there;
And thy commandment all alone shall live
Within the book and volume of my brain,
Unmix'd with baser matter: yes, by heaven!—
O most pernicious woman!
O villain, villain, smiling, damned villain!
My tables,—meet it is I set it down,
That one may smile, and smile, and be a villain;
At least, I am sure, it may be so in Denmark:

[*Writing*]

So, uncle, there you are. Now to my word;
It is 'Adieu, adieu! remember me.'
I have sworn't.

Marcellus   [*Within*] My lord, my lord,—
& Horatio

Marcellus   [*Within*] Lord Hamlet,—

Horatio   [*Within*] Heaven secure him!

Marcellus   [*Within*] So be it!

'ej nIm rur, nonmo' 'oHDaq wIbchoHDI'.
nom 'e' chav rIntaH. jeDchoHpu' je 'IwwIj.
'ej vaQbogh porghwIj Dech DIrnaghHey letqu'.
'ej muroSHa'moH HIghbogh rop DIr mo'Hey
web'e'.
vaj jIHvo' be'nal, yIn je, ta'mIv je
nge'pu' loDnI'wI' ghop, jIQongDI'; quq.
murInmoHta', jIchun'eghchoHmoHpa'.
mInDu'wIj bej, 'ej lomDaq jach pagh vaj.
yo' qIj vI'elrupbe'. loj paymcH 'ebwIj.
Qu'vatlh! Hoch Duy'meywIj vIqengtaHvIS,
tugh mughIpDIjchu'meH veqlargh, mungeH.
QI'yaH! Ha', QI'yaH! vav Davuvrupchugh,
vaj ghu'vam yISIQQo'. qorDu'wIj wemmeH
'ej ngaghmeH neH taHqeq, lI' ta' QongDaq,
Qo'noSDaq 'e' yIbot. 'ach Qu' DanIDDI',
SoSlI' DaQIHmeH SoH, 'oghbe'nIS qa'lI'.
'ej joch'eghQo'jaj yablInlS. ghaH lubljnIS
veqlargh meqba"a', tIqDaj 'oy'moHbogh
'ej 'aw'taHbogh pach jejqu"e' je. QI'yaH!
naDev jIratlhlaHbe'. tugh qaSchoH po,
'e' 'ang ghargh wov. 'ej quIDaj tIhIb rIHHa' 'oH.
Qapla'. qamej! qamej! Hamlet, HIqaw!

[mej]

Hamlet	QI'tu' mangghom! ngeHbej! QI'yaH, nuq latlh? ghe"or vIpongnIS'a' je? SuH, SIQ, SIQ, Somrawwlj, 'ej SIbI' peqanchoHQo'. jIQamlaHmeH HIboQ! peHoS! "HIqaw?" lomqa' Do'Ha'qu', tamey leHlaHtaHvIS maw'rupbogh nachvam! chay'? "HIqaw?" HIja', yabwIj HabII'vo', rambogh Hoch ta Dogh vIQaw'. Hoch paq paQDI'norgh. Hoch qawHaq. Hoch ngoDmey'e' ben qonpu'bogh qoj tu'bogh yablaHwIj Qup. nIteb yab paqwIjDaq, HabII'Daq je ratlh Qu' chora'pu'bogh. pa' lam quvHa' DuDbe'lu'bej. ghuy'cha'! be' mIghqu'! taHqeq! taHqeq! monbogh webbogh taHqeq! nuqDaq ghItlhpaqwIj? ngoD vIqonnISba': monlaH 'ej montaH je taHqeq quvHa'. Qo'noSDaq qaSlaH DaH 'e' tobbej ghu'.

[ghItlh]

pItlh, vavloDnI'. DaH SoQ vIqeInISqa'.
nuq jatlhpu' ghaH? "qamej! qamej! HIqaw!"
jI'Ipchu' rIntaH.

marSe'luS Horey'So je	['emvo'] joHwI'! joH!
marSe'luS	['emvo'] Hamlet joH!
Horey'So	['emvo'] ghaH Qanjaj qeylIS!
marSe'luS	['emvo'] toH, vaj qaSjaj.

Horatio	[*Within*] Hillo, ho, ho, my lord!
Hamlet	Hillo, ho, ho, boy! come, bird, come.
	[*Enter HORATIO and MARCELLUS*]
Marcellus	How is't, my noble lord?
Horatio	What news, my lord?
Hamlet	O, wonderful!
Horatio	Good my lord, tell it.
Hamlet	No; you'll reveal it.
Horatio	Not I, my lord, by heaven.
Marcellus	Nor I, my lord.
Hamlet	How say you, then; would heart of man once think it?— But you'll be secret?
Horatio & *Marcellus*	Ay, by heaven, my lord.
Hamlet	There's ne'er a villain dwelling in all Denmark But he's an arrant knave.
Horatio	There needs no ghost, my lord, come from the grave To tell us this.
Hamlet	Why, right; you are i' the right;— And so, without more circumstance at all, I hold it fit that we shake hands and part: You, as your business and desire shall point you,— For every man has business and desire, Such as it is;—and for mine own poor part, Look you, I'll go pray.
Horatio	These are but wild and whirling words, my lord.
Hamlet	I'm sorry they offend you, heartily; Yes, 'faith heartily.
Horatio	There's no offence, my lord.
Hamlet	Yes, by Saint Patrick, but there is, Horatio, And much offence too. Touching this vision here; It is an honest ghost, that let me tell you: For your desire to know what is between us, O'ermaster 't as you may. And now, good friends, As you are friends, scholars and soldiers, Give me one poor request.
Horatio	What is't, my lord? we will.
Hamlet	Never make known what you have seen to-night.
Horatio & *Marcellus*	My lord, we will not.
Hamlet	Nay, but swear't.

Horey'So	[*'emvo'*] Ha'! Ha'! Ha' joHwI'!
Hamlet	HaHaHa! Haghlaw' mang!
	[*'el* HOREY'SO MARSE'LUS *je*]
marSe'luS	joH, DotlhlIj nuq?
Horey'So	De' chu' Daghoj; yIDel.
Hamlet	toH! merqu' De'!
Horey'So	vaj 'oH glioja'neS.
Hamlet	Qo'.
	De' DapeghHa'ba' SoH.
Horey'So	jIjatlhpa', jatlhbej Hovmey.
marSe'luS	jatlhbej Hov, joH.
Hamlet	vuDraj nuq? toH! 'oH HarlaH'a' tIq vay'?
	'a De' bopegh, qar'a'?
Horey'So	wIpeghbejneS.
marSe'luS je	
Hamlet	Qo'noSDaq yInbogh wa' taHqeq web law',
	Qo'noS Hoch latlh web puS. 'ej—toH, petaQ ghaH.
Horey'So	De'vam nuja'meH 'utba' molvo' cheghbogh
	pagh qa', joHwI'.
Hamlet	HIja', bIlugh. bIlughba'.
	vaj lIHmeH wa' latlh mu' vIja'choHbe' je.
	mavanchuq 'ej matlheDchuq 'e' vIwuq.
	Qu', neHtaHghach je pabnIS Hoch, qar'a',
	Hoch Sar wIqelchugh. vay' vIpabnISmo' je—
	vaj SuH: jImI' jIjaH.
Horey'So	maw' neH 'ej taQqu' mu'meyvam, joH quv.
Hamlet	Dumawmo' bIH, jIQoSqu', jup. jIQoSqu'.
	HIja'. jIQoS.
Horey'So	ghobe'. mawbe'ba', joH.
Hamlet	qarbe', Horey'So. 'oljaj ghe''or Qang.
	chIch mawqu'lu'bejta'. HoSDo' vIqelDI'—
	yuDHa'bej qa'vetlh. De'vam'e' Saja'laH.
	'a ghu' wIbuSbogh, pa' maja'chuqtaHvIS—
	boSovqangbe'choHchugh, vaj DaH petung'egh.
	'ej tugh, Do', Qap SutammeH Qu'. toH, jup:
	SuvwI', HaDwI' je, jupna'wI' je tlhIHmo',
	jIHvaD wa' Qu'Hom neH ylta'.
Horey'So	Qu' nuq?
	wIta'rup.
Hamlet	wanI'mey'e' DaHjaj boleghpu'bogh
	not bopeghHa'.
Horey'So	luq, joH.
marSe'luS je	
Hamlet	pe'Ip je.

Horatio	In faith, My lord, not I.
Marcellus	Nor I, my lord, in faith.
Hamlet	Upon my sword.
Marcellus	We have sworn, my lord, already.
Hamlet	Indeed, upon my sword, indeed.
Ghost	[*Beneath*] Swear.
Hamlet	Ah, ha, boy! say'st thou so? art thou there, truepenny?— Come on—you hear this fellow in the cellarage— Consent to swear.
Horatio	Propose the oath, my lord.
Hamlet	Never to speak of this that you have seen, Swear by my sword.
Ghost	[*Beneath*] Swear.
Hamlet	Hic et ubique? then we'll shift our ground.— Come hither, gentlemen, And lay your hands again upon my sword: Never to speak of this that you have heard, Swear by my sword.
Ghost	[*Beneath*] Swear.
Hamlet	Well said, old mole! canst work i' the earth so fast? A worthy pioner!—Once more remove, good friends.
Horatio	O day and night, but this is wondrous strange!
Hamlet	And therefore as a stranger give it welcome. There are more things in heaven and earth, Horatio, Than are dreamt of in your philosophy. But come;— Here, as before, never, so help you mercy, How strange or odd soe'er I bear myself,— As I, perchance, hereafter shall think meet To put an antic disposition on,— That you, at such times seeing me, never shall, With arms encumber'd thus, or this headshake, Or by pronouncing of some doubtful phrase, As 'Well, well, we know;'—or 'We could, an if we would;'— Or 'If we list to speak;'—or 'There be, an if they might;'— Or such ambiguous giving out, to note That you know aught of me:—this not to do, So grace and mercy at your most need help you, Swear.
Ghost	[*Beneath*] Swear.
Hamlet	Rest, rest, perturbed spirit! [*They swear*] So, gentlemen,

Horey'So Hu'tegh,
not vIpeghHa'bej, joH.

marSe'luS not vIpeghHa' je.

Hamlet 'etlhwIjDaq 'e' yI'Ip.

marSe'luS wI'Ipta', joH.

Hamlet ghobe'. ghobe'. 'ach 'etlhwIjDaq pe'Ipqa'.

Iomqa' [*bIngvo'*] pe'Ip.

Hamlet baQa', nuqjatlh? Ha' Iomoy! pa' SoH'a'?
juppu', Ha'. SomDaq ghotvetlh chuS boQoy.
pe'Ipqang.

Horey'So 'Ip wI'IpnISbogh ghoQljneS.

Hamlet not ghu'meyvam boleghpu'bogh boja',
'etlhwIjDaq 'e' yI'Ip.

Iomqa' [*bIngvo'*] pe'Ip.

Hamlet chay'? *Here and everywhere?* vaj Daq wIchoHmoH.
qaH, naDev ghoS.
'ej 'etlhwIjDaq ghopDu'raj'e' tIlanqa'.
'eH, 'etlhwIjDaq yI'Ip:
not ghu'meyvam boleghpu'bogh boja',

Iomqa' [*bIngvo'*] 'eH, 'etlhDajDaq pe'Ip.

Hamlet majQa', Iamto'baj! nom yav bIng DalenglaH!
po'qu' tlhIlwI'vam! Daq yIchoHmoH, jup.

Horey'So Hu'tegh! baQa'! Hat ghu'!

Hamlet vaj Hat yISIQ,
'ej tujDI', DopIlj qul yIchenmoHQo'.
chalDaq, ghorDaq je law'bej Doch, Horey'So.
'ej puSqu' Dochmey'e' neH najbogh QeDIlj.
toH Ha'.
jaS peDaQo'. 'ej batlh yo' qIj bo'elmeH:
jItaQchugh qoj jIHujchoHchugh jIDaDI',
IeS chIch qoH tlhaQ vIDa chaq 'e' vIwuqDI'—
qaStaHvIS poHmeyvetlh, tuleghDI' tlhIH,
'eH, not DeSDu' tIbagh. not nach tIjoqmoH.
not Honbogh mu'tlhegh vay' tIja' je jay'—
vaj not "toH, toH, ghu''e' wISov,"
"mata'laH, mata'qangchugh" joq, "maja'qangchugh neH" joq,
"net chaw'chugh, vaj 'e' ta'meH Iutu'lu'" joq.
'ej not SuloymoHmeH SoQghoch yIjunmoH.
vaj ghu'wIj'e' boSov, not 'e' yIqImmoH.
'ej "Hochvam wIta'Qo'" SIbI' pe'Ip.
vaj rInDI' Heraj, 'ej bo'elrupDI',
Do' IomrajDaq yo' qIjvaD jachlu'jaj!

Iomqa' [*bIngvo'*] pe'Ip!

Hamlet yIleS, yIleS, qa' Sot.

[*'Ip chaH*]

vaj, juppu'wI',

With all my love I do commend me to you:
And what so poor a man as Hamlet is
May do, to express his love and friending to you,
God willing, shall not lack. Let us go in together;
And still your fingers on your lips, I pray.
The time is out of joint:—O cursed spite,
That ever I was born to set it right!—
Nay, come, let's go together.

[*Exeunt*]

ACT II
SCENE I *A room in Polonius' house.*

[*Enter POLONIUS and REYNALDO*]

Polonius	Give him this money and these notes, Reynaldo.
Reynaldo	I will, my lord.
Polonius	You shall do marvellous wisely, good Reynaldo Before you visit him, to make inquire Of his behavior.
Reynaldo	My lord, I did intend it.
Polonius	Marry, well said; very well said. Look you, sir, Inquire me first what Danskers are in Paris; And how, and who, what means, and where they keep, What company, at what expense; and finding By this encompassment and drift of question, That they do know my son, come you more nearer Than your particular demands will touch it: Take you, as 'twere, some distant knowledge of him; As thus, 'I know his father and his friends, And in part him; ' do you mark this, Reynaldo?
Reynaldo	Ay, very well, my lord.
Polonius	'And in part him;—but' you may say 'not well: But, if't be he I mean, he's very wild; Addicted so and so;' and there put on him What forgeries you please; marry, none so rank As may dishonour him; take heed of that; But, sir, such wanton, wild and usual slips As are companions noted and most known To youth and liberty.
Reynaldo	As gaming, my lord.
Polonius	Ay, or drinking, fencing, swearing, quarrelling, Drabbing: you may go so far.
Reynaldo	My lord, that would dishonour him.
Polonius	'Faith, no; as you may season it in the charge. You must not put another scandal on him, That he is open to incontinency; That's not my meaning: but breathe his faults so quaintly That they may seem the taints of liberty;

Savan 'ej jupna'ra' vIDarupbej.
llvuv 'ej llparHa'taH Hamlet puj,
Do' not net 'angmeH Dachjaj 'eb, chavlaH je.
Qo', HItlha'Qo'; matay'. patlh tIgh yIblv.
'ej SuH: lojmItvetlh poSDaq DaqlaH pagh.
pupHa'law' bov. va, noDbogh San vIpay.
va, qatlh vIlughmoHmeH jIboghpu' jay'!
Qo'. Ha' matay'.

[mej chaH]

LUT 'AY' CHA'
LUT 'AY'HOM WA' polonyuS juH pa'.

['el POLONYUS REYNALDO je]

polonyuS	'eH, ghaHvaD Huchvam ghItlhvam je tInob.
reynalDo	luq, joH.
polonyuS	reynalDo QaQ, bIvalqu', Qu' Data'chugh: "chay' Da layerteS," latlh tIghel DaSuchpa'.
reynalDo	joH, 'e' vIHech.
polonyuS	majQa'! majQa'! yIqIm: wa': romuluS Dabbogh Qo'noSnganpu''e' vISovchoHmeH yIghel. chay' ghoSta' chaH. 'Iv chaH. chay' chep chaH. Huchchaj law'moH nuq. 'Iv lutlhej. chay' wagh mIp. puqwI' luSov, QIt 'e' Datu'DI', DechII'mo' moDQo'bogh bIghelmeH SoQ, ghu' potlh yIcholchoHchu'— 'oH chollaHbe'mo' yu'chu'wI' yuDHa'. DaSovqu'be'law' pa' 'e' HarnIS Hoch. "vavDaj, juppu'Daj puS je neH vISov. 'ach ghaH vISovchu'be'." qIm'a', reynalDo?
reynalDo	jIqImchu', joH.
polonyuS	"vISovchu'be'bej jIH" bIjatlh net chaw'. "toH, ghot vIqelbogh ghaHchugh, vaj DaHa'taH. qaghmeyvam HoHtaH ghaH." 'ej DaH DapummeH, DubelmoHbogh ngoD ngeb tl'ogh. 'ach Hu'tegh, not luquvHa'moHlaw'meH, ramnIS bIH. Qu'vaD yIqIm. wej SuvchoHbogh loD Qup tlhejtaHmo' reHbogh tlhIvtaHghachmey motlhqu', vaj HeSHommeyvam ghov 'ej SovtaH Hoch. qaH, HeSvammo' yIpum.
reynalDo	chaq SuDlaw', joH.
polonyuS	HIja'. chaq chechlaw'; Hay'law'; tIchlaw'; Sollaw'; toH, chaq ngaghHa'law'—pumvam'e' qachaw' je.
reynalDo	'ach joH, ghaytan bong ghaH quvHa'moH pumvam.
polonyuS	Hu'tegh, ghobe'. DamaqDI', pum yIpujmoH. ngaghqangDI' SeH'eghbe' ghaH, yIja'Qo'— naDHa'ghach taghlaHmo'. not 'oH vIHechpu'. pumDaj DatlhuptaHvIS, qapHa'nIS SoQlIj. wej vaj Duj chIjbogh mangHom'e' lulammoH

The flash and outbreak of a fiery mind;
A savageness in unreclaimed blood,
Of general assault.

Reynaldo   But, my good lord,—

Polonius   Wherefore should you do this?

Reynaldo   Ay, my lord,
I would know that.

Polonius   Marry, sir, here's my drift;
And I believe, it is a fetch of wit:
You laying these slight sullies on my son,
As 'twere a thing a little soil'd i' the working,
Mark you,
Your party in converse, him you would sound,
Having ever seen in the prenominate crimes
The youth you breathe of guilty, be assur'd
He closes with you in this consequence,
'Good sir,' or so; or 'friend,' or 'gentleman,'—
According to the phrase or the addition
Of man and country.

Reynaldo   Very good, my lord.

Polonius   And then, sir, does he this—he does—what was I
about to say?—By the mass, I was about to say
something:—where did I leave?

Reynaldo   At 'closes in the consequence,' at 'friend or so,'
and 'gentleman.'

Polonius   At—'closes in the consequence,'—ay, marry;
He closes thus:—'I know the gentleman,
I saw him yesterday, or t' other day,
Or then, or then; with such, or such; and, as you say,
There was a' gaming; there o'ertook in's rouse;
There falling out at tennis:' or perchance,
'I saw him enter such a house of sale,'—
Videlicet, a brothel,—or so forth.—
See you now;
Your bait of falsehood takes this carp of truth:
And thus do we of wisdom and of reach,
With windlasses, and with assays of bias,
By indirections find directions out:
So, by my former lecture and advice,
Shall you my son. You have me, have you not?

Reynaldo   My lord, I have.

Polonius   God be wi' you; fare you well.

Reynaldo   Good my lord!

Polonius   Observe his inclination in yourself.

Reynaldo   I shall, my lord.

HeSHomvam neH vaj 'e' luHarnIS latlh.
Daw'choH 'ej joq neH meQlI'bogh wa' yab.
vaQ 'IwDaj'e' wej lobmoHpu'bogh Sun,
'ej Hoch Doch HIvqang ghaH.

| reynalDo | luq. 'ach joHwI'— |

polonyuS   qatlh Qu'vam yuD Data'nIS?

| reynalDo | joH, HIja', |

vISov vIneH.

polonyuS   qaH, ghu'vam'e' vIHech.
'ej maytaH tu'meH mIwvam 'e' vIHar.
puqwI' puqHeSHomvam Damaqpu'DI';
'ej "pIpyuS ghornIS pIpyuS pach Sopwi'"
bIjatlhDI'; vaj yIqIm:
HeSmo', Daja'bogh, DIv QupwI' DajoSbogh,
wa'logh 'e' leghchugh ghot DangonglI'bogh,
Suja'chuqtaHvIS, vaj, qaH, DIch yIghaj:
Suja'chuqtaH 'e' rInchoHmoHmeH ghotvetlh,
Dujatlh: "vajna'," "jupwI'" ghap, "qaH QaQ" ghap,
Segh wo' je tlgh, pongmIw je pabtaHvIS.

| reynalDo | lu', joH. |

polonyuS   toH, qaH, ta'vam vang—chay' vang—
va nuq vIjatlhruppu'? Hu'tegh, vay' vIjatlhruppu'.
nuqDaq vIja' 'e' vImev?

| reynalDo | "Suja'chuqtaH 'e' rInmoHmeH," |

"jupwI'" latlh ghap je, "qaH QaQ" je.

polonyuS   "Suja'chuqtaH 'e' rInmoHmeH."—HIja'!
vaj SoHvaD jatlh: "toH, loDvetlh Qup vISov.
wa'Hu' vIleghlaw', pagh wejHu' vIleghlaw',
pagh qaSDI' vay', pagh qaSpu'DI' wanI'vetlh,"
'ej vay'vam tlhejpu' ghaH, pagh vay'vetlh tlhejpu'.
'ej qarbej ghu' Daja'bogh. SuDtaH chaH.
pagh, chechqu'mo' lengHa'taHvIS, loQ vul.
pagh, SolchoH, 'ovmeH vI'qeq jeStaHvIS.
pagh, chaq vIlegh, malja' qach 'eltaHvIS."
—vaj, ngagh 'e' DIlmeH qach. "pagh, latlhDaq ghaH."
toH, qIm:
vIt Qa'vam jonba' tojbogh chablIj ngeb.
'ej DoS wIpuSmeH Sup 'ej SoDnIS pu'maj.
maQoDpu'DI' maDoQ, mavalqu'mo',
matu'chu'mo' je. SoQwIj qeSwIj je
Dapabchu'mo', puqloDwI'"e' DapuS je.
'ej peghDaj Sov DaDoQ je SoH, bIQoDDI'.
choyaj, qar'a'?

reynalDo	HIja', joH.
polonyuS	maj. Qapla'.
reynalDo	lu', joH.
polonyuS	'ej DameH mIw yItu' je SoH.
reynalDo	luq.

Polonius	And let him ply his music.
Reynaldo	Well, my lord.
Polonius	Farewell!

[*Exit REYNALDO*]

[*Enter OPHELIA*]

How now, Ophelia! what's the matter?

Ophelia	Alas, my lord, I have been so affrighted!
Polonius	With what, i' the name of God?

Ophelia My lord, as I was sewing in my closet,
Lord Hamlet,—with his doublet all unbraced;
No hat upon his head; his stockings foul'd,
Ungarter'd, and down-gyved to his ankle;
Pale as his shirt; his knees knocking each other;
And with a look so piteous in purport
As if he had been loosed out of hell
To speak of horrors,—he comes before me.

Polonius Mad for thy love?

Ophelia   My lord, I do not know;
But truly, I do fear it.

Polonius   What said he?

Ophelia He took me by the wrist and held me hard;
Then goes he to the length of all his arm;
And, with his other hand thus o'er his brow,
He falls to such perusal of my face
As he would draw it. Long stay'd he so;
At last,—a little shaking of mine arm,
And thrice his head thus waving up and down,—
He raised a sigh so piteous and profound
As it did seem to shatter all his bulk
And end his being: that done, he lets me go:
And, with his head over his shoulder turn'd,
He seem'd to find his way without his eyes;
For out o' doors he went without their help,
And to the last bended their light on me.

Polonius Come, go with me: I will go seek the king.
This is the very ecstasy of love;
Whose violent property fordoes itself
And leads the will to desperate undertakings,
As oft as any passion under heaven
That does afflict our natures. I am sorry.—
What, have you given him any hard words of late?

Ophelia No, my good lord; but, as you did command,
I did repel his letters, and denied
His access to me.

Polonius   That hath made him mad.
I am sorry that with better heed and judgment
I had not quoted him: I fear'd he did but trifle,
And meant to wreck thee; but, beshrew my jealousy!

polonyuS	'ej QoQDaj nID 'e' yInISQo'.
reynalDo	lu', joH.
polonyuS	Qapla'.

[*mej REYNALDO*]

['*el 'OVELYA*]

nuqneH, 'ovelya! qay'law' nuq?

'ovelya	QI'yaH, vIghIjqu'lu', joHwI', joHwI'!
polonyuS	Hu'tegh! DughIj maQmIghHey nuq?

'ovelya

joHwI',
pa'HomwIjDaq SutDegh vIchenmoHtaHvIS,
jIHDaq chol Hamlet joH. QeyHa'chu' wepDaj.
mIvDaj tuQbe' ghaH. ghIH paSIoghmeyDaj;
pumpu' bIH, 'ej qama' qammIrmey rur.
yIvbeHDaj rur ghaH, chISmo'. mupchuq qIvDaj.
'oy"a' luQummeH Hechlaw'mo' mInDu'Daj,
Qugh ja'meH, ghe"orvo' ghaH ghImlu'law'pu'.

polonyuS   parmaqIIjmo' maw"a'?

'ovelya

'e' vISovbe', joH.
'ach 'e' vIpIHbejneS.

polonyuS   toH, nuq Dujatlh?

'ovelya

yebDu'wIj tlhapchoH, 'ej jIHaw' 'e' nISchu'.
DeSDaj naQ tIqmoH. Huy'Daq latlhDaj IanmeH,
mIwvam pab. qaSDI', qabwIj bejchoHchu'mo',
'oH HotIhlaw'. DotIhvam IeHmeH nI'qu' poHDaj.
rInmoHmeH, DeSwIj QomchoHmoHlaw'DI',
'ej, wejlogh joqmeH nachDaj, mIwvam pabDI',
tlhuHqu' ghaH. vupmoHmo' 'ej HoSmo' tlhuHDaj,
vaj roDaj DejmoHlaw', 'ej qa'Daj HoHlaw'.
rInpu'DI', muweghHa'. volchaHDajDaq
mubejmeH nachDaj tlhe'taH; HeDaj SammeH,
mInDu' lo'be'law' ghaH, pa' HurDaq ghoSpa'.
'ej HurDaq mejpa', reH mubuSII' tlHchaj.

polonyuS

HItlhej, Ha'. ta' vISam. parmaqmo' maw'.
teHbej. 'ej ralmo' Dotlhvetlh, Qaw"egh bang,
'ej SuDbogh Qu'mey nIDmeH, yabDaj tlhu'moH.
ghu'vam motlh law', latlh' ghu"e' chavchoHmeH
nutlhu'moHbogh tIq rop motlh puS. jIQoSbej.
toH, qen Daqunta"a'?

'ovelya

ghobe', joH QaQ. 'ach qeSmeylIj vIpabta'.
jabbI'IDmeyDaj vIlajQo'. mucholII'
reH 'e' vIbot.

polonyuS

wanI'vammo' DaH maw'law'.
jIQoS: vInuDtaHvIS ghaH vInoHHa'
'ej muj leSSovwIj. SoHvaD reHpu' neH,
'ej leS SoH DuquvHa'moH, 'e' vIpIH.

It seems it is as proper to our age
To cast beyond ourselves in our opinions
As it is common for the younger sort
To lack discretion. Come, go we to the king:
This must be known; which, being kept close, might
move
More grief to hide than hate to utter love.

[*Exeunt*]

SCENE II *A room in the castle.*

[*Enter KING CLAUDIUS, QUEEN GERTRUDE, ROSENCRANTZ,
GUILDENSTERN, and Attendants*]

Claudius	Welcome, dear Rosencrantz and Guildenstern!
	Moreover that we much did long to see you,
	The need we have to use you did provoke
	Our hasty sending. Something have you heard
	Of Hamlet's transformation; so I call it,
	Sith nor the exterior nor the inward man
	Resembles that it was. What it should be,
	More than his father's death, that thus hath put him
	So much from the understanding of himself,
	I cannot dream of: I entreat you both,
	That being of so young days brought up with him,
	And sith so neighbour'd to his youth and havior,
	That you vouchsafe your rest here in our court
	Some little time: so by your companies
	To draw him on to pleasures, and to gather,
	So much as from occasion you may glean,
	Whether aught, to us unknown, afflicts him thus,
	That, open'd, lies within our remedy.

Gertrude
Good gentlemen, he hath much talk'd of you;
And sure I am two men there are not living
To whom he more adheres. If it will please you
To show us so much gentry and good will
As to expend your time with us awhile,
For the supply and profit of our hope,
Your visitation shall receive such thanks
As fits a king's remembrance.

Rosencrantz
       Both your majesties
Might, by the sovereign power you have of us,
Put your dread pleasures more into command
Than to entreaty.

Guildenstern
       But we both obey,
And here give up ourselves, in the full bent
To lay our service freely at your feet,
To be commanded.

Claudius Thanks, Rosencrantz and gentle Guildenstern.

Gertrude Thanks, Guildenstern and gentle Rosencrantz:
And I beseech you instantly to visit
My too much changed son.—Go, some of you,
And bring these gentlemen where Hamlet is.

'a Hu'tegh! jIpIHHa'ta'! qanDI' ghot,
vuD bo'Dagh'a' lo' ghaH; 'ej QuptaHvIS,
Sun bo'DaghHom lo' ghaH. Ha', ta' wIghoS.
De' SovnISlu'. wIpeghtaHvIS, maSoy'DI',
pegh lot Qob law', ta' QeH Qob puS—De' QoyDI'.

[*mej chaH*]

LUT 'AY'HOM CHA' *ta'qach pa'*.

['*el* TLHAW'DIYUS TA', GHERTLHUD TA'BE', ROSENQATLH,
GHILDESTEN, *tlhcjwI'pu' je*]

tlhaw'DIyuS
maj, roSenQatlh, maj, ghIlDeSten, nuqneH!
Salegh vIneHba'. jIHvaD 'ut je Qu'
SachavmoHbogh. vaj "tugh pechol" jIra'DI',
jImoDnIS. Hamlet chol lHey De' boQoypu'.
vIpongmeH, "choH" jIjatlhnIS; DotlhDaj ngo"e'
DaH luleHbe'mo' tIqDaj, porghDaj je.
pay' yaj'eghghachDaj nISba' vavDaj Hegh
'a nISmeH je latlh meq vIloylaHbe'.
vaj tlhIH Satlhob. qaStaHvIS jajraj Qup,
Sutay' tlhIH ghaH je, batlh boghojtaHvIS.
boSumtaH je, SuQupmo' 'ej SuvIDmo'.
vaj loQ naDev monjuHwIjDaq peratlhqang.
chaq ghaH botlhejmo', belmey nejqangqa' ghaH.
ghaH SotmoHtaH vay"e' wej Do' vISovbogh
chaq 'e' botu', IlloymoHlaHDI' 'eb.
'ej Seng bo'angDI', Do' chaq 'oH vIvorlaH.

ghertlhuD
jatlhtaHvIS, pIj IIbuSpu' ghaH, qaH QaQ.
'ej qarbej: tlhIHvaD tIqDaj SumtaH law',
yInbogh cha' vay'vaD tIqDaj SumtaH puS.
yInmeH 'ej chepmeH ghu' wItulll'bogh,
Suquvqang 'ej Suvupqang, 'e' che'angchugh,
'ej loQ naDev SumImchugh, vaj, SuSuchmo',
ta' vanvaD 'umbej tlho' boSuqlI'bogh.

roSenQatlh
maHvaD voDleH DIbHoS boghajneSmo',
Qu' chav boneHneSbogh boraDlaHbej.
chetlhobnISbe'.

ghIlDeSten
                    'ach batlh relobrupbej.
'ej tlhIH retoy'rupqu'mo', baHbogh pu'HIch
wIDaqangbej. vaj DaH majegh'eghneS.
chera'meH, qamrajDaq Hoch laHmeymaj
DIlan, cheraDpa'.

tlhaw'DIyuS
roSenQatlh, ghIlDeSten je quv, retlho'.

ghertlhuD
ghIlDeSten, roSenQatlh je quv, retlho'.
'ej 'eH: tugh choHqu'pu'bogh puqloDwI'
yISuch; Satlhob. Ha', 'eH, peghoS, mang puS.
'ej Hamlet DaqDaq loDvam quv tIDor.

| Guildenstern | Heavens make our presence and our practises |
| | Pleasant and helpful to him! |

| Gertrude | Ay, amen! |

[*Exeunt ROSENCRANTZ, GUILDENSTERN, and some Attendants*]

[*Enter POLONIUS*]

| Polonius | The ambassadors from Norway, my good lord, |
| | Are joyfully return'd. |

| Claudius | Thou still hast been the father of good news. |

Polonius	Have I, my lord? Assure you, my good liege,
	I hold my duty, as I hold my soul,
	Both to my God and to my gracious king:
	And I do think,—or else this brain of mine
	Hunts not the trail of policy so sure
	As it hath us'd to do,—that I have found
	The very cause of Hamlet's lunacy.

| Claudius | O, speak of that; that do I long to hear. |

| Polonius | Give first admittance to the ambassadors; |
| | My news shall be the fruit to that great feast. |

| Claudius | Thyself do grace to them, and bring them in. |

[*Exit POLONIUS*]

| | He tells me, my sweet queen, he hath found |
| | The head and source of all your son's distemper. |

| Gertrude | I doubt it is no other but the main;— |
| | His father's death, and our o'erhasty marriage. |

| Claudius | Well, we shall sift him. |

[*Re-enter POLONIUS, with VOLTIMAND and CORNELIUS*]

| | Welcome, my good friends! |
| | Say, Voltimand, what from our brother Norway? |

Voltimand	Most fair return of greetings and desires.
	Upon our first, he sent out to suppress
	His nephew's levies; which to him appear'd
	To be a preparation 'gainst the Polack;
	But, better look'd into, he truly found
	It was against your highness: whereat griev'd,
	That so his sickness, age, and impotence
	Was falsely borne in hand,—sends out arrests
	On Fortinbras; which he, in brief, obeys;
	Receives rebuke from Norway; and, in fine,
	Makes vow before his uncle never more
	To give the assay of arms against your majesty.
	Whereon old Norway, overcome with joy,
	Gives him three thousand crowns in annual fee;
	And his commission to employ those soldiers,
	So levied as before, against the Polack:
	With an entreaty, herein further shown,

[*Giving a paper*]

| | That it might please you to give quiet pass |

ghIlDeSten	maSaHmo' 'ej maQorghmo', beljaj Hamlet, 'ej ghaHvaD QaHjaj ghu'!
ghertIhuD	'e' chaw'jaj San!

[*mej* ROSENQANTLH, GHILDESTEN, 'op tlhejwI'pu' je]

['el POLONYUS]

polonyuS	DuraSvo' cheghpu'neS Duypu', joHwI'. 'ej cheghDI' Quchqu'.
tlhaw'DIyuS	reH De' QaQ vav DaDa.
polonyuS	qar'a', joH quv? toH DIch yIghajneS: jIHvaD potIhchugh qa'wI', vaj jIHvaD potIhqu' ta'vaD, qa"a'vaD je Qu'wIj vIpabbogh. Hamlet maw'moHwI"e' DaH Do' vItu'bej—mujchugh, vaj jISammeH po'Ha'choHlaw' ben po'qu'taHbogh yabwIj, ngoDmey vIwamtaHvIS—DaH 'e' vIHarqu'.
tlhaw'DIyuS	yIja'choH. De'vetlh lI' vIQoyqangqu'.
polonyuS	nISuch Duypu'ma' 'e' yIchaw', jIjatlhpa'. rInDI' 'uQ'a'Daj, naHHey DalaH De'wIj.
tlhaw'DIyuS	vaj nay' tIlIHneS SoH. naDev tIDor.

[*mej* POLONYUS]

puqlI' QuchHa'ghach Hoch HaI, meqHey je
tu'pu' ghaH, 'e' muSovmoH, ghertIhuD, bang.

ghertIhuD	'a wa' meq potIhmo' qaSpu', 'e' vIHar: Heghmo' vavDaj 'ej moDqu'pu'mo' tlhoghmaj.
tlhaw'DIyuS	toH, tuQDoqna' vIlo'rup.

['elqa' POLONYUS. lutIhej VOLTIMAD QORNELYUS je]

jup, nuqneH!
'eH, voltImaD, nuq Qum DuraS loDnI'wI'?

voltImaD	DurI' ghaH 'ej Duvan, Davanpu'mo'. maja'chuqDI', vaj muvmoH vortIbraS tugh 'e' lumevmeH, pa' Duypu' ngeH pIn. qInSaya HIvmeH qeqtaH Hu' 'e' Har ghaH. 'ach nuDchu'DI', nIQojmeH qeqtaH chaH 'e' tu'bej pIn. 'ej Qay'qu'—tojlu'pu'mo', roptaHvIS, qantaHvIS, HoSHa'taHvIS ghaH. vaj mevmeH vortIbraS, jabbI'ID lab. nom ghu' vIja': lob latlh. ghaH qunqu' pIn. 'ej not DuQoj 'e' nIDqa', vavIoDnI'vaD 'e' 'IpnIS ghaH. vaj Quchqu'mo' pIn qan, qInSaya HIvmeH neghvetlh muvmoHta'bogh, DaH ghaHvaD woQDaj nobpu' pIn. 'ej Qu'vaD DISHuchDaj bIHmeH wejSaD DeQmey nob je. tlhobmeH ghItlh'e' lu'angbogh navvam qon je:

[ta'vaD nav nob]

Qu'vetlhvaD SepIlj lenglaHlI' mangghomDaj
tugh 'e' yIchaw'neS. Qob SIQbe'meH 'oH,
'ej chaw'lIj leHmeH, Qu"e' Delbogh navvetlh

Through your dominions for this enterprise,
On such regards of safety and allowance
As therein are set down.

ClaudiusS   It likes us well;
And at our more consider'd time we'll read,
Answer, and think upon this business.
Meantime we thank you for your well-took labour:
Go to your rest; at night we'll feast together:
Most welcome home!

[*Exeunt VOLTIMAND and CORNELIUS*]

Polonius   This business is well ended.
My liege, and madam,—to expostulate
What majesty should be, what duty is,
Why day is day, night night, and time is time,
Were nothing but to waste night, day and time.
Therefore, since brevity is the soul of wit,
And tediousness the limbs and outward flourishes,
I will be brief:—your noble son is mad:
Mad call I it; for to define true madness,
What is't but to be nothing else but mad?
But let that go.

Gertrude   More matter, with less art.

Polonius   Madam, I swear I use no art at all.
That he is mad, 'tis true: 'tis true 'tis pity;
And pity 'tis 'tis true: a foolish figure;
But farewell it, for I will use no art.
Mad let us grant him, then: and now remains
That we find out the cause of this effect;
Or rather say, the cause of this defect,
For this effect defective comes by cause:
Thus it remains, and the remainder thus.
Perpend.
I have a daughter.—have while she is mine—
Who, in her duty and obedience, mark,
Hath given me this: now gather, and surmise.

[*Reads*]

'To the celestial and my soul's idol, the most
beautified Ophelia,'—
That's an ill phrase, a vile phrase;—'beautified' is
a vile phrase: but you shall hear. Thus:

[*Reads*]

'In her excellent white bosom, these, &c.'

Gertrude   Came this from Hamlet to her?

Polonius   Good madam, stay awhile; I will be faithful.

[*Reads*]

    'Doubt thou the stars are fire;
        Doubt that the sun doth move;
    Doubt truth to be a liar;

yIpab je.

tlhaw'DIyuS	toH, mubelqu'moHbej ghu'vam.

vIqelmeH chaw'DI' poHwIj, ghItlh vIlaD.
ghu'vam'e' tugh vIbuSchu' 'ej vIjang je.
'a qaSpa', tlhIH SatIho' Suvumchu'ta'mo'.
peleS. yupma' wItaghbej, qaSDI' ram.
majQa' Sucheghmo'!

[*mej* VOLTIMAD QORNELYUS *je*]

polonyuS	Qu' luchavchu'ta'.

ta', ta'be' je: nuq 'oHnIS ta'Dotlh'e';
nuq 'oH Qu''e'; nuqmo' pem 'oH pem'e';
qatlh ram—ram'e'; 'ej qatlh poH 'oH poH'e':
Hochvetlh vIQIjchugh, vaj pem ram je poH je
Hoch vIlo'Ha' neH. toH SovlaHvaD qa'botlh
'oHmo' SoQ vI''e', 'ej Sov DeS, HaQchor je
'oHmo' SoQ DaI'e', vaj DaH nom jIja'.
maw'neS puqra'. toH, maw' ghaH, 'e' vIpong neH.
maw'lu' net QIjchu'chugh, vaj maw' QIjwI'.
'ach ramjaj SoQvetlh.

ghertlhuD	law'nIS De'na'lIj,

'ej puSnIS mu'QujlIj.

polonyuS	qa'Iprup, joH:

not mu' vIQuj. toH maw'mo', teHbej SoQwIj.
teHmo', Do'Ha' 'oH. 'ej Do'Ha'bej: teH.
Dogh mu'QujvetlIh. 'ach 'oH vIghImbej rIntaH,
mu' vIQujQo'mo'. maw' ghaH 'e' wIloy.
'ej yabDaj nISchoHwI''e' DaH wItu'nIS.
toH, "yabDaj mISmoHwI'" DaH jaS jIjatlhnIS:
qaSba'taH nISbogh mISvam, lISmo' vay'.
vaj ratlhtaH ghu', 'ej ratlhII' ghu' vIDelbogh.
peqImchu'.
puqbe' vIghaj. vIghaj vIghatlhtaHvIS.
'ej batlh mulobmo' ghaH 'ej Qu'Daj pabmo',
SuH: navvam nobta' ghaH. peqIm; penoH.

[*laD*]

"HovoywI'vaD—qa'wI' Ho'vaD—'ovelya 'IHchu'vaD"
mujbej mu'vetlh. moHbej mu'vetlh. moHbej "'IHchu'vaD."
'a tugh Hoch boQoy. ghItlh:

[*laD*]

povqu'bogh roDaj DoqDaq, Dochvam, [*taH*]

ghertlhuD	Hamletvo' De'vam Hevpu''a'?
polonyuS	joH quvqu', IoQ yIloS. ghItlh naQ vIlaDchu'.

[*laD*]

meQ Hovmey 'e' yIghoH.
    ratlh pemHov 'e' HIpon.
ngeb vIt chIch 'e' yInoH.

But never doubt I love.
'O dear Ophelia, I am ill at these numbers,
I have not art to reckon my groans: but that
I love thee best, O most best, believe it. Adieu.
'Thine evermore, most dear lady, whilst
this machine is to him, HAMLET.'

This, in obedience, hath my daughter shown me:
And more above, hath his solicitings,
As they fell out by time, by means, and place,
All given to mine ear.

Claudius	But how hath she
	Receiv'd his love?

Polonius	What do you think of me?

Claudius	As of a man faithful and honourable.

Polonius	I would fain prove so. But what might you think,
	When I had seen this hot love on the wing—
	As I perceiv'd it, I must tell you that,
	Before my daughter told me—what might you,
	Or my dear majesty your queen here, think,
	If I had play'd the desk or table-book;
	Or given my heart a winking, mute and dumb;
	Or look'd upon this love with idle sight;—
	What might you think? No, I went round to work,
	And my young mistress thus I did bespeak:
	'Lord Hamlet is a prince, out of thy sphere;
	This must not be:' and then I precepts gave her,
	That she should lock herself from his resort,
	Admit no messengers, receive no tokens.
	Which done, she took the fruits of my advice;
	And he, repulsed—a short tale to make—
	Fell into a sadness; then into a fast;
	Thence to a watch; thence into a weakness;
	Thence to a lightness; and, by this declension,
	Into the madness wherein now he raves,
	And all we mourn for.

Claudius	Do you think 'tis this?

Gertrude	It may be, very likely.

Polonius	Hath there been such a time—I'd fain know that—
	That I have positively said 'Tis so,'
	When it proved otherwise?

Claudius	Not that I know.

Polonius	[Pointing to his head and shoulder]

Take this from this, if this be otherwise:
If circumstances lead me, I will find
Where truth is hid, though it were hid indeed
Within the centre.

Claudius	How may we try it further?

Polonius	You know, sometimes he walks for hours together
	Here in the lobby.

bang jIH, not 'e' yIHon.
'ovelya'oy, bom mu' vIqontaHvIS jIpo'be'. Hoch 'ItmoHwI'meywIj
QumlaHchu'be' ghItlhlaHwIj. 'ach bangII' jIHbejbogh
nong law', bangmey Dabogh latlh'e' nong puS; toH nongbe'
latlhvetlh 'e' yIHar. Qapla', jawoy. reH bangII', porghDaj
yInmoHtaHvIS neH QuQDaj, HAMLET'e'.

mulobmo', jIHvaD navvam 'ang puqwI'.
'ej ghaHvaD tlhobDI' Hamlet, teSwIjvaD
Hoch poII, Hoch mIw je, Daq je ja'chu' ghaH.

tlhaw'DIyuS	'ach ghaH muSHa'choH Hamlet, chay' 'e' laj?
polonyuS	toH, 'Iv jIH 'e' DaHar?
tlhaw'DIyuS	loD quv, loD matlh je.
polonyuS	vItob vIneH. 'a nuq DaQublaH, joH, moDchoH parmaqchaj tuj, bong 'e' vItu'DI' ('ej 'e' vItu'bej, ja'choHpa' puqbe'wI'— tlhIHvaD vIchIDnIS), nuq boQubneS, ta', ta'be'lI' quv je, peghghItlhpaq vIDachugh; qoj, tIqwIjvaD mInDu' vISoQmoHchugh, QIchwIj vIlojmoHDI'; qoj, ghu' vIleghDI', nochDu'wIj vIyajbe'chugh; nuq boQubneS? ghobe'. SIbI' jIvang. puqbe'wI' QupvaD jIjatlh: "chavqo'lIj HurDaq Hamlet tu'lu'. qaSbe'nIS." 'ej vIra'choH: SuchtaH Hamlet 'e' nISmeH wegh'eghnIS. 'oSwI' lajbe'nIS. nobmey Suqbe'nIS. 'ej jIra'DI' rIntaH, yabDajDaq qeSwIj poch. vaj nom vIja': HamletvaD janglu'Qo'DI', 'ItchoH ghaH. Sopbe'choH. tugh Qongbe'choH. tugh HoSbe'choH. tugh mISchoH. ghaHvaD qaSpu'DI' Hoch choHvam, DaH maw'. DaH wam'egh yabDaj. DaH ma'IQ.
tlhaw'DIyuS	ghu'vetlhmo' SabchoH ghaH 'e' DaHar'a'?
ghertlhuD	ghaytan, ghaytan.
polonyuS	joH, qaSDI' vay'—jISovqang—ghu' vI'olmeH, "qaS" jIjatlh'a', qaSbe'bej 'oH net tobpa'?
tlhaw'DIyuS	wanI'vetlh vISovbe'.
polonyuS	[*nachDaj volchaHDaj je 'ang*] teHbe'chugh vuDwIj, Dochvamvo' Dochvam'e' yIteqneS jay'. muchaw'chugh 'eb, So'meH Daq'e' 'angHa'bogh vIt tugh vItu'—yuQbotlhDaq So'chugh je.
tlhaw'DIyuS	toH chay' wItobchoH?
polonyuS	qaStaHvIS rep law', rut vaSvam HeDaq yIttaH. 'e' DaSov.

Gertrude	So he does, indeed.
Polonius	At such a time I'll loose my daughter to him:
	Be you and I behind an arras then;
	Mark the encounter: if he love her not,
	And be not from his reason fall'n thereon,
	Let me be no assistant for a state,
	But keep a farm and carters.
Claudius	We will try it.
Gertrude	But look, where sadly the poor wretch comes reading.
Polonius	Away, I do beseech you, both away:
	I'll board him presently.—O, give me leave:

[*Exeunt KING CLAUDIUS, QUEEN GERTRUDE, and Attendants*]

[*Enter HAMLET, reading*]

How does my good Lord Hamlet?

Hamlet	Well, God-a-mercy.
Polonius	Do you know me, my lord?
Hamlet	Excellent, excellent well; you are a fishmonger.
Polonius	Not I, my lord.
Hamlet	Then I would you were so honest a man.
Polonius	Honest, my lord!
Hamlet	Ay, sir; to be honest, as this world goes, is to be
	one man picked out of ten thousand.
Polonius	That's very true, my lord.
Hamlet	For if the sun breed maggots in a dead dog, being a
	god kissing carrion,—Have you a daughter?
Polonius	I have, my lord.
Hamlet	Let her not walk i' the sun: conception is a
	blessing: but not as your daughter may conceive:—
	Friend, look to 't.
Polonius	[*Aside*]
	How say you by that? Still harping on my
	daughter:—yet he knew me not at first; he said I
	was a fishmonger: he is far gone, far gone: and
	truly in my youth I suffered much extremity for
	love; very near this. I'll speak to him again.—
	What do you read, my lord?
Hamlet	Words, words, words.
Polonius	What is the matter, my lord?
Hamlet	Between who?
Polonius	I mean, the matter that you read, my lord.
Hamlet	Slanders, sir: for the satirical rogue says here
	that old men have grey beards; that their faces are

ghertlhuD	yItbej.
polonyuS	vaj pa' puqbe'wI' vIweghHa'. 'ej qaStaHvIS, nuSo'taHlaH HaSta. ghomchuqmeH mIw yItu'. ghaH muSHa'be'chugh, 'ej ghaH muSHa'qu'mo' Sabbe'chugh yabDaj, vaj wo' qumboQ jIHbe'jaj. Du', veQDuj je vIvu'choHjaj jay'.
tlhaw'DIyuS	maj, tugh nab wInID.
ghertlhuD	peqIm. DaH chol Do'Ha'wI'. Sagh 'ej laD.
polonyuS	pemejneS, joH. SatIhob, pemejneS, cha'. SIbI' vIDorchoH. Ha' HIchaw'neS, joH.
	[*mej* TLHAW'DIYUS TA', GHERTLHUD TA'BE', *toy'wI'pu' je*]
	['el HAMLET *laDtaHvIS*]
	DotlhIlj nuq, joHwI'?
Hamlet	jIquv!
polonyuS	choghov'a', joHwI'?
Hamlet	qaghovchu'; verengan mut 'oH mutlIj'e'
polonyuS	ghobe', joHwI'.
Hamlet	vaj bImutbe'mo' qanaD.
polonyuS	jImutbe''a', joHwI'?
Hamlet	HISlaH, wa'netlh nuvvo' le' wa' mutbe'wI'.
polonyuS	teHqu', joHwI'.
Hamlet	"pe'vIl targh lomDaq SISDI' 'otlh vID, gharghHom nenmoHchugh, yInroHHom notlhHa'moHlaHchu'mo' woj'a'..." puqbe' Daghaj'a'?
polonyuS	HIja', joHwI'.
Hamlet	SISbogh Sep'e' bong 'el ghaH 'e' yIbot. lopmoHbej ghu muvtay, 'ach SeplaHmo' puqbe'lI'—jup, qeS yIqel.
polonyuS	[*pegh'egh*] nuqjatlh jay'? puqbe'wI' buStaH qar'a'? 'a mughovbe'pu'. verengan jIH 'e' noHHa'. loj, lojqu' yabDaj. 'a jIQuptaHvIS je jIH, reH muSHa'qu'bogh tlqwIjmo' jIbechbej— ghaH vIrurba'pu'. jIljatlhqa'. nuq DalaD, joHwI'?
Hamlet	mu', mu', mu'.
polonyuS	nuq luqel, joHwI'?
Hamlet	vangmeH qel 'Iv?
polonyuS	'ach De''e' luqelbogh mu' 'oH nuq'e', joHwI'?
Hamlet	mu'qaD. qon qoH tlhIv, "loD qan porghDaq chIS rol, Hab Quch, DughHa' 'ej Hurgh bIQ jeD nljbogh mInDu''e',

	wrinkled; their eyes purging thick amber and plum-tree gum; and that they have a plentiful lack of wit, together with most weak hams: all which, sir, though I most powerfully and potently believe, yet I hold it not honesty to have it thus set down; for you yourself, sir, should be old as I am, if, like a crab, you could go backward.
Polonius	[*Aside*] Though this be madness, yet there is method in 't.—Will you walk out of the air, my lord?
Hamlet	Into my grave?
Polonius	Indeed, that is out o' the air.—
	[*Aside*]
	How pregnant sometimes his replies are! A happiness that often madness hits on, which reason and sanity could not so prosperously be delivered of. I will leave him, and suddenly contrive the means of meeting between him and my daughter.—My honourable lord, I will most humbly take my leave of you.
Hamlet	You cannot, sir, take from me any thing that I will more willingly part withal:—except my life, except my life, except my life.
Polonius	Fare you well, my lord.
Hamlet	These tedious old fools!
	[*Enter ROSENCRANTZ and GUILDENSTERN*]
Polonius	You go to seek the Lord Hamlet; there he is.
Rosencrantz	[*To POLONIUS*] God save you, sir!
	[*Exit POLONIUS*]
Guildenstern	Mine honoured lord!
Rosencrantz	My most dear lord!
Hamlet	My excellent good friends! How dost thou, Guildenstern? Ah, Rosencrantz! Good lads, how do ye both?
Rosencrantz	As the indifferent children of the earth.
Guildenstern	Happy, in that we are not over-happy; On fortune's cap we are not the very button.
Hamlet	Nor the soles of her shoe?
Rosencrantz	Neither, my lord.
Hamlet	Then you live about her waist, or in the middle of her favours?
Guildenstern	'Faith, her privates we.
Hamlet	In the secret parts of fortune? O, most true; she is a strumpet. What's the news?
Rosencrantz	None, my lord, but that the world's grown honest.
Hamlet	Then is doomsday near: but your news is not true.

'ongHa'chu' yab, 'ej pujqu' 'uS." may tIchbogh Hoch mu'vam,
'ach maybe' mIw, mu'qaD veSvam noDlaHbe'mo' qanwI'.
nawloghwIj Qup Damuvlah, bIHeDmeH vetlh nuch
DaDachugh.

polonyuS	[*pegh'egh*] maw'bej, 'ach meqlaw'taH.—muDvo' bIyItqang'a', joHwI'?
Hamlet	molDaq.
polonyuS	toH, muDvo' 'oH mol'e'.—
	[*pegh'egh*]
	pIj jangDI' 'ongqu' SoQDaj. SoQvam 'ong lo'laHbe' nuj pIv, Dupvam tuchmo' mISbe'ghach. vImej, 'ej ghomchuq ghaH puqbe'wI' je tugh 'e' vInab.—SoHvo' jIjaHnISneS, joHwI' quvqu'.
Hamlet	jIHvo' bIyaHDI' SoH, jIH Quch law'; yaHDI' HochHom, jIH Quch puS—wa' neH latlh vImaS: yaHjaj yInwIj neH, yInwIj neH, yInwIj neH.
polonyuS	SoHvo' jIyaHnIS.
Hamlet	qetlh qoHvam qan.
	['*el ROSENQATLH GHILDESTEN je*]
polonyuS	Hamlet quv bonejlaw'. pa' ghaHtaH.
roSenQatlh	[*POLONYUSvaD*] Dutlho'jaj qeylIS, qaH.
	[*mej POLONYUS*]
ghIlDeSten	joHwI' quv!
roSenQatlh	joHwI' webHa'!
Hamlet	juppu'wI' QaQqu'! Dotlhraj nuq, ghIlDeSten, roSenQatlh je? nuqneH?
roSenQatlh	wa'Hu' vIq yoS wutlhDaq 'Iwghargh yontaHghach 'oH Dotlhmaj'e'.
ghIlDeSten	Do' yapmo' neH Do'taHghachmaj, maQuch. mIvDaq tuQbogh San maQambe'.
Hamlet	DaSmeyDaj bIngDaq SuQambe' qar'a' je?
ghIlDeSten	HISlaH.
Hamlet	vaj qoghDaq tuQbogh, botlhDaj yonDaq joq SuQam.
ghIlDeSten	loQ. jojDajDaq neH maQam.
Hamlet	jojporgh'ay'Daq? wejpuH, teHqu'! ngaghHa'wI' ghaH. De' chu' HIja'.
roSenQatlh	chu'law' ghu'vam neH—maychoH 'u'.
Hamlet	qaS maQmIgh'a'! 'ach teHbe' De'raj.

	Let me question more in particular: what have you, my good friends, deserved at the hands of fortune, that she sends you to prison hither?
Guildenstern	Prison, my lord!
Hamlet	Denmark's a prison.
Rosencrantz	Then is the world one.
Hamlet	A goodly one; in which there are many confines, wards, and dungeons, Denmark being one o' the worst.
Rosencrantz	We think not so, my lord.
Hamlet	Why, then, 'tis none to you; for there is nothing either good or bad, but thinking makes it so: to me it is a prison.
Rosencrantz	Why, then, your ambition makes it one; 'tis too narrow for your mind.
Hamlet	O God, I could be bounded in a nut shell, and count myself a king of infinite space, were it not that I have bad dreams.
Guildenstern	Which dreams, indeed, are ambition; for the very substance of the ambitious is merely the shadow of a dream.
Hamlet	A dream itself is but a shadow.
Rosencrantz	Truly, and I hold ambition of so airy and light a quality that it is but a shadow's shadow.
Hamlet	Then are our beggars bodies, and our monarchs and outstretched heroes the beggars' shadows. Shall we to the court? for, by my fay, I cannot reason.
Rosencrantz & Guildenstern	We'll wait upon you.
Hamlet	No such matter: I will not sort you with the rest of my servants; for, to speak to you like an honest man, I am most dreadfully attended. But, in the beaten way of friendship, what make you at Elsinore?
Rosencrantz	To visit you, my lord; no other occasion.
Hamlet	Beggar that I am, I am even poor in thanks; but I thank you: and sure, dear friends, my thanks are too dear a halfpenny. Were you not sent for? Is it your own inclining? Is it a free visitation? Come, deal justly with me: come, come; nay, speak.
Guildenstern	What should we say, my lord?
Hamlet	Why, anything,—but to the purpose. You were sent for; and there is a kind of confession in your looks, which your modesties have not craft enough to colour: I know the good king and queen have sent for you.
Rosencrantz	To what end, my lord?
Hamlet	That you must teach me. But let me conjure you, by the rights of our fellowship, by the consonancy of our youth, by the obligation of our ever-preserved

Saghelqa'qu'. nuq boHeSbogh
bIjmeH San, naDev bIghHa'Daq lIngeH.

ghIlDeSten	bIghHa'Daq?
Hamlet	bIghHa' 'oH Qo'noS'e'.
roSenQatlh	vaj, 'oH je 'u''e'.
Hamlet	bIghHa' tIn'e' 'oH; 'oHDaq weghbogh pa'mey, Surchemmey je, qama'DISmey je lutu'lu'; Qo'noS qab law', Hochvetlh qab puS.
roSenQatlh	'e' wIQoch.
Hamlet	vaj 'oH boqelDI' bIghHa' botu'be'. QaQbe' 'ej qabbe' ghu' 'a QaQ, pagh qab 'e' tu' qelwI' neH. vIqelDI' bIghHa' vItu'.
roSenQatlh	toH, bIchav 'e' Danabmo' bIghHa' Datu'. chavnablIj wegh.
Hamlet	QI'yaH, muweghchu'chugh je naH yub, mIch'a'mey'e' not luvuSlu'bogh vIche' 'e' vInoHlaH. 'ach vInoHbe' muSujmo' wanI' vInajbogh.
ghIlDeSten	tugh bIchav 'e' Danajbej. QIb najlu'bogh 'oH chav'e' nablu'bogh.
Hamlet	QIb neH 'oH je Hoch wanI''e' najlu'bogh.
roSenQatlh	teH. tISmo' 'ej tunmo' chavnab, QIb QIb neH 'oH 'e' vInoH.
Hamlet	vaj porgh 'oH qoHma''e', 'ej qoH QIb neH chaH chuQunma''e', chavbogh Subma''e' je. vaS'a'Daq wIghoS'a', Hu'tegh jImeqlaHbe'mo'.
roSenQatlh ghIlDeSten je	pItlhej.
Hamlet	baQa' Qo'! latlh tlhejwI'wI' tIDaQo', toy'Ha'qu'mo' mutlhejtaHvIS. 'ach jupwI' tlhIH, pIj ben 'e' botobmo' DaH peyuDHa'. qatlh tlhInDaq tlhIH?
roSenQatlh	pISuch. latlh wIneHbe'.
Hamlet	mIpHa'wI' vIDamo', jItlho'DI' jIchuSbe', 'ach Satlho'. 'ej, jupoy, yapqu' mu'DeQwIj. naDev SupawmeH bora'lu''a'? boneH'a' tlhIH? boSap'a'? Ha' Ha' pechuH. Ha' Ha'. Qo', pejatlh.
ghIlDeSten	nuq wIjatlh DaneH?
Hamlet	jISaHbe', 'a yIjangchu'. SupawmeH lIra' vay' 'e' luDISlaw' qabraj DIv'e' jechlaHbe'bogh SunaDmeH mIw. lIra' ta' ta'be' je QaQ 'e' vISov.
roSenQatlh	qatlh, qaH?
Hamlet	tuja'nIS. 'a taHmeH boqmaj yuDHa' pevlt. boqmaj matlhmo', parHa'ghachmaj Qupmo', jupbatlhmaj yuDHa'mo', Hoch potlhmo' je DellaHbogh gharwI'na' jIHbe'bogh HIlob 'ej pevlt,

love, and by what more dear a better proposer could
charge you withal, be even and direct with me,
whether you were sent for, or no?

Rosencrantz	[*Aside to GUILDENSTERN*] What say you?
Hamlet	[*Aside*] Nay, then, I have an eye of you.—If you love me, hold not off.
Guildenstern	My lord, we were sent for.
Hamlet	I will tell you why; so shall my anticipation prevent your discovery, and your secrecy to the king and queen moult no feather. I have of late—but wherefore I know not—lost all my mirth, forgone all custom of exercises; and, indeed, it goes so heavily with my disposition that this goodly frame, the earth, seems to me a sterile promontory; this most excellent canopy, the air, look you, this brave o'erhanging firmament, this majestical roof fretted with golden fire,—why, it appears no other thing to me than a foul and pestilent congregation of vapours. What a piece of work is a man! how noble in reason! how infinite in faculty! in form and moving, how express and admirable! in action, how like an angel! in apprehension how like a god! the beauty of the world! the paragon of animals! And yet, to me, what is this quintessence of dust? man delights not me; no, nor woman neither, though by your smiling you seem to say so.
Rosencrantz	My lord, there was no such stuff in my thoughts.
Hamlet	Why did you laugh, then, when I said 'man delights not me'?
Rosencrantz	To think, my lord, if you delight not in man, what lenten entertainment the players shall receive from you: we coted them on the way; and hither are they coming, to offer you service.
Hamlet	He that plays the king shall be welcome;—his majesty shall have tribute of me; the adventurous knight shall use his foil and target; the lover shall not sigh gratis; the humourous man shall end his part in peace; the clown shall make those laugh whose lungs are tickled o' the sere; and the lady shall say her mind freely, or the blank verse shall halt for't.—What players are they?
Rosencrantz	Even those you were wont to take delight in,—the tragedians of the city.
Hamlet	How chances it they travel? their residence, both in reputation and profit, was better both ways.
Rosencrantz	I think their inhibition comes by the means of the late innovation.
Hamlet	Do they hold the same estimation they did when I was in the city? are they so followed?
Rosencrantz	No, indeed, are they not.

SupawmeH bora'lu' qar'a'?

roSenQatlh	[*GHILDESTENvaD pegh*] nuq DanoH?
Hamlet	[*pegh'egh*] vaj Qo', jIDughrup. tuparHa'chugh vaj pemImQo'.

ghIlDeSten	joHwI', mapawmeH wIra'lu'.
Hamlet	Sulay' 'e' boquvmoHlaHmeH 'ej notlhchoHbe'meH

'Ipraj, lIra'meH meq vIloychu' jIH.
bong qen belwIj vIjegh; meq vIyajbe' je.
jIHaghqangbe'law'; jIreHqangbe'law'; 'ej 'u' qo"a'vam
je qelDI' maw'wI' vImojlaw'pu'bogh, Dalbogh
ghe"orHey'e' tu'. maH Dung'a' pov'e', SuS'e',
nuDechbogh moQ'a' 'IH'e' yItu'. toH chalvetlh
jenDaq HuS meQbogh Hovmey wov—
wejpuH, jIHvaD He'So'bogh SIptlhoQ ngIm rur.
toH, chovnatlh Doj ghaH tlhIngan'e'. valqu'
meqlaHDaj; HoSqu' porghlaHDaj; chentaHvIS 'ej
vIHtaHvIS po' 'ej le'.
Dol'a' jub rur SuvtaHvIS. QI'tu' moch rur QubtaHvIS.
'IHchu'bogh qo"a'Daq pupchu' mutvam 'IH.
'a jIHvaD ramlaw' chenmeH porghmeyvam lam'e'
tlholHa'moHbogh 'u'. mubelmoHbe' loD—be"e' je,
'ach SuHaghmo' jaS SuQublaw'.

roSenQatlh	joHwI', yabwIjDaq 'oHpu'be' qech tlhaQ'e'.
Hamlet	qatlh bIHagh, jIjatlhDI' "mubelmoHbe' loD..."
roSenQatlh	nIbelmoHbe'chugh loD, vaj DawI'pu' DabejDI', Human

tejpu'Hey DaqIHlaw'. chaH DIjuS naDev maqughtaHvIS.
toH, naDev nItIvmoHmeH chol chaH.

Hamlet	batlh paw ta'qoq. ghaH vIvanchu' jIH. SuvmeH vaj yoH,

'etlh yoD je lo'jaj. jachDI' parmaqqay, lI'chu'jaj HughDaj.
SoQ naQ rInmoHchu'jaj nongwI'. taghDu"e' reH
luchu'beHlu'bogh jormoHjaj HaghmoHwI'. bom mu'tlhegh
pabjaj be"a', pagh ghaH lupab bIH, jatlhtaHvIS.
DawI'ghomvam nuq?

roSenQatlh	vengvo' lot ja'wI"e', reH DatIvqangbogh ben DabejtaHvIS.
Hamlet	nuqmo' DaH lengtaH? juHvengchajDaq chepchu' batlhchaj

maljma'chaj je.

roSenQatlh	Qapla'chaj lutunglaw' noywI' chu'.
Hamlet	ben, DaHjaj je rap'a' naD luHevbogh? DaH lunaDlu"a'?
roSenQatlh	ghobe'.

Hamlet	How comes it? do they grow rusty?
Rosencrantz	Nay, their endeavour keeps in the wonted pace: but there is, sir, an aery of children, little eyases, that cry out on the top of question, and are most tyrannically clapped for't: these are now the fashion; and so berattle the common stages—so they call them—that many wearing rapiers are afraid of goose-quills and dare scarce come thither.
Hamlet	What, are they children? who maintains 'em? how are they escoted? Will they pursue the quality no longer than they can sing? will they not say afterwards, if they should grow themselves to common players—as it is most like, if their means are no better—their writers do them wrong, to make them exclaim against their own succession?
Rosencrantz	'Faith, there has been much to do on both sides; and the nation holds it no sin to tarre them to controversy: there was for a while no money bid for argument, unless the poet and the player went to cuffs in the question.
Hamlet	Is't possible?
Guildenstern	O, there has been much throwing about of brains.
Hamlet	Do the boys carry it away?
Rosencrantz	Ay, that they do, my lord; Hercules and his load too.
Hamlet	It is not very strange; for mine uncle is king of Denmark, and those that would make mouths at him while my father lived, give twenty, forty, fifty, an hundred ducats a-piece for his picture in little. 'Sblood, there is something in this more than natural, if philosophy could find it out.

[*Flourish of trumpets within*]

Guildenstern	There are the players.
Hamlet	Gentlemen, you are welcome to Elsinore. Your hands, come: the appurtenance of welcome is fashion and ceremony: let me comply with you in this garb; lest my extent to the players, which, I tell you, must show fairly outward, should more appear like entertainment than yours. You are welcome: but my uncle-father and aunt-mother are deceived.
Guildenstern	In what, my dear lord?
Hamlet	I am but mad north-north-west: when the wind is southerly I know a hawk from a handsaw.

[*Enter POLONIUS*]

Polonius	Well be with you, gentlemen!
Hamlet	Hark you, Guildenstern;—and you too;—at each ear a hearer: that great baby you see there is not yet out of his swaddling-clouts.

Hamlet	chay' qaS? ragh'a'?
roSenQatlh	ghobe', chaHvaD laH po' polmoH qeqchaj. 'ach nIS puqtlhoQ chu''e', Qa'Hompu''e'. DataHvIS SoQchaj chuS lachmo', chaH naDqu' je bejwI' Seyqu'. DaH noychoHpu' 'ej Qoplaw'bogh DawI'yaHmeyqoq tIchqu'mo', ghItlhtaj vaQ law', 'etlh vaQ puS 'ej 'elvIp 'etlh qengwI'.
Hamlet	toH puq chaH'a'? Qorgh 'Iv? je' 'Iv? bomlaHbe'DI' ghoghchaj notlhchoH'a' Qu'chaj? nem beprup'a', DawI' qan mojDI' ('ej ghaytan qaS wanI'vam, jaS malja' ghajlaHbe'chugh), "nunuS qonwI'ma', DawI' qan DIcho'nISbogh naDHa'qu'mo'?"
roSenQatlh	QI'yaH pIj Qay'qu' cha' jaghHeyvam. SoltaH DawI'pu' 'e' lutungHa'DI' rewbe', Qu'chaj lunaDtaH. qaStaHvIS benvam, lut ghItlh'e' reH DIlQo' Hoch muchwI', lutDaq DawI' noHmo' tonSaw' luqaSmoHbe'chugh je ghItlhwI' DawI' je.
Hamlet	qarqu''a'?
ghIlDeSten	va yabtonSaw'na' luqaSmoHqu'bejtaH cha'.
Hamlet	Qapla' lunge''a' QupwI'?
roSenQatlh	toH, HIja' jay'—qo'qengwI' tepDaj je lunge' je.
Hamlet	net pIHbej. ta' ghaH vavloDnI'wI''e', 'ej DaH DeghDaj DIlmeH cha'maH, loSmaH, vaghmaH, wa'vatlh ghap DeQ nobqang ben ghaH luvanHa'qu'bogh ghotpu''e', yIntaHvIS vavwI'. Qu'vatlh, ghu'vam SIghbe' 'u'pab neH; ghu' QIjjaj QeD.
	[chuS DawI'pu' maqmeH QoQ]
ghIlDeSten	paw DawI'pu'.
Hamlet	batlh tlhInDaq bopawpu'. DeS tIlo', pevan. vanwI'vaD tay quv ra' lurDech tIgh je. SavanmeH jIjatlh, pagh DawI'pu'vaD (jaqnISba'bogh) vanwIj jaq law', tlhIHvaD jaq puS net HarlaH. batlh Supawpu'. 'ach vavqoqwI' SoSHeywI' je toj ghu'.
ghIlDeSten	ghu' nuq, joHwI'?
Hamlet	000 DoD 2 QuvDaq jImaw'. choHDI' lurghvetlh pIm toQDuj to'baj je, 'e' vIghovlaH.
	['el POLONYUS]
polonyuS	Saghom, loDpu'.
Hamlet	pe'lj, ghIlDeSten—SoH je—cha' qoghDaq cha' QoywI''e'. ghuSutHom tuQ, wej 'e' mev loDqoqvetlh.

Rosencrantz	Happily he's the second time come to them; for they say an old man is twice a child.
Hamlet	I will prophesy he comes to tell me of the players; mark it.—You say right, sir: o' Monday morning; 'twas so indeed.
Polonius	My lord, I have news to tell you.
Hamlet	My lord, I have news to tell you. When Roscius was an actor in Rome,—
Polonius	The actors are come hither, my lord.
Hamlet	Buz, buz!
Polonius	Upon mine honour,—
Hamlet	Then came each actor on his ass,—
Polonius	The best actors in the world, either for tragedy, comedy, history, pastoral, pastoral-comical, historical-pastoral, tragical-historical, tragical-comical-historical-pastoral, scene individable, or poem unlimited: Seneca cannot be too heavy. nor Plautus too light. For the law of writ and the liberty, these are the only men.
Hamlet	O Jepthah, judge of Israel, what a treasure hadst thou!
Polonius	What a treasure had he, my lord?
Hamlet	Why,— 'One fair daughter and no more, The which he loved passing well.'
Polonius	[*Aside*] Still on my daughter.
Hamlet	Am I not i' the right, old Jephthah?
Polonius	If you call me Jephthah, my lord, I have a daughter that I love passing well.
Hamlet	Nay, that follows not.
Polonius	What follows, then, my lord?
Hamlet	Why,— 'As by lot, God wot,' and then, you know, 'It came to pass, as most like it was,'— the first row of the pious chanson will show you more; for look, where my abridgement comes.

[*Enter four or five Players*]

You are welcome, masters; welcome, all.—I am glad to see thee well.—Welcome, good friends.—O, my old friend! thy face is valenced since I saw thee last; comest thou to beard me in Denmark?—What, my young lady and mistress! By'r lady, your ladyship is nearer to heaven than when I saw you last, by the altitude of a chopine. Pray God, your voice, like a piece of uncurrent gold, be not cracked within the

roSenQatlh   chaq cha'logh 'oH tuQ. puq chaHqa' loD qan'e', rut net joS.

Hamlet   paw DawI', muja' 'e' nabba'. yItu'—toH bIlugh. Hoghjaj
                 wa' qaS. lughqu' mu'.

polonyuS   joHwI', De' qaja'.

Hamlet   joHwI', De' qaja' jIH. rIymuS luDanchoHDI' romuluSngan...

polonyuS   paw DawI'pu', joHwI'.

Hamlet   not mev peghmeyHey!

polonyuS   baQa' qavIt.

Hamlet   'ej targhDaj lIghchoH Hoch DawI'.

polonyuS   laHchaj Doj law', Hoch laH Doj puS; lotlut,
                 tlhaQbogh lut, qunlut, noybogh lut tlhaQ,
                 tlhaQbogh lut noy, qunlut noy, qunlotlut,
                 tlhaQbogh qunlotlut noy, 'ay' wavbe'lu'bogh,
                 bom tlhab joq ja'meH DataHvIS. "morab qeylIS je" ja'meH
                 'IQqu'be' qoj "verengan'a' Qagh" ja'meH Quchqu'be'.
                 DataHvIS, lurDechvaD pablaHchu' pagh bIvlaHchu' chaH.

Hamlet   bo'DIj pIn'a', toH ghaw'ron qan!
                 tev'a' Daghajbejpu'!

polonyuS   tev'a' ghajbogh yIngu'.

Hamlet   toH,
                         'ej ghaHvaD wa' puqbe' neH tu'lu'.
                         puqvetlh muSHa'taH ghaH 'ej Qan.

polonyuS   [*pegh'egh*] puqbe'wI' buStaH.

Hamlet   lugh qar'a' mu'wIj, ghaw'ronoy?

polonyuS   chopongmeH "ghaw'ron" bIjatlhchugh, vaj wa' puqbe'
                 vImuSHa'taHbogh 'ej vIQanbogh vIghajbej.

Hamlet   ghobe', qarbe'.

polonyuS   vaj qar nuq?

Hamlet   toH,
                         ra'taHvIS San, Dach Sun.
                 'ej qaS wanI'"e' DaSovbogh:
                         vaj ghaHvaD DoqchoH bIQtIq bIQ.
                 SoHvaD ghu' naQ Del bomvam mu'tlheghmey wa'DIch'e'.
                 toH, ghoS mevmoHwI'wI'.

                 ['*el DawI' puS*]

                 batlh naDev Supawpu', pInpu', batlh Savan. naDev
                 tlhIHmo' jIlop. Savan, juppu' QaQ—toH, jupwI' nI',
                 ben qaleghbogh, DaH jIbvam chu' Suqba'pu' qab.
                 qab laHlIj 'e' chotemmeH naDev Qo'noSDaq SoH'a'.—
                 toH, be'oywI', bang je. Hu'tegh, chalDaq SaltaH nachlIj;
                 DaH qajuvmeH, DaSpu' vIchel. ghuy'cha' bombogh
                 HoS lIngwI' rurmo' ghoghlIj Qup, va 'oH Sorghbe'lu'jaj.—
                 pInpu', batlh Savan. romuluSngan wamwI' DIDa,

| | ring.—Masters, you are all welcome. We'll e'en to't like French falconers, fly at any thing we see: we'll have a speech straight: come, give us a taste of your quality; come, a passionate speech. |

First Player   What speech, my lord?

Hamlet   I heard thee speak me a speech once,—but it was
never acted; or, if it was, not above once; for the
play, I remember, pleased not the million; 'twas
caviare to the general: but it was—as I received
it, and others whose judgments in such matters
cried in the top of mine—an excellent play, well
digested in the scenes, set down with as much
modesty as cunning. I remember, one said there
were no sallets in the lines to make the matter
savoury, nor no matter in the phrase that might
indict the author of affectation; but called it an
honest method, as wholesome as sweet, and by very
much more handsome than fine. One speech in it I
chiefly loved: 'twas Aeneas' tale to Dido; and
thereabout of it especially where he speaks of
Priam's slaughter: if it live in your memory, begin
at this line: let me see, let me see—
'The rugged Pyrrhus, like the Hyrcanian beast,'—
it is not so:—it begins with Pyrrhus:—
'The rugged Pyrrhus,—he whose sable arms,
Black as his purpose, did the night resemble
When he lay couched in the ominous horse,—
Hath now this dread and black complexion smear'd
With heraldry more dismal; head to foot
Now is he total gules; horridly trick'd
With blood of fathers, mothers, daughters, sons,
Bak'd and impasted with the parching streets,
That lend a tyrannous and damned light
To their vile murders: roasted in wrath and fire,
And thus o'er-sized with coagulate gore,
With eyes like carbuncles, the hellish Pyrrhus
Old grandsire Priam seeks.'—
So, proceed you.

Polonius   'Fore God, my lord, well spoken, with good accent and
good discretion.

First Player   'Anon he finds him
Striking too short at Greeks; his antique sword,
Rebellious to his arm, lies where it falls,
Repugnant to command: unequal match'd,
Pyrrhus at Priam drives; in rage strikes wide;
But with the whiff and wind of his fell sword
The unnerved father falls. Then senseless Ilium,
Seeming to feel this blow, with flaming top
Stoops to his base; and with a hideous crash
Takes prisoner Pyrrhus' ear: for, lo! his sword,
Which was declining on the milky head
Of reverend Priam, seem'd i' the air to stick:
So, as a painted tyrant, Pyrrhus stood;
And like a neutral to his will and matter,

HochDaq wIleghbogh wISupqangmo'. qul DIr wISop.
SIbI' SoQ wIQoy. Ha', laHraj po' yItob. Ha',
SoQ nong.

DawI' wa'DIch	SoQ DapoQbogh yIngu', joHwI' QaQ.
Hamlet	ben SoQ choja', 'ach not naQ lutDaj. naQbejchugh vaj

wa'logh neH naQ. rewbe' motlh vuD vIqaw: chaH belmoHbe'
lut. to'baj 'IISDu' SopQo', qaSbe'taHvIS QI'Iop. 'ach QaQqu' lut,
'e' wInoH jIH, vuD nIv ghajwI'pu' je. pov lut; 'ay'meyDaj
buvchu'; 'ej mu'mey 'ongmoHqu', lachbe'taHvIS qonwI'.
mu'tlhegh wIbHa'moHbe' HaQchorHey, net joS; 'ej mu'Daq
qech ngeb chellaw'pu' net pumlaHbe'. 'ach yuDHa'chu' net
maq; belmoHbejtaHvIS pov, 'ej reH mIybe'law'taHvIS Doj.
lutvo' wa' SoQ'e' vIparHa'chu': DI'Do'vaD SoQ'e' ja'bogh
'enyaS. Hegh pIray'am 'e' qelDI' SoQ vIparHa'qu'. qawbogh
yablIjDaq yIntaHchugh vaj mu'tlheghvamvo' yIruch:
toH jIQub, jIQub—
"rughtlhoQ rurlaw' pob qIj pay'ruS—"
qarbe'. SoQ tagh pay'ruS mu'tlhegh.
"ramjep rurlaw' pob qIj pay'ruS
DeSDu' Dugh, HoH 'e' Hechmo',
Sanchaj SomDaq QojrupmeH QottaHvIS.
pe'vII porghDaj qIjqu'Daq qu'moHtaHbogh
DuQwI' DeghHey DaH ngoHpu' ngotlhwI'.
qabDaq qamDu'Daq je Doqchu' DevwI'.
ghaHDaq ghomHa'pu' qorDu' quppu' je
'Iw'e' 'uybogh 'ej QIt QaDmoHbogh
qechmey qul'a'. vaj che'wI'chaj chotrupwI'vaD
HeSrupbogh HoSDo' QIbHey Qobqu'
qemlaw' qul'a'vetlh. meQmo' 'ej muSmo'
DaSpu'DajDaq DuD'egh Hommey HuH je.
puyjaq pImbe' mInDu'Daj maw'.
pay' pIray'am, qup'a' qan
noDmeH nejtaH pejqangbogh pay'ruS,
ghe''or ghungwI'."
vaj yItaH.

polonyuS	Hu'tegh, joHwI', bIjatlhchu', 'ej ghogh DalISchu', 'ej mu'
	DanongmoH.
DawI' wa'DIch	"tugh ghaH tu'.

mangpu' mupHa' gholvetlh. ghopDaj
lobHa'mo' letbogh betleHDaj, buDlaw'
pumDI' 'oH. poQDI' tlhaptaHwI'Daj 'e' tlhIvlaw'.
HIghbejmeH HI', Hay'choH pIray'am pay'ruS je.
mayHa' may'chaj. HIv Hurghwl'.
QeHmo', QapHa' 'etlhDaj. 'ach 'aw'mo'
naSbogh nuHDaj SuSHey Sey,
vulchoH vavnI''a' Doy'. Dej je
vanglaHbe'bogh veng, DungDaj DechtaHvIS
qorqanglaw'bogh qul. ghatlh ghaH 'e' ghovlaw' 'oH.
chuSqu'mo' chenHa'taHvIS, tojwI' teSDu'
vonglaw' veng. vaj peplu'DI' pumlaw'Qo'
nurnuv nach chISDaq chungbeHbogh

Did nothing.
But as we often see, against some storm,
A silence in the heavens, the rack stand still,
The bold winds speechless, and the orb below
As hush as death, anon the dreadful thunder
Doth rend the region; so, after Pyrrhus' pause,
A roused vengeance sets him new a-work;
And never did the Cyclops' hammers fall
On Mars his armour, forg'd for proof eterne,
With less remorse than Pyrrhus' bleeding sword
Now falls on Priam.—
Out, out, thou strumpet, Fortune! All you gods,
In general synod, 'take away her power;
Break all the spokes and fellies from her wheel,
And bowl the round nave down the hill of heaven,
As low as to the fiends!'

Polonius	This is too long.
Hamlet	It shall to the barber's, with your beard.—Prithee, say on:—he's for a jig, or a tale of bawdry, or he sleeps:—say on: come to Hecuba.
First Player	'But who, O, who had seen the mobled queen—'
Hamlet	'The mobled queen?'
Polonius	That's good; 'mobled queen' is good.
First Player	'Run barefoot up and down, threatening the flames With bisson rheum; a clout upon that head Where late the diadem stood; and for a robe, About her lank and all o'er-teemed loins, A blanket, in the alarm of fear caught up;— Who this had seen, with tongue in venom steep'd, 'Gainst Fortune's state would treason have pronounc'd: But if the gods themselves did see her then, When she saw Pyrrhus make malicious sport In mincing with his sword her husband's limbs, The instant burst of clamour that she made, Unless things mortal move them not at all,— Would have made milch the burning eyes of heaven, And passion in the gods.'
Polonius	Look, whether he has not turn'd his colour and has tears in's eyes.—Pray you, no more.
Hamlet	'Tis well; I'll have thee speak out the rest soon.— Good my lord, will you see the players well bestowed? Do you hear, let them be well used; for they are the abstracts and brief chronicles of the time; after your death you were better have a bad epitaph than their ill report while you live.

tochDaj taj'a'. HI' Hotlhlu'bogh
rurchoH rojQo'wI'. QeHDaj Qu'Daj je
vangbe'choH vIHbe'wI'.
'ach rut ralpa' muD, morgh 'e' mevlaw'
chal. chuSQo' Sachbogh SuSmey.
'ughlaw' 'engmey. peghlaw' je puH,
HeghvIplaw'mo'. 'a HatlhDaq tIHmeyDaj'e' tugh
mupmoH muD. jaS ja'be'lu'.
yevpu'DI' je yovwI', ghaH vumqa'moH vembogh
bortaS. baSDaq qIptaHvIS qeylIS
yovwI' yayyoD chenmoHbogh chamwI'pu''e',
vaQbej. 'a vIDchu' 'Iwmey 'etlhDaj,
pIray'amDaq pumDI'. Sorghqang neH San!
laHmeyDaj lIqjaj qa''a'pu' qep.
gho'a'Daj gho'wI'mey naQmey je notlhmoHjaj.
QI'tu' QuQvo' botlhDaj bachjaj.
laghlu'DI', luchvetlh ghupjaj ghe''or!"

polonyuS	tIqqu' SoQ.

Hamlet	vaj chIpwI'Daq rollIj tlhej. SuH, yIltaH. chaq DaH ghaHvaD
	qaq SoQ tlhaQ, lut Qut joq. jaS yonbe'. yIjatlhtaH. He'quba
	yIqelchoH.

| DawI' wa'DIch | "bortaS be'nal'e', Huy''a'Du' He'quba'e'—" |

| Hamlet | Huy''a'Du' He'quba? |

| polonyuS | QaQbej mu'vetlh. QaQbej "Huy''a'Du' He'quba." |

DawI' wa'DIch	"tu''a' toDlaHwI'? DachtaHvIS DaSmey,
	qevpobDajvo' qulmey boch buQlaw'
	leghmoHbogh laHDaj mISmoHbogh mInbIQ'e'.
	Dat DughtaH. nachDajDaq narghpu'
	qutmey qogh. DaHjaj 'oH Dech
	qatwI' qutlh. mopDaj mechpu' je.
	boghmeH batlhvaj law' QeyHa'lI'bogh 'ej Qopbogh
	chorDaj chIS'e' ma'nIS mep'ay' neH.
	ghumtaHvIS ghong, vubvam vupnISlu'.
	be'nalvetlh bejchoHchugh vay', vaj vaQnIS.
	'urmang 'oghpu' SotmoHbogh San,
	'e' maqnIS meqwI'vetlh, SuQtaHvIS SoQDaj.
	bIjmeH, ghaH bejchugh qa''a' qep—
	QujmeH QutwI', loDnalDaj lommey
	puy pIray'uS 'etlh 'e' 'oIDI' ghaH—
	vaj vItmo' vI'bogh ghoghDaj ghum'a',
	qa''a'pu' qImmoHlaHchugh jubbe'wI' jIp,
	vaj vangrup je veSmey joH'a', 'ej jeDnIS
	meQbogh muDmIn'a'."

| polonyuS | toH, yIltu': choHbej qabDaj, qoj nIjbeHbej mInDaj. va, mevyap. |

Hamlet	pItlh, maj. tugh SoQ naQ Daja', 'e' vIchaw'.—
	joHwI' QaQ, DawI'pu' Dama'meH yIHeQ. yaj'a'?
	Dotlhchaj yIqel. bovmaj ta qengwI', qun qawwI' je chaH.
	HeghlIjvaD SonchIy Hat qaq law', yInlIjvaD
	naDHa'ghachchaj qaq puS.

Polonius	My lord, I will use them according to their desert.
Hamlet	Odd's bodkin, man, better: use every man after his desert, and who should 'scape whipping? Use them after your own honour and dignity: the less they deserve the more merit is in your bounty. Take them in.
Polonius	Come, sirs.
Hamlet	Follow him, friends: we'll hear a play to-morrow.—

[*Exit POLONIUS with all the Players but the First*]

Dost thou hear me, old friend; can you play the
Murder of Gonzago?

First Player	Ay, my lord.
Hamlet	We'll ha't to-morrow night. You could, for a need, study a speech of some dozen or sixteen lines which I would set down and insert in't? could you not?
First Player	Ay, my lord.
Hamlet	Very well.—Follow that lord; and look you mock him not.—

[*Exit First Player*]

My good friends, I'll leave you till night: you are
welcome to Elsinore.

Rosencrantz	Good my lord!

[*Exeunt ROSENCRANTZ and GUILDENSTERN*]

Hamlet	Ay, so, God be wi' ye! Now I am alone. O, what a rogue and peasant slave am I! Is it not monstrous that this player here, But in a fiction, in a dream of passion, Could force his soul so to his own conceit That from her working all his visage wan'd; Tears in his eyes, distraction in's aspect, A broken voice, and his whole function suiting With forms to his conceit? And all for nothing! For Hecuba! What's Hecuba to him or he to Hecuba, That he should weep for her? What would he do, Had he the motive and the cue for passion That I have? He would drown the state with tears, And cleave the general ear with horrid speech; Make mad the guilty, and appal the free; Confound the ignorant, and amaze, indeed, The very faculties of eyes and ears. Yet I, A dull and muddy-mettled rascal, peak, Like John-a-dreams, unpregnant of my cause, And can say nothing; no, not for a king Upon whose property and most dear life A damn'd defeat was made. Am I a coward? Who calls me villain? breaks my pate across? Plucks off my beard and blows it in my face?

polonyuS	joHwI', 'umchugh Hochvam vIma'chu'.
Hamlet	ghuy'cha', qaH. 'umbe'chugh tIma' je. 'umlu'chugh neH ma'lu'DI', vaj Hoch wImuHlu'. Dama'meH ra'jaj batlhlIj nurlIj je neH. reH 'umbe'chugh, vI'bej tevlIj. yI'elmoH.
polonyuS	Ha', qaHpu'.
Hamlet	yItlha', juppu'. wa'leS lut wIbej. [*mej* POLONYUS *DawI'pu' je, ratlhtaHvIS wa'DIch*] choQoylaH'a', jup. "ghonja'gho Hegh"'e' boja'meH SuDalaH'a'.
DawI' wa'DIch	lu', joHwI'.
Hamlet	wa'leS ram 'oH wIbej. wa'maH cha' jav joq mu'tlhegh'e' vI'oghbogh 'ej vIchelbogh, chIch DaHaDlaH, qar'a'?
DawI' wa'DIch	lu', joHwI'.
Hamlet	majQa'. qupvetlh yItlha', 'ej yIvaqbejQo'.
	 [*mej DawI' wa'DIch*] juppu'wI' QaQ, DaHjaj ram Saghomqa'. batlh tlhInDaq bopawpu'.
roSenQatlh	maj. [*mej* ROSENQATLH GHILDESTEN *je*]
Hamlet	vaj taHjaj wo'. DaH jImob. baQa', Qovpatlh, toy'wI''a' qal je jIH! nonglaw' 'e' najmo' neH ghaH, wa' lutmo' neH, qechlaHDaj qu'vaD qa'Daj raD DawI'vam. webmoH, qar'a'? 'oH raDDI', chISchoH qabDaj. yIQ mInDu'Daj. buSHa''egh DataHvIS. ghor ghoghDaj. chenlI'mo' porghlaHmeyDaj, qechDaj luDelchu' bIH. 'ej paghvaD qaS jay'. He'qubavaD neH! qatlh He'qubamo' SaQmeH wIchvetlh SaH ghaH? nongchu'meH meq, tungHa'wI' je vIghajbogh ghajchugh ghaH, vaj chay' vangrup ghaH? nuq ta'? DawI' yaH SoDnISlaw' mInblQDaj ngeng. ghom'a' teSDu' Hoch DuQnIS ghljbogh QIchDaj. DIvwI'pu' maw'nISmoH. chunwI'pu' 'ItmoH. HeS Sovbe'wI'pu' mISnISmoH. mInDu', teSDu' je laHmey yay'nISmoHbej ghaH. 'ach jIH? lam DataHbogh toDSaH neH qetlhqu' jIH. najbogh vulqangan neH vIrur, jItammo'. Qu'wIjvaD vay' vIchavmeH jIyatlhQo'. 'ej pagh vIjatlhlaH. ta'vaD pagh vIjatlh je, 'ej ta'vetlh mIpmey, yInDaj quvqu' je QIHlu'chu'pu'! va nuch jIH'a'? "taHqeq SoH" jatlh 'Iv? va nachwIj qIpmeH ngIlqang 'Iv? rolwIjvo' jotlh 'ej qabDaq pob vo' 'Iv?

Tweaks me by the nose? gives me the lie i' the throat,
As deep as to the lungs? who does me this, ha?
'Swounds, I should take it: for it cannot be
But I am pigeon-liver'd, and lack gall
To make oppression bitter; or ere this
I should have fatted all the region kites
With this slave's offal:—bloody, bawdy villain!
Remorseless, treacherous, lecherous, kindless villain!
O, vengeance!
Why, what an ass am I! This is most brave,
That I, the son of a dear father murder'd,
Prompted to my revenge by heaven and hell,
Must, like a whore, unpack my heart with words,
And fall a-cursing like a very drab,
A scullion!
Fie upon't! foh!—About, my brain! I have heard
That guilty creatures, sitting at a play,
Have by the very cunning of the scene
Been struck so to the soul that presently
They have proclaim'd their malefactions;
For murder, though it have no tongue, will speak
With most miraculous organ. I'll have these players
Play something like the murder of my father
Before mine uncle: I'll observe his looks;
I'll tent him to the quick: if he but blench,
I know my course. The spirit that I have seen
May be the devil: and the devil hath power
To assume a pleasing shape; yea, and perhaps
Out of my weakness and my melancholy,—
As he is very potent with such spirits,—
Abuses me to damn me: I'll have grounds
More relative than this:—the play 's the thing
Wherein I'll catch the conscience of the king.

[*Exit*]

ACT III
SCENE I *A room in the castle.*

[*Enter KING CLAUDIUS, QUEEN GERTRUDE, POLONIUS,
OPHELIA, ROSENCRANTZ, and GUILDENSTERN*]

Claudius And can you, by no drift of circumstance,
Get from him why he puts on this confusion,
Grating so harshly all his days of quiet
With turbulent and dangerous lunacy?

Rosencrantz He does confess he feels himself distracted;
But from what cause he will by no means speak.

Guildenstern Nor do we find him forward to be sounded;
But, with a crafty madness, keeps aloof
When we would bring him on to some confession
Of his true state.

Gertrude   Did he receive you well?

Rosencrantz Most like a gentleman.

va ghIchwIj bochmoH 'Iv? "HughDaq bInep"
taghwIjDaq pumvam yuvmeH je jatlh 'Iv?
Hu'tegh! vISIQnISba' jIH. be'tatlheDngan
HuHqoq vIghaj; jIHvaD wIbbe'law' HI'tuy,
pujqu'mo' HuHwIj. chaq puSbe'chugh 'oH,
vaj wa'Hu' Hoch chal toQ vIrornISmoH,
bIHvaD toDSaH luHDu' vIje'pu'mo'.
ngaghHa'bogh chotqangbogh taHqeq! quvHa'bogh
payQo'bogh qurbogh 'ongchu'bogh taHqeq!
bortaS!
toH SuS vIvuvmoH. wejpuH yoHlaw' ghu'.
vav vImuSHa'bogh chotlu'. DaH bortaSvaD
puqloDDaj ra'lI' ghe''orHey, QI'tu' je.
'a chay' jIvang? tera'ngan neH vIDa,
mu'meyDaq tIqwIj vI'ughHa'moHlaw'mo'.
'ej mu'qaD vIjawHa'mo', chom vIDa.
tach toy'wI''a'!
Hu'tegh! wejpuH! Ha' yabwIj. ngoD vIQoypu':
DawI' lut bejmeH ba'taHvIS DIvwI',
po'mo' neH lut muchwI'pu', qa'Daj'e'
pIj qIpchu' lut. SIbI' vaj HeSDaj maq.
jatDu' ghajbe' chotwI' Dotlh. teH. 'a jatlhmeH
Hoch porgh laH lo'rupmo', vaj HochvaD mer.
bejtaHvIS vavloDnI'wI' ror, vav HoH
rurlaw'bogh lutHom'e' lumuch DawI'vam,
'e' vIqaSmoH. 'ej qabDaj Dotlh vItu'.
vI'oymoHmeH vIDaj. 'ej bItlaw'chugh neH,
vaj He vISov. chaq ghe''orvo' nucholta'
lomqa' vIleghbogh. chenDI' belmoHmeH
laH ghaj veqlargh. jIpujmo' 'ej jI'Itmo',
muqIchmeH rIntaH chaq mughongpu'. DuH,
ghaH HoSmoHlaw' 'Iw 'It net Sovmo'. toH,
'olmeH, ngoD meq qaq law', qa' QIch qaq puS.
ta' ghob vIchu'meH DawI' lut vIghuS.

[mej]

LUT 'AY' WEJ
LUT 'AY'HOM WA' *ta'qach pa'.*

[*'el* TLHAW'DIYUS TA*', GHERTLHUD TA'BE', POLONYUS,
'OVELYA, ROSENQATLH, GHILDESTEN je*]

tlhaw'DIyuS	'ej mISwI' DameH meq boghojlaHbe',
	mu'tlheghmeyraj boSeHtaHvIS, qar'a'?
	DaH maw'mo', Qobmo', ngojmo', Hoch jaj jot
	Sujchu' ghaH jay'!
roSenQatlh	teH. bItlaw' ghaH 'e' DIS.
	'a maHvaD bItmoHwI' QIjQo' ghaH, joH.
ghIlDeSten	ghaH yu'lu'DI' jIjQo' ghaH 'e' wItu' je.
	'ach 'ongmo' maw'taHvIS, maHvaD jangQo',
	yabDaj Dotlhna' nuDISmeH pIj manIDDI'.
ghertlhuD	qej'a' IIIeghDI'?
roSenQatlh	toH, vaj chongqu' Dabej.

Guildenstern	But with much forcing of his disposition.
Rosencrantz	Niggard of question, but, of our demands, Most free in his reply.
Gertrude	Did you assay him To any pastime?
Rosencrantz	Madam, it so fell out that certain players We o'er-raught on the way: of these we told him; And there did seem in him a kind of joy To hear of it: they are about the court; And, as I think, they have already order This night to play before him.
Polonius	'Tis most true: And he beseech'd me to entreat your majesties To hear and see the matter.
Claudius	With all my heart; and it doth much content me To hear him so inclin'd.— Good gentlemen, give him a further edge, And drive his purpose on to these delights.
Rosencrantz	We shall, my lord.

[*Exeunt ROSENCRANTZ and GUILDENSTERN*]

Claudius	Sweet Gertrude, leave us too; For we have closely sent for Hamlet hither That he, as 'twere by accident, may here Affront Ophelia: Her father and myself,—lawful espials,— Will so bestow ourselves that, seeing, unseen, We may of their encounter frankly judge; And gather by him, as he is behav'd, If 't be the affliction of his love or no That thus he suffers for.
Gertrude	I shall obey you.— And for your part, Ophelia, I do wish That your good beauties be the happy cause Of Hamlet's wildness: so shall I hope your virtues Will bring him to his wonted way again, To both your honours.
Ophelia	Madam, I wish it may.

[*Exit QUEEN GERTRUDE*]

Polonius	Ophelia, walk you here.—Gracious, so please you, We will bestow ourselves.—

[*To OPHELIA*]

Read on this book;
That show of such an exercise may colour
Your loneliness.—We are oft to blame in this,—
'Tis too much prov'd—that with devotion's visage
And pious action we do sugar o'er
The devil himself.

Claudius	[*Aside*] O, 'tis too true!

ghIlDeSten	'ach DameH raD'egh je.
roSenQatlh	nughelqangbe'.
	'ach ghaH wIghelDI', maHvaD jatlhruptaH.
ghertlhuD	yupma'Daq jeSmeH botungHa'pu"a'?

roSenQatlh   joH: lut DawI' DIjuS malengtaHvIS.
ghaHvaD DIDel, 'ej QoyDI' QuchchoHlaw'.
ta'qachDaq chaII. DaHjaj ram ghaHvaD DameH,
chaH ra'pu' ghaH.

polonyuS   qar. "lut yIleghneS, joH"
SatlhobmeH jIH muqoy'pu'.

tlhaw'DIyuS   vIleghqangbej, 'ej ghu'vetlh neHlaw'mo'
buy' ngop. yIneHqu'moH.
'ej belvam tIvmeH yItungHa', qaH QaQ.

roSenQatlh   luq, joH.

[*mej ROSENQATLH GHILDESTEN je*]

tlhaw'DIyuS   SuH, ghertlhuD 'IH, ghomej je SoH.
jIH neH mughommeH Hamlet DaH jIra'pu'.
vaj bong naDev 'ovelya ghomlaw' ghaH.
maSo'mo' vavDaj jIH je—mub IInDabmaj—
mabejtaHvIS maH nubejbe'taHvIS,
ghomchuqmeH mIw wIchovDI' vaj maqarlaH.
'ej DameH mIwDaj teH wIqelchu'mo',
wIwuq: parmaqDaj 'oy'mo' bechtaH'a'?
pagh, latlh meqmo' bech'a'?

ghertlhuD   qalobrupbej.
'ovelya, Hujlaw' Hamlet; Do' 'e' qaSmoH
qa'IIj QaQ neH, bI'IHba'mo', vIneH.
vaj DotlhDaj motlhDaq ghaH DacheghmoHlaH
bI'IImo' 'e' vItul. 'ej tugh Suquvjaj.

'ovelya   joHwI', vIqaSmoHjaj.

[*mej GHERTLHUD TA'BE'*]

polonyuS   'ovelya, 'eH:
naDev yIyIt. joH quv, maSo"eghneS.

['*OVELYAvaD jatlh*]

paqvam yIlaD. bImobmeH meqHey 'anglaH
lalDanIIj Qu'Heyvetlh, DuleghDI' Hamlet.
ghuy'cha', lalDan vuvwI' DIDataHvIS,
'ej tay DItaghtaHvIS, veqlargh wIjun je.
pIj pIchvam'e' wIghaj; net tobqu'.

tlhaw'DIyuS   teHlaw'.

How smart a lash that speech doth give my conscience!
The harlot's cheek, beautied with plastering art,
Is not more ugly to the thing that helps it
Than is my deed to my most painted word:
O heavy burden!

Polonius

I hear him coming: let's withdraw, my lord.

[*Exeunt KING CLAUDIUS and POLONIUS*]

[*Enter HAMLET*]

Hamlet

To be, or not to be:—that is the question:—
Whether 'tis nobler in the mind to suffer
The slings and arrows of outrageous fortune,
Or to take arms against a sea of troubles,
And by opposing end them?—To die:—to sleep;—
No more; and by a sleep to say we end
The heart-ache and the thousand natural shocks
That flesh is heir to,—'tis a consummation
Devoutly to be wish'd. To die,—to sleep;—
To sleep! perchance to dream:—ay, there's the rub;
For in that sleep of death what dreams may come,
When we have shuffled off this mortal coil,
Must give us pause: there's the respect
That makes calamity of so long life;
For who would bear the whips and scorns of time,
The oppressor's wrong, the proud man's contumely,
The pangs of despis'd love, the law's delay,
The insolence of office and the spurns
That patient merit of the unworthy takes,
When he himself might his quietus make
With a bare bodkin? who would fardels bear,
To grunt and sweat under a weary life,
But that the dread of something after death,—
The undiscover'd country, from whose bourn
No traveller returns,—puzzles the will,
And makes us rather bear those ills we have
Than fly to others that we know not of?
Thus conscience does make cowards of us all;
And thus the native hue of resolution
Is sicklied o'er with the pale cast of thought;
And enterprises of great pith and moment,
With this regard, their currents turn awry,
And lose the name of action.—Soft you now!
The fair Ophelia! Nymph, in thy orisons
Be all my sins remember'd.

Ophelia

                                        Good my lord,
How does your honour for this many a day?

Hamlet

I humbly thank you; well, well, well.

Ophelia

My lord, I have remembrances of yours,
That I have longed long to re-deliver;
I pray you, now receive them.

Hamlet

                                        No, not I;
I never gave you aught.

[*pegh'egh*] va, ghobwIj HIvchu' SoQvam 'oy'naQ jay'!
ngaghwI' qevpobDaq tojbogh rItlhmey ngoHDI',
qevpob moH law', rItlh boch moH puS. vIrur je.
ta'wIj HoS law', SoQwIj vInguvmoHbogh
HoS puS. baQa', tep 'ugh!

polonyuS   chol 'e' vIQoy. maSo"eghneS, joH quv.

               [*mej* TLHAW'DIYUS TA' POLONYUS *je*]

               ['el HAMLET]

Hamlet   taH pagh taHbe'. DaH mu'tlheghvam vIqelnIS.
               quv'a', yabDaq San vaQ cha, pu' je SIQDI'?
               pagh, Seng bIQ'a'Hey SuvmeH nuHmey SuqDI',
               'ej, Suvmo', rInmoHDI'? Hegh. Qong—Qong neH—
               'ej QongDI', tIq 'oy', wa'SanID Daw"e' je
               cho'nISbogh porghDaj rInmoHlaH net Har.
               yIn mevbogh mIwvam'e' wIruchqangbej.
               Hegh. Qong. QongDI' chaq naj. toH, waQlaw' ghu'vam!
               HeghDaq maQongtaHvIS, tugh vay' wInajlaH,
               volchaHmajvo' jubbe'wI' bep wIwoDDI';
               'e' wIqelDI', maHeDnIS. Qugh DISIQnIS,
               SIQmoHmo' qechvam. Qugh yIn nI'moH 'oH.
               reH vaq 'ej qIpqu' bov; mayHa'taH HI';
               Dochchu' HemwI'; ruv mImlu'; tIchrup patlh;
               'oy'moH muSHa'ghach 'Il vuvHa'lu'bogh;
               quvwI'pu' tuv quvHa'moH quvHa'wI'pu';
               qatlh Hochvam lajqang vay'? wa' taj neH lo'DI',
               Qu'Daj Qatlh qIllaH ghaH! tep qengqang 'Iv?
               Doy'moHmo' yInDaj, bepmeH bechqang 'Iv,
               mISbe'chugh neHtaHghach, ghaH ghljmo' DuHvam:
               Hegh tlha' vay': Hegh tlha' qo"e' tu'bogh pagh.
               not chegh lengwI'ma', qo'vetlh veHmey 'elDI'.
               vaj Seng DIghajbogh, lajtaHmeH qaq law';
               latlh DISovbe'bogh, ghoSchoHmeH qaq puS.
               vaj nuch DIDa 'e' raDlaw' ghobmaj, qelDI'.
               'ej, pIvmo', wovqu'taHvIS wuqbogh qab,
               'oH ropmoH rIntaH Sotbogh qech ghom Hurgh.
               'ej Qu'mey potlh DItulbogh qIl je qechvam.
               vIDHa'choH nab. baQa'! 'ovelya 'IH!
               toH be', qa"a'pu'vaD bItlhobtaHvIS,
               jIyempu' 'e' yIQIjchoH je.

'ovelya   joH QaQ,
               qaStaHvIS Hu'vam chay' bIpIvneS SoH?

Hamlet   qatlho'; choquvmoHbej. jIchep, jIchep.

'ovelya   SoHvo' qaqawmeH nobmey law' vISuqta'.
               qaStaHvIS jajmey, bIH vItatlh vIneH.
               qatlhobneS, joH. tItlhap.

Hamlet   ghobe'. nobbe'.
               paghna' qanobta'.

Ophelia	My honour'd lord, you know right well you did; And, with them, words of so sweet breath compos'd As made the things more rich: their perfume lost, Take these again; for to the noble mind Rich gifts wax poor when givers prove unkind. There, my lord.
Hamlet	Ha, ha! are you honest?
Ophelia	My lord?
Hamlet	Are you fair?
Ophelia	What means your lordship?
Hamlet	That if you be honest and fair, your honesty should admit no discourse to your beauty.
Ophelia	Could beauty, my lord, have better commerce than with honesty?
Hamlet	Ay, truly; for the power of beauty will sooner transform honesty from what it is to a bawd than the force of honesty can translate beauty into his likeness: this was sometime a paradox, but now the time gives it proof. I did love you once.
Ophelia	Indeed, my lord, you made me believe so.
Hamlet	You should not have believed me; for virtue cannot so inoculate our old stock but we shall relish of it: I loved you not.
Ophelia	I was the more deceived.
Hamlet	Get thee to a nunnery: why wouldst thou be a breeder of sinners? I am myself indifferent honest; but yet I could accuse me of such things that it were better my mother had not born me: I am very proud, revengeful, ambitious; with more offences at my beck than I have thoughts to put them in, imagination to give them shape, or time to act them in. What should such fellows as I do crawling between heaven and earth? We are arrant knaves, all; believe none of us. Go thy ways to a nunnery. Where's your father?
Ophelia	At home, my lord.
Hamlet	Let the doors be shut upon him, that he may play the fool no where but in's own house. Farewell.
Ophelia	O, help him, you sweet heavens!
Hamlet	If thou dost marry, I'll give thee this plague for thy dowry:—be thou as chaste as ice, as pure as snow, thou shalt not escape calumny. Get thee to a nunnery, go: farewell. Or, if thou wilt needs marry, marry a fool; for wise men know well enough what monsters you make of them. To a nunnery, go; and quickly too. Farewell.
Ophelia	O heavenly powers, restore him!

'ovelya	Danobta' 'e' DaSovbejneS, joH quv. bIH tlhejmeH, 'IHqu'mo' bang QIch DatlhuHbogh vaj waghqu'choH. 'a DaH Dajbe'choH plwchaj. vaj tItlhapqa'. yab quvvaD qutlh nob wagh, SuqwI' maghDI' nobwI'. vaj boq vIlagh. tItlhapneS, joH.
Hamlet	wejpuH! wejpuH! be'batlh Daghaj'a'?
'ovelya	nuqjatlhneS?
Hamlet	bI'IH'a'?
'ovelya	nuq jatlhmeH bIHech, joH?
Hamlet	be'batlh Daghajchugh 'ej bI'IHchugh, vaj be'batlhvaD tamnIS 'IHtaHghachIlj.
'ovelya	joHwI', be'batlh van tamlaH'a' 'IHtaHghach?
Hamlet	HIja', teH. batlh rurwI' moj 'IHwI' 'e' qaSmoHpa' batlh HoS, DotlhDaj ngo' lon batlh 'ej ngaghwI' quvHa' moj batlh 'e' qaSmoHbej 'IHwI'. ben Hujpu' mu'tlheghvetlh. 'ach DaH 'oH tob bov. qamuSHa'pu'.
'ovelya	HISlaH, joH, qen SoHmo' 'e' vIHar.
Hamlet	choHarbe'nISpu'. ropmaj ngo' ngejHa'moHlaHbe' batlhqoq. reH He'So'taH ropvetlh. not qamuSHa'.
'ovelya	vaj vItojlu'bej.
Hamlet	Ha'! ngaghQo'wI' nawlogh yImuv. qatlh yemwI'pu' DaboghqangchoHmoH? machbe'bogh quv vIghaj. 'a HeS Dunmo' jIpum'eghlaHmo', vaj qaq, not muboghmoHchugh SoSwI'. jIHemqu'. jInoDqang. jItlhIv. HeSmey vIta'qangbogh law' law', HeSvetlh vInabmeH qechmeywIj law' puS; HeSvetlh vIchenmoHmeH laHmeywIj law' puS; HeSvetlh vIta'meH 'ebmeywIj law' puS. yav chal je jojDaq yIttaHvIS mururbogh petaQpu', chay' mavangnIS? taHqeq maH Hoch'e'. pagh yIvoq. tugh ngaghQo'wI' nawlogh yImuv. nuqDaq vavlI'?
'ovelya	juHDajDaq ghaH, joHwI'.
Hamlet	ghaHvaD SoQjaj lojmItmey. vaj juHDajDaq neH qoH Dajaj. qamej.
'ovelya	va, yIboQ, qa'pu' quv!
Hamlet	bInaychugh, vaj tlhogh nob tammeH, maQmIghvam qanob. chuch Darurchugh je bIngaghHa'Qo'mo', peDwI' Darurchugh je bIquvmo', vaj Dapumlu' 'e' DabotlaHbe'. ngaghQo'wI' nawlogh yImuv. Ha', qamej. pagh, bInaynISchugh, vaj qoH yInay. Qovpatlh moj loDnalra' 'e' boqaSmoHmeH mIwraj luSov loD val. ngaghQo'wI' nawlogh'e' nom yImuv. qamej.
'ovelya	qeylIS HoS, ghaH yIQaw'Ha'!

| Hamlet | I have heard of your paintings too, well enough; God has given you one face, and you make yourselves another: you jig, you amble, and you lisp, and nick-name God's creatures, and make your wantonness your ignorance. Go to, I'll no more on't; it hath made me mad. I say, we will have no more marriages: those that are married already, all but one, shall live; the rest shall keep as they are. To a nunnery, go. |

[*Exit*]

| Ophelia | O, what a noble mind is here o'erthrown! The courtier's, soldier's, scholar's eye, tongue, sword: The expectancy and rose of the fair state, The glass of fashion and the mould of form, The observ'd of all observers, quite, quite down! And I, of ladies most deject and wretched That suck'd the honey of his music vows, Now see that noble and most sovereign reason, Like sweet bells jangled, out of tune and harsh; That unmatch'd form and feature of blown youth Blasted with ecstasy: O, woe is me, To have seen what I have seen, see what I see! |

[*Re-enter KING CLAUDIUS and POLONIUS*]

| Claudius | Love! his affections do not that way tend; Nor what he spake, though it lack'd form a little, Was not like madness. There's something in his soul O'er which his melancholy sits on brood; And I do doubt the hatch and the disclose Will be some danger: which for to prevent, I have in quick determination Thus set it down:—he shall with speed to England For the demand of our neglected tribute: Haply, the seas and countries different With variable objects, shall expel This something-settled matter in his heart; Whereon his brains still beating puts him thus From fashion of himself. What think you on't? |

| Polonius | It shall do well: but yet do I believe The origin and commencement of his grief Sprung from neglected love.—How now, Ophelia! You need not tell us what Lord Hamlet said; We heard it all.—My lord, do as you please; But if you hold it fit, after the play, Let his queen mother all alone entreat him To show his grief: let her be round with him; And I'll be plac'd, so please you, in the ear Of all their conference. If she find him not, To England send him; or confine him where Your wisdom best shall think. |

| Claudius | It shall be so: Madness in great ones must not unwatch'd go. |

[*Exeunt*]

Hamlet   qabraj bochoHmoHmeH rItlh Doqqu' lo'raj
         vIQoybej je. 'u'vo' wa' qab boghaj, 'a tIhIHvaD latlh
         bochenmoH. SuyItHa' 'ej SureHHa' 'ej SujawHa'.
         'u' DolmeyvaD Saj pongoyqoq bonob.
         SuDaHa' 'e' boQIjmeH, Sujlv 'e' boqap. yIDoH,
         vISIQQo'. mumaw'moHpu'. not tlhogh wIqelqa'.
         wa'leS yInlaw'taH tlhogh jeSbogh HochHom'e'.
         yInbe' wa' neH. choHbe' Hoch latlh Dotlh.
         ngaghQo'wI' nawlogh yImuv.

         [mej HAMLET]

'ovelya   baQa' DaH Sab yab quv! tej, vaj, gharwI' je
         'etlh, jat, mIn je! wo' Do' ro', nembatlhna' je!
         ghaH Dapu' 'ej ghaH rurqangpu' Hoch vaj.
         ghaH tu'qang Hoch tu'wI'. 'a va, DaH Sabchu'.
         'IpDaj QoQ yuch vISoppu'. DaH jIH'e'
         'It 'ej Do'Ha' law', Hoch latlh be' 'It puS.
         DaH che'pu'bogh meqlaHvetlh quv yItu'.
         DIron qebHa'lu'bogh rur: tlhov 'ej taQ.
         QuptaHghach 'oSbogh chenchu'wI''e' Qaw'pu'
         meqHa'ghach QIH. Do'Ha'! Qugh 'ongvaD jeghtaH.
         wIgh naQ vIleghpu' 'ej maQmIgh vIleghtaH!

         ['elqa' TLHAW'DIYUS TA' POLONYUS je]

tlhaw'DIyuS   muSHa''a'? 'e' 'angbe'ba' neHtaHghachDaj.
         maw' 'e' tobbe' je SoQDaj ja'pu'bogh,
         chenHa'taHvIS je. qa'Daj nuQtaH vay'.
         'oH 'avmeH retlhDaq ba'lI' 'IttaHghach.
         chaq Qob 'avwI' Qu', Qubmo' ghaH 'ej nabmo';
         'e' vIpIH. Qob vIbotmeH nom jIwuqDI',
         jIra': tugh vanmaj luSaHHa'pu'bogh
         poQmeH tera'Daq ghoSnIS ghaH. vaj Do',
         pImmo' yuQ logh je, Dechbogh Dochmey je,
         tugh tIqDajvo' qech buStaHbogh lughIm.
         reH yabDaj mupmo' qechvetlh, DotlhDaj motlhvo'
         Hop ghaH. HopHa'qa'nIS. SuH, chay' choqeS?

polonyuS   Qaplaw'. muSHa'ghachDaj jangHa'lu'mo'
         chenlaw'pu' 'IQtaHghachDaj mung taghwI' je,
         toH, wej 'e' vIHarQo'. nuqneH, 'ovelya.
         Hamlet joH mu'tlheghmey juja'nISbe'.
         Hoch mu' wIQoypu'. nab yIwIvneS, joH.
         'ach latlh yIchaw' je. 'IQ ghaH; rInDI' lut,
         SoSvaD 'e' 'angmeH ghaH, nIteb ghaH tlhob
         SoS'e', ta'be''e'. ghaHvaD qu'nIS qunDI'.
         ja'chuq chaH 'e' vIDaqneSmeH jIlan'egh.
         ghu'Daj tu'be'chugh SoS, vaj nom tera'Daq
         bIghHa'Daq ghap yIngeH. Daq lugh yIwIv,
         bIvalbejmo'.

tlhaw'DIyuS   Ha'. DaH SIbI' vIruch.
         maw'DI' ghot potlh, tugh QoblaH 'e' wItuch.

         [mej chaH]

SCENE II *A hall in the castle.*

[*Enter HAMLET and Players*]

Hamlet	Speak the speech, I pray you, as I pronounced it to you, trippingly on the tongue: but if you mouth it, as many of your players do, I had as lief the town-crier spoke my lines. Nor do not saw the air too much with your hand, thus; but use all gently: for in the very torrent, tempest, and, as I may say, the whirlwind of passion, you must acquire and beget a temperance that may give it smoothness. O, it offends me to the soul, to hear a robustious periwig-pated fellow tear a passion to tatters, to very rags, to split the ears of the groundlings, who, for the most part, are capable of nothing but inexplicable dumbshows and noise: I would have such a fellow whipped for o'erdoing Termagant; it out-herods Herod: pray you, avoid it.
First Player	I warrant your honour.
Hamlet	Be not too tame neither, but let your own discretion be your tutor: suit the action to the word, the word to the action; with this special observance, that you o'erstep not the modesty of nature: for any thing so overdone is from the purpose of playing, whose end, both at the first and now, was and is, to hold, as 'twere, the mirror up to nature; to show virtue her own feature, scorn her own image, and the very age and body of the time his form and pressure. Now, this overdone or come tardy off, though it make the unskilful laugh, cannot but make the judicious grieve; the censure of the which one must, in your allowance, o'erweigh a whole theatre of others. O, there be players that I have seen play,—and heard others praise, and that highly,—not to speak it profanely, that, neither having the accent of Christians nor the gait of Christian, pagan, nor man, have so strutted and bellowed that I have thought some of nature's journeymen had made men, and not made them well, they imitated humanity so abominably.
First Player	I hope we have reformed that indifferently with us, sir.
Hamlet	O, reform it altogether. And let those that play your clowns speak no more than is set down for them: for there be of them that will themselves laugh, to set on some quantity of barren spectators to laugh too; though, in the mean time, some necessary question of the play be then to be considered: that's villanous, and shows a most pitiful ambition in the fool that uses it. Go, make you ready.

[*Exeunt Players*]

[*Enter POLONIUS, ROSENCRANTZ, and GUILDENSTERN*]

How now, my lord! will the king hear this piece of work?

LUT 'AY'HOM CHA'. *ta'qach'a' vaS.*

['el HAMLET, wej DawI' je]

Hamlet

SoQ'e' Daja'taHvIS, HIDa—
jat yISupmoH. DawI' motlh mIw QIch Dalo'chugh,
vaj chetvI'vo' mu'meywIj baH DIvI'may'Duj
'e' vImaS. muD yISIjlaw'Qo', ghop DajoqmoHtaHvIS,
'ach Hoch yISeH. SIStaHvIS, jevtaHvIS,
'ej (chaq vIDellaH) jorlaw'taHvIS QeHHeyIIj,
vIt rurlaw'meH SoQ Daja'bogh QeH jot
yIchenmoH. va, SoQ SangDI' mIybogh toDSaH ral,
SoQ Qaw'DI', qa'wI' tIch. yavDaq bejwI' teSDu' neII
DuQlu'bogh belmoH, lut tam luQIjbe'lu'bogh,
QIch chuS je neH yajlaHmo'.
chIch veqlargh DameH lachchugh DawI',
vaj vImuHrup. molor rurmeH, ghaH 'um law';
molor 'um puS. yIbot.

DawI' wa'DIch

qaHeQneS.

Hamlet

'a yIjotqu'Qo' je; bIDachu'meH Duj yIvoqtaH.
mu' DallSmeH yIvangchu' 'ej bIvangmeH mu' tIlISchu'.
ngeHbej vIt yIwemQo' 'ej wa' qech'e' yIqelchu':
DawI' Qu' ta'Ha'qu' lachbogh 'ej wembogh DawI';
ben DaHjaj je, 'u'vaD qabna'Daj 'angmeH, quvvaD
batlhna'Daj 'angmeH, quvHa'ghachvaD porghDaj moH
'angmeH, chentaHvIS 'ej tlhetlhtaHvIS bov ro,
lupDaj je mIwna' cha'chu'meH Qu''e' ghaj DawI'.
bIlachchugh pagh bIyapbe'chugh, vaj bejwI' Soy'
DaHaghmoH 'ach noHchu'wI' DabepmoH neH.
bIqeltaHvIS, SoHvaD wa' noHchu'wI' yoj potlh law',
qach naQDaq latlhpu' yoj potlh puS. va, rut lachmo'
DawI''e' vIbejbogh 'ej naDqu'bogh latlhpu', vaj QI'yaH.
tlhInganna' rurHa'qu' jatlhDI'; 'ej tlhInganna',
novna' ghap, yaghna' ghap rurHa'qu' jay' vIHDI'.
'ej Soy'chu'taHmo' 'ej chuSchu'taHmo' chaH,
chenmeH chaH lam lutlholHa'moHlaw'pu' yo' qIj jonwI'
ghojwI'pu'. (lalDan vItlchQo', 'ach) 'e' vIHarqang,
ghotna' DaHa'qu'mo', DataHvIS chaH.

DawI' wa'DIch

malIS'eghlaw'pu'neS.

Hamlet

toH, pelIS'eghchu' jay'.
'ej chIch ghItlh neH lupabnIS HaghmoHbogh DawI'ra'.
toH HaghmoHmeH HaghmoHwI', Hagh ghaH neH,
'ej lururmeH bejwI' Dogh, Hagh je chaH.
'ach HaghtaHvIS Hoch, lut potlhmey'e' wej
lumuchlu'bogh mIm. Hat 'ej tlhetlhHa'ghach
neH Hech Dupqoqvam lo'bogh qoH'e'.
'eH peDarupchoH.

[mej DawI'pu']

['el POLONYUS ROSENQATLH GHILDESTEN je]

toH jay', qaH, lutvam Qoyrup'a' ta'?

Polonius	And the queen too, and that presently.
Hamlet	Bid the players make haste.

[*Exit POLONIUS*]

Will you two help to hasten them?

Rosencrantz & Guildenstern	We will, my lord.

[*Exeunt ROSENCRANTZ and GUILDENSTERN*]

Hamlet	What ho! Horatio!

[*Enter HORATIO*]

Horatio	Here, sweet lord, at your service.
Hamlet	Horatio, thou art e'en as just a man As e'er my conversation coped withal.
Horatio	O, my dear lord,—

Hamlet

     Nay, do not think I flatter;
For what advancement may I hope from thee,
That no revenue hast, but thy good spirits,
To feed and clothe thee? Why should the poor be flatter'd?
No, let the candied tongue lick absurd pomp;
And crook the pregnant hinges of the knee
Where thrift may follow fawning. Dost thou hear?
Since my dear soul was mistress of her choice,
And could of men distinguish, her election
Hath seal'd thee for herself: for thou hast been
As one, in suffering all, that suffers nothing;
A man that Fortune buffets and rewards
Hast ta'en with equal thanks: and bless'd are those
Whose blood and judgment are so well commingled
That they are not a pipe for fortune's finger
To sound what stop she please. Give me that man
That is not passion's slave, and I will wear him
In my heart's core, ay, in my heart of heart,
As I do thee.—Something too much of this.—
There is a play to-night before the king;
One scene of it comes near the circumstance
Which I have told thee of my father's death:
I prithee, when thou seest that act afoot,
Even with the very comment of thy soul
Observe mine uncle: if his occulted guilt
Do not itself unkennel in one speech,
It is a damned ghost that we have seen;
And my imaginations are as foul
As Vulcan's stithy. Give him heedful note:
For I mine eyes will rivet to his face;
And, after, we will both our judgments join
In censure of his seeming.

Horatio

     Well, my lord:
If he steal aught the whilst this play is playing,
And 'scape detecting, I will pay the theft.

polonyuS   ta'be' je—SIbI'!

Hamlet   moDmeH DawI' tIra'.

                  [*mej POLONYUS*]

                  moDmoHmeH, SuH, yItlhej tlhIH.

roSenQatlh   luq, joH.
ghIlDeSten je

                  [*mej cha'*]

Hamlet   Horey'So! SuH!

                  ['*el HOREY'SO*]

HOREY'SO   naDev jIH, joH. qatoy'rup.

Hamlet   Horey'So, SoH quv law', jIjatlhtaHmeH
                  Hoch ghot vIqIHpu'bogh quv puS.

Horey'So   toH, joH—

Hamlet   qatoj 'e' yIHarQo'. chochepmoHlaH,
                  chay' 'e' vIHarlaH jIH? Soj, SutmeyIIj je
                  Daje'laHmeH yapbe'ba' mIp Daghajbogh,
                  yablaHIIj QaQ qelbe'lu'chugh. Horey'So,
                  qatlh mIpbe'wI' vItojqang? va, patlh Dogh neH
                  roSnIS HaQchorHey jat. 'ej chep'eghmoHmeH
                  mIpqangbogh qIvDaj SIHmoHnIS yuDwI' neH.
                  vaj naDDI', numchoHlu' 'e' tul. 'Ij'a'?
                  wIvlaHmeH ra''eghchoHDI' qa'wI' quv,
                  'ej ghotpu'vo' QaQwI'na' ngu'laHDI',
                  DuwuvmeH vaj DuDoQ, Dutu'taHmo'.
                  bIbechlaw'be', Hochmo' bIbechtaHvIS je.
                  DutIchDI' 'ej DunaDDI' San, Hoch ghu'
                  DaSIQmeH nIbtaH tlho'IIj. Do'bej ghot,
                  ghotvamDaq 'IwDaj, qelbogh laHDaj je
                  DuDlu'chu'chugh. Hoch QoQmey maSbogh IIngmeH,
                  luHengmeH San nItlhDu', vaj, San Dov'agh
                  DaQo' batlhghotvam. ghotvam'e' HI'ang.
                  'ej nongtaHghach toy'wI''a' puj DaQo'chugh,
                  vaj tIqwIj botlhDaq, tIq tIqna'wIjDaq
                  ghotvam vIqeng. HIja'. vaj SoH qaqeng.
                  'a pItlh. DaHjaj ram ta'vaD lutHom muchlu'.
                  vavwI' Hegh ghu' qaja'bogh Dellaw' 'ay'Daj.
                  qatlhob, jup. 'ay'vam muchlu' 'e' DabejDI',
                  QaptaHvIS tu'chu'meH je qa'll' botlh,
                  ta'ma' yIbej. wa' SoQ lumuchtaHvIS,
                  'ejyo'waw'vo' narghQo'chugh DujDaj DIv
                  reH So'taHbogh, vaj qa' quvHa' wIleghpu',
                  'ej tlhIvmo' Hoch qech Dogh vI'oghpu'bogh,
                  bajor mangghom lurur neH. ghaH yIbejchu'.
                  'ej qabDajDaq mInDu'wIj tIH vIpuS je.
                  'ej rInDI' ghu', DameH ghaH mIw wIchovmeH,
                  cha' yojmeymaj DIchelchu'.

Horey'So   lu', joHwI'.
                  lut muchlu'DI', batlhDotlhHey nIHchugh ghaH,
                  ghaH tu'lu'pa', vaj lojbogh Hoch vIDIlrup.

Hamlet	They are coming to the play; I must be idle: Get you a place.
	[*Danish march. A flourish. Enter KING CLAUDIUS, QUEEN GERTRUDE, POLONIUS, OPHELIA, ROSENCRANTZ, GUILDENSTERN, and others*]
Claudius	How fares our cousin Hamlet?
Hamlet	Excellent, i' faith; of the chameleon's dish: I eat the air, promise-crammed: you cannot feed capons so.
Claudius	I have nothing with this answer, Hamlet; these words are not mine.
Hamlet	No, nor mine now.—
	[*To POLONIUS*]
	My lord, you played once i' the university, you say?
Polonius	That did I, my lord, and was accounted a good actor.
Hamlet	What did you enact?
Polonius	I did enact Julius Caesar: I was killed i' the Capitol; Brutus killed me.
Hamlet	It was a brute part of him to kill so capital a calf there.—Be the players ready?
Rosencrantz	Ay, my lord; they stay upon your patience.
Gertrude	Come hither, my dear Hamlet, sit by me.
Hamlet	No, good mother, here's metal more attractive.
Polonius	[*To KING CLAUDIUS*] O, ho! do you mark that?
Hamlet	Lady, shall I lie in your lap?
	[*Lying down at OPHELIA's feet*]
Ophelia	No, my lord.
Hamlet	I mean, my head upon your lap?
Ophelia	Ay, my lord.
Hamlet	Do you think I meant country matters?
Ophelia	I think nothing, my lord.
Hamlet	That's a fair thought to lie between maids' legs.
Ophelia	What is, my lord?
Hamlet	Nothing.
Ophelia	You are merry, my lord.
Hamlet	Who, I?
Ophelia	Ay, my lord.
Hamlet	O, your only jig-maker. What should a man do but be merry? for, look you, how cheerfully my mother looks, and my father died within 's two hours.
Ophelia	Nay, 'tis twice two months, my lord.

Hamlet	lutDaq chollI' chaH. pagh vIbuSlaw' 'e' vI'angnIS. yIlan'egh.
	[*chuS yItmeH Qo'noS QoQ. chuS maqmeH QoQ.* '*el TLHAW'DIYUS TA'*, *GHERTLHUD TA'BE'*, *POLONYUS*, '*OVELYA*, *ROSENQATLH*, *GHILDESTEN*, *latlhpu' je*]
tlhaw'DIyuS	pIv'a' qorDu' ghotma', Hamlet?
Hamlet	pIv, pov. ghew vIDa, muDDaq ngoSpu'bogh 'Ipmcy'e' vISopmo'. to'baj nay' tamlaHbe'.
tlhaw'DIyuS	mu'wIj Daqelbe'law', Hamlet. mu'wIj jangpu'be' mu'lIj.
Hamlet	jangbe''egh je bIH.
	[*POLONYUSvaD*]
	toH, ben DuSaQ'a'Daq DawI' SoH, qar'a'?
polonyuS	HISlaH, 'ej vIqellu'DI' DawI' QaQqu' jIH net noH.
Hamlet	'Iv DaDa?
polonyuS	yulyuS qaySar vIDa. monDaq jIHegh. muHeghmoH beru'tuS.
Hamlet	Sor rur ghaH, QamtaHvIS. yol yoSDaq qay' Sor. vaj val HeghmoHwI'Daj.—Darup'a' DawI'pu'?
roSenQatlh	HISlaH, joHwI'. DaQoyqangchoH 'e' luloS.
ghertlhuD	Ha' naDev, Hamletoy, jIba'taHvIS HItlhej.
Hamlet	Qo', SoSoy QaQ, pa' jIghoS. muSIgh peQvetlh 'IHqu'.
polonyuS	[*TLHAW'DIYUS TA'vaD pegh*] toH Hu'tegh, yItu' jay'!
Hamlet	be'oy, 'uSDu'lIjDaq jIQot 'e' Dachaw''a'?
	['*OVELYA qamDu'Daq Qot*]
'ovelya	Qo', joHwI'.
Hamlet	'a 'uSDu'lIjDaq nachwIj'e' vIQotmoH 'e' vIHech neH.
'ovelya	lu', joHwI'.
Hamlet	ngaghlu' 'e' vIHech 'e' DaQub'a'?
'ovelya	pagh vIQub, qaH.
Hamlet	be' 'uSDu'Daq QotmeH QaQba' qechvam.
'ovelya	qech nuq, qaH?
Hamlet	0 DaHub.
'ovelya	bItlhaQ, qaH.
Hamlet	'Iv? jIH?
'ovelya	HIja'.
Hamlet	baQa', tagh QommoHwI''a'lI' jIH. Qombe'chugh taghDu', vaj chay' jaS vanglaH porgh. toH, Quchqu'bej SoSwI' 'e' yItu', 'ach Heghpu'DI' vavwI', qaS cha' rep neH.
'ovelya	ghobe', qaS loS jarmey, joH.

Hamlet	So long? Nay, then, let the devil wear black, for I'll have a suit of sables. O heavens! die two months ago, and not forgotten yet? Then there's hope a great man's memory may outlive his life half a year: but, by'r lady, he must build churches, then; or else shall he suffer not thinking on, with the hobby-horse, whose epitaph is 'For, O, for, O, the hobby-horse is forgot.'

[*Hautboys play. The dumb-show enters*]

[*Enter a King and a Queen very lovingly; the Queen embracing him, and he her. She kneels, and makes show of protestation unto him. He takes her up, and declines his head upon her neck: lays him down upon a bank of flowers: she, seeing him asleep, leaves him. Anon comes in a fellow, takes off his crown, kisses it, and pours poison in the King's ears, and exit. The Queen returns; finds the King dead, and makes passionate action. The Poisoner, with some two or three Mutes, comes in again, seeming to lament with her. The dead body is carried away. The Poisoner wooes the Queen with gifts: she seems loath and unwilling awhile, but in the end accepts his love*]

[*Exeunt*]

Ophelia	What means this, my lord?
Hamlet	Marry, this is miching mallecho; it means mischief.
Ophelia	Belike this show imports the argument of the play.

[*Enter Prologue*]

Hamlet	We shall know by this fellow: the players cannot keep counsel; they'll tell all.
Ophelia	Will he tell us what this show meant?
Hamlet	Ay, or any show that you'll show him: be not you ashamed to show, he'll not shame to tell you what it means.
Ophelia	You are naught, you are naught: I'll mark the play.
Prologue	For us, and for our tragedy, Here stooping to your clemency, We beg your hearing patiently.

[*Exit*]

Hamlet	Is this a prologue, or the posy of a ring?
Ophelia	'Tis brief, my lord.
Hamlet	As woman's love.

[Enter two Players, King and Queen]

Player King	Full thirty times hath Phoebus' cart gone round Neptune's salt wash and Tellus' orbed ground, And thirty dozen moons with borrow'd sheen About the world have times twelve thirties been,

Hamlet	qaS'a'? Qo' jay', San Quch choS veqlargh. choS SutwIj vItuQHa'. QI'yaH, Heghpu' Hu' ta', 'ej qaS cha' jar neH, ghaH lIjlu'pa'. Heghpu'DI' DunwI', chaq batlh ghaH qawlu'taH, qaStaHvIS DIS bID'e' net tul je. 'ach Hu'tegh, yuQmey pongnIS. pongbe'chugh, vaj qawbe'lu' 'e' SIQ, 'ej qolotlh San ghaj. ghaH qaw bom mu'vam'e' neH: "toH va, toH va, qolotlh pong gho' Serman."

[*chuS meSchuS; 'el DawI' tam*]

['el ta'qoq ta'be'qoq je. muSHa'chuqlaw' 'e' luDa.
DeSDaq QIDchuqmeH pachDu'chaj lo'.
ta' qIvDu' jojDaq HIvmeH tor ta'be'.
ta'be' Hu'moH 'ej mong chop ta'.
ta' woH 'ej yavDaq pummoH ta'be'.
belpu'mo' Qonglaw' ta' 'e' leghDI' mej ta'be'.
tugh 'el latlh loD. ta' mIv'a' teq 'ej roS.
ta' qoghDaq tar qang 'ej mej. chegh ta'be'.
Heghpu' ta' 'e' leghmo' pe'vIl SaQ.
'elqa' chotwI' tlhejwI' puS je. luvuplaw'.
vIHbe'bogh ta' lomHey lunge'. ta'be' bang moj 'e'
nID chotwI'. nayqangmoHmeH nobmey Hev ta'be'.
lajqangbe', 'ach tugh latlh muSHa' ghaH
'ej bang DalI'bogh chotwI''e' laj.]

[*mej*]

'ovelya	qaSpu' nuq jay', joH.
Hamlet	va, HeS'a' 'ong'e'. qaSbeH lot 'e' 'ang 'oH.
'ovelya	ghaytan lut'a' lumuchmeH mIw QIj lutHomvam.

['el *lIHwI'*]

Hamlet	'e' luQIjbej nuvvam'e'. peghlaHbe' DawI'pu'. Hoch luchID.
'ovelya	De''e' luja'meH nIDbogh DawI'vetlh luQIjqang'a'?
Hamlet	HISlaH, De' law' luja'mo', QIDtaHvIS chaH. bIQIDqangchugh vaj bIghoj. QIDmeH 'ay'Du'lIj jej ghov QIjwI' 'ej ghojmoH.
'ovelya	bIQut, bIQut! DawI' lut'e' vIbej.
lIHwI'	DaH lutmaj 'It wIjeSqu'nIS. checherghchoHmeH matortaHvIS, pe'Ij. petuv. 'ej wej ghonIS.

[*mej*]

Hamlet	lIHbogh SoQ 'oH'a' SoQvam'e'? Degh mu'tlheghHom 'oH'a' neH?
'ovelya	ngaj, joH.
Hamlet	vaj be' parmaq rur.

['el *ta'qoq ta'be'qoq je*]

ta'qoq	wejmaHlogh bIQ SoD wIb, yuQ moQ je bavpu' pemHov Duj; wejvatlh javmaHlogh DIS wavpu' maSwovDaj ngIpbogh maS, rInpu'DI' ghu': tlq muv tlq, bang DIDamo'. Qap je Qu':

Since love our hearts, and Hymen did our hands
Unite commutual in most sacred bands.

Player Queen So many journeys may the sun and moon
Make us again count o'er ere love be done!
But, woe is me, you are so sick of late,
So far from cheer and from your former state,
That I distrust you. Yet, though I distrust,
Discomfort you, my lord, it nothing must:
For women's fear and love holds quantity;
In neither aught, or in extremity.
Now, what my love is, proof hath made you know;
And as my love is siz'd, my fear is so:
Where love is great, the littlest doubts are fear;
Where little fears grow great, great love grows there.

Player King 'Faith, I must leave thee, love, and shortly too;
My operant powers their functions leave to do:
And thou shalt live in this fair world behind,
Honour'd, belov'd and haply one as kind
For husband shalt thou—

Player Queen   O, confound the rest!
Such love must needs be treason in my breast:
In second husband let me be accurst!
None wed the second but who kill'd the first.

Hamlet [*Aside*] Wormwood, wormwood.

Player Queen The instances that second marriage move
Are base respects of thrift, but none of love:
A second time I kill my husband dead
When second husband kisses me in bed.

Player King I do believe you think what now you speak;
But what we do determine oft we break.
Purpose is but the slave to memory;
Of violent birth, but poor validity:
Which now, like fruit unripe, sticks on the tree;
But fall unshaken when they mellow be.
Most necessary 'tis that we forget
To pay ourselves what to ourselves is debt:
What to ourselves in passion we propose,
The passion ending, doth the purpose lose.
The violence of either grief or joy
Their own enactures with themselves destroy:
Where joy most revels grief doth most lament;
Grief joys, joy grieves, on slender accident.
This world is not for aye; nor 'tis not strange
That even our loves should with our fortunes change;
For 'tis a question left us yet to prove
Whether love lead fortune or else fortune love.
The great man down, you mark his favourite flies;
The poor advanc'd makes friends of enemies.
And hitherto doth love on fortune tend:
For who not needs shall never lack a friend;
And who in want a hollow friend doth try,
Directly seasons him his enemy.
But, orderly to end where I begun,—

matay'taH, tlhoghvaD muvchuqmo' ghopDu'maj.

ta'be'qoq   pIj maS pemHov je leng DItoghqa'pu'jaj,
               rInpa' muSHa'ghachmaj! 'ach DaH bIropmo'
               qaStaHvIS Hu', 'ej Dotlh ngo'vo' bIHopmo',
               pay' bI'IQtaHvIS, QI'yaH! Qugh vIpIH.
               toH, joH, jIpIHchugh jIH, vaj not DuQIH,
               SaHqu'mo' be'nal, loD muSHa'taIIvIS je.
               muSHa'DI' be', 'ej SaHDI', rap. reH Dach cha',
               pagh (qamuSHa'qu' 'e' Datu') reH lach cha'.
               ngojDI' muSHa'wI', ngojnIS je SaHwI'.
               muSHa'chugh nuv, vaj HajnIS HonchoHDI'.
               'ach Hajqu'chugh ghaH, vaj muSHa'rupchu'.

ta'qoq   bangwI', va, tugh qalonnIS. puj 'ej ru'
               porghlaHmeywIj. qo' 'IHDaq leS bImob.
               bIquv. 'ej Do' DuSaw—

ta'be'qoq   not latlh vIlob!
               not tIqwIjDaq 'urmangvetlh web vIlaj.
               loDnalqoq cha'mo' jIquvHa'nIS. vaj,
               loD cha'DIch nay neH be'—loD wa'DIch HoHDI'!

Hamlet   [pegh'egh] maQmIgh! maQmIgh!

ta'be'qoq   muSHa'be' be', tlhogh cha'DIch ruchmeH boHDI'.
               'ej chepmeH neH quvHa"eghmoH. jImatlh!
               loDnal vIHoHqa', wuSwIj chopDI' latlh.

ta'qoq   DaH vuD Daja' DaQubmo'. 'e' vIHar.
               'ach nuQbogh nabmaj qIlmeH pIj maghar.
               leS qawtaHghachmaj wuv DaH nabbogh Duj.
               vIDqang 'oH boghDI', 'a wIDajDI' luj.
               DaH naH Qup rur 'oH. SorDaq HuS, qar'a'?
               'ach qanDI' pum 'oH, Sorchaj yuvlu'pa'.
               Qu'maj DIlay'pu'bogh DIlIjnISlaw'.
               chavvetlh, wIchuppu'bogh manongDI', Qaw'
               SaHQo'ghachmaj, manongqu' 'e' wImevmo'.
               Sorgh'egh Dotlh Quch, Dotlh 'IQ joq ral, QIt jevmo'.
               lopchugh QuchwI', vaj SaQnIS je 'IQwI';
               butlhmo' neH 'IQ yonwI' 'ej Quch 'ItwI'.
               ru'nIS ngeHbejmaj. vaj Hujbe' wanI':
               choHnIS muSHa'ghachmaj, choHDI' San vI.
               wej ngoD wIwuq: parmaq wuv'a' neH San?
               pagh, San wuv'a' parmaqvetlh? toH, ghaytan
               quvHa'DI' potlh, Haw' bangDaj. jup moj ghol
               'e' SIgh mIpbe'pu'wI', ghaH DuvDI' yol.
               San toy' muSHa'ghach. vay'vaD 'utlaHbe'DI'
               SaH juppu'Hey. 'a boQmeH jup leS nge'DI'
               vay', ghaHvaD tlhobmo', tugh jupna'vo' cheH.
               'ach taghbogh DaqDaq SoQ vIrInmoHmeH:
               Sanmaj DonHa'moH neHtaHghachmeymaj.
               'ej reH Hoch nabmaj ngeplu'. qech DIghaj
               'ach qechvam ghochmey DIghajbe'. toH mub:

	Our wills and fates do so contra'ry run That our devices still are overthrown; Our thoughts are ours, their ends none of our own: So think thou wilt no second husband wed; But die thy thoughts when thy first lord is dead.
Player Queen	Nor earth to me give food, nor heaven light! Sport and repose lock from me day and night! To desperation turn my trust and hope! An anchor's cheer in prison be my scope! Each opposite, that blanks the face of joy, Meet what I would have well, and it destroy! Both here and hence, pursue me lasting strife, If, once a widow, ever I be wife!
Hamlet	[to OPHELIA] If she should break it now!
Player King	'Tis deeply sworn. Sweet, leave me here awhile; My spirits grow dull, and fain I would beguile The tedious day with sleep. [Sleeps]
Player Queen	Sleep rock thy brain, And never come mischance between us twain! [Exit]
Hamlet	Madam, how like you this play?
Gertrude	The lady protests too much, methinks.
Hamlet	O, but she'll keep her word.
Claudius	Have you heard the argument? Is there no offence in 't?
Hamlet	No, no, they do but jest, poison in jest; no offence i' the world.
Claudius	What do you call the play?
Hamlet	The Mouse-trap. Marry, how? Tropically. This play is the image of a murder done in Vienna: Gonzago is the duke's name; his wife, Baptista: you shall see anon; 'tis a knavish piece of work: but what o' that? your majesty and we that have free souls, it touches us not: let the galled jade wince, our withers are unwrung. [Enter LUCIANUS] This is one Lucianus, nephew to the king.
Ophelia	You are as good as a chorus, my lord.
Hamlet	I could interpret between you and your love, if I could see the puppets dallying.
Ophelia	You are keen, my lord, you are keen.
Hamlet	It would cost you a groaning to take off my edge.
Ophelia	Still better, and worse.
Hamlet	So you must take your husbands.—Begin, murderer; pox, leave thy damnable faces, and begin. Come:—

loD cha'DIch DanayQo' DaH 'e' yIQub.
'ach HeghnIS vuDvam HeghDI' je loD wa'.

ta'be'qoq   yavvo' Soj vISuqbe'jaj; Hurghjaj qa';
        reH jIHvo' Quj leSpoH je nge'jaj moch;
        jIvoqtaH 'ej jItul 'e' mevjaj ngoch;
        bIghHa' Saj'uQ vIpIHjaj; qaqbogh ghu'
        ghomjaj 'ej Qaw'jaj qab Quch Hoch ghol qu';
        Dat naDev je mutlha'jaj nI'bogh Seng—
        be'nal vImojqa'chugh jIH. 'Ip vIqeng!

Hamlet   ['*OVELYAvaD*] DaH 'Ip pabHa'jaj!

ta'qoq   bI'Ipchu'ta'. 'ach bang, DaH loQ HImej.
        Doy'choHtaH qa'wI'. Qatlhmo' pem, jIDej.
        vaj DaH jIQong.

        [*Qong*]

ta'be'qoq   bIQongDI', jotjaj yablIj.
        not' qabwIjvo' lotmo' SumHa'jaj qablIj.

        [*mej*]

Hamlet   joH, DubelmoH'a' lutvam?

ghertlhuD   wejpuH Hoch 'Iprup be'.

Hamlet   'ach 'Ip quvmoHbej ghaH.

tlhaw'DIyuS   lut DaSov'a'? luja'taHvIS HeS'a'?

Hamlet   ghobe' jay'! SaghHa' neH HeS. SaghHa' tar. HeSbe'chu'.

tlhaw'DIyuS   lutvam pong nuq?

Hamlet   "ghew jonwI'." toH, qatlh? wejpuH, lutDaj Del pongDaj.
        romuluSDaq HoHwanI' rur lutvam. ghonja'gho ghaH
        ta'qorDu'loD'e'; batlhISta ghaH be'nalDaj'e'. tugh Dabej.
        HeSwI' ghu' luDel. 'a maSaHbe'ba'. ta', qa' chun polwI' je
        ghob'e' muplaHbe'. chut DIlobbogh maH'e' nujoy'laHbe'
        pe'vIl nov DIv DISmoHbogh tuQDoq'e'.

        ['*el LUQYANUS*]

        luqyanuS ghaH. ta'qorDu'loD ghaH je.

'ovelya   lut DaQIjmeH SoH val law', QIjbogh DawI' val puS.

Hamlet   SoH bangHeylI' je jojDaq Quj vIQIjmeH jIval je, taj'e'
        vItu'laHchugh.

'ovelya   bIjej, jawwI', bIjej.

Hamlet   tajwIj DajejHa'qangmoHchugh bIboghnISmoH.

'ovelya   Dub 'ej Sab mu'

Hamlet   nayqangmeH be' Dup SapmoH mu'.—yIchot yIruch SoH.
        Qu'vatlh, Ha'DIbaH qablIj tIlon 'ej yIruch. Ha', bortaS QaQ

'the croaking raven doth bellow for revenge.'

Lucianus	Thoughts black, hands apt, drugs fit, and time agreeing; Confederate season, else no creature seeing; Thou mixture rank, of midnight weeds collected, With Hecate's ban thrice blasted, thrice infected, Thy natural magic and dire property On wholesome life usurp immediately.

[*Pours the poison into the sleeper's ears*]

Hamlet	He poisons him i' the garden for's estate. His name's Gonzago: the story is extant, and writ in choice Italian: you shall see anon how the murderer gets the love of Gonzago's wife.
Ophelia	The king rises.
Hamlet	What, frighted with false fire!
Gertrude	How fares my lord?
Polonius	Give o'er the play.
Claudius	Give me some light:—away!
All	Lights, lights, lights!

[*Exeunt all but HAMLET and HORATIO*]

Hamlet	Why, let the stricken deer go weep, The hart ungalled play; For some must watch, while some must sleep: So runs the world away. Would not this, sir, and a forest of feathers— if the rest of my fortunes turn Turk with me—with two Provincial roses on my razed shoes, get me, a fellowship in a cry of players, sir?
Horatio	Half a share.
Hamlet	A whole one, I. For thou dost know, O Damon dear, This realm dismantled was Of Jove himself and now reigns here A very, very—pajock.
Horatio	You might have rhymed.
Hamlet	O good Horatio, I'll take the ghost's word for a thousand pound. Didst perceive?
Horatio	Very well, my lord.
Hamlet	Upon the talk of the poisoning?
Horatio	I did very well note him.
Hamlet	Ah, ha!—Come, some music! come, the recorders!— For if the king like not the comedy, Why then, belike,—he likes it not, perdy. Come, some music!

[*Re-enter ROSENCRANTZ and GUILDENSTERN*]

Guildenstern	Good my lord, vouchsafe me a word with you.

jablu'DI' reH bIrqu' nay'.

luqyanuS	qech qIj, ghop po', tar 'um, poH lugh: Samuv.

boq jeS 'eb poH. 'ej DaH mulegh pagh nuv.
ramjep tI boSlu'mo' bIchen, molDargh.
wejlogh Dungej 'ej DunaDHa' veqlargh.
pay' pIvbogh yInDaj lurIHHa'meH jIj je
wIchlaHIlj motlh, ghIjbogh toDujHeylIj je.

[*ta' qoghDu'Daq tar qang*]

Hamlet   patlhDaj nIHmeH, ngemHomDaq QottaHvIS ghaHDaq
tar Ilch; ghonja'gho 'oH pongDaj'e'. noy lut 'ej
romuluSngan Hol pov lo' qonwI'. ta'be' parmaq
SuqmeH mIw'e' tugh Dalegh.

'ovelya   Qam ta'.

Hamlet   nuq? yay'moH'a' ghum muj?

ghertlhuD   joHwI' Dotlh nuq?

polonyuS   lut rInmoH.

tlhaw'DIyuS wov! tlheD!

Hoch   wov! wov! wov!

[*mej Hoch, ratlhtaHvIS* HAMLET HOREY'SO *je*]

Hamlet   vaj rIQDI' Haw'jaj to'baj jay',
'ej reHjaj pIvbogh Qa'.
reH yepnIS vay'; reH QongnIS vay';
reH ghu'vetlh ngo' wIma'.
chavvammo', Qa'pobngemmo' je vISuqbogh—
jIcho'meH SanHeywIj'e' wa'leS Sorghchugh
SermanyuQngan 'ej mInwIj nIjmoHlaHchugh Haq—
vaj DawI'tlhoQDaq ghuv jIHlaH qar'a'.

Horey'So   ghuv bID SoH.

Hamlet   naQ jIH.
loDnI', yISov: chIch wo'vamvo'
qeylIS lunge'pu' chaH.
povpu' voDleH, 'a DaH ghaH cho'
'ej DaH wo' che'—pujwI'.

Horey'So   bommu'tlhegh DarInmoHlaHchu'pu'.

Hamlet   majQa', Horey'So, Iom qa' 'Ip quv law', Qojta'bogh
wa'SanID 'utlh quv puS. Datu"a'?

Horey'So   vItu'chu', joHwI'.

Hamlet   tar mIw vIDelDI'.

Horey'So   ghaH vItu'chu'qu'.

Hamlet   Hu'tegh! Ha' QoQ! Ha' may'ronmey.
toH, lutmaj parchugh ta',
ghaytan vaj—par, baQa'!
Ha' QoQ.

[*'elqa'* ROSENQATLH GHILDESTEN *je*]

ghIlDeSten   joHwI', wa' mu' qapeghnIS.

Hamlet	Sir, a whole history.
Guildenstern	The king, sir,—
Hamlet	Ay, sir, what of him?
Guildenstern	Is, in his retirement, marvellous distempered.
Hamlet	With drink, sir?
Guildenstern	No, my lord, rather with choler.
Hamlet	Your wisdom should show itself more richer to signify this to his doctor; for, for me to put him to his purgation would perhaps plunge him into far more choler.
Guildenstern	Good my lord, put your discourse into some frame, and start not so wildly from my affair.
Hamlet	I am tame, sir:—pronounce.
Guildenstern	The queen, your mother, in most great affliction of spirit, hath sent me to you.
Hamlet	You are welcome.
Guildenstern	Nay, good my lord, this courtesy is not of the right breed. If it shall please you to make me a wholesome answer, I will do your mother's commandment: if not, your pardon and my return shall be the end of my business.
Hamlet	Sir, I cannot.
Guildenstern	What, my lord?
Hamlet	Make you a wholesome answer; my wit's diseased: but, sir, such answer as I can make, you shall command; or, rather, as you say, my mother: therefore no more, but to the matter: my mother, you say,—
Rosencrantz	Then thus she says: your behavior hath struck her into amazement and admiration.
Hamlet	O wonderful son, that can so astonish a mother!—But is there no sequel at the heels of this mother's admiration?
Rosencrantz	She desires to speak with you in her closet ere you go to bed.
Hamlet	We shall obey, were she ten times our mother. Have you any further trade with us?
Rosencrantz	My lord, you once did love me.
Hamlet	So I do still, by these pickers and stealers.
Rosencrantz	Good my lord, what is your cause of distemper? you do, surely, bar the door upon your own liberty if you deny your griefs to your friend.
Hamlet	Sir, I lack advancement.
Rosencrantz	How can that be, when you have the voice of the king himself for your succession in Denmark?

Hamlet	vaj gharwI' SoQ naQ vItu'qang je.
ghIlDeSten	toH ta'—
Hamlet	ghaHvaD qaS nuq jay'?
ghIlDeSten	pa'DajDaq ghaH ngejqu'lu'law'.
Hamlet	chaq ngej ghew.
ghIlDeSten	ghobe', joH; QeH.
Hamlet	bIval 'e' DatobmeH, QelvaD bIja'nIS. toH, ghew QeHvo' ghaH vIvormeH jInIDchugh jIH, vaj ghaytan ngejtaHbogh ghew puq vISepmoHqu'. lumej bIH 'ej tugh chegh, tlhejtaHvIS porghDaj yIvqangtaHbogh ghew negh'e'.
ghIlDeSten	joHwI' QaQ, meqDaq SoQlIj yIlan, 'ej pay' Qu'wIj yIjunQo'.
Hamlet	jIjotneS. yIjatlh.
ghIlDeSten	ta'be'vaD, SoSlI'vaD nuQlu'mo' 'ej qay'lu'mo', SoHDaq mungeHta' ghaH.
Hamlet	majQa'.
ghIlDeSten	ghobe', DaH chonaD 'e' vIHechbe'. 'ach chojangqangchu'chugh vaj SoSlI' vIloblaH. bIjangchu'Qo'chugh vaj rInmeH mIwvam yIchaw' 'ej jImej.
Hamlet	qaSlaHbe'.
roSenQatlh	nuq'e', joHwI'?
Hamlet	jIjanglaHchu'be'. pIvHa' yabwIj. 'ach jIjanglaHmeH jInIDqu'qangmo' chaq chotu', pagh mutu' SoSwI''e' (pongHeyDaj'e' Dalo'pu'bogh). 'a yap. vaj yIjatlhqa'. bIjatlh, SoSlI'vaD nuQlu'—
roSenQatlh	jatlh ghaH: nuq Da Hamlet? Damo' muyay'moHpu' 'ej muSIvmoHpu'.
Hamlet	puqloD yaymo' SIvnISbe' SoS. 'ach DaH SoSwI'vaD nuq qaSmoH yay'moHlaw'pu'bogh wanI'wIj'e'? yIja'.
roSenQatlh	pa'DajDaq Suja'chuq neH ghaH, bIQongchoHpa'.
Hamlet	'e' vIlobchu', wa'maHlogh SoSwI''e' (pongvetlh Dalo') ghaHchugh. latlh tujatlhnIS'a'.
roSenQatlh	joHwI', ben choparHa'.
Hamlet	DaH qaparHa'taHmeH je jagh HuH lungaS ghopwIj.
roSenQatlh	pIvHa'moHwI'lIj nuq? pIvtaHghachvaD lojmIt DawaQ, juplI'vo' Sengmeylij Dapeghchugh je.
Hamlet	qaH, qaSHa' cho'wIj.
roSenQatlh	'a qItbe' ghu'vam, Qo'noSDaq bIcho'meH ta' woQna' 'oHmo' woQlIj'e'.

Hamlet	Ay, but, 'While the grass grows,'—the proverb is something musty.

[*Re-enter Players with recorders*]

O, the recorders!—let me see one.—To withdraw with you:—why do you go about to recover the wind of me, as if you would drive me into a toil?

Guildenstern	O, my lord, if my duty be too bold, my love is too unmannerly.
Hamlet	I do not well understand that. Will you play upon this pipe?
Guildenstern	My lord, I cannot.
Hamlet	I pray you.
Guildenstern	Believe me, I cannot.
Hamlet	I do beseech you.
Guildenstern	I know no touch of it, my lord.
Hamlet	'Tis as easy as lying: govern these ventages with your finger and thumb, give it breath with your mouth, and it will discourse most eloquent music. Look you, these are the stops.
Guildenstern	But these cannot I command to any utterance of harmony; I have not the skill.
Hamlet	Why, look you now, how unworthy a thing you make of me! You would play upon me; you would seem to know my stops; you would pluck out the heart of my mystery; you would sound me from my lowest note to the top of my compass: and there is much music, excellent voice, in this little organ; yet cannot you make it speak. 'Sblood, do you think I am easier to be played on than a pipe? Call me what instrument you will, though you can fret me you cannot play upon me.

[*Enter POLONIUS*]

God bless you, sir!

Polonius	My lord, the queen would speak with you, and presently.
Hamlet	Do you see yonder cloud that's almost in shape of a camel?
Polonius	By the mass, and 'tis like a camel, indeed.
Hamlet	Methinks it is like a weasel.
Polonius	It is backed like a weasel.
Hamlet	Or like a whale?
Polonius	Very like a whale.
Hamlet	Then I will come to my mother by and by.—They fool me to the top of my bent.—I will come by and by.
Polonius	I will say so.
Hamlet	By and by is easily said.—

Hamlet	HIja', qaH, 'ach "yaptaHvIS loSpev"—mu'tlheghvam noy DaSovbej.

['el Dov'aghmey qengbogh DawI'pu"e']

toH Dov'agh! wa' HInob. 'a qapegh: nIteb jIjuntaHvIS, qatlh choyu'meH bIjonqang?

ghIlDeSten	baQa', qaqeSmeH chaq jIvaQ, vaQmo' je parI Ia'ghachwIj neH.
Hamlet	'e' vIyajchu'be'. Dov'aghvam DaHeng'a'?
ghIlDeSten	joHwI', laH vIghajbe'.
Hamlet	yIHengneS.
ghIlDeSten	laH vIghajbe' jay'.
Hamlet	qara'neS.
ghIlDeSten	vIHengmeH mIw vISovbe'.
Hamlet	HengmeH mIw ngeD law', nepmeH mIw ngeD puS. naQvam DaQoDmeH nItlh tIlo'. ngujlep Dachu'meH nuj yISuSmoH. vaj QoQ 'IH lIng. SuH, QoQSeHlaw bIH Dochvam'e'.
ghIlDeSten	'ach 'IHmeH QoQ vIQoDlaHbe'. vIHengmeH jIpo'qu'be'.
Hamlet	vaj chorammoH. jIH choqelDI' Dov'agh neH Datu"a'? jIH'e' choHengqang; SeHlawwIj DachuSqangmoHlaw'; SengwIj ghogh DabomqangmoH; Se'wIj DalISmeH jIH chochu'qang; ghogh 'IHqu' IIngIaH chuSwI'vam mach, 'ach 'oH DajatlhmoHlaHbe'. Qu'vatlh, jIH choHengmeH mIw ngeD law', Dov'agh DaHengmeH mIw ngeD puS, 'e' DaHar'a'? Dov'agh vIrur 'e' DaHarmoH—jISaHbe'; Se'wIj DalISmeH SeHlaw'e' Daghaj 'ach choSeHlaw' 'e' vIchaw'Qo'.

['el POLONYUS]

pIghov, qaH.

polonyuS	joHwI', SoHvaD jatlh neHtaH ta'be'. SIbI'!
Hamlet	loQ Qogh rurbogh 'engvetlh Dalegh'a'?
polonyuS	Hu'tegh, Qogh rurbej 'oH.
Hamlet	'er'e' rur 'e' vItu'.
polonyuS	'er Dub ghaj.
Hamlet	ghargh ghap rur.
polonyuS	ghargh rurbej.
Hamlet	vaj tugh SoSwI' vIghoS. *[pegh'egh]* muDoghmoHlaw'mo' jIpuQqu'.—tugh vIghoS.
polonyuS	vIja'.
Hamlet	ngeD "tugh" jatlhmeH Qu'.

[*Exit POLONIUS*]

Leave me, friends.

[*Exeunt all but HAMLET*]

Tis now the very witching time of night,
When churchyards yawn, and hell itself breathes out
Contagion to this world: now could I drink hot blood,
And do such bitter business as the day
Would quake to look on. Soft! now to my mother.—
O heart, lose not thy nature; let not ever
The soul of Nero enter this firm bosom:
Let me be cruel, not unnatural:
I will speak daggers to her, but use none;
My tongue and soul in this be hypocrites,—
How in my words soever she be shent,
To give them seals never, my soul, consent!

[*Exit*]

SCENE III   *A room in the castle.*

[*Enter KING CLAUDIUS, ROSENCRANTZ, and GUILDENSTERN*]

Claudius	I like him not; nor stands it safe with us

To let his madness range. Therefore prepare you;
I your commission will forthwith dispatch,
And he to England shall along with you:
The terms of our estate may not endure
Hazard so dangerous as doth hourly grow
Out of his lunacies.

Guildenstern   We will ourselves provide:
Most holy and religious fear it is
To keep those many many bodies safe
That live and feed upon your majesty.

Rosencrantz   The single and peculiar life is bound,
With all the strength and armour of the mind,
To keep itself from 'noyance; but much more
That spirit upon whose weal depend and rest
The lives of many. The cease of majesty
Dies not alone but like a gulf doth draw
What's near it with it: it is a massy wheel,
Fix'd on the summit of the highest mount,
To whose huge spokes ten thousand lesser things
Are mortis'd and adjoin'd; which, when it falls,
Each small annexment, petty consequence,
Attends the boisterous ruin. Never alone
Did the king sigh, but with a general groan.

Claudius   Arm you, I pray you, to this speedy voyage;
For we will fetters put upon this fear,
Which now goes too free-footed.

Rosencrantz   We will haste us.
& Guildenstern

[*Exeunt ROSENCRANTZ and GUILDENSTERN*]

[*Enter POLONIUS*]

[*mej* POLONYUS]

pemej juppu'.

[*mej Hoch, ratlhtaHvIS* HAMLET]

DaH qaS wIchHoSmey rep. DaH Hoblaw' molmey.
DaH qo'Daq ngejmeH tlhIchDaj tlhuchlaw' ghe''or.
DaH 'aD 'Iw tuj vItlhutlhlaH. 'ej jIwemchu'
DaH 'e' vIruchlaHmo', vaj HajnIS pem,
'oH leghchugh neH. SuH, DaH SoSwI' vIjaHnIS.
'eH, tIqwIj, matlhbogh DujIlj yIchIlQo'.
not rowIj letDaq 'eljaj molor qa'.
jInaSjaj, 'ach qorDu'wIj vIbolQo'jaj.
tajmey vIjatlhnIS, 'ach pagh taj vIlo'nIS.
Qu'wIjvaD tojjaj jatwIj, qa'wI' je.
mu'wIjmo' tuHjaj ghaH. 'ach mu'wIj tob
ta'wIj'e'—qa'wI', 'eH, not 'e' yIlob.

[*mej*]

LUT 'AY'HOM WEJ *ta'qach'a' pa'*.

['*el* TLHAW'DIYUS TA', ROSENQATLH, GHILDESTEN *je*]

tlhaw'DIyuS	mubItmoH ghaH. 'ej jIHvaD QIHtaH ghu', maw'taH ghaH 'e' vIweghpu'pa'. vaj SuH: tugh Qu'ghItlhraj vIqonmoH, 'ej tera'Daq lItlhejnIS ghaH. Huy'Du'Dajvo' chen Qob, qaSDI' Hoch rep. 'ej jIH muSumqu' Qobvetlh 'e' SIQlaHbe'ba' ta'Dotlh.
ghIlDeSten	Qu' wIQorghchu'. je'meH 'ej yIntaHmeH, nIwuv ghot law'qu'. Qobvo' DIleHneSmeH, lalDanvaD potlhqu' 'ej quvqu' Qu'.
roSenQatlh	reH lotvo' leH'eghmeH, yab Hoch yoD, HoS je lo' wa' yInwI' neH ram. vaj lo'nISbe' qa' Dunqu'—cheptaH ghaH reH 'e' luwuvmo' yIn law', 'ej Do' ghaHmo' chaHvo' Hop QIH. rInDI' ta' poH, nIteb Heghbe'ba' ta'Dotlh. luSpet Da. Sumchugh vay', vaj Hochvetlh tlha'moH. gho'a' 'ugh rur ghaH. 'ej HuD jenqu' DungDaq 'oH lanlu'law'. ghonaQmey tInqu'Daq muvchuq 'ej HuStaH wa'netlh Dochmey ram. vaj pumDI' gho, pe'vIl QIH chuS lutlhej Hoch chachmey machqu', Hoch tlha'wI'Hom ram je. vaj not nIteb vIng ta'. DaH 'ItDI' potlh, tugh bepnIS je mangghom, 'ej jegh vaj rotlh.
tlhaw'DIyuS	'eH, nom tera' wo'Daq yIleng'eghrupmoH. DaH tlhabqu' Qob qamDu'Hey. DaH Dat yIt. 'a tugh qamDu'Daq mIr wIlan.
roSenQatlh ghIlDeSten je	mamoDIl'.

[*mej* ROSENQATLH GHILDESTEN *je*]

['*el* POLONYUS]

Polonius	My lord, he's going to his mother's closet:

My lord, he's going to his mother's closet:
Behind the arras I'll convey myself
To hear the process; and warrant she'll tax him home:
And, as you said, and wisely was it said,
'Tis meet that some more audience than a mother,
Since nature makes them partial, should o'erhear
The speech, of vantage. Fare you well, my liege:
I'll call upon you ere you go to bed,
And tell you what I know.

Claudius   Thanks, dear my lord.

[*Exit POLONIUS*]

O, my offence is rank, it smells to heaven;
It hath the primal eldest curse upon't,—
A brother's murder!—Pray can I not,
Though inclination be as sharp as will:
My stronger guilt defeats my strong intent;
And, like a man to double business bound,
I stand in pause where I shall first begin,
And both neglect. What if this cursed hand
Were thicker than itself with brother's blood,—
Is there not rain enough in the sweet heavens
To wash it white as snow? Whereto serves mercy
But to confront the visage of offence?
And what's in prayer but this two-fold force,—
To be forestalled ere we come to fall,
Or pardon'd being down? Then I'll look up;
My fault is past. But, O, what form of prayer
Can serve my turn? Forgive me my foul murder!
That cannot be; since I am still possess'd
Of those effects for which I did the murder,—
My crown, mine own ambition, and my queen.
May one be pardon'd and retain the offence?
In the corrupted currents of this world
Offence's gilded hand may shove by justice;
And oft 'tis seen the wicked prize itself
Buys out the law: but 'tis not so above;
There is no shuffling,—there the action lies
In his true nature; and we ourselves compell'd,
Even to the teeth and forehead of our faults,
To give in evidence. What then? what rests?
Try what repentance can: what can it not?
Yet what can it when one can not repent?
O wretched state! O bosom black as death!
O limed soul, that, struggling to be free,
Art more engag'd! Help, angels! Make assay:
Bow, stubborn knees and, heart, with strings of steel,
Be soft as sinews of the newborn babe!
All may be well.

[*Retires and kneels*]

polonyuS joH, SoSDaj pa'Hom ghoS. wanI' vItu'meH
tugh HaSta'a'DajDaq jISo''eghneS.
ghaH qunqu'bej ta'be'. 'ej vuD Daja'pu',
'ej valqu' vuDIlj: ja'chuqtaHvIS chaH,
SoQchaj tu'be'nIS SoSDaj neH, qar'a';
SoS SIghtaHmo' qorDu'. 'ej boQbogh DaqDaq
Hoch DaqnIS vay'. vaj DaH qamej, ta' quv.
qaSuch, QongDaq DaghoSpa'. 'ej qaSuchDI'
SoHvaD Hoch De' vIQum.

tlhaw'DIyuS   qatlho', jawwI'.

[*mej* POLONYUS]

He'So'ba' HeSwIj. va, QI'tu'Daq He' je.
naDHa'ghach wa'DIch ngo'mo' bechmoH 'oH.
loDnI' vIchot! qa''a'pu'vaD jItlhob
vIneHqu'bej vIHechDI', 'ach jIluj.
vIHechmeH HoSwIj jey jIDIvmeH HoS.
'ej cha' malja'vaD vumnISwI' vIrur:
Qu' wa'DIch'e' vIwIvnISbogh vIqelDI',
jIyev, 'ej tugh cha' Qu'vetlh vIbuSHa'nIS.
loDnI'wI' 'Iwmo' jeD quvHa'bogh ghopvam
net tu'chugh je, vaj ram, qar'a'? chal quvDaq
SISbeHba' bIQ; peDwI' chIS rurmeH ghopwIj,
Say'moHmeH yap, qar'a', tugh SISbogh bIQ.
HeS qabHey puSmeH 'oH, qar'a', pung tu'lu'.
'ej cha' Qu' ta'meH, qa''a'vaD tlhob Hoch,
qar'a'? wIbotlu'meH, mapumruppa',
pagh, wInoDHa'lu'meH, mapumpu'DI'.
vaj chal vIbejchoH. pIch vIqIlbej rIntaH.
'ach DotlhwIj ngo' vIleHmeH, chay' jItlhoblaH?
"jIchotmeH jIquvHa' 'e' yInoDQo'."
DuHbe'. mIp law' vIghajchoHmeH jIchotpu'.
'ej mIpmeyvetlh vIpoltaH: ta' mIv'a',
Hoch'e' vItulbogh je, ta'be'nalwI' je.
chay'? toH, wej HeSDaj pop ghajQo'chugh vay',
vaj ghaH noDHa'laH'a' ruvpIn? jIchID:
pIj qo'vam mIwmey qalDaq, ruv lujotlhlaH
DIlbogh HeSwI' DeQghopqoq. 'ach veqlarghvaD
moSlaHlaw' pagh. pa' tojlaH pagh 'oghwI'.
pa' chavmeymaj DotIhna' luleghlaH Hoch.
'ej pIchmeymaj Ho' QuchHey je DIbej
net ra'taHvIS, mapum'eghchu' net raD.
tlha' nuq? ratlh nuq? toH, vay' vIchavlaHchugh
jIpayDI', vaj vInIDchoH. SuH, vInID!
Hoch chavlaHlaw' paywI' jay'! 'ach nuq chavlaH
paylaHbe'wI'? baQa', Dotlh 'It! baQa',
Hegh rurbogh tlqwIj qIjqu''e'! baQa',
qa'wI''e' vonlu'bogh! bItlhabqa'meH
bInoghDI', vaj Dubaghqu'choH chon jan!
HIQaH, boQqa'pu'! SuH, jInIDqu'jaj!
peSIH, qIvDu'wIj mul! baS tlhogh Daghajlaw',
tIqwIj. yItun. ghu to'waQmey yIrur.
tugh QaQjaj Hoch.

['emDaq jaH 'ej tor]

[*Enter HAMLET*]

Hamlet   Now might I do it pat, now he is praying
           And now I'll do't;—And so he goes to heaven;
           And so am I reveng'd:—That would be scann'd:
           A villain kills my father; and for that,
           I, his sole son, do this same villain send
           To heaven.
           O, this is hire and salary, not revenge.
           He took my father grossly, full of bread;
           With all his crimes broad blown, as flush as May;
           And how his audit stands who knows save heaven?
           But in our circumstance and course of thought
           'Tis heavy with him: and am I, then, reveng'd,
           To take him in the purging of his soul,
           When he is fit and season'd for his passage?
           No.
           Up, sword; and know thou a more horrid hent:
           When he is drunk, asleep, or in his rage;
           Or in the incestuous pleasure of his bed;
           At gaming, swearing; or about some act
           That has no relish of salvation in't;—
           Then trip him, that his heels may kick at heaven;
           And that his soul may be as damn'd and black
           As hell, whereto it goes. My mother stays:
           This physic but prolongs thy sickly days.

           [*Exit*]

Claudius   [*Rising*] My words fly up, my thoughts remain below:
           Words without thoughts never to heaven go.

           [*Exit*]

           SCENE IV *The Queen's closet.*

           [*Enter QUEEN MARGARET and POLONIUS*]

Polonius   He will come straight. Look you lay home to him:
           Tell him his pranks have been too broad to bear with,
           And that your grace hath screen'd and stood between
           Much heat and him. I'll sconce me even here.
           Pray you, be round with him.

Hamlet   [*Within*] Mother, mother, mother!

Gertrude   I'll warrant you,
           Fear me not:—withdraw, I hear him coming.

           [*POLONIUS hides behind the arras*]

           [*Enter HAMLET*]

Hamlet   Now, mother, what's the matter?

Gertrude   Hamlet, thou hast thy father much offended.

['el *HAMLET*]

Hamlet	DaH jIHvaD vIHtaH gho. DaH tlhobtaH ghaH.
	vaj DaH vIta': yo' qIjDaq Suvjaj ghaH.
	chay'! mIwvammo' bortaSwIj vIchav'a'?
	vIqelqu'nIS. vavwI"e' HoH taHqeq.
	latlh puq ghajbe' vav. HoHpu'mo' taHqeqvetlh,
	yo' qIjDaq ghaH ngeH puqvam.
	vaj ghaHvaD boQ vIDIllaw'! luj bortaS jay'!
	qen vavwI' chotmeH merDI', pI' vavwI',
	'ej Suvrupbe'. HeS paymeH, yempu'DI',
	'eb SuqlaHbe'. 'ej lomDaq jach pagh vaj.
	vaj ghaH lulajmeH yo' qIj negh, pa' pawDI',
	lengchaw'Daj Dotlh luSovlaw' chaH neH. 'ach,
	ghobmaj wIHarbogh, yo' qIj qechmaj je
	qellu'chugh, vaj DaH ghaHvaD 'ughlaw' ghu'.
	'ach DaH bortaS vISuqmeH, vIHoH'a',
	qa'qoqDaj Say'moHtaHvIS? vIHoH'a',
	yo' qIjDaq tlheDmeH ghuHDI' ghaH 'ej 'umDI'?
	Qo'.
	Ha', 'etlh, qaroQ. Qu' naSvaD tugh qalel.
	chechDI', pagh, QongDI', vupDI', pagh, QongDaqDaq
	qorDu' ngaghwI' HeSbelmey tIvtaHvIS;
	SuDtaHvIS, ghartaHvIS; vay' ruchtaHvIS,
	ghe"orvo' qa'Daj pollaHbe'chugh chavvam.
	'ej qaSDI' chavvam 'eb, SIbI' yIjop.
	DaqIpDI', chalDaq pupqu'jaj qamDu'Daj.
	vaj webmo' 'ej He'So'mo' qa'Daj non,
	ghe"or'e' rurbej, ghe"or ghoStaHvIS.
	muloStaH SoS. qa'll'vaD, wej bIllmmeH
	ghobHergh Danoblaw'. 'ach bIHegh 'e' mIm neH.

[*mej*]

tlhaw'DIyuS	[*Hu'*] puv mu'meywIj, 'ach bIngDaq ratlhtaH yab.
	mu'mey DorQo'DI' yab, QI'tu'vo' ngab.

[*mej*]

LUT 'AY'HOM LOS. *ta'be' pa'Hom.*

['el *ta'be' POLONYUS je*]

polonyuS	tugh naDev chol. SuH, ghaH yIqunqu'neS.
	yIja'neS: "tlhIvqu'pu'mo' QujIIj taQ,
	luSIQlu'Qo'. 'ej SoH, QeHtuj je botlhDaq
	jIQampu' 'ej qayoDpu', yoD DaraDmo'."
	naDev jIjtam'eghmoH. qatlhob, joHwI':
	ghaHvaD yIvaQ, bIjatlhDI'.
Hamlet	['*emvo'*] SoS! SoS! SoS!
ghertlhuD	DIch yIghaj.
	'ej HIHonQo'—yISo"egh. cholII' ghaH.

[*HaStaDaq So"egh POLONYUS*]

['el *HAMLET*]

Hamlet	toH, SoS, qay' nuq?
ghertlhuD	Hamlet, vavlI' Damawqu'bejpu' SoH.

Hamlet	Mother, you have my father much offended.
Gertrude	Come, come, you answer with an idle tongue.
Hamlet	Go, go, you question with a wicked tongue.
Gertrude	Why, how now, Hamlet!
Hamlet	What's the matter now?
Gertrude	Have you forgot me?
Hamlet	No, by the rood, not so:

You are the queen, your husband's brother's wife;
And,—would it were not so!—you are my mother.

Gertrude	Nay, then, I'll set those to you that can speak.

Hamlet	Come, come, and sit you down; you shall not budge;

You go not till I set you up a glass
Where you may see the inmost part of you.

Gertrude	What wilt thou do? thou wilt not murder me?—

Help, help, ho!

Polonius	[*Behind*] What, ho! help, help, help!
Hamlet	[*Drawing*] How now! a rat? Dead, for a ducat, dead!

[*Makes a pass through the arras*]

Polonius	[*Behind*] O, I am slain!—

[*Falls and dies*]

Gertrude	O me, what hast thou done?
Hamlet	Nay, I know not:

Is it the king?

[*Lifts up the array and discovers POLONIUS*]

Gertrude	O, what a rash and bloody deed is this!
Hamlet	A bloody deed!—almost as bad, good mother,

As kill a king, and marry with his brother.

Gertrude	As kill a king!
Hamlet	Ay, lady, 'twas my word.—

[*to POLONIUS*]

Thou wretched, rash, intruding fool, farewell!
I took thee for thy better: take thy fortune;
Thou find'st to be too busy is some danger.—
Leave wringing of your hands: peace; sit you down,
And let me wring your heart: for so I shall,
If it be made of penetrable stuff;
If damned custom have not braz'd it so
That it is proof and bulwark against sense.

Gertrude	What have I done, that thou dar'st wag thy tongue

In noise so rude against me?

Hamlet	SoS, vavna'wI' Damawqu'pu'neS SoH.
ghertlhuD	Ha', Ha'. bIjangDI' Doghlaw' jatlIj jay'.
Hamlet	va, va. bIghelDI' mIghlaw' jatlIj jay'.
ghertlhuD	toH, Hamlet! chay'!
Hamlet	nuqneH?
ghertlhuD	cholljlaw"a'?
Hamlet	Qu'vatlh! ghobe'. qalljta'be', joHwI'. ta'be' SoH. loDnalII' loDnI'vaD be'nal. SoSwI'Hey SoH je. va, Do'Ha'.
ghertlhuD	baQa', nIvuvmoH lobmoHwI' tugh 'e' vIpoQ.
Hamlet	yIba'. Ha'. naDevvo' bIvIHchoHbe'. 'ej bItlheDbe', HotlhwI' vIchenmoHpa'. HotlhwI'vetlhDaq tIqlIj Somraw DaleghlaH.
ghertlhuD	QI'yaH! DaH nuq Data'qang? chochot'a'? QaH! QaH! 'eH!
polonyuS	['emvo'] QI'yaH! QaH!
Hamlet	['etlhDaj leI] chay'? jach'a' 'er? DaH Hegh ghaH! 'e' vISuDmeH DeQ vInobrup!
	[HaSta bIngDaq DuQ Hamlet]
polonyuS	['emvo'] Hu'tegh! muHoHpu'!
	[pum 'ej Hegh]
ghertlhuD	QI'yaH! nuq Data'?
Hamlet	Sovbe'. va, ta' ghaH'a'?
	[HaSta teq, 'ej POLONYUS tu']
ghertlhuD	chav boH, chav ralqu' je Data'!
Hamlet	chav ral. 'ej mIghmo' chavwIj, latlh HeS rurlaw' 'oH. ta' HoHlu', 'ej loDnI'Daj naylu' je.
ghertlhuD	ta' HoHlu'!
Hamlet	mu'tlheghvetlh vIjatlhbejneS.
	[POLONYUSvaD]
	qoH puj, qoH boHqu', munbogh qoH, Qapla'! mochlI' SoH 'e' vIHar qaleghchu'pa'. SanlIj yIlaj. De' pegh DaSovqangDI', vaj chaq Do'Ha' DaH 'e' Datu'. yImev. ghopDu' DaqIptaHvIS tIQopmoHQo'. yIba'. DaH tIqlIj'e' vIQopmoHnIS. vIQopmoHbej, Somraw Hap ghajchugh 'oH, 'ej pay 'oH wej 'e' nISqu'chugh 'ej botchugh motlhtaHghach webqu', tIqlIj letmoHpu'mo'.
ghertlhuD	nuq jay' vIHeSpu'mo', mupummeH rIntaH chuS jatlIj tlhIvqu' 'e' DangII?

Hamlet   Such an act
That blurs the grace and blush of modesty;
Calls virtue hypocrite; takes off the rose
From the fair forehead of an innocent love,
And sets a blister there; makes marriage-vows
As false as dicers' oaths: O, such a deed
As from the body of contraction plucks
The very soul, and sweet religion makes
A rhapsody of words: heaven's face doth glow;
Yea, this solidity and compound mass,
With tristful visage, as against the doom,
Is thought-sick at the act.

Gertrude   Ay me, what act,
That roars so loud, and thunders in the index?

Hamlet   Look here, upon this picture, and on this,—
The counterfeit presentment of two brothers.
See, what a grace was seated on this brow;
Hyperion's curls; the front of Jove himself;
An eye like Mars, to threaten and command;
A station like the herald Mercury
New-lighted on a heaven-kissing hill;
A combination and a form, indeed,
Where every god did seem to set his seal,
To give the world assurance of a man:
This was your husband.—Look you now, what follows:
Here is your husband, like a mildew'd ear,
Blasting his wholesome brother. Have you eyes?
Could you on this fair mountain leave to feed,
And batten on this moor? Ha! have you eyes?
You cannot call it love; for at your age
The hey-day in the blood is tame, it's humble,
And waits upon the judgment: and what judgment
Would step from this to this? Sense, sure, you have,
Else could you not have motion: but sure that sense
Is apoplex'd; for madness would not err;
Nor sense to ecstasy was ne'er so thrall'd
But it reserv'd some quantity of choice,
To serve in such a difference. What devil was't
That thus hath cozen'd you at hoodman-blind?
Eyes without feeling, feeling without sight,
Ears without hands or eyes, smelling sans all,
Or but a sickly part of one true sense
Could not so mope.
O shame! where is thy blush? Rebellious hell,
If thou canst mutine in a matron's bones,
To flaming youth let virtue be as wax,
And melt in her own fire: proclaim no shame
When the compulsive ardour gives the charge,
Since frost itself as actively doth burn,
And reason panders will.

Gertrude   O Hamlet, speak no more:
Thou turn'st mine eyes into my very soul;
And there I see such black and grained spots

Hamlet   ta' mIghqu'.
quvmoH 'ej tuHlaH batlhmaj 'e' ghItlhHa' 'oH.
ngeb Hoch matlhwI' 'e' maq. va, bang Quch chunvo'
Hommey ghegh teqDI', tam naDHa'ghach Degh.
tlhogh 'Ipmey nepmoHmo', SuDwI' 'Ip rurchoH.
baQa'! paywI' tay porghqoqvo' qa"e'
yaHmoHbej ta'vetlh. 'ej verengan ghItlh neH
moj je lalDanmaj quv. chal wewmoH, tuHmo',
va, ta'vetlh qelDI', Haj je yuQmaj Sub.
'IQmo' tlhoQ'a'vetlh mIn, San bIjHey pIHlaw'.

ghertlhuD   va, lIH'eghtaHvIS chuS 'ej buQII' nuq?

Hamlet   naDev, 'eH, Deghvam, Deghvetlh je yIlegh.
DeghmeyDaq cha' loDnI'pu' HotlhmeH 'oghlu'.
Huy'vamDaq ba' batlhna', 'eH, 'e' yIlegh.
qeylIS Quch. ghorqon jIb. ra'meH 'ej buQmeH
veSmey joH'a' mIn. Qumbogh qa"a' 'uS,
chal yuvbogh HuDDaq pawmeH moDta'DI'.
chenchu'mo' ghaH, 'ej joDaj DuDlu'chu'mo',
loDna' ghaH, qo'vaD 'e' lu'olmeH woQ
lunoblaw' qa'pu'. loDnalII"e' ghaHpu'.
tlha'wI' yIchov. DaH loDnalII"e' ghaHtaH
chovnatlhvetlh'e'. loDnI'Daj pIvqu' ngejmeH,
pomrop tIr'etlh Da ghaH. mIn DaHutlh'a'?
HuDHeyvam 'IH DalonDI', Debvetlh moHDaq
bIrorchoH'a' 'ej pa' bISopqang'a'?
yIja'! mIn DaHutlh'a'? bImuSHa"a'?
net HarQo'. qanDI' ghot, 'ej benIlj SIchDI',
jot 'ej HemHa'nIS reHpu'bogh 'Iw tuj,
'ej noHDI' yab, yab lob. 'ach ghotvamvo'
ghotvetlhDaq gho'ta'meH qatlh noHqang yab?
bIQublaHba'. bIQublaHbe'taHchugh,
bIvIHlaHbe' je. 'ach bIQubmeH laH
roSHa'moHlu'law'. Qaghchugh je maw'wI',
'ej vay' yab che'chugh je valHa'ghach jay',
vaj pIm ghotpu'vam tugh net ghovlaHba',
wej lojchu'mo' wIvmeH Hoch jo. Dutojlaw'
veqlarghHey jay', "leghbe'wI' wIv" DaQujDI'.
QIpqu'meH mISlaHbe' HotQo'bogh mIn,
bejQo'bogh nItlh joq, cha' teSDu"e' joq
boQQo'bogh mIn nItlhDu' je, wa' ghIch'e' joq
boQQo'bogh Hoch, nochDu'lIj 'ay'Hom rop joq.
qatlh bIDoqQo', tuHwI'?
lotIhtaHbogh ghe"or, chuQunbe' HomDu'
DaqIQmoHchugh, vaj meQII'bogh QupwI'vaD
weQ rurjaj batlh. 'ej qulDajDaq neH tetjaj.
vaj petuHQo', IlraDDI' 'IwlIj tujqu';
ngaghqangmeH meQtaHmo' je SISbogh chuchHey;
ngaghwI'Du' toy'taH neH meqlaH—

ghertlhuD   'eH, Hamlet,
yIjatlhlI'be'. qa'wI' lutu'taH mInwIj
DaraDmo'. tlherbogh ghItlhmey qIj vIlegh.

As will not leave their tinct.

Hamlet   Nay, but to live
In the rank sweat of an enseamed bed,
Stew'd in corruption, honeying and making love
Over the nasty sty,—

Gertrude   O, speak to me no more;
These words, like daggers, enter in mine ears;
No more, sweet Hamlet.

Hamlet   A murderer and a villain;
A slave that is not twentieth part the tithe
Of your precedent lord; a vice of kings;
A cutpurse of the empire and the rule,
That from a shelf the precious diadem stole,
And put it in his pocket!

Gertrude   No more!

Hamlet   A king of shreds and patches,—

[*Enter Ghost*]

Save me, and hover o'er me with your wings,
You heavenly guards!—What would your gracious figure?

Gertrude   Alas, he's mad!

Hamlet   Do you not come your tardy son to chide,
That, laps'd in time and passion, lets go by
The important acting of your dread command? O, say!

Ghost   Do not forget: this visitation
Is but to whet thy almost blunted purpose.
But, look, amazement on thy mother sits:
O, step between her and her fighting soul,—
Conceit in weakest bodies strongest works,—
Speak to her, Hamlet.

Hamlet   How is it with you, lady?

Gertrude   Alas, how is't with you,
That you do bend your eye on vacancy,
And with the incorporal air do hold discourse?
Forth at your eyes your spirits wildly peep;
And, as the sleeping soldiers in the alarm,
Your bedded hair, like life in excrements,
Starts up, and stands on end. O gentle son,
Upon the heat and flame of thy distemper
Sprinkle cool patience. Whereon do you look?

Hamlet   On him, on him! Look you, how pale he glares!
His form and cause conjoin'd, preaching to stones,
Would make them capable.—Do not look upon me;
Lest with this piteous action you convert
My stern effects: then what I have to do
Will want true colour; tears perchance for blood.

'ej bIH nguvHa'moHbe'lu'.

Hamlet   Qo'. QongDaq
ghIHqu' DIrHuH He'So'Daq yInlu' neH.
naDHa'ghach'a'Daq HaH'egh. targh puchpa'Daq
yachchuq 'ej chopchuq—

ghertlhuD   jIHvaD yIjatlhQo'.
teSDu'wIj 'eIDI' mu'vam, tajmey Da.
yImev neH, Hamlet 'IH.

Hamlet   chotwI', mIghwI' je.
toy'wI''a' neH ghaH. wa'ben loDnalII' Dun
bID bID vatlhvI' ghaHbe' je. qoH voDleH ghaH.
chIch wo'vaD qumvaD je nIHwI''a' Da:
raS'a'vo' ta' mIv'a' wagh nIHpu'DI',
yopwaHDajDaq 'oH So'!

ghertlhuD   yImev!

Hamlet   tera'
voDleHqoq Da neH—

[*'el lomqa'*]

HIboQII', 'ej jIH DungDaq tel tIpuvmoH,
chal'a' 'avwI'pu'! nuq DaneHneS, joH?

ghertlhuD   QI'yaH, DaH maw'.

Hamlet   moDHa'bogh puq DaqunmeH DaH bIchol,
qar'a'? 'eb, nongtaHghachwIj je vImImmo',
HajmoHbogh Qu'wIj pav Dara'pu'bogh
vIlon neH. Ha', yIja'!

lomqa'   Qu' yIIIjQo'. DaH tlhoS jejHa'beH ngoQIIj.
vIjejqa'moHmeH neH qaSuch. yIqIm!
SoSII'Daq Danqu' yaytaHghach. yIHu'.
Suv'eghbogh qa'Daj 'It yImun. porgh pujDaq
HoSqu' qech Qobqu'. ghaHvaD, 'eH, yIjatlh.

Hamlet   nuqneH, joHwI'?

ghertlhuD   baQa', nuqneH, Do'Ha'wI'?
logh chImDaq neH mInDu' DaQeqlaw'taH,
'ej pagh porgh ghajbogh muDvaD neH bIjatlh!
mInDu'IIjDaq jotHa'qu' bejbogh qa'II'.
'ej Qongbogh negh, pay' ghumDI', Dalaw' jIblIj.
QottaHvIS, yInchoHlaw' porgh'ay'vetlh buD:
yay'law' 'ej QamchoH 'oH. yIjot, puqwI' quv.
tujII' 'ej meQII' QeHIIj. DaH meQHa'meH
QeHIIjDaq tuvbogh bIQHey yIghomHa'moH.
nuq'e' Dabej?

Hamlet   ghaH'e'! ghaH'e'! yIqIm neH. chIS 'ej qej.
muvchuqmo' porghDaj, Qu'Daj Hechbogh je,
vaj naghmey ra'DI' je, lujangqangbej.—
'eH, HIbejQo'. Qu' Sagh vIHechtaHbogh
DaqIIIaH, vupmoHmo' bIDameH mIw.
jIvupDI', loj jIvangnISmeH qab qu'.
'ej 'Iw vIIIchnISDI', mInbIQ vIIIchlaH.

Gertrude	To whom do you speak this?
Hamlet	Do you see nothing there?
Gertrude	Nothing at all; yet all that is I see.
Hamlet	Nor did you nothing hear?
Gertrude	No, nothing but ourselves.
Hamlet	Why, look you there! look, how it steals away! My father, in his habit as he lived! Look, where he goes, even now, out at the portal!

[*Exit Ghost*]

Gertrude	This the very coinage of your brain: This bodiless creation ecstasy Is very cunning in.
Hamlet	Ecstasy! My pulse, as yours, doth temperately keep time, And makes as healthful music: it is not madness That I have utter'd; bring me to the test, And I the matter will re-word; which madness Would gambol from. Mother, for love of grace, Lay not that mattering unction to your soul, That not your trespass, but my madness speaks: It will but skin and film the ulcerous place, Whilst rank corruption, mining all within, Infects unseen. Confess yourself to heaven; Repent what's past; avoid what is to come; And do not spread the compost on the weeds, To make them ranker. Forgive me this my virtue; For in the fatness of these pursy times Virtue itself of vice must pardon beg, Yea, curb and woo for leave to do him good.
Gertrude	O Hamlet, thou hast cleft my heart in twain.
Hamlet	O, throw away the worser part of it, And live the purer with the other half. Good night: but go not to mine uncle's bed; Assume a virtue, if you have it not. That monster custom, who all sense doth eat, Of habits devil, is angel yet in this,— That to the use of actions fair and good He likewise gives a frock or livery That aptly is put on. Refrain to-night; And that shall lend a kind of easiness To the next abstinence: the next more easy; For use almost can change the stamp of nature, And either curb the devil, or throw him out With wondrous potency. Once more, good night: And when you are desirous to be bless'd, I'll blessing beg of you.—For this same lord,

[*Pointing to POLONIUS*]
I do repent: but Heaven hath pleased it so,
To punish me with this, and this with me,

ghertlhuD	'IvvaD mu'vam Dajatlh?
Hamlet	pagh Dalegh'a'?
ghertlhuD	paghna'. 'ej Hoch Doch tu'lu'bogh vIlegh.
Hamlet	pagh DaQoy'a' je?
ghertlhuD	maH vIQoylaH neH.
Hamlet	Ha', pa' yIqIm! Ha' So''eghtaHvIS mej! ben yInDaj Sutmey tuQhogh tuQ vavwI'! yIqIm! DaH mej ghaH! DaH lojmItDaq mej!

[*mej lomqa'*]

ghertlhuD	wanI'vam 'oghbejpu' yabqechIIj neH. HoSDo'Hey chenmoHmeH reH po' ghot maw'.
Hamlet	maw''a'? tIqlIj rur tIqwIj, Se'Daj moDmoHbe'mo', 'ej pIvmo' QoQDaj. maw'pu'be'neS mu'wIj. HIngong! 'ej ghu' vIja'meH mu' vIjatlhqa', mu'vetlh pabbe'nIStaHvIS je maw'wI'qoq. SoS, quv yIquvmoH. SoHvaD jatlh ghot maw'DI', 'ej jatlhbe' wemIIj, qa'II'Daq 'e' maqmeH DunaDbogh Herghvetlh yIngoHQo'. Daq ragh So' neH 'ej yoD 'oH, porghIIj ngejtaHvIS rolIjDaq tlhIIII'bogh quvHa'ghach yuD. 'ej wej 'oH leghlu'. chalvaD HeS tIDIS. qaSpu'bogh ta' tIpay. qaSbeHbogh ta' tIjunchoH je. 'ej webqu'meH nov tI bIHDaq chorDI yIlanqa'Qo'. toH, SoS, jIquvqanglaw' 'e' yIbIjQo'. baQa'! bIjQo'meH, HeSvaD tlhobnISlaw' je batlh, reH pI'taHvIS tlhuHHa'bogh bovvam! vannIS! 'ej HeS vor batlh, net chaw'meH naDnIS je!
ghertlhuD	va, Hamlet, jIHvaD bIDDaq tIq Dachevta'.
Hamlet	Ha', bIDDaj qab yIwoD. latlh bID Dapolmo', bIquvtaHmeH yIyIn. Qapla'. 'ach SoS, vavloDnI'wI' QongDaqDaq yIjaHQo'. wej ghobvam'e' Daghajchugh, vaj yISuq. mIwmeymaj motlhmoHmeH veqlarghHey Da tlgh buD, 'ej qay' 'e' tlhojbogh laHmaj Sopchu' moH chu'. 'ach Qu'vamvaD QI'tu'ngan Da 'oH: QaQbogh 'ej quvbogh chav DIta'II'meH HIp mop joq nob je. tuQmeH ngeDqu' bIH. DaHjaj ram yIngaghQo'. bIngaghqa'Qo'meH latlh 'eblIj ngeDmoH ghu'. tugh ngeD Hoch 'eb. Duj'e' ben ghitlhbogh Sanmaj choHmoHlaH ghu' motlh. vaj veqlargh'e' Do' SevlaH 'oH, pagh, ghImmeH rIntaH, merqu' HoSDaj. toH, Qapla'. DunaDchoH bortaSqa' DaneHDI', chonaDqa' 'e' vItlhob. jaw HoHvam'e'—

[*POLONYUS 'ang*]

vIpay. 'ach SanvaD belmoHlaw' wanI'vam.
SanvaD vIbIjlaw' 'ej mubIjlaw' lomvam.

That I must be their scourge and minister.
I will bestow him, and will answer well
The death I gave him. So, again, good night.—
I must be cruel, only to be kind:
Thus bad begins and worse remains behind.—
One word more, good lady.

Gertrude   What shall I do?

Hamlet   Not this, by no means, that I bid you do:
Let the bloat king tempt you again to bed;
Pinch wanton on your cheek; call you his mouse;
And let him, for a pair of reechy kisses,
Or paddling in your neck with his damn'd fingers,
Make you to ravel all this matter out,
That I essentially am not in madness,
But mad in craft. 'Twere good you let him know;
For who that's but a queen, fair, sober, wise,
Would from a paddock, from a bat, a gib,
Such dear concernings hide? who would do so?
No, in despite of sense and secrecy,
Unpeg the basket on the house's top,
Let the birds fly, and, like the famous ape,
To try conclusions, in the basket creep,
And break your own neck down.

Gertrude   Be thou assur'd, if words be made of breath
And breath of life, I have no life to breathe
What thou hast said to me.

Hamlet   I must to England; you know that?

Gertrude   Alack,
I had forgot: 'tis so concluded on.

Hamlet   There's letters seal'd: and my two schoolfellows,—
Whom I will trust as I will adders fang'd,—
They bear the mandate; they must sweep my way
And marshal me to knavery. Let it work;
For 'tis the sport to have the engineer
Hoist with his own petard: and 't shall go hard
But I will delve one yard below their mines,
And blow them at the moon: O, 'tis most sweet,
When in one line two crafts directly meet.—
This man shall set me packing:
I'll lug the guts into the neighbour room.—
Mother, good night.—Indeed this counsellor
Is now most still, most secret, and most grave,
Who was in life a foolish prating knave.
Come, sir, to draw toward an end with you.—
Good night, mother.

[*Exeunt severally; HAMLET dragging in POLONIUS*]

ACT IV
SCENE I *A room in the castle.*

[*Enter KING CLAUDIUS, QUEEN GERTRUDE,
ROSENCRANTZ, and GUILDENSTERN*]

vaj SanvaD 'oy'naQ 'oy'yaS je vIDa.
lomvam vIlan. 'ej ghaHvaD Hegh vInobmo',
jIbechnIS. pItlh. qaboQmeH neH qabuQ.
DaH qaSnIS Qugh, 'ach Do' latlh lotvaD SuQ.
'ach wa' latlh mu' vIja'neS.

ghertlhuD	chay' jIvangnIS?
Hamlet	not Qu' vIDelchoHbogh tIruchhej. 'cH.

QongDaqDajDaq DutIhu'qa'moH ta' ror.
bIngaghqangmeH qevpobIlj qIp. "ghghgh" jatlh.
'ej wuSIlj chopmeH ghIHDI', mongIljDaq
yachmeH ghaH, nItlhDaj webqu' lo'taHvIS,
ghaHvaD ghu' naQ DayajmoHlaH 'e' pon:
maw'be'taH mIwwIj, 'ach jImaw'law'meH
jI'ong. maj! ghaHvaD 'e' yISovchoHmoH.
chIch yIntaghvo', targhvo', ngIbna'vo' potlhvetlh
qelnISbogh peghba'Qo' ta'be'nal 'IH,
ta'be'nal quv, ta'be'nal valqu' je.
not peghba'. yab peghDuj je yIllobQo'.
qach DungDaq mo' yIpoSmoH. Haw'meH puvjaj
chalHa'DIbaHmey. 'ej qoH noy yIDa.
bIngongmeH, mo' yI'el. 'ej ghorjaj mongIlj,
bIpuvchoH 'e' DanIDDI'.

<table>
<tr><td>ghertlhuD</td><td>tlhuHmeymo' chenmo' mu'maj, 'ej yInmo'</td></tr>
</table>

ghertlhuD	tlhuHmeymo' chenmo' mu'maj, 'ej yInmo'

chenmo' je tlhuHmeymaj, vaj DIch yIghaj:
mu'Ilj choja'pu'bogh vIja'qa'meH
yInlaH pagh tlhuHwIj.

Hamlet	tera' vIghoSnIS. DaSov'a'?
ghertlhuD	va, QI'yaH,

vIlIjpu'. wuqlu'.

Hamlet	SoQtaH pum peghghItlh.

'ej ghItlh luqeng cha' DuSaQjupqoqwI'.
vIvoqchugh, vaj verengan'e' vIvoqrup.
HewIj luHuvmoHII' 'ej tojbogh nabvaD
muDevII' chaH. toH ruchjaj. tlhaQbej ghu',
ngatpIn luSangchu'DI' jorwI'mey lanbogh.
'ej chIch jorwI'meyHeychaj bIngDaq 'och
vIchenmoHbe'chugh, 'ej, latlh ngat vIyongDI',
maSDaq chaH vIjorbe'chugh, vaj jItlhIb.
Do' vaj, wa' Qu'vaD muvchuqDI' 'och nIb.
mulengnISmoHlaw' ghotvam.
retlh pa'HomDaq chorDu' vIteq. Qapla', SoS.
DaH tam 'ej Sagh 'ej peghqanglaw' qeSIa'.
'ach yIntaHvIS, jawbogh Qovpatlh Dogh Da.
Ha', jaw. Qu' ta'DI' Hegh 'e' tul Hoch tlhIngan.
Qapla', SoS.

[*nIteb mej chaH, pa'Daq* POLONYUS *lom teqtaHvIS* HAMLET]

LUT 'AY' LOS
LUT 'AY'HOM WA'. *ta'qach'a' pa'.*

['*el* TLHAW'DIYUS TA', GHERTLHUD TA'BE',
ROSENQATLH, GHILDESTEN *je*]

Claudius   There's matter in these sighs, these profound heaves:
You must translate: 'tis fit we understand them.
Where is your son?

Gertrude   Bestow this place on us a little while.

[Exeunt ROSENCRANTZ and GUILDENSTERN]

Ah, my good lord, what have I seen to-night!

Claudius   What, Gertrude? How does Hamlet?

Gertrude   Mad as the sea and wind, when both contend
Which is the mightier: in his lawless fit,
Behind the arras hearing something stir,
Whips out his rapier, cries, 'A rat, a rat!'
And, in this brainish apprehension, kills
The unseen good old man.

Claudius   O heavy deed!
It had been so with us, had we been there:
His liberty is full of threats to all;
To you yourself, to us, to every one.
Alas, how shall this bloody deed be answer'd?
It will be laid to us, whose providence
Should have kept short, restrain'd, and out of haunt
This mad young man: but so much was our love,
We would not understand what was most fit;
But, like the owner of a foul disease,
To keep it from divulging, let it feed
Even on the pith of Life. Where is he gone?

Gertrude   To draw apart the body he hath kill'd:
O'er whom his very madness, like some ore
Among a mineral of metals base,
Shows itself pure; he weeps for what is done.

Claudius   O Gertrude, come away!
The sun no sooner shall the mountains touch
But we will ship him hence: and this vile deed
We must, with all our majesty and skill,
Both countenance and excuse.—Ho, Guildenstern!

[Re-enter ROSENCRANTZ and GUILDENSTERN]

Friends both, go join you with some further aid:
Hamlet in madness hath Polonius slain,
And from his mother's closet hath he dragg'd him:
Go seek him out; speak fair, and bring the body
Into the chapel. I pray you, haste in this.

[Exeunt ROSENCRANTZ and GUILDENSTERN]

Come, Gertrude, we'll call up our wisest friends;
And let them know, both what we mean to do
And what's untimely done: so haply slander,—
Whose whisper o'er the world's diameter,
As level as the cannon to his blank,
Transports his poison'd shot,—may miss our name,

tlhaw'DIyuS   vay' Qumbej tlhutlhmeyllj Datlhovquʼboghʼ.
                     tImughʼ. vIyajnISʼ. nuqDaq ghaH puqlI"eʼ?

ghertlhuD   loQ maHvaD Daq yIjegh.

[*mej ROSENQATLH GHILDESTEN je*]

                                    ghuy'cha', joHwI',
                     DaHjaj maQmIgh vIleghpuʼ!

tlhaw'DIyuS   toH, nuq, ghertlhuD?
                     nuq Hamlet Dotlh?

ghertlhuD   va, SuS. bIQ'a' je Da,
                     chaHvoʼ HoSwI'na' ngu'meH ghoHchoHDIʼ.
                     maw'quʼ ghaH. chut lobHa'taHvIS yab Sab,
                     HaStawlj bIngDaq vIHchoH vay' 'eʼ QoyDIʼ,
                     pay' 'etlhDaq lel. pay' jachchoH "ghew! vIH ghew!"
                     'ej qechvam mulqu' najtaHvIS, qup QaQ'e'
                     wej leghbogh HoH.

tlhaw'DIyuS   HeS'aʼ! 'ej jIHvaD qaS je,
                     jISaHchugh neHʼ. DaH Hoch nubuQtaH tlhabDaj.
                     SoH, jIH je, Hoch je buQlI' ghaH. baQaʼ!
                     chay' 'Iwvam chav vIQlj? tugh jIH vIpumluʼ.
                     Qupwl'vetlh maw' vISeHmeH 'ej vIvuSmeH,
                     Hochvoʼ vIweghlI'meH leSSov vIghajnISʼ.
                     'ach vIparHa'qu'mo', vIvorchu'meH
                     mIw vIyajQoʼ. rop web SIQwI' vIDapuʼ.
                     Sovbe'meH latlh, chIch ropvaD yInwIj 'Iw
                     vIje' je, reH vIpeghmoʼ. DaqDaj nguʼ!

ghertlhuD   lom HoHbogh rIntaH lelll'. tlhIlHey ramDaq
                     la'tInum rur ghaH, 'ang'eghchu'mo' batlhDaj,
                     maw'taHvIS je ghaH. paymo' SaQtaH ghaH.

tlhaw'DIyuS   va, ghertlhuD, Haʼ. mamej.
                     HuD HotchoHDIʼ pemHov, nom naDevvoʼ
                     vIngeHnISʼ. 'ej HeSchavvam mIgh vIngoy'mo',
                     vIQljDIʼ, Huy' rur woQwIj; po'qu'nISʼ.
                     'eH, ghIlDeSten!

['*elqaʼ ROSENQATLH GHILDESTEN je*]

                              juppuʼ, boQwI' tImuvmoHʼ.
                     polonyuS HoHpu' Hamlet maw'taHvISʼ.
                     'ej SoSDaj pa'voʼ lomDaj jotlhpu' ghaHʼ.
                     Haʼ, ghaH yInejʼ. peghar. 'ej chIrghHomDaq
                     lomvetlh yIqengʼ. SatIhob: SIbI' pemoDʼ.

[*mej ROSENQATLH GHILDESTEN je*]

                     ghertlhuD, HItlha'. juppu'ma' val wISuchʼ.
                     qaSbeHbogh ngoQwIj, qaSpu'bogh Qugh ghoQ je
                     Sov chaH, tugh 'e' vIchaw'laHʼ. roD tar voʼ
                     pum'aʼ, pum tlhuplu'DIʼ je, yuQ bIngvoʼ
                     'oH QeqDIʼ je. 'ej qarmoʼ baHtaHvIS,
                     tlhevjaQ rur: ghuSDIʼ, vaQ. DaH pongwIj'e'

And hit the woundless air.—O, come away!
My soul is full of discord and dismay.

[*Exeunt*]

SCENE II *Another room in the castle.*

[*Enter HAMLET*]

Hamlet	Safely stowed.
Rosencrantz & Guildenstern	[*Within*] Hamlet! Lord Hamlet!
Hamlet	What noise? who calls on Hamlet? O, here they come.

[*Enter ROSENCRANTZ and GUILDENSTERN*]

Rosencrantz	What have you done, my lord, with the dead body?
Hamlet	Compounded it with dust, whereto 'tis kin.
Rosencrantz	Tell us where 'tis, that we may take it thence, And bear it to the chapel.
Hamlet	Do not believe it.
Rosencrantz	Believe what?
Hamlet	That I can keep your counsel, and not mine own. Besides, to be demanded of a sponge!—what replication should be made by the son of a king?
Rosencrantz	Take you me for a sponge, my lord?
Hamlet	Ay, sir; that soaks up the king's countenance, his rewards, his authorities. But such officers do the king best service in the end: he keeps them, like an ape, in the corner of his jaw first mouthed, to be last swallowed: when he needs what you have gleaned, it is but squeezing you, and, sponge, you shall be dry again.
Rosencrantz	I understand you not, my lord.
Hamlet	I am glad of it: a knavish speech sleeps in a foolish ear.
Rosencrantz	My lord, you must tell us where the body is, and go with us to the king.
Hamlet	The body is with the king, but the king is not with the body. The king is a thing,—
Guildenstern	A thing, my lord!
Hamlet	Of nothing: bring me to him. Hide fox, and all after.

[*Exeunt*]

SCENE III *Another room in the castle.*

[*Enter KING CLAUDIUS, attended*]

Claudius	I have sent to seek him, and to find the body.

Do' chuHlaHbe'jaj pum, 'ej muD neH mupjaj,
'oH rIQmoHbe'ba'mo'. Ha', bang. ylylt.
jotHa'qu' qa'wI' Doy'. lotmo' jI'It.

[*mej*]

LUT 'AY'HOM CHA'. *ta'qach'a' latlh pa'.*

['el HAMLET]

Hamlet	vIpegh, vIpol.
roSenQatlh ghIlDeSten je	['emvo'] Hamlet! Hamlet joH!
Hamlet	'eH jay'! chuSlu'! Hamlet jach 'Iv? toH, mughoSlI'.

['el ROSENQATLH, GHILDESTEN *je*]

roSenQatlh	lom'e', joHwI', nuqDaq Datlhappu'neS?
Hamlet	lam mojqa', vIchenHa'moHmo'; no' DornIS.
roSenQatlh	wItlhapmeH 'ej batlh chIrghHomDaq wIlupmeH, DaqDaj yIDIS.
Hamlet	'e' yIHarQo'.
roSenQatlh	nuq HarQo'?
Hamlet	Satey' jItey"eghlaHbe'taHvIS, Qo'. 'ach wem je ghu'vam: yu'DI' HerghwI', chay' jangnIS ta'puqloD'e'?
roSenQatlh	choqelDI' HerghwI'"e' Datu"a', joHwI'?
Hamlet	HISlaH, qaH, ta' DIb, HoS, woQ je Qay 'oH'e'. 'a reH ta' lutoy'chu' yaSpu'vam'e'. nuj HeHDaq chaH pol, Sopbogh mughato' rurtaHvIS: DaH vup, 'a nem ghup. De' DaQay 'e' poQDI', Du'uy neH 'ej, HerghwI', bIQaDqa'.
roSenQatlh	qayajbe', joHwI'.
Hamlet	vaj jIQuch: qoH qoghDaq Qong QIch 'ong.
roSenQatlh	lom Daq ghopeghHa' 'ej ta'Daq ghotlhej.
Hamlet	ta' tlhej lom 'a lom tlhejta'be'. ta' qa' 'oH—
ghIlDeSten	ta', joHwI'?
Hamlet	'oH Doch'e'. 'oHDaq HIqem. Dejpu'bogh Hov rur qablIj!

[*mej*]

LUT 'AY'HOM WEJ. *ta'qach'a' latlh pa'.*

['el TLHAW'DIYUS TA', *toy'wI'pu'Daj je*]

tlhaw'DIyuS	ghaH, lom je Samta'meH, toy'wI' vIngeHta'.

How dangerous is it that this man goes loose!
Yet must not we put the strong law on him:
He's lov'd of the distracted multitude,
Who like not in their judgment, but their eyes;
And where tis so, the offender's scourge is weigh'd,
But never the offence. To bear all smooth and even,
This sudden sending him away must seem
Deliberate pause: diseases desperate grown
By desperate appliance are reliev'd,
Or not at all.

[*Enter ROSENCRANTZ*]

How now! what hath befall'n?

Rosencrantz	Where the dead body is bestow'd, my lord, We cannot get from him.
Claudius	But where is he?
Rosencrantz	Without, my lord; guarded, to know your pleasure.
Claudius	Bring him before us.
Rosencrantz	Ho, Guildenstern! bring in my lord.

[*Enter HAMLET and GUILDENSTERN*]

Claudius	Now, Hamlet, where's Polonius?
Hamlet	At supper.
Claudius	At supper! where?
Hamlet	Not where he eats, but where he is eaten: a certain convocation of politic worms are e'en at him. Your worm is your only emperor for diet: we fat all creatures else to fat us, and we fat ourselves for maggots: your fat king and your lean beggar is but variable service,—two dishes, but to one table: that's the end.
Claudius	Alas, alas!
Hamlet	A man may fish with the worm that hath eat of a king, and eat of the fish that hath fed of that worm.
Claudius	What dost you mean by this?
Hamlet	Nothing but to show you how a king may go a progress through the guts of a beggar.
Claudius	Where is Polonius?
Hamlet	In heaven; send hither to see: if your messenger find him not there, seek him i' the other place yourself. But, indeed, if you find him not within this month, you shall nose him as you go up the stairs into the lobby.
Claudius	Go seek him there.
	[*To some Attendants*]
Hamlet	He will stay till ye come.

Qu'vatlh! reH Qobqu', ghotvam weghlu'pa'.
'ach ghaHvaD chut HoS Hoch vIlo'laHbe'.
ghaH luparHa'taH Dachba'bogh ghom'a',
wIvbe'mo' yojchaj. wIvlaH mInchaj neH.
'ej wIvDI' chaH, HeSwI''e' bIjlu'chugh,
vaj bIj lunoH, 'ej HeSDaj lunoHQo'.
pay' ghaH vIghImnIS. 'a vIghImtaHvIS,
wo'Daq jIrojmeH 'ej jImaylaw'meH,
vIqelchu' jImoDHa'taI IvIS—net HarnIS.
ghurqu'DI' rop, 'ej SuQDI', vorlu'meH
SuQnIS je Hergh. SuQbe'chugh, vaj not vor.

[*'el ROSENQATLH*]

nuqneH. qaS nuq?

roSenQatlh	joH, lomvetlh So'meH DaqDaj wISovlaHbe', wej DISmo'.
tlhaw'DIyuS	nuqDaq ghaH?
roSenQatlh	HurDaq ghaH, joH. ghaH 'avlu'. chay' jura'neS?
tlhaw'DIyuS	'eH, jIHDaq ghaH yIqem.
roSenQatlh	SuH, ghIlDeSten! naDev joH quv yIqem.

[*'el HAMLET GHILDESTEN je tlhejwI'pu' je*]

tlhaw'DIyuS	SuH Hamlet, nuqDaq ghaHtaH polonyuS'e'.
Hamlet	'uQDaq.
tlhaw'DIyuS	'uQDaq? nuqDaq?
Hamlet	pa' Sopbe' ghaH 'a ghaH Soplu'. ghaH DantaH wutlhwo' nglvbogh ghewQaS'e'. wo' pIvDaq ghatlhlaH ghew ruv neH. mapI'meH Hoch Ha'DIbaH wIpI'moHtaH maH, 'ej maHmo' pI'taH ghewmey. Soj Sar bIH ta' pI''e', qoH lang'e' je— cha' nay' chaH, qaStaHvIS wa' 'uQ neH. ghu' Qav 'oH.
tlhaw'DIyuS	va, va.
Hamlet	chaq ta' Soppu'bogh ghew'e' lo' wamwI'. chaq ghew Soppu'bogh to'baj'e' jon wamwI' 'ej Sop ghaH.
tlhaw'DIyuS	nuq choyajmoHmeH bIHech.
Hamlet	paghHey, 'a petaQ burghDaq DuvIl'meH ta' mIw'e' qa'ang neH.
tlhaw'DIyuS	nuqDaq ghaHtaH polonyuS'e'?
Hamlet	QI'tu'Daq. pa' SammeH vay' yIngeH. pa' Sambe'chugh nejwI' vaj latlhDaq DaSammeH yIngeH'egh SoH. 'ach qaStaHvIS jarvam DaSambe'chugh, tlhonIIj mupbej ghaH, 'ochDaq bIyItDI' 'ej vaSHom Da'elDI'.
tlhaw'DIyuS	pa' yInejII'.

[*toy'wI'pu' puSvaD*]

Hamlet	Supawpa' mejbe'.

[Exeunt Attendants]

Claudius	Hamlet, this deed, for thine especial safety,—
	Which we do tender, as we dearly grieve
	For that which thou hast done,—must send thee hence
	With fiery quickness: therefore prepare thyself;
	The bark is ready, and the wind at help,
	The associates tend, and every thing is bent
	For England.

Hamlet	For England!
Claudius	Ay, Hamlet.
Hamlet	Good.
Claudius	So is it, if thou knew'st our purposes.
Hamlet	I see a cherub that sees them.—But, come; for
	England!—Farewell, dear mother.
Claudius	Thy loving father, Hamlet.
Hamlet	My mother: father and mother is man and wife; man
	and wife is one flesh; and so, my mother.—Come, for England!

[Exit]

Claudius	Follow him at foot; tempt him with speed aboard;
	Delay it not I'll have him hence to-night:
	Away! for every thing is seal'd and done
	That else leans on the affair: pray you, make haste.

[Exeunt ROSENCRANTZ and GUILDENSTERN]

And, England, if my love thou hold'st at aught—
As my great power thereof may give thee sense,
Since yet thy cicatrice looks raw and red
After the Danish sword, and thy free awe
Pays homage to us—thou mayst not coldly set
Our sovereign process; which imports at full,
By letters conjuring to that effect,
The present death of Hamlet. Do it, England;
For like the hectic in my blood he rages,
And thou must cure me: till I know 'tis done,
Howe'er my haps, my joys were ne'er begun.

[Exit]

SCENE IV   *A plain in Denmark.*

[Enter FORTINBRAS, a Captain, and Soldiers, marching]

Fortinbras	Go, captain, from me greet the Danish king:
	Tell him that, by his licence, Fortinbras
	Craves the conveyance of a promis'd march
	Over his kingdom. You know the rendezvous.
	If that his majesty would aught with us,
	We shall express our duty in his eye,
	And let him know so.
Captain	I will do't, my lord.

[*mej toy'wI'pu'*]

tlhaw'DIyuS 'eH, Hamlet: Qob DaSIQchoHbe'taHmeH—
'ej DaSIQbe'taH 'e' vIQorghqangbej,
HeSchavlIjmo' jI'IQqu'taHvIS je—
DaH naDevvo' Dunge'nISmoHbej HeSlIj.
'ej tugh bItlheDtaHvIS, qul Do DaleHnIS.
vaj DaH yIghuHchoH. jaHbeH DujHomlIj.
ma'beH pIvghor. nIloSlI' je tlhejwI'lI'.
tera'Daq ghuS.

Hamlet   tera'Daq?

tlhaw'DIyuS   HIja'.

Hamlet   maj!

tlhaw'DIyuS toH, "maj" bIjatlhqangbej, nabwIj DaSovchugh.

Hamlet lubejbogh lInDab naw'wI' vIbej. 'a Ha', tera'Daq. qamej, SoSoy.

tlhaw'DIyuS 'a DuparHa'qu'bogh vavlI' jIH, Hamlet.

Hamlet SoSwI'! loDnal be'nal je chaH vav'e' SoS'e' je; tay' loDnal
be'nal je porgh; vaj SoSwI''e' SoH. Ha' tera'Daq.

[*mej*]

tlhaw'DIyuS yItlha' yISum. nom tIjmeH ghaH yIraD.
Qu' yImImQo'. DaHjaj ram mejnIS ghaH.
Ha'. Qu' vI'olmeH Hoch nav 'ut vIqonta',
'ej wuvbogh Hoch vIqI'ta'. SuH, pemoD.

[*mej* ROSENQATLH GHILDESTEN *je*]

tera', parHa'ghachwIj Davuvqangchugh—
DavuvmeH meq Dunobbejta' HoS'a'wIj.
wej, Qo'noSngan 'etlhmo', DoqHa', qoj Hab
porghghItlhlIj roQqu', 'ej van'a'wIj DIllI'
HajIl'ghachlIj vIleHbogh—ta'ghItlh'e'
vaj DavuvHa'laHbe' je. ra'chu' ghItlh,
'ej Qu'vam lutlhochHa' latlh ghItlh: DalaDDI',
tugh HeghnIS Hamlet. 'eH, yIchav, tera'.
tujrop Da, 'IwwIj weHmo'. 'ej chovornIS.
chavvam vISovpa', Do'taHvIS je ghu',
'ej cheptaHvIS je Dotlh, reH jIHvaD ru'.

[*mej*]

LUT 'AY'HOM loS. *Qo'noS Hatlh.*

['*el* VORTIBRAS, HoD, negh je, yIttaHvIS]

vortIbraS 'eH, HoD. DaH jIHvaD Qo'noS ta' yIrI'.
yIja': "Dachaw'mo', wo'lIj Sep lujuS
vortIbraS negh. DaDormoHmeH bIlay'pu'.
DaDormoH DaH 'e' poQ." qep Daq DaSov.
QumqangDI' ta', vaj QummeH Qu' luchavnIS
mInDaj vIbejDI'. ghaHvaD 'e' yISovmoH.

HoD   lu', joH.

Fortinbras	Go softly on.

[Exeunt FORTINBRAS and Soldiers]

[Enter HAMLET, ROSENCRANTZ, GUILDENSTERN, and others]

Hamlet	Good sir, whose powers are these?
Captain	They are of Norway, sir.
Hamlet	How purpos'd, sir, I pray you?
Captain	Against some part of Poland.
Hamlet	Who commands them, sir?
Captain	The nephews to old Norway, Fortinbras.
Hamlet	Goes it against the main of Poland, sir, Or for some frontier?
Captain	Truly to speak, and with no addition, We go to gain a little patch of ground That hath in it no profit but the name. To pay five ducats, five, I would not farm it; Nor will it yield to Norway or the Pole A ranker rate should it be sold in fee.
Hamlet	Why, then the Polack never will defend it.
Captain	Yes, it is already garrison'd.
Hamlet	Two thousand souls and twenty thousand ducats Will not debate the question of this straw: This is the imposthume of much wealth and peace, That inward breaks, and shows no cause without Why the man dies.—I humbly thank you, sir.
Captain	God be wi' you, sir.

[Exit]

Rosencrantz	Wilt please you go, my lord?
Hamlet	I'll be with you straight. Go a little before.

[Exeunt all except HAMLET]

How all occasions do inform against me.
And spur my dull revenge! What is a man,
If his chief good and market of his time
Be but to sleep and feed? a beast, no more.
Sure he that made us with such large discourse,
Looking before and after, gave us not
That capability and god-like reason
To fust in us unus'd. Now, whether it be
Bestial oblivion, or some craven scruple
Of thinking too precisely on the event,—
A thought which, quarter'd, hath but one part wisdom
And ever three parts coward,—I do not know

vortIbraS	'eH, QIt peyIt.
	[*mej VORTIBRAS negh je*]
	['*el HAMLET, ROSENQATLH, GHILDESTEN, latlh je*]
Hamlet	ylja', qaH QaQ.
	nuqvo' chol neghvam?
HoD	DuraSvo', qaH quv.
Hamlet	chay' Hech?
HoD	qInSaya Sep luHIvrup, qaH.
Hamlet	Dev 'Iv?
HoD	DuraS pIn qan loDnI'puqloD:
	vortIbraS.
Hamlet	Sepchaj botlh luHIvqang'a'?
	veH neH luHIvqang'a'?
HoD	jIvIt 'ej jImIyQo', qaH, ghu' qaja'DI'.
	yav 'ay'Hom ram wIDoQmeH, pa' maghoS.
	'ej maHvaD pongDaj neH 'oH joDaj'e'.
	yavvetlh vIwIjchoHmeH vIDIllaHchugh,
	vagh DeQmey neH vInobnISchugh je jay',
	vaj vIwIjQo'. 'ej Sepvetlhvo' vagh'e'
	not Suq qInSaya, DuraS joq, qaH quv—
	bIH 'oStaHvIS, tlhongchu'chugh je verengan.
Hamlet	vaj Hubrupbe' qInSaya negh.
HoD	qarbe'.
	'oHDaq Surchem lucherta'.
Hamlet	mavjopHey Sengqoqvam luwuqlaHbe'law'
	cha'SanID qa'pu', cha'netlh DeQmey je.
	rojmo' mIpmo' je ghur ropHuHvam Hal.
	'aDDu'Daq lIchtaH taS, 'a Hur wIbejDI',
	ghot Hegh pagh meq wIlegh.—qatlho'neS, qaH.
HoD	DuQanjaj qeylIS.
	[*mej HoD*]
roSenQatlh	joH, bIghoSrup'a'?
Hamlet	SIbI' Satlhej. DaH loQ HInungchoH neH.
	[*mej ROSENQATLH GHILDESTEN je*]
	mupumII' Hoch wanI'. bortaSwIj buD'e'
	lurIHqang. QongmeH neH 'ej SopmeH poH
	'oHchugh ghot Qu''a''e', malja''e' je,
	vaj quvlaH'a' ghot? vaj targhna' neH ghaH!
	bov 'em, bov tlhopHey je DIleghlaHmeH,
	SIjbogh yablaH wIghaj, machenpu'DI'.
	nonmeH neH yabmaj, bIH DIlo'taHQo'mo',
	meqlaHvetlh, qa''a' yab je wIghajbe'.
	targh vIDa'a' neH, reH jIlIjnISmo'?
	pagh, chaq rejmorgh vIDameH Qu'wIj San
	vIqelchu''a' 'ej QIt vIHonqang'a'?
	'ej cha'logh qelbogh yabvam wavlu'chugh,

Why yet I live to say, 'This thing's to do;'
Sith I have cause, and will, and strength, and means
To do't. Examples, gross as earth, exhort me:
Witness this army, of such mass and charge,
Led by a delicate and tender prince;
Whose spirit, with divine ambition puff'd,
Makes mouths at the invisible event;
Exposing what is mortal and unsure
To all that fortune, death, and danger dare,
Even for an egg-shell. Rightly to be great
Is not to stir without great argument,
But greatly to find quarrel in a straw
When honour's at the stake. How stand I then,
That have a father kill'd, a mother stain'd,
Excitements of my reason and my blood,
And let all sleep? while, to my shame, I see
The imminent death of twenty thousand men,
That, for a fantasy and trick of fame,
Go to their graves like beds; fight for a plot
Whereon the numbers cannot try the cause,
Which is not tomb enough and continent
To hide the slain?—O, from this time forth,
My thoughts be bloody, or be nothing worth!

[*Exit*]

SCENE V   *Elsinore. A room in the castle.*

[*Enter QUEEN GERTRUDE, HORATIO, and a Gentleman*]

Gertrude	I will not speak with her.
Gentleman	She is importunate; indeed distract: Her mood will needs be pitied.
Gertrude	What would she have?
Gentleman	She speaks much of her father; says she hears There's tricks i' the world; and hems, and beats her heart; Spurns enviously at straws; speaks things in doubt, That carry but half sense: her speech is nothing, Yet the unshaped use of it doth move The hearers to collection; they aim at it, And botch the words up fit to their own thoughts; Which, as her winks, and nods, and gestures yield them, Indeed would make one think there might be thought, Though nothing sure, yet much unhappily.
Horatio	'Twere good she were spoken with; for she may strew Dangerous conjectures in ill-breeding minds.
Gertrude	Let her come in.

[*Exit HORATIO*]

To my sick soul, as sin's true nature is,
Each toy seems prologue to some great amiss:

vaj val wa' 'ay'Daj neH, 'ej vangvIp wej.
"wej ta' vIchav," wej vImaqHa'meH meq
vISovlaHbe'. vIchavmeH neHtaHghach,
meqna' je, HoS je, 'eb je vIHutlhbe'.
'ej mutungHa' yuQ rurmeH 'ughbogh mo'mey.
yIqIm: qevbogh 'ej waghqu'bogh mangghomvam
Dev vajvetlh nong. 'ej qa'Daj ghoDpu'mo'
num'eghmeH Duj, wanI'meyvaD wej leghbogh
qabDaj 'ang ghaH. jubbc'bogh HapDaj ru'
yoDHa'taHmo' ghaH, tugh 'oH muplaH rIntaH
Hoch lotmey baHlaHbogh San, Hegh je, Qob je.
nuqvaD qaS Hochvam? va, choljaHHomvaD jay'!
quvqangchugh vay', vaj qaSpa' Qay'meH meq,
reH DeghqangQo'; 'ach batlhDaj buQlu'chugh,
vaj ghormo' je HIvje' neH SolrupnIS.
vaj qatlh jIloStaH neH? vav chotlu', QI'yaH!
SoS webmoHlu'. 'ej 'IwwIj yabwIj je
tungHa'bej ghu'. 'ach Qong Hoch 'e' vIchaw'.
'ej tugh Hegh cha'maHSaDvam 'e' vIleghDI',
jItuHnIS. noyqangmo' 'ej najmo' neH,
DaH molchaj 'el, QonqDaqchaj 'ellaw'taHvIS.
yotlhHomvaD Qoj, 'ej ghu' luwuqmeH negh,
yapbe'law' yotlhvetlh logh, 'ej lommey So'meH,
molghom ngaSwI' je mojmeH je yapbe'law'.
Hu'tegh, DaH 'Iw lubuSjaj qechmeywIj.
pagh, ramjaj. Qu'wIj qu''e' not vIIIj!

[*mej*]

    LUT 'AY'HOM VAGH. *Qo'noS ta'qach'a' pa'.*

['*el GHERTLHUD TA'BE', HOREY'SO, 'utlh je*]

ghertlhuD	Qo'. ghaHvaD jIjatlhQo'.
'utlh	tlhobqu' ghaH. mISchoH je. 'ej yabDaj Dotlh vuplu'bejneS.
ghertlhuD	jIHvo' nuq'e' neH ghaH?
'utlh	reH vavDaj buS ghaH, jatlhtaHvIS. reH jatlh "qo'vamDaq tojlu' 'e' vItu'." "toH" jatlh. 'ej tIqDaj qIptaH. pe'vIl Quj jeSQo'. jatlhDI', QumHa'bogh mu'meyDaj ngoQna' wIwuqchu'be'. Dap jatlh. 'ach tlholmo' Dapvetlh, vaj yajchoHrup 'IjwI'pu', chaHvaD motlhDI'. SoQDaj luQeq, 'ej qechmeychaj Qochbe'meH, mu'Daj ngongHa'. 'ej mu'Daj qattaHmo' nach, mIn je, porgh je mIwDaj, vaj vay''e' luQubmoHlaH. DIch lughajbe'bej QubDI', 'ach pIch lughaj, 'ej pIchvaD Soy' 'ej QIHlaH.
Horey'So	ghaHvaD jatlhnISlu'. QuSmey Sepbogh yabvaD loyHa'moHlaH. loyHa'DI', maHvaD QoblaH.
ghertlhuD	'el chaw'.

[*mej HOREY'SO*]

va reH yemwI'vaD qaStaH. qa'wI' 'oy'vaD
lot Doj lununglaw' Hoch ghu' ram. 'ej joy' qaD.

So full of artless jealousy is guilt,
It spills itself in fearing to be spilt.

[*Re-enter HORATIO, with OPHELIA*]

Ophelia   Where is the beauteous majesty of Denmark?

Gertrude   How now, Ophelia!

Ophelia   [*Sings*]

> How should I your true love know
> From another one?
> By his cockle hat and staff,
> And his sandal shoon.

Gertrude   Alas, sweet lady, what imports this song?

Ophelia   Say you? nay, pray you, mark.

[*Sings*]

> He is dead and gone, lady,
> He is dead and gone;
> At his head a grass-green turf,
> At his heels a stone.

Gertrude   Nay, but, Ophelia,—

Ophelia   Pray you, mark.

[*Sings*]

> White his shroud as the mountain snow,—

[*Enter KING CLAUDIUS*]

Gertrude   Alas, look here, my lord.

Ophelia   [*Sings*]

> Larded with sweet flowers;
> Which bewept to the grave did go
> With true-love showers.

Claudius   How do you, pretty lady?

Ophelia   Well, God 'ild you! They say the owl was a baker's
               daughter. Lord, we know what we are, but know not
               what we may be. God be at your table!

Claudius   Conceit upon her father.

Ophelia   Pray you, let's have no words of this; but when they
               ask you what it means, say you this:

[*Sings*]

> To-morrow is Saint Valentine's day,
> All in the morning betime,
> And I a maid at your window,
> To be your Valentine.
> Then up he rose, and donn'd his clothes,
> And dupp'd the chamber-door;
> Let in the maid, that out a maid
> Never departed more.

DIvDI' ghot, pIHqu' ghaH. HeS ghItlhDaq Hotlh'egh.
'ej Qotlh 'e' pIHtaHmo' ghot DIv, tugh Qotlh'egh.

['elqa' HOREY'SO. ghaH tlha' 'OVELYA]

'ovelya	SuH, nuqDaq 'IHbogh rIntaH Qo'noS be''a'?
ghertlhuD	nuqneH, 'ovelya.
'ovelya	[*bom*]

> IcS chay' bangna' vIngu'?
> chay' latlh vIDoH?
> lengmIv, baSDaS je tuQ.
> jeqqIj tIq woH.

ghertlhuD	QI'yaH, be' quv, nuq HechlI' bom Daja'bogh?
'ovelya	nuqjatlh? Qo', Qo', yIqImneS.
	[*bom*]

> Heghpu' 'ej lojpu', joH.
> Heghpu' 'ej loj.
> DaH porghDajvo' Haw' qa'.
> yo' qIjDaq Qoj.
> ghuy'cha'!

ghertlhuD	'a SuH, 'ovelya—
'ovelya	Qo'. yIqIm.
	[*bom*]

> lomSut chIS law', peDwI' chIS puS.

['el TLHAW'DIYuS TA']

ghertlhuD	QI'yaH, naDev yIbej.
'ovelya	[*bom*]

> luDech SuvwI'na' Degh.
> 'a molDaj retlhDaq jach pagh wuS,
> ghaH mupDI' rIntaH Hegh.

tlhaw'DIyuS	nuqneH, be' 'IH.
'ovelya	toH, Duvanjaj qeylIS. pIpyuS moj yonmang puqbe' net ja'. DaHjaj Dotlhmaj DISov 'a leS Dotlhmaj DISovbe'. Dunumjaj qeylIS.
tlhaw'DIyuS	vav buSba'.
'ovelya	qechvam qelqa'lu'neSQo'jaj; 'a "nuq Hech", ghelDI', yIja' neH:

> [*bom*]

> DaHjaj 'oH bangjaj'e'. nuqneH!
> SuH, 'eqDI' po, qaghoS.
> 'ej batlh tugh mamuSHa'chuqmeH
> QorwaghDaq jIloS.
> vaj Hu'DI' loD, lojmItDaq joD.
> vay' tuQpa', poSmoHpu'.
> 'el be'. bel be'. 'ej be'batlh woD.
> tugh be' lon loD net tu'.

Claudius	Pretty Ophelia!
Ophelia	Indeed, la, without an oath, I'll make an end on't:

[*Sings*]

> By Gis and by Saint Charity,
> Alack, and fie for shame!
> Young men will do't, if they come to't;
> By cock, they are to blame.
> Quoth she, before you tumbled me,
> You promised me to wed.
> So would I ha' done, by yonder sun,
> An thou hadst not come to my bed.

Claudius How long hath she been thus?

Ophelia I hope all will be well. We must be patient: but I
cannot choose but weep, to think they should lay him
i' the cold ground. My brother shall know of it:
and so I thank you for your good counsel.—Come, my
coach!—Good night, ladies; good night, sweet ladies;
good night, good night.

[*Exit*]

Claudius Follow her close; give her good watch,
I pray you.

[*Exit HORATIO*]

O, this is the poison of deep grief; it springs
All from her father's death. O Gertrude, Gertrude,
When sorrows come, they come not single spies
But in battalions. First, her father slain:
Next, your son gone; and he most violent author
Of his own just remove: the people muddied,
Thick and unwholesome in their thoughts and whispers,
For good Polonius' death; and we have done but greenly
In hugger-mugger to inter him: poor Ophelia
Divided from herself and her fair judgment,
Without the which we are pictures, or mere beasts:
Last, and as much containing as all these,
Her brother is in secret come from France;
Feeds on his wonder, keeps himself in clouds,
And wants not buzzers to infect his ear
With pestilent speeches of his father's death;
Wherein necessity, of matter beggar'd,
Will nothing stick our person to arraign
In ear and ear. O my dear Gertrude, this,
Like to a murdering-piece, in many places
Gives me superfluous death.

[*A noise within*]

Gertrude   Alack, what noise is this?

Claudius Where are my Switzers? Let them guard the door.

[*Enter another Gentleman*]

tlhaw'DIyuS	'ovelya 'IH!
'ovelya	Su', qatlchqangbe', 'a latlh HIvje'Daq bIQ bIr yIqang. vIrInmoHbej.

[*bom*]

> ghay'cha' chomaghpu'. qatlh choHup?
> ghay'cha' yIltuH! yISaH!
> ngaghmeH loD Qup, pIj tojqu'rup.
> 'ej pIch lughajbej chaH.
> jatlh be'. qanay not 'e' DanIS;
> chongaghpa' 'e' Da'ol.
> qar, 'a jIDIS: jIlay'taHvIS,
> qangaghmeH wej chochol.

tlhaw'DIyuS	ghorgh qaSchoH DotIhvam?
'ovelya	QapmeH ghu' QaQ jItul. matuvnIS.

'ach wutlh bIrDaq lulan 'e' vIqelDI' jISaQ,
'ej jaS jIvanglaHbe'. SovchoHbej loDnI'wI'.
vaj Satlho', batlh tuqeSpu'mo'.
Ha' tlhejwI'wI'. revan, be'pu',
revan, be'oypu', revan, revan.

[*mej*]

tlhaw'DIyuS	yItlha' peSum! yI'avchu' 'e' Satlhob.

[*mej* HOREY'SO]

'IQchu'ghach tar wISIQ. va, vavDaj HeghDaq
Hal ghaj ghu' naQ. 'ej QI'yaH! ghertlhuD, ghertlhuD,
nucholDI' lot, nIteb ghoqwI' DaQo' bIH.
nawloghDaq ghomlaw' jay'! wa': vavDaj HoHlu'.
cha': tlheD puqII'. ruvna'vaD ghaH vIghIm,
pe'vII 'e' raDmoH ghaH. wej: jorrup wo'.
jeDlaw' 'ej roplaw' QubtaHvIS 'ej joSDI',
Heghpu' polonyuS QaQqu' 'e' lubuSmo'.
'ej ghaH wImoIDI', mabachHa'bejpu',
Qu'vetlh wIpeghmo' 'ej wImoDmoHmo'.
Do'Ha' je: yabDajvo' 'ovelya wavlu'.
meqlaHDajvo' ghaH wav je. yaHDI' laHvetlh,
Ha'DIbaH neH, Dep Hotlhlu'bogh ghap maH.
ghu' Qav'e' ram law'be' latlh ram puSbe':
romuluSvo' chegh loDnI'Daj, pegh'eghtaHvIS.
ghaH je' yay'II'ghach. 'engmey SepDaq pol'egh.
'ej vavDaj qan Hegh Delbogh SoQmeyqoq
luja'II' teSDaj ngejbogh petaQ'e'.
ngoDna' ghajbe'mo' chaH, vaj 'utDI' ghu',
qoghmeyDaq jIH mupummeH Hoch lu'oghqang,
'ej Ha'quj nge'vIpQo'. baQa', bang, ghertlhuD,
DIHom ghorwI' rur ghu'vam. 'ay'wIj law'Daq
mumup; Hegh law' vIHeghnIS.

['emDaq chuSlu']

ghertlhuD	va! chuS nuq?
tlhaw'DIyuS	nuqDaq 'avwI'pu'wI'? lojmIt lu'avnIS.

['el latlh 'utlh]

What is the matter?

Gentleman	Save yourself, my lord:

The ocean, overpeering of his list,
Eats not the flats with more impetuous haste
Than young Laertes, in a riotous head,
O'erbears your officers. The rabble call him lord;
And, as the world were now but to begin,
Antiquity forgot, custom not known,
The ratifiers and props of every word,
They cry 'Choose we: Laertes shall be king:'
Caps, hands, and tongues applaud it to the clouds:
'Laertes shall be king, Laertes king!'

Gertrude How cheerfully on the false trail they cry!
O, this is counter, you false Danish dogs!

Claudius The doors are broke.

[*Noise within*]

[*Enter LAERTES, armed; Danes following*]

Laertes Where is this king?—Sirs, stand you all without.

Danes No, let's come in.

Laertes   I pray you, give me leave.

Danes We will, we will.

[*They retire without the door*]

Laertes I thank you:—keep the door.—O thou vile king,
Give me my father!

Gertrude   Calmly, good Laertes.

Laertes That drop of blood that's calm proclaims me bastard;
Cries cuckold to my father; brands the harlot
Even here, between the chaste unsmirched brow
Of my true mother.

Claudius What is the cause, Laertes,
That thy rebellion looks so giant-like?—
Let him go, Gertrude; do not fear our person:
There's such divinity doth hedge a king,
That treason can but peep to what it would,
Acts little of his will.—Tell me, Laertes,
Why thou art thus incensed.—Let him go, Gertrude:—
Speak, man.

Laertes   Where is my father?

Claudius   Dead.

Gertrude   But not by him.

Claudius Let him demand his fill.

Laertes How came he dead? I'll not be juggled with:
To hell, allegiance! vows, to the blackest devil!
Conscience and grace, to the profoundest pit!
I dare damnation:—To this point I stand,—
That both the worlds I give to negligence,

	qaS nuq?
'utlh	yItoD'egh, joH. veHHeHDaj juSDI'
	vupQo' bIQ'a', 'ej puHmey SoDmeH moDbej.
	yaSpu'lI' SoDqu' je layerteS Qup,
	Daw'meH DuHIvDI'! jachtaHvIS chaH "joH",
	lupong ghom'a'. 'ej chaHvaD chu'law' 'u':
	bov tIQ lulIjlaw'. tlghmey luSovbe'law'.
	Hoch mu' 'ol bIH 'ej tob; 'a DaH bIH juS.
	'ej jach: "mawIvnIS maH. ta' moj layerteS."
	'ej 'engmey SovmoH mIvmey, ghop je, jat je.
	"ta' moj layerteS, polonyuS puqloD."

ghertlhuD	jachlI' chaH, Quchmo', HeS larghHa'taHvIS!
	va, SuwamHa'bej, maghbogh Qo'noS targhmey!
tlhaw'DIyuS	lojmIt lughormoHlu'.
	['emvo' chuSlu']
	['el LAYERTES, nuH qengtaHvIS. lutlha' Qo'noSngan]
layerteS	'eH, nuqDaq ta'qoqvetlh?—HurDaq peratlh, qaH.
Qo'noSnganpu'	Qo', joH. ma'el.
layerteS	'eb neH HIchaw', juppu'.
Qo'noSnganpu'	luq, luq.
	[lojmIt HurDaq tlheD chaH]
layerteS	Satlho'. lojmIt yI'av.—'eH, ta'qoq mIghqu',
	vavwI' HInob.
ghertlhuD	yIjot, layerteS QaQ.
layerteS	va, jotchugh 'IwwIj 'ay'Hom neH, vaj maq 'oH:
	"ben bIboghHa'. vavlI''e' toj SoSlI'."
	tlhIvbe'bejbogh SoSwI' Quch chunqu'Daq
	ngaghHa'wI' DeghHey nan 'oH.
tlhaw'DIyuS	qatlh, layerteS,
	tengchaH rur Daw'lIj, Dojqu'mo'? 'eH, ghertlhuD,
	ghaH yInISQo', 'ej jIHvaD ylyepQo'.
	ta' yoDbej San. 'ej yoDDI' San, bejHa' neH
	'urmang, 'ej Qu' vID Hechbogh chavlaHbe' 'oH.
	yIja', layerteS, qatlh bIQeHqu'taH?
	ghertlhuD, ghaH yInISQo'. yIjatlhchoH, qaH.

layerteS	nuqDaq vavwI''e'?
tlhaw'DIyuS	Heghpu'.
ghertlhuD	'ach HoHbe' ghaH.
tlhaw'DIyuS	ghellI' 'e' yInISQo'.
layerteS	qatlh Heghpu'? Hu'tegh, jIH vItojlu'Qo'!
	matlhjaj veqlargh neH! 'Ipmey ngaSjaj ghe"or!
	ghob, chut je ghupjaj rIntaH wa' luSpet jay'!
	yo' qIj Hoch bIj vISISQrup. pavmo' Qu'wIj,
	ghe"or, QI'tu' je vISaHHa'. bIQ'a'Daq

Let come what comes; only I'll be reveng'd
Most throughly for my father.

Claudius   Who shall stay you?

Laertes   My will, not all the world:
And for my means, I'll husband them so well,
They shall go far with little.

Claudius   Good Laertes,
If you desire to know the certainty
Of your dear father's death, is't writ in your revenge
That, sweepstake, you will draw both friend and foe,
Winner and loser?

Laertes   None but his enemies.

Claudius   Will you know them, then?

Laertes   To his good friends thus wide I'll ope my arms;
And like the kind life-rendering pelican,
Repast them with my blood.

Claudius   Why, now you speak
Like a good child and a true gentleman.
That I am guiltless of your father's death,
And am most sensible in grief for it,
It shall as level to your judgment pierce
As day does to your eye.

Danes   [*Within*] Let her come in.

Laertes   How now! what noise is that?

[*Re-enter OPHELIA frantically dressed, with straws and flowers*]

O heat, dry up my brains! tears seven times salt,
Burn out the sense and virtue of mine eye!—
By heaven, thy madness shall be paid by weight,
Till our scale turn the beam. O rose of May!
Dear maid, kind sister, sweet Ophelia!—
O heavens! is't possible a young maid's wits
Should be as moral as an old man's life?
Nature is fine in love; and where 'tis fine
It sends some precious instance of itself
After the thing it loves.

Ophelia   [*Sings*]

They bore him barefaced on the bier;
Hey non nonny, nonny, hey nonny;
And in his grave rain'd many a tear:—
Fare you well, my dove!·

Laertes   Hadst thou thy wits, and didst persuade revenge,
It could not move thus.

Ophelia   [*Sings*]

You must sing a-down a-down,
An you call him a-down-a.

'oHtaH 'etlh'e'. 'ach DaH vavwI' Heghmo'
bortaS vISuqbej.

tlhaw'DIyuS   toH, Dubotrup 'Iv?

layerteS   mubotlaH neHtaHghachwIj. botlaHbe'
qo' naQ latlh HoS jay'.
'ej SupmeywIj vIvu'chu'mo', vaj Qapqu',
puStaHvIS je bIH.

tlhaw'DIyuS   SuH, layerteS QaQ,
vavlI' Hegh vIt DaSov DaneHqu'chugh,
vaj jupDaj, jaghDaj je DayotlhnIS'a'?
pe'vIl DabI'chu''a'? 'ej bech ngup, Hom je,
DaH SoHvaD 'e' poQ'a' bortaS?

layerteS   ghobe',
bech jaghDaj neH.

tlhaw'DIyuS   'ej jupDaj Daghov'a'?

layerteS   HIja'. juppu'DajvaD DeSDu' vIpoSmoH.
'ej qeylIS SoS vIDarup. chaH vIje'meH,
'IwwIj vInobrup je.

tlhaw'DIyuS   toH, DaH vajna' SoH.
puq quv DaDabej. HeghtaHvIS vavlI',
jIchun. 'ej Heghmo' ghaH jIQoSqu'bej.
yojlIjDaq baHDI' vItmeyvam, vaj mInvaD
jajlo' luDalaw'.

Qo'noSnganpu'   ['etDaq] 'el chaw'. yIbotQo'.

layerteS   chay'? chuStaH nuq?

          ['el 'OVELYA. Sut taQ, tI beQ QaD, tlpuqmey je tuQ]

Ha' QeDjaj yabwIj! Ha'. mInblQ na', Sochlogh
mInDu'wIj HoS, noch laHmey je yImeQjaj!
bImaw'taH tugh net DIl. 'ej DIllu' rIntaH,
Huch nobbogh 'ughDI' law' SoH 'ughDI' puS.
Qu'vatlh! SuH wo'maj naDmoHbogh Degh'e'!
be' 'IH! be'nI'wI' matlh! 'ovelya quv!
ghuy'cha'! DuH'a' wanI'? DuQaw'pu''a'?
Heghpu'DI' loD qan yIn, SIbI' Hegh'a' je
be'Hom Qup yab? muSHa'taHvIS nong puq.
'ej nongDI', Dol muSHa'bogh tlhejtaHmeH,
wa' 'ay'Daj waghqu' ngeH.

'ovelya   [*bom*]

                    molghomDaq porghDaj tlhol luqeng;
                    QI'yaH QI'yaH QI'yaH.
                    'ej molDaq SaQlu'mo', chen ngeng.
bIplvjaj, Qa'oy.

layerteS   wej Sabchugh yablIj, 'ej bortaS chora'chugh,
bIponmeH SoH po' law', yab plv po' puS.

'ovelya   [*bom*]

                    "baQa' baQa'" yIbom.
                    'ej "yIra' ghuy'cha'" yIbom SoH.

O, how the wheel becomes it! It is the false
steward, that stole his master's daughter.

Laertes   This nothing's more than matter.

Ophelia   There's rosemary, that's for remembrance; pray,
love, remember: and there is pansies, that's for thoughts.

Laertes   A document in madness,—thoughts and remembrance fitted.

Ophelia   There's fennel for you, and columbines:—there's rue
for you; and here's some for me:—we may call it
herb-grace o' Sundays:—O you must wear your rue with
a difference.—There's a daisy:—I would give you
some violets, but they withered all when my father
died:—they say he made a good end,—

                [*Sings*]

                        For bonny sweet Robin is all my joy.

Laertes   Thought and affliction, passion, hell itself,
She turns to favour and to prettiness.

Ophelia   [*Sings*]

                        And will he not come again?
                        And will he not come again?
                        No, no, he is dead,
                        Go to thy death-bed,
                        He never will come again.

                        His beard was as white as snow,
                        All flaxen was his poll:
                        He is gone, he is gone,
                        And we cast away moan:
                        God ha' mercy on his soul!

                And of all Christian souls, I pray God.—God be wi' ye.

                [*Exit*]

Laertes   Do you see this, O God?

Claudius   Laertes, I must commune with your grief,
Or you deny me right. Go but apart,
Make choice of whom your wisest friends you will
And they shall hear and judge 'twixt you and me:
If by direct or by collateral hand
They find us touch'd, we will our kingdom give,
Our crown, our life, and all that we call ours,
To you in satisfaction; but if not,
Be you content to lend your patience to us,
And we shall jointly labour with your soul
To give it due content.

Laertes   Let this be so;
His means of death, his obscure burial—
No trophy, sword, nor hatchment o'er his bones,
No noble rite nor formal ostentation—
Cry to be heard, as 'twere from heaven to earth,
That I must call't in question.

               toH, QoQ 'IHmoHchu' je QuQ.
               HoD puqbe' tlhu'moH qalmoHbogh lagh'e'.

layerteS   yajmoHmo' DapHeyvam, SoQ'a' 'utbe'moH.

'ovelya   Dargh qanob. DIch 'oS. DIch yIghajneS, bang. Dom qanob je.
               yoj 'oS.

layerteS   maw'taHvIS ghaH maghojqu'laH. tlhejchuqchu' 'IQmoHbogh
               qechDaj, qawmoHbogh qechDaj je.

'ovelya   SoHvaD noSvagh, ngat je vInob. 'Iw qanob,
               'ej 'IwHom jInob'egh je. chaq QI'lop vaj nIn wIpong.
               'IwlIj DatuQtaHvIS DapImnISmoH. Qab vInob.
               toplIn qanobqangpu' je 'ach ngoS 'oH HeghDI' vavwI'.
               batlh rInta' ghaH net jatlh—

               [*bom*]

                       muQuchqu'moHmo' qoreQ 'IH,—

layerteS   'It ghaH 'ej roptaH. bech, 'ej ghe"or SIQ.
               'a ghaHvaD bel, 'IHwI' je mojlaw' Hochvetlh.

'ovelya   [*bom*]

                   naDev not cholqa"a'?
                   naDev not cholqa"a'?
                   ghobe'. Hu' Hegh.
                   SIbI' yIjegh.
                    naDev not cholqa'ba'.

                   peDwI' rur rolDaj chIS.
                   ram qIj rur patlhDaj ngup.
                   DaH yaH. DaH yaH.
                   maSaQnIStaH.
                   QI'tu' Da'eljaj, qup!

               'ej Hoch SuvwI' Hugh vIjachmoHDI', qeylIS vItlhob. qeylIS
               boghomjaj.

               [*mej*]

layerteS   QI'yaH! Daleghpu"a'?

tlhaw'DIyuS   bI'IQtaHvIS, layerteS, DaH qatlhej.
               'ej DIbvam HIbotQo'. 'a loQ yIDoH neH.
               juppu'lI'vo' vay' val DawIvpu'DI',
               tugh ghu'maj lut luQoylaH 'ej lunoHlaH.
               'ej DuQmoHmo' pagh DuQmo', ghIHtaH ghopwIj,
               chaq 'e' lutu'chugh, yonchu'meH bortaSlIj,
               vaj wo'wIj, ta'mIv'a' je, yInwIj je,
               Hoch je vIghajpu'bogh qanobrupneS.
               'a ghIH 'e' lutu'be'chugh, vaj yIloS,
               'ej DaH bItultaH jIHvaD 'e' yIchav.
               'ej yonmeH rIntaH qa'lI', batlh jIyeqrup.

layerteS   qaSjaj. 'a morghmeH chalDaq yuQDaq je
               jach HeghDaj meq, 'ej jachqu' nolDaj moD—
               HomDu'Daj DungDaq Dach nagh, 'etlh je, ghItlh je;
               Dach je noltay, 'ej Dach SuvwI'na' van—
               'ej Hochvam QIjlu' 'e' vIpoQ.

Claudius   So you shall;
And where the offence is let the great axe fall.
I pray you, go with me.

[*Exeunt*]

SCENE VI *Another room in the castle.*

[*Enter HORATIO and a Servant*]

Horatio   What are they that would speak with me?

Servant   Sailors, sir: they say they have letters for you.

Horatio   Let them come in.—

[*Exit Servant*]

I do not know from what part of the world
I should be greeted, if not from Lord Hamlet.

[*Enter Sailors*]

First Sailor   God bless you, sir.

Horatio   Let him bless thee too.

First Sailor   He shall, sir, an't please him. There's a letter for
you, sir; it comes from the ambassador that was
bound for England; if your name be Horatio, as I am
let to know it is.

Horatio   [*Reads*] 'Horatio, when thou shalt have overlooked
this, give these fellows some means to the king:
they have letters for him. Ere we were two days old
at sea, a pirate of very warlike appointment gave us
chase. Finding ourselves too slow of sail, we put on
a compelled valour; and in the grapple I boarded
them: on the instant they got clear of our ship; so
I alone became their prisoner. They have dealt with
me like thieves of mercy: but they knew what they
did; I am to do a good turn for them. Let the king
have the letters I have sent; and repair thou to me
with as much haste as thou wouldst fly death. I
have words to speak in thine ear will make thee
dumb; yet are they much too light for the bore of
the matter. These good fellows will bring thee
where I am. Rosencrantz and Guildenstern hold their
course for England: of them I have much to tell
thee. Farewell.
                    'He that thou knowest thine, HAMLET.'

Come, I will make you way for these your letters;
And do't the speedier, that you may direct me
To him from whom you brought them.

[*Exeunt*]

SCENE VII *Another room in the castle.*

[*Enter KING CLAUDIUS and LAERTES*]

Claudius   Now must your conscience my acquaintance seal,

tlhaw'DIyuS	bIlugh.

'ej HeSta'bogh petaQDaq pumjaj ghIt.
HItlhej; qatlhob.

[mej chaH]

LUT 'AY'HOM JAV. ta'qach'a' latlh pa'.

['el HOREY'SO, toy'wI' je]

Horey'So	toH, jIllvaD jatlhqang 'Iv?
toy'wI'	yo' negh, jawwI'.

jatlh chaH: "jabbI'IDmey DIghajII'."

Horey'So	'el chaw'.

[mej toy'wI']

Horey'So	yuQDaq 'Ivvo' van ghItlh vISuq, labbe'chugh

Hamlet joH'e'? 'oH labba'pu' pagh latlh.

['el mangpu']

mang	DuHoSmoHjaj qeylIS qa'.
Horey'So	DuHoSmoHjaj je ghaH.
mang	muHoSmoHbej, qaH, taHvIS neH wo'. DarI'lu'—lab tera'Daq

Hechpu'bogh Duy'a'—SoH Dungu'chugh Horey'So pong'e',
qapongmeH vISovmoHlu'bogh.

Horey'So	[jabbI'ID laD] Horey'So, QInvam Dayajta'DI',

ta' luSammeH ghotpu'vam He yIngeDmoH.
ghaHvaD jabbI'ID ghajII' chaH. loghDaq qaSpu'DI'
cha' jajHom nutlha'choH nuH vIDqu' lo'bogh HeS
mech Duj'e'. maHaw'meH yapbe'mo' chuyDaHmaj pe'vIl
mavaQchoH. HotDI' HIchDalmaj nIteb vItlj.
Dujmaj cholHa'choHDI' Dujchaj, vaj qama'chaj
vImoj jIH neH. gharqoqvaD vangtaHvIS
lotlhwI' yuDHa' Da chaH, 'a gharwI' 'ong Da je
SutlhtaHvIS: vaj chaHvaD DIb vInobnIS.
ta'vaD jabbI'ID vIlabpu'bogh yIngeH,
'ej jIHDaq bIchlj'eghmeH yo' qIj la'Duj pIvlob'e'
yIchu'. teSDu'lIj DuQbej mu'mey vIja'rupbogh,
'a De'wIj nIch baHmeH 'umchu'be' moy'bI'vam.
QIvwIjDaq nIqem ghotpu'vam QaQ.
tera'Daq He polba' roSenQatlh ghIlDeSten je.
chaH qelbogh De' law"e' qaja'nIS. pItlh.
    jupna'Il Daghovbogh, Hamlet.

Ha', jup. jabbI'"IDlIjvaD He vI'ang.
'ej nom yIHev. jabbI'IDvam labwI'vo'
De'vam Daqengmo', Do' tugh ghaH choSammoH.

[mej chaH]

LUT 'AY'HOM SOCH. ta'qach'a' latlh pa'.

['el TLHAW'DIYUS TA', LAYERTES je]

tlhaw'DIyuS	jIchunqu' DaH 'e' 'olbej ghoblIj pov;

And you must put me in your heart for friend,
Sith you have heard, and with a knowing ear,
That he which hath your noble father slain
Pursu'd my life.

Laertes   It well appears:—but tell me
Why you proceeded not against these feats,
So crimeful and so capital in nature,
As by your safety, wisdom, all things else,
You mainly were stirr'd up.

Claudius   O, for two special reasons;
Which may to you, perhaps, seem much unsinew'd,
But yet to me they are strong. The queen his mother
Lives almost by his looks; and for myself,—
My virtue or my plague, be it either which,—
She's so conjunctive to my life and soul,
That, as the star moves not but in his sphere
I could not but by her. The other motive,
Why to a public count I might not go,
Is the great love the general gender bear him;
Who, dipping all his faults in their affection,
Would, like the spring that turneth wood to stone,
Convert his gyves to graces; so that my arrows,
Too slightly timber'd for so loud a wind,
Would have reverted to my bow again,
And not where I had aim'd them.

Laertes   And so have I a noble father lost;
A sister driven into desperate terms,—
Whose worth, if praises may go back again,
Stood challenger on mount of all the age
For her perfections:—but my revenge will come.

Claudius   Break not your sleeps for that: you must not think
That we are made of stuff so flat and dull
That we can let our beard be shook with danger,
And think it pastime. You shortly shall hear more:
I lov'd your father, and we love ourself;
And that, I hope, will teach you to imagine—

[*Enter a Messenger*]

How now! what news?

Messenger   Letters, my lord, from Hamlet:
This to your majesty; this to the queen.

Claudius   From Hamlet! who brought them?

Messenger   Sailors, my lord, they say; I saw them not:
They were given me by Claudio;—he receiv'd them
Of him that brought them.

Claudius   Laertes, you shall hear them.—
Leave us.

[*Exit Messenger*]

[*Reads*]

'High and mighty,—You shall know I am set naked on

'ej jup vIDamo', tIqlIjDaq cholannIS—
qen yInwIj wampu' je vavII' HoHwI',
DaH 'e' DaQoymo', valbejtaHvIS teSIIj.

layerteS   net QochlaHbe'. 'ach jIHvaD ghu' yIQIj:
chavvam DabIjmeH qatlh bIvangpu'be'?
HeS webqu' bIH, 'ej Hegh 'oH bIjchaj'e'.
bInurmeH 'ej bIche'meH 'ej bIvalmeH
bInoDqangqu'bej.

tlhaw'DIyuS   toH, cha' meqmey potlhmo'.
chaq SoHvaD pujqu'law', 'ach jIHvaD HoS bIH.
yInmeH, Hamlet mInDu' neH wuvlaw' SoSDaj,
'ej jIHvaD—batlh, QIH ghap 'oH ghu'vam'e';
ram wIv—toH yInvaD, qa'wI'vaD je 'ut ghaH.
bavtaHvIS, ghoDajvo' Haw'be'ba' yuQ;
ghaHvo' jIHaw'laHbe' je jIH. meq cha'DIch:
meqba'Daq peghlu'be'bogh vIngeHbe'nIS,
ghaH luparHa'qu'ba'taHmo' ghom'a' Qut.
parHa'ghachchajDaq ngoSmo' Duy'meyDaj,
Hap choHmoHwI' luDa. qammIr lurIHDI',
chenchoH batlhDeghHey. vaj ghaH puSDI' pu'wIj,
ghom'a' ghoghHoS luSpetDaq pujqu' tIH.
'ej pu'HIchwIjDaq chegh tIH, lujmo' vI'wIj.

layerteS   vaj jIHvaD loj vav quv. 'Itqu' be'nI'wI'
net ral. 'ej qun potlhwI' DInaDqa'DI' je,
vaj bov Hoch potlhHey qaDIaHchu' be'nI'wI',
po'bejmo' ghaH. 'a tugh bortaS vIchav.

tlhaw'DIyuS   bortaS DanabII'meH bIQongHa'Qo'.
pujmo' 'ej buDmo' Hapwlj, vaj jItlvlaH,
rolwljvaD Qomlu'DI'—'e' yIHarQo'.
toH, tugh De' chu' DaQoy. vavII' vIvuvpu';
jIvuv'egh je. Do' ghu'vammo' qaponbej:—

['*el QumwI'*]

nuqneH. De' nuq?

QumwI'   Hamlet jabbI'ID, joH.
SuH, SoHvaD ghItlhvam, 'ej ta'be'vaD ghItlhvetlh.

tlhaw'DIyuS   chay'? Hamletvo'! qem 'Iv?

QumwI'   yo'mang, net jatlhneS. chaH vIleghpu'be'.
bIH HevDI', bIH munobpu' tlhaw'DIyo.

tlhaw'DIyuS   yI'Ij, layerteS.—DoH.

[*mej QumwI'*]

[*laD*]

SuH, patlh woQ je, wo'IIjDaq nuHmey vIHutlhtaHvIS

your kingdom. To-morrow shall I beg leave to see
your kingly eyes: when I shall, first asking your
pardon thereunto, recount the occasion of my sudden
and more strange return.
    'HAMLET.'

What should this mean? Are all the rest come back?
Or is it some abuse, and no such thing?

Laertes	Know you the hand?
Claudius	'Tis Hamlet's character.—'Naked!—

And in a postscript here, he says 'alone.'
Can you advise me?

Laertes   I am lost in it, my lord. But let him come;
It warms the very sickness in my heart,
That I shall live, and tell him to his teeth,
'Thus didest thou.'

Claudius   If it be so, Laertes,—
As how should it be so? how otherwise?—
Will you be rul'd by me?

Laertes   Ay, my lord;
So you will not o'errule me to a peace.

Claudius   To thine own peace. If he be now return'd,—
As checking at his voyage, and that he means
No more to undertake it,—I will work him
To an exploit, now ripe in my device,
Under the which he shall not choose but fall:
And for his death no wind of blame shall breathe;
But even his mother shall uncharge the practise,
And call it accident.

Laertes   My lord, I will be ruled;
The rather, if you could devise it so
That I might be the organ.

Claudius   It falls right.
You have been talk'd of since your travel much,
And that in Hamlet's hearing, for a quality
Wherein they say, you shine: your sum of parts
Did not together pluck such envy from him
As did that one; and that, in my regard,
Of the unworthiest siege.

Laertes   What part is that, my lord?

Claudius   A very riband in the cap of youth,
Yet needful too; for youth no less becomes
The light and careless livery that it wears
Than settled age his sables and his weeds,
Importing health and graveness.—Two months since,
Here was a gentleman of Normandy,—
I've seen myself, and serv'd against, the French,
And they can well on horseback: but this gallant
Had witchcraft in't; he grew unto his seat;
And to such wondrous doing brought his horse,
As he had been incorps'd and demi-natur'd

jIleng. wa'leS chuQunqabllj tlhopDaq jISaHmeH
qatlhob, 'ej qatlhljpu'DI', pay' jlcheghmeH wanI' taQ'e'
DuHmoHta'bogh San Do' qaQIj.
    HAMLET

nuq Hcch ghaH ghItlhDI'? cheghpu"a' Hoch latlh?
chaq mutoj'a' neH? chaq qaSbe"a' Hochvam?

layerteS   ghItlhmIwvetlh Daghov'a'?

tlhaw'DIyuS   nav ghItlhbej Hamlet.
"nuHmey vIHutlh." ghItlhbIngDaq chel: "jImob."
jIHvaD DaQIjlaH'a'?

layerteS   mumISmoHbejneS, joH. 'a choljaj neH.
pay' tIqwlj ropHey vor wanI'vam Do':
jIHeghpa' Ho'Du'DajvaD pum vImaq:
"HeSvetlh Dachavta'."

tlhaw'DIyuS   teHchugh ghu', layerteS—
toH teHlaH'a'? 'a ngeblaHbe'ba' je—
vaj chIch cholobqang'a'?

layerteS   HIja', joH quv,
ghaHvaD jIrojmeH chora'be'chugh neH.

tlhaw'DIyuS   Qo'. SoHvaD rojbej yab, bortaS Dachavmo'.
cheghpu'chugh—lengDaj Qu'vo' Haw'law'mo',
'ej DaH 'oH HechlI'Qo'—vaj San mIqta'Daq
vIghuSmoHlI'bogh, tugh ghaH'e' vIqIch.
mIqta'mo' pumnISbej. jaS wIvlaHbe' ghaH.
'ej HeghDaj pIch lutlhutlhlaHbe' vay' ghogh.
'a nabmaj 'ongqu' pIHlaHbe' je SoSDaj,
'ej "bong qaS" jatlhqang.

layerteS   luq, joHwI'. qalobrup.
qalobrupqu' je, nab chavwI' vIDameH
Da'oghlaHneSchugh.

tlhaw'DIyuS   jIHvaD lI'bej. maj.
bIlengtaHvIS, nIbuStaH naD joSwI'—
'ej Qoy je Hamlet—Dojqu'mo' wa' laHllj.
qu' 'oH net jatlh. 'oH, tIqDajvaD qay' law',
Hoch laHmeylIj qay' puS. 'a vuD vI'angnIS:
ramba' neH laHvetlh ghIgh.

layerteS   yIngu', joH quv.

tlhaw'DIyuS   Suvwl' Qup mIvDaq naDbogh DeghHom neH 'oH.
'ach 'ut je 'oH. mop paH je ghajnIS qup,
'ej chep 'ej Sagh ghaH 'e' lu'ang, 'ej 'um.
'ach reHmeH Sutmey tISqu' ghaj vaj Qup,
net pIH, 'ej 'um je bIH. DaH rIn cha' jar,
nuSuchpu'DI' wa' rIymuS yaS. jItu'pu',
'ej romuluS vIQojpu': lIghchu' chaH.
'a lIghDI', qa'pu' SeHlaw' yaSvam yoH.
porgh'ay'Daj mojlaw' yaS. lupDujHom'e'
SeHchu'mo', jo'vetlh vIDqu' QuQHey mojpu'.
laH'e' vIpIHbogh juSmo' rIntaH ghaH,

With the brave beast: so far he topp'd my thought,
That I, in forgery of shapes and tricks,
Come short of what he did.

Laertes   A Norman was't?

Claudius   A Norman.
Laertes   Upon my life, Lamond.

Claudius   The very same.

Laertes   I know him well: he is the brooch, indeed,
And gem of all the nation.

Claudius   He made confession of you;
And gave you such a masterly report
For art and exercise in your defence,
And for your rapier most especially,
That he cried out, 'twould be a sight indeed
If one could match you: the scrimers of their nation,
He swore, had had neither motion, guard, nor eye,
If you opposed them. Sir, this report of his
Did Hamlet so envenom with his envy,
That he could nothing do but wish and beg
Your sudden coming o'er, to play with him.
Now, out of this,—

Laertes   What out of this, my lord?

Claudius   Laertes, was your father dear to you?
Or are you like the painting of a sorrow,
A face without a heart?

Laertes   Why ask you this?

Claudius   Not that I think you did not love your father;
But that I know love is begun by time;
And that I see, in passages of proof,
Time qualifies the spark and fire of it.
There lives within the very flame of love
A kind of wick or snuff that will abate it;
And nothing is at a like goodness still;
For goodness, growing to a plurisy,
Dies in his own too much: that we would do
We should do when we would; for this 'would' changes,
And hath abatements and delays as many
As there are tongues, are hands, are accidents;
And then this 'should' is like a spendthrift sigh
That hurts by easing. But to the quick o' the ulcer:—
Hamlet comes back: what would you undertake
To show yourself your father's son in deed
More than in words?

Laertes   To cut his throat i' the church.

Claudius   No place, indeed, should murder sanctuarize;
Revenge should have no bounds. But, good Laertes,
Will you do this, keep close within your chamber.
Hamlet return'd shall know you are come home:
We'll put on those shall praise your excellence,
And set a double varnish on the fame

vaj way' 'ej jop ghaH 'e' vIDelchu'meH
Human vImojchugh je, vaj lujbej Qu'wIj.

layerteS   toH, rIymuSngan ghaH'a'?

tlhaw'DIyuS   rIymuSngan'e'.
layerteS   baQa'! lamoD ghaH.

tlhaw'DIyuS   ghaHbej.

layerteS   ghaH vISovchu'.
wo' Degh joqwI' je ghaH.

tlhaw'DIyuS   toH, maHvaD laHIlj chID ghaH.
bIHub'eghmeH bIpo'qu' 'ej bIqeqchu',
'e' naDDI', 'ej 'etlhvI'lIj naDqu'DI',
tugh jach: "chaq rapchugh vI'Daj, vay' vI' je,
vaj Dunbej 'etlhchaj Quj. DaHay'moHchugh,
vaj HIvmeH chaH, pagh HubmeH chaH, pagh tu'meH,
Soy' wo'Daj Hoch yanwI', ghaH qellu'DI'."
'ej naDDaj QoyDI' Hamlet, tarHey tlhutlhlaw',
qeHqu'mo' ghaH. 'ej SoHvaD vI'Daj tobmeH,
SIbI' bIchegh 'e' loS 'ej neHqu' ghaH.
toH. ghu'vammo'—

layerteS   ghu'vammo' qaSneS nuq?

tlhaw'DIyuS   layerteS, vavlI"e' DamuSHa"a'?
pagh, lotHey HotIhlu'bogh neH DaDa'a'?
SaHba' qab QeHqu'. 'ach SaH'a' tIqna'?

layerteS   Ha'! nuq DaghojmeH mu'tlheghvam Dajatlh?

tlhaw'DIyuS   vavlI' DamuSHa'be', 'e' vIghojbe'meH;
muSHa'ghach taghtaH poH—'ach 'e' vISov.
'ej qulDaj, HatDaj je qIl rIntaH poH—
tobtaHmo' ghu'mey, vaj reH 'e' vItu'.
muSHa'ghach qulDaq wa' weQ tlheghHom tu'lu'.
meQtaH, pagh, meQpu' tlhegh. vaj qul HoSHa'moH.
'ej tIqDaj QaQqu' leHlaH pagh QaQwI'.
lach'eghDI' tIqvam—SoD'eghmo', tugh Hegh.
wIneHDI', mojnIS Qu' wIneHtaHbogh:
roD choHtaHmo' "wIneH"vetlh. mogh 'ej mIm 'oH,
law'mo' 'ej law'moHmo' jat, ghop je, ghu' je.
vaj tlhuHmey buDqu' DanISchoH "wIchavnIS":
leSmoHDI', QIH 'oH. 'ach Daq potlh vIDuQ:
DaH cheghII' Hamlet. vaj, vavlI' puqna' SoH,
batlh 'e' DatobmeH, SoQmey yIlo'Qo'.
'ach ta' yIlo'. vaj ta'na'lIj yIwIv.

layerteS   chIrghDaq HughDaj vIpe'qang.

tlhaw'DIyuS   toH, bIlugh.
chotwI' Qanbe'nIS qechmey. bortaS'e'
vuSbe'nIS Hoch. 'ach pa'lIjDaq yIratlhtaH,
layerteS QaQ. bIcheghpu', 'e' Sov Hamlet,
cheghDI' je ghaH. bIpo'qu' 'e' vInaDmoH.
batlh'e' Dunobbogh romuluSnganlI'

The Frenchman gave you; bring you, in fine, together
And wager on your heads: he, being remiss,
Most generous, and free from all contriving,
Will not peruse the foils; so that, with ease,
Or with a little shuffling, you may choose
A sword unbated, and, in a pass of practise
Requite him for your father.

Laertes   I will do't:
And, for that purpose, I'll anoint my sword.
I bought an unction of a mountebank,
So mortal that but dip a knife in it,
Where it draws blood no cataplasm so rare,
Collected from all simples that have virtue
Under the moon, can save the thing from death
That is but scratch'd withal: I'll touch my point
With this contagion, that, if I gall him slightly,
It may be death.

Claudius   Let's further think of this;
Weigh what convenience both of time and means
May fit us to our shape: if this should fail,
And that our drift look through our bad performance,
'Twere better not assay'd: therefore this project
Should have a back or second, that might hold
If this should blast in proof. Soft! let me see:—
We'll make a solemn wager on your cunnings:
I ha't,
When in your motion you are hot and dry,—
As make your bouts more violent to that end,—
And that he calls for drink I'll have prepar'd him
A chalice for the nonce; whereon but sipping
If he by chance escape your venom'd stuck,
Our purpose may hold there.

[*Enter QUEEN GERTRUDE*]

                                         How now, sweet queen!

Gertrude   One woe doth tread upon another's heel,
So fast they follow:—your sister's drown'd, Laertes.

Laertes   Drown'd! O, where?

Gertrude   There is a willow grows aslant a brook,
That shows his hoar leaves in the glassy stream;
There with fantastic garlands did she come
Of crow-flowers, nettles, daisies, and long purples,
That liberal shepherds give a grosser name,
But our cold maids do dead men's fingers call them.
There, on the pendent boughs her coronet weeds
Clambering to hang, an envious sliver broke;
When down her weedy trophies and herself
Fell in the weeping brook. Her clothes spread wide;
And, mermaid-like, awhile they bore her up:
Which time she chanted snatches of old tunes;
As one incapable of her own distress,
Or like a creature native and indu'd
Unto that element: but long it could not be

lubochqa'moH. tugh SoH ghaH je SaghommoH.
'ovmeH SuHay'DI', yaylljvaD jISuD.
pIHQo'mo', 'IImo', 'ej tojQo'mo' ghaH,
Quj'etlhmey nuDchu'be'. vaj bIH DatammeH
loQ ghaH Datojpu'DI', pagh 'eqDI' wIvllj,
'etlh jej DawIvlaH. 'ej SuQujlaw'taHvIS,
vavlI'vaD ghaH DanoD.

layerteS   maj, Qu' vIta'rup.
'ej Qu'vaD 'etlh vInguH je. Qelqoqvo'
wa' tar vIje'pu'. HeghmoHqu'bej 'oH.
vaj tajwIjDaq vIllchDI', 'ej jaghwI'vo'
'IwHom vIlelDI' 'aw'mo' tajwIj neH,
Heghbe'meH ghaH yapbe' Hoch Herghmey qubqu'—
maSwovDaq Hoch tIvo' DIboSlaHbogh
chenchugh je Hergh. HoHtaSvamDaq 'etlhHeHwIj
vInguvmoH. vaj vIqotlhmeH neH vIDuQDI',
Hegh rIntaH.

tlhaw'DIyuS   maj. vaj nab wIQubchu'lI'.
nabvaD mavanglI', 'e' lungeDmoHlaHmeH
poH, 'eb je, bIH DIchovnIS. lujchugh Qu',
'ej nabmaj tu'choHlu'chugh mata'Ha'mo',
vaj qaqbej wInIDbe'chugh. vaj nab chach,
nab cha' joq tu'nISlu'. 'ej jorchugh wa'DIch
wIDajtaHvIS, vaj ratlhlaH latlh. jIQubnIS.
SuHay'DI', yaylljvaD jISuD. 'ej SeQnIS.
tu'!
SuSuvtaHvIS SutujchoH 'ej SuQaDchoH.
'ej qaSmeH ghu'vam, ralqu'nIStaH 'etlhlIj.
toH, tlhutlhmeH tlhobDI', may'qoqraj vIlopmeH
HIvje"a' Dun vIlI'moH. tlhutlhchoHDI' neH,
bong tarlljvo' DaDuQbogh narghpu'chugh,
vaj tarwIjmo' Qap ngoQ.

     ['el GHERTLHUD TA'BE']

         nuqneH, ta'be'?

ghertlhuD   va, wa' lot nglb gho' latlh lot bem. baQa'!
moDqu'lI' lot. layerteS, Hegh be'nI'lI'.

layerteS   Hegh'a'? nuqDaq?

ghertlhuD   bIQtIqHom DungDaq banglojwI'Sor tu'lu'.
pa' baSHey bIQDaq tIHomDaj qlj 'ang 'oH.
pa' Sor tItlheghmey taQqu' chenmoH ghaH.
Qa'tIvo', DuStIvo', naHjejmeyvo',
nI'wI'mey Doqvo' je bIH chenmoHtaH.
nI'wI' lupongmeH Doch wIjwI'pu' mu',
ngIlmo' chaH jatlhDI'. pongmeH chuQunbe'pu',
"lomnItlh" jatlh chaH. pa' Dung SorDeSmeyDaq
mIvHey tItlheghDaj HuSmoHmeH ghaH toSDI',
ghor DeSHom mIgh. 'ej SaQtaHbogh bIQHaIDaq
pum tImey popDaj, ghaH je. beQchoH SutDaj.
'ej qaStaHvIS poH ngaj, DungDaq lupep.
vaj wIch ngengqa' rur. bom ngo' DImey bomtaH,
'ej SengDaj yajlaHbe'law'; qoj, bIQyInvaD
ghaH 'ummoHlaw'pu' DujDaj, porghDaj je.

Till that her garments, heavy with their drink,
Pull'd the poor wretch from her melodious lay
To muddy death.

Laertes   Alas, then, she is drown'd?

Gertrude   Drown'd, drown'd.

Laertes   Too much of water hast thou, poor Ophelia,
And therefore I forbid my tears: but yet
It is our trick; nature her custom holds,
Let shame say what it will: when these are gone,
The woman will be out.—Adieu, my lord:
I have a speech of fire, that fain would blaze,
But that this folly douts it.

                [*Exit*]

Claudius   Let's follow, Gertrude:
How much I had to do to calm his rage!
Now fear I this will give it start again;
Therefore let's follow.

                [Exeunt]

ACT V
SCENE I   *A churchyard.*

[*Enter two Clowns, with spades, &c*]

First Clown   Is she to be buried in Christian burial that
wilfully seeks her own salvation?

Second Clown   I tell thee she is; and therefore make her grave
straight: the crowner hath sat on her, and finds it
Christian burial.

First Clown   How can that be, unless she drowned herself in her
own defence?

Second Clown   Why, 'tis found so.

First Clown   It must be 'se offendendo;' it cannot be else. For
here lies the point: if I drown myself wittingly,
it argues an act: and an act hath three branches; it
is, to act, to do, to perform: argal, she drowned
herself wittingly.

Second Clown   Nay, but hear you, goodman delver,—

First Clown   Give me leave. Here lies the water; good: here
stands the man; good; if the man go to this water
and drown himself, it is, will he, nill he, he
goes,—mark you that: but if the water come to him
and drown him, he drowns not himself: argal, he
that is not guilty of his own death shortens not his own life.

Second Clown   But is this law?

First Clown   Ay, marry, is't; crowner's quest law.

Second Clown   Will you ha' the truth on't? If this had not been
a gentlewoman she should have been buried out o'
Christian burial.

'ach tugh qaSHa'. 'ugh SutDaj, tlhuHqu'pu'mo'.
'ej belDaj bommeyvo' bIQlammey HeghDaq
Qugh ghot luyaHmoH.

layerteS   QI'yaH! vaj Hegh'a'?

ghertlhuD   Hegh ghaH. Hegh rIntaH.

layerteS   SoHvaD law'qu'pu' bIQ, 'ovelya quv.
jISaQ vaj 'e' vIbot. 'a ghotvaD motlh 'oH.
tIghDaj leH tlqwIj Duj. vaj DaH jISaQnIS,
'ej ram tuHwI' pum. yaHpu'DI' mInbIQvetlh,
yaHbej je pujbogh tIqwIj. joH, Qapla'.
qul SoQ vIghaj. 'ej meQqang 'oH. 'ach QI'yaH!
SoQvetlh luSoD mInDu' Dogh.

[*mej ghaH*]

tlhaw'DIyuS   Ha', wItlha'nIS.
QeHqu' ghaH 'e' vIqIlmeH, Qatlhpu' Qu'wIj!
QeHqa' 'e' taghlaH ghu'vam chu'. Do'Ha'.
vaj ghertlhuD, ghaH wItlha'.

[*mej chaH*]

LUT 'AY' VAGH
LUT 'AY'HOM WA'. *molghom.*

[*'el cha' HaghmoHwI'; molmeH luch luqeng*]

molwI'   quv'a' nol mIw, yo' qIj 'elmeH qIghqoq nejpu'chugh je.

latlh   HISlaH, qaja'. vaj yImolchu'. Matlh ghu' qelpu' 'ej nol
quv ra' Heghutlh'a'.

molwI'   nuqmo' NuH, HuM'eghmeH SoN'eghMe'chugh.

latlh   toH, NuHmoHlu'Mej.

molwI'   *In Self Offense* qaSMejpu'. jaS qaSlaHMe'pu'.
toH qar meqvam'e': chIch taghNu'wIj vISoNchugh,
vaj mIw vIta'. wej Qu' ghaj mIw—Hechghach,
vangghach, chavghach je ghaj.
tlherevore chIch SoN'eghpu'.

latlh   'a ghoMe', HInISMe', molneSwI'.

molwI'   MIjatlh 'e' yImev. naNev MIQ tu'lu', maj.
naNev ghot tu'lu', maj. SoN'eghmeH MIQvam lo'chugh,
pollaH pagh polHa'laH, loj—'e' yItu'.
'ach chIch ghaH SoNchugh MIQ'e' vaj SoN'eghqu'Me'.
tlherevore yInpoH rInmoHMe' HoH'eghMe'wI'.

latlh   'ach 'e' ra''a' ruv?

molwI'   HISlaH, vIt. ruvvam'e' Matlh wuq Heghutlh'a'.

latlh   vItna' NanuSHa'qang'a'? yaS ghaHMe'chugh vaj nolNaj
quvMe'nISmoHlu'.

First Clown   Why, there thou say'st: and the more pity that
                 great folk should have countenance in this world to
                 drown or hang themselves more than their even
                 Christian.—Come, my spade. There is no ancient
                 gentleman but gardeners, ditchers, and grave-makers:
                 they hold up Adam's profession.

Second Clown   Was he a gentleman?

First Clown   He was the first that ever bore arms.

Second Clown   Why, he had none.

First Clown   What, art a heathen? How dost thou understand the
                 Scripture? The Scripture says 'Adam digged:'
                 could he dig without arms? I'll put another
                 question to thee: if thou answerest me not to the
                 purpose, confess thyself—

Second Clown   Go to.

First Clown   What is he that builds stronger than either the
                 mason, the shipwright, or the carpenter?

Second Clown   The gallows-maker; for that frame outlives a
                 thousand tenants.

First Clown   I like thy wit well, in good faith: the gallows
                 does well; but how does it well? it does well to
                 those that do ill: now thou dost ill to say the
                 gallows is built stronger than the church: argal,
                 the gallows may do well to thee. To't again, come.

Second Clown   'Who builds stronger than a mason, a shipwright, or
                 a carpenter?'

First Clown   Ay, tell me that, and unyoke.

Second Clown   Marry, now I can tell.

First Clown   To't.

Second Clown   Mass, I cannot tell.

                 [Enter HAMLET and HORATIO, at a distance]

First Clown   Cudgel thy brains no more about it, for your dull
                 ass will not mend his pace with beating; and when
                 you are asked this question next, say a
                 grave-maker; the houses that he makes last till
                 doomsday. Go, get thee to Yaughan; fetch me a
                 stoup of liquor.

                 [Exit Second Clown]

                 [He digs and sings]

                     In youth, when I did love, did love,
                     Methought it was very sweet,
                     To contract, O, the time, for, ah, my behove,
                     O, methought, there was nothing meet.

Hamlet   Has this fellow no feeling of his business, that he
                 sings at grave-making?

molwI'   toH, MIvItMa'. 'ej SoN'eghchu'meH pagh
       voQ'eghchu'meH NIM ghajMogh yaS muM law',
       NIM ghajMogh latlhpu' tlhIvHa' muM puS.
       Ha' molluchwIj. ben negh chaH pochwI',
       lamwI', molwI' je neH. Qu' naMpu'Mogh qeng lutaH.

latlh   muvmoH'a' qeng.

molwI'   wo'mangghom'a' wa'NIch muvmoH 'ej qeqmoHqu'. SevNI' jagh,
       Haw' 'ej ghatlhqa' yo' tuH.

latlh   'a SevvaN tuHMe'Ma'.

molwI'   nuqjatlh? vajMatlh NanuS'a'? chay' vajMatlhHeylIj
       NapaM. vajMatlh paMlu'meH, 'ut tuH'e', Sevmo' jagh.
       tlhoMMogh mu'tlhegh cha'NIch qaQoymoH 'ej
       qoghlIjNaq Nap rarchugh, vaj Hov ghajMe' ram.

latlh   vIwovrupmoH.

molwI'   'Iv lo'laH law', latlhvam lo'laH puS: jonwI', QumpIn,
       chamwI' joq?

latlh   yIH je'wI''e'. yIH roghvaH vu' 'e' lo'laH ghaH'e'.

molwI'   MI'ong 'e' vInuSHa', majQa'. yIH je'wI''e'
       vInuSHa'. 'a nuqmo' vInuSHa'. yIH ghung je'.
       Nol Naje'laHMe'chugh, nol Natu'. 'a Soj
       NamechmeH yIH Nalo'laHMe'. *tlherevore*
       yIH roghvaH tInmo' MIMechjaj. yIjangqa', Ha'.

latlh   'Iv lo'laH law', latlhvam lo'laH puS: jonwI', QumpIn,
       chamwI' joq?

molwI'   HISlaH, HIjangpu' 'ej yIvergh.

latlh   Hu'tegh, NaH jIjanglaH.

molwI'   Ha'.

latlh   MaQa', jIjanglaHMe'.

       [*'el* HAMLET HOREY'SO *je,* HoptaHvIS]

molwI'   yaMIlj yIngepMe', qoq MuN NaraNmeH je
       MuQ HIch net lo'laHMe'mo'. tlhoMMogh
       tlheghvam NatlhoMlu'meH NaQoyqa'moHlu'NI'
       "molwI''e'" yIjatlh. San puyjaq SIQ juH
       chenmoHMogh. ruch, yavnganNaq yIjaH.
       jIHvaN ghargh 'Iw puMmeH yIra'.

       [*mej latlh*]

       [*mol HaghmoHwI' 'ej bom*]

         jIQuptaHvIS muSoN
         Melna', vay' vImuSHa'NI'.
         jIchepmeH—Ha'—poH—Hu'tegh—vItoN,
         'e' poQlaw' pagh, ghoM ra'NI'.

Hamlet   malja' Qu' ta'taHvIS QorghHa'qu'law''a' ghotvam'e', bommo'
       moltaHvIS.

Horatio	Custom hath made it in him a property of easiness.
Hamlet	'Tis e'en so: the hand of little employment hath the daintier sense.
First Clown	[*Sings*]

> But age, with his stealing steps,
> Hath claw'd me in his clutch,
> And hath shipped me intil the land,
> As if I had never been such.

[*Throws up a skull*]

Hamlet	That skull had a tongue in it, and could sing once: how the knave jowls it to the ground, as if it were Cain's jaw-bone, that did the first murder! This might be the pate of a politician, which this ass now o'er-reaches; one that would circumvent God, might it not?
Horatio	It might, my lord.
Hamlet	Or of a courtier; which could say 'Good morrow, sweet lord! How dost thou, good lord?' This might be my lord such-a-one, that praised my lord such-a-one's horse, when he meant to beg it,—might it not?
Horatio	Ay, my lord.
Hamlet	Why, e'en so: and now my Lady Worm's; chapless, and knocked about the mazzard with a sexton's spade: here's fine revolution, an we had the trick to see't. Did these bones cost no more the breeding, but to play at loggats with 'em? mine ache to think on't.
First Clown	[*Sings*]

> A pick-axe, and a spade, a spade,
> For and a shrouding sheet:
> O, a pit of clay for to be made
> For such a guest is meet.

[*Throws up another skull*]

Hamlet	There's another: why may not that be the skull of a lawyer? Where be his quiddits now, his quillets, his cases, his tenures, and his tricks? why does he suffer this rude knave now to knock him about the sconce with a dirty shovel, and will not tell him of his action of battery? Hum! This fellow might be in's time a great buyer of land, with his statutes, his recognizances, his fines, his double vouchers, his recoveries: is this the fine of his fines, and the recovery of his recoveries, to have his fine pate full of fine dirt? will his vouchers vouch him no more of his purchases, and double ones too, than the length and breadth of a pair of indentures? The very conveyances of his lands will hardly lie in this box; and must the inheritor himself have no more, ha?
Horatio	Not a jot more, my lord.

Horey'So	Qorghchu'meH ghopDaj ruQHa'moHlaH roD molbogh DujDaj'e'.
Hamlet	qarbej. Qu' Qorghqu'nIS laH buD'e' tambogh Duj.

molwI' [*bom*]

> 'ach ro'NajNaq mujonpu'
> Mov qu'. mujonNI' MIvlaw'.
> yav MIrqu'Naq mulonpu',
> 'ej Mcn jIQup 'e' JIvlaw'.

[*nach Hom woD*]

Hamlet jat ngaSpu' Homvetlh, 'ej ben bomlaH. va Dochqu' petaQ, Doch pummoHDI', molorHey pIgh pumlaw'taHvIS. yabvaH'e' ghajpu'bogh HeSwI"a' chaq DaH Sev je QovpatIhvam. chaq yejquv junqang qar'a' HeSwI"a'vetlh.

Horey'So chaq HIja', joHwI'.

Hamlet chaq 'oH ghajpu' bochmoHwI': jatlhlaHpu', "qavan, joH webHa'. pIvtaHghachlIj 'oH nuq'e', joH quv?" chaq joHwI' pong vay' ghaH, 'ej joHDaj pong vay' Qogh'e' naDqu', Qochbogh vuD QubtaHvIS je, chaq qar'a'?

Horey'So HISlaH, joHwI'.

Hamlet toH qarba'! 'a DaH Su', ghaH yIvqang ghew yo' 'aj, Dej woS, 'ej lamDaq nachmey pIgh DuD molwI' luch. naDev jaS Qeq San pu' net tu', bortaS QaQqu' jabtaHbogh San nuH'e' DItu'laHchugh. DaH HomDu' QujmeH neH, ben 'ItlhHa'choHpu'a' bIH? vIqeltaHvIS 'oy'qu' HomDu'wIj'e'.

molwI' [*bom*]

> wa' lamnge'wI', wa' naghghorwI',
> lomSut je MIH jan'e'.
> 'ej lamNaq NIS vIchenmoHNI',
> vaj yonnIS mol ngan'e'.

[*latlh nach Hom woD*]

Hamlet toH latlh. chaq bo'DIj meqwI' nach Hom 'oH qar'a'? DaHjaj nuqDaq bIH pojbogh 'ej ponbogh mu'Daj'e', yojDaj'e', chaw'Daj'e', meqDaj'e' je. DaH pIpDegh qIptaH lamluch qatlh 'e' SIQ ghaH, qIpmeH meq mub QIjbe'taHvIS vIDwI'. va, qaStaHvIS yInbovDaj chaq malja' gharwI"a' ghaH, ngIpHa'moHbogh 'ej nojHa'moHbogh woQ, vu'meH, qummeH, 'ej loHmeH chaw' je ghajtaHvIS. naDev nglpmoHbogh 'ej nojmoHbogh woQ nej, lamDaq nujvo' nIj 'e' najmo'. HuqtaHghach vu' 'e' chaw'lu'meH 'um ghaH DaH 'e' lu'olQo"a' 'ummoHwI'Daj'e', 'ummoHbogh cha'rIp'e' je, jochlaHbe'mo' chopDI' pe'vIl SutIhbogh 'ej tlhongbogh mu'meyDaj. yoS malja' ta ngaSlaHbe'mo' 'Ibvam, vaj je'wI' QavvaD chuvbe'nIS yoSDaj naQ, Ha' qar'a'?

Horey'So yoSDaq chuvbe' je wa' naghHom, joHwI'.

Hamlet	Is not parchment made of sheepskins?
Horatio	Ay, my lord, and of calf-skins too.
Hamlet	They are sheep and calves which seek out assurance in that. I will speak to this fellow. Whose grave's this, sirrah?
First Clown	Mine, sir.

[*Sings*]

> O, a pit of clay for to be made
> For such a guest is meet.

Hamlet	I think it be thine, indeed; for thou liest in't.
First Clown	You lie out on't, sir, and therefore it is not yours: for my part, I do not lie in't, and yet it is mine.
Hamlet	'Thou dost lie in't, to be in't and say it is thine: 'tis for the dead, not for the quick; therefore thou liest.
First Clown	'Tis a quick lie, sir; 'twill away gain, from me to you.
Hamlet	What man dost thou dig it for?
First Clown	For no man, sir.
Hamlet	What woman, then?
First Clown	For none, neither.
Hamlet	Who is to be buried in't?
First Clown	One that was a woman, sir; but, rest her soul, she's dead.
Hamlet	How absolute the knave is! we must speak by the card, or equivocation will undo us. By the Lord, Horatio, these three years I have taken a note of it; the age is grown so picked that the toe of the peasant comes so near the heel of the courtier, he gaffs his kibe.—How long hast thou been a grave-maker?
First Clown	Of all the days i' the year, I came to't that day that our last king Hamlet overcame Fortinbras.
Hamlet	How long is that since?
First Clown	Cannot you tell that? every fool can tell that: it was the very day that young Hamlet was born,—he that is mad, and sent into England.
Hamlet	Ay, marry, why was he sent into England?
First Clown	Why, because he was mad: he shall recover his wits there; or, if he do not, it's no great matter there.
Hamlet	Why?
First Clown	'Twill not be seen in him there; there the men are as mad as he.
Hamlet	How came he mad?
First Clown	Very strangely, they say.
Hamlet	How strangely?

Hamlet	malja' Huqlu'meH tera'ngan De'wI' lulo'lu' qar'a'?
Horey'So	HISlaH, joHwI', verengan De'wI' je.
Hamlet	tera'nganbatlh verenganbatlh je ghaj De'wI' luvoqbogh nuv'e'. ghotvamvaD jIjatlh— molvam ghaj 'Iv, qaHHom?
molwI'	vIghaj, qaH.

[*bom*]

'ej lamNaq NIS vIchenmoHNI',
vaj yonnIS mol ngan'e'.

Hamlet	Daghajbej, SoHvaD lulIghHom 'oHmo'.
molwI'	ghoMe', NIS 'oH neH. lulIghlaHMe' Hom. vIghaj 'ach 'oHNaq jIMa'Me'.
Hamlet	chonISbej, Duma' 'e' DaDISQo'mo'. pa' bIQamlaHbe'. vaj bIpum.
molwI'	QamMe' pumlIj. chojun 'a MIchunMe'.
Hamlet	loD DamollI'bogh yIngu'.
molwI'	loNvaN vImolMe'.
Hamlet	toH, be' yIngu'.
molwI'	Me'vaN vImolMe' je.
Hamlet	pa' 'Iv Damol?
molwI'	Me' ghaHpu', qaH. 'a qeylIS ghomjaj, Heghmo'.
Hamlet	reH mu' Donqu' Qovpatlh, yajtaHvIS. machuHnISchu', QIch wIwobtaHvIS. jaS Deghmeymaj Qotlh DuDchuqlaw'taHbogh rI'Se' ngoqmaj. qeng HoS, Horey'So, qaStaHvIS wej benvam vItu'taH: 'Itlhqu'mo' nugh, chuQun quvDaq Sumqu'mo' tlha'bogh rewbe' Qut, movDaq yaDbutlh ngoH.— ghorgh molwI' Damoj?
molwI'	NIS jajmey Hochvo', vImoj vortIMraS jeyNI' che'pu'Mogh ta' Hamletma'.
Hamlet	ghorgh qaS wanI'vetlh?
molwI'	'e' NajanglaHMe''a'? 'e' janglaH qoH Hoch. quq wanI'vetlh wanI'vam je: Mogh Hamlet Qup—NaHjaj maw'moHlu'pu'Mogh 'ej tera'Naq ngeHlu'pu'Mogh.
Hamlet	HISlaH, vIt, qatlh tera'Daq ghaH ngeHlu'?
molwI'	maw'mo'. pa' mISNaj SuqHa'qa'. SuqHa'Me'chugh pa' ram ghu'.
Hamlet	qatlh?
molwI'	pa' ghaHNaq mIS lutu'Me'. Sung mIS law' ghaH mIS puS.
Hamlet	maw'moH nuq?
molwI'	Hujqu' maw'meH mo' net joS.
Hamlet	chay' Huj?

First Clown	Faith, e'en with losing his wits.
Hamlet	Upon what ground?
First Clown	Why, here in Denmark: I have been sexton here, man and boy, thirty years.
Hamlet	How long will a man lie i' the earth ere he rot?
First Clown	Faith, if he be not rotten before he die—as we have many pocky corses now-a-days, that will scarce hold the laying—he will last you some eight year or nine year: a tanner will last you nine year.
Hamlet	Why he more than another?
First Clown	Why, sir, his hide is so tanned with his trade, that he will keep out water a great while; and your water is a sore decayer of your whoreson dead body. Here's a skull now; this skull has lain in the earth three and twenty years.
Hamlet	Whose was it?
First Clown	A whoreson mad fellow's it was: whose do you think it was?
Hamlet	Nay, I know not.
First Clown	A pestilence on him for a mad rogue! a' poured a flagon of Rhenish on my head once. This same skull, sir, was Yorick's skull, the king's jester.
Hamlet	This?
First Clown	E'en that.
Hamlet	Let me see.—

[*Takes the skull*]

Alas, poor Yorick!—I knew him, Horatio; a fellow of infinite jest, of most excellent fancy: he hath borne me on his back a thousand times, and now, how abhorred in my imagination it is! my gorge rises at it. Here hung those lips that I have kissed I know not how oft. Where be your gibes now? your gambols? your songs? your flashes of merriment, that were wont to set the table on a roar? Not one now, to mock your own grinning? quite chap-fallen? Now get you to my lady's chamber, and tell her, let her paint an inch thick, to this favour she must come; make her laugh at that. Prithee, Horatio, tell me one thing.

Horatio	What's that, my lord?
Hamlet	Dost thou think Alexander looked o' this fashion i' the earth?
Horatio	E'en so.
Hamlet	And smelt so? pah!

[*Puts down the skull*]

molwI'	Su', yaHlaw' yaM.
Hamlet	meq nuq?
molwI'	Su', naNev Qo'noSNaq molghomvam Meq jIH neH. wejmaH NIS mol vIQan, jIqanNI' 'ej jIQupNI'.
Hamlet	qaStaHvIS DIS 'ar wutlhDaq QottaH lom, nonpa'?
molwI'	Heghpa' nonMe'chugh—toH, law'qu' roplom'e' NItlhapnISMogh, 'ej tlhoS NIQotmoHNI', Nej—wej non, qaSpa' chorgh Hut ghap NIS. qaSpa' Hutna' wej non SurghwI'.
Hamlet	qatlh poHDaj nI' law', latlh poH nI' puS?
molwI'	toH, malja' Qu'Najmo' letchu'mo' NIrNaj, HurNajNaq MIQ pol, qaStaHvIS wa'maHcha' pemmey wa'maHcha' rammey je. reH Quch HaM lom nonmoHqu' MIQ. toH nach Hom 'oH: wutlhNaq 'oHtaH Homvam, qaStaHvIS cha'maH wej NIS.
Hamlet	ghajpu' 'Iv?
molwI'	ghajpu' Quch HaM ghot Nogh. ghajpu' 'Iv 'e' yIloy.
Hamlet	Qo', 'e' vISovbe'.
molwI'	naSjaj yIntagh Nogh yIvqangMogh ghewmey. ben HIvje"a' teMHa'meH nachwIjNaq puMtaHMogh gharghHIq chagh. nach Homvam'e' ghajpu' yorIq, ta' HaghmoHwI'.
Hamlet	Dochvam'e'?
molwI'	Nochvetlh'e'.
Hamlet	HItu'moH.
	[*nach Hom tlhap*]
	va Do'Ha' yorIq. yIntaHvIS vISov, Horey'So. HaghmoH not 'e' mevqang. tIvmoH reH 'e' tob. wa'SanIDlogh DubDaj vIIIgh 'ej DaH qech qIch najbogh yabwIj. vIqawDI' poqwIj laQ. naDev HuS woS'e' pIj vIchopbogh—"pIj"vetlh vItoghlaHbe'. DaH nuqDaq bIH jIpHommeyIIj tlhaQ'e'? QujIIj'e', QoQIIj'e', pay' Hoch meb HaghmoHtaHbogh lutIIj tlhaQ'e' je DaH tIvlaH 'Iv? bIHagh DaH 'e' vaq qar'a' paghna'? Dej'a' woS? DaH be'oywI' quv pa'Daq yIjaH 'ej yIja', bI'IH'eghmoHmeH wa'SaD Haq DaSIQchugh je, rurchuq qabDu'maj 'e' DabotlaHbe'. HaghmeH yIja'. vay' yISovmoH, Horey'So.
Horey'So	nuq DaSovrup, joHwI'?
Hamlet	wutlhDaq pIghvam rur qeylIS pIgh 'e' DaHar'a'?
Horey'So	rurbej.
Hamlet	pIwvam rur'a' je pIwDaj. QI'yaH.
	[*nach Hom roQ*]

Horatio	E'en so, my lord.
Hamlet	To what base uses we may return, Horatio! Why may not imagination trace the noble dust of Alexander till he find it stopping a bung-hole?
Horatio	'Twere to consider too curiously to consider so.
Hamlet	No, faith, not a jot; but to follow him thither with modesty enough, and likelihood to lead it: as thus; Alexander died, Alexander was buried, Alexander returneth into dust; the dust is earth; of earth we make loam; and why of that loam whereto he was converted might they not stop a beer-barrel?

> Imperious Caesar, dead and turn'd to clay,
> Might stop a hole to keep the wind away:
> O, that that earth, which kept the world in awe
> Should patch a wall to expel the winter flaw!

But soft! but soft! aside: here comes the king.

[Enter Priest, &c. in procession; the Corpse of OPHELIA, LAERTES and Mourners following; KING CLAUDIUS, QUEEN GERTRUDE, their trains, &c]

The queen, the courtiers: who is that they follow?
And with such maimed rites? This doth betoken
The corse they follow did with desperate hand
Fordo its own life: 'twas of some estate.
Couch we awhile, and mark.

[Retiring with HORATIO]

Laertes	What ceremony else?
Hamlet	That is Laertes, A very noble youth: mark.
Laertes	What ceremony else?
First Priest	Her obsequies have been as far enlarg'd As we have warrantise: her death was doubtful; And, but that great command o'ersways the order, She should in ground unsanctified have lodged Till the last trumpet; for charitable prayers, Shards, flints, and pebbles should be thrown on her, Yet here she is allow'd her virgin rites, Her maiden strewments, and the bringing home Of bell and burial.
Laertes	Must there no more be done?
First Priest	No more be done: We should profane the service of the dead To sing a requiem, and such rest to her As to peace-parted souls.
Laertes	Lay her i' the earth,— And from her fair and unpolluted flesh May violets spring!—I tell thee, churlish priest, A ministering angel shall my sister be When thou liest howling.

Horey'So	HIja', He'So'bej.
Hamlet	lo'mey ramqu' wIcheghlaH, Horey'So. HIq HIvje"a' SoQmoHchu'bogh lamHom'e' qellu'DI', qeylIS lom Dunvo' 'oH ghochlaH qar'a' 'oghbogh yoj?
Horey'So	Dalach 'e' vItu', ghu'vetlh vIqelDI'.
Hamlet	ghobe', vIt, vIlachbe'chu'. 'a ghaH ghochmeH, San DuH lachbe'taHvIS 'ej yojmey qItqu' neH buStaHvIS, vaj qaS: Hegh qeylIS, wutlh ghoS qeylIS, tlholqa' qeylIS Hap, lam 'oH Hap tlhol'e', SoQmeH HIvje"a' lam lo'lu', 'ej HIq polmeH qegh, lam'e' (bong mojpu'bogh qeylIS) ghoDmoHlu', chaq qar'a'.

	lom mojDI' qeylIS, lam moj je voDleH.
	       SuS waQmeH, pa'Dop DISHom ghoDlaH neH.
	       nunuQ bov bIr 'e' botmeH vaj nuboQ
	       'e' laj ben qo'maj HajmoHbogh lamtlhoQ.
	'a tam! 'eH, tam! yInech. DaH cholIl' ta'.

	[*'el lalDanyaSpu' latlh je, 'ej Sagh yIttaHvIS.* *tlha' 'OVELYA lom, LAYERTES, nolwI'pu' je. tlha'TLHAW'DIYUS TA',* *GHERTLHUD TA'BE', toy'wI'pu' je*]
	ta'be'! toy'wI'pu' je! 'ach 'Iv lutlha'? 'ej tayDaj nupqu'lu'. vaj pIHmoH ghu'vam: quvHa'law' lomvetlh ghop lutlha'll'bogh, yInDaj polHa'mo', Heghvetlh raDpa' batlh. 'ej chuQunghotHey ghaHpu'. loQ maba'. naDev maqImIl'.
	[*'emDaq ghoS HAMLET HOREY'So je*]
layerteS	tay veb yIngu'.
Hamlet	layerteS ghaH. loD quvqu'. yIqIm.
layerteS	DaH tlha' tay nuq?
lalDanyaS wa'DIch	nolDaj wInI'moHmeH, chaw'maj wIpabta'. nub HeghDaj'e'. 'ej lalDantIgh ngepbe'chugh nura'pu'bogh DunwI', vaj yav quvHa'Daq QotnISbej porgh, ghIpDIjpa' ghe"orpIn. ghaHDaq vanbommey DIjachbe'nISpu'. 'ej naghmey, DI je, veQ je jaDnISlu'. 'a ghaHvaD nuH luqenglu' DaH net chaw'; 'ej ghItlh wIlanpu'; 'ej tlhogh Qav wIqaSmoH; 'ej jaq chuS'ugh, noltay je.
layerteS	chay'? Hat'a' latlh?
lalDanyaS wa'DIch	Hatjaj jay'! lommey tay wIwebmoHbej, mInDu'DajDaq majachchugh, 'ej yo' qIjDaq pe'vIl Heghbogh vajpu"e' tlha'chugh ghaH.
layerteS	yavDaq yIlan. 'ej 'IHbogh porghDaj chunvo' boghjaj DuStImey! yaSqoq qej, qajatlh: yo' qIjDaq boQbogh qa"a' moj be'nI'wI', Dujoy'taHvIS veqlargh.

Hamlet	What, the fair Ophelia!
Gertrude	Sweets to the sweet: farewell!

[*Scattering flowers*]

I hop'd thou shouldst have been my Hamlet's wife;
I thought thy bride-bed to have deck'd, sweet maid,
And not have strew'd thy grave.

Laertes   O, treble woe
Fall ten times treble on that cursed head
Whose wicked deed thy most ingenious sense
Depriv'd thee of!—Hold off the earth awhile,
Till I have caught her once more in mine arms:

[*Leaps into the grave*]

Now pile your dust upon the quick and dead,
Till of this flat a mountain you have made,
To o'ertop old Pelion, or the skyish head
Of blue Olympus.

Hamlet   [*Advancing*] What is he whose grief
Bears such an emphasis? whose phrase of sorrow
Conjures the wandering stars, and makes them stand
Like wonder-wounded hearers? This is I,
Hamlet the Dane.

[Leaps into the grave]

Laertes   The devil take thy soul!

[Grappling with him]

Hamlet   Thou pray'st not well.
I prithee, take thy fingers from my throat;
For, though I am not splenitive and rash,
Yet have I something in me dangerous,
Which let thy wiseness fear: hold off thy hand.

Claudius   Pluck them asunder.

Gertrude   Hamlet, Hamlet!

All   Gentlemen,—

Horatio   Good my lord, be quiet.

[*The Attendants part them, and they come out of the grave*]

Hamlet   Why, I will fight with him upon this theme
Until my eyelids will no longer wag.

Gertrude   O my son, what theme?

Hamlet   I loved Ophelia; forty thousand brothers
Could not, with all their quantity of love,
Make up my sum.—What wilt thou do for her?

Claudius   O, he is mad, Laertes.

Gertrude   For love of God, forbear him.

Hamlet   'Swounds, show me what thou'lt do:

Hamlet	'ovelya! chay'!
ghertlhuD	'IHwI'na'vaD 'IHwI'Hommey. Qapla'!

[*vanmeH tImey ghomHa'moH*]

HamletwI' be'nal SoHchoH reH vIneH.
be' 'IH, bInayDI', tlhogh QongDaqrajDaq
tImey vIchaghrupmoH. 'a nolDaq chagh
not 'e' vIpIH.

layerteS	baQa'! SuH, wejlogh qIch,

wa'maHlogh wejlogh nachvetlh webDaq pumjaj
qIch, yablIj valqu' nge'mo' chavDaj mIghqu'!
loQ lam yImIm. DeSDu'wIjDaq vIvanqa'.

[*mol bIngDaq Sup*]

SIbI' yInwI'Daq lomDaq je yav lam
yIghommoH. Daqvam beQDaq chenjaj HuD.
peDSoS HuD ngo'qu', qa'HuD'a' chalnach je
juSjaj 'oH jay'!

Hamlet	[*tlhopDaq yIt*] Ha', 'IQtaHghach lach 'Iv?

lengtaHbogh yuQmey yay'moH 'Iv SoQ 'It?
'ej 'Iv ghogh QoymeH yev bIH, QIDmo' merDI'?
Qo'noSngan Hamlet jIH.

[*mol bIngDaq Sup*]

layerteS	Dughupjaj ghe"or!

[*Sol chaH*]

Hamlet	QaQbe'law' mu' DajatlhbogH.

'eH, HughwIjvo' nItlhDu' tIteq; qatlhob.
jIvIDqang 'ej jImoDqang 'e' vISeH.
'ach jIHDaq QoblaH vay'. vaj Hojjaj yojlIj.
'eH, ghop yIyaHmoH.

tlhaw'DIyuS	Ha' tIchev.
ghertlhuD	SuH, Hamlet!
	Hamlet!
Hoch	joHpu'!
Horey'So	joHwI' QaQ, SuH, yIjot.

[*chaH chev tlhejwI'pu', 'ej molvo' DoH chaH*]

Hamlet	baQa'! vItobmeH pe'vIl ghaH vISuvrup,

jIleghmeH vIHlaHtaHvIS mInyoDDu'wIj!

ghertlhuD	va, puqoy! nuq DatobmeH?
Hamlet	'ovelya vImuSHa'. mujuSlaHbe'

loSnetlh loDnI' muSHa'ghachHom tlhoQ naQ.
'ej not mururchoH. ghaHvaD nuq Data'rup?

tlhaw'DIyuS	va, maw'ba' ghaH, layerteS.
ghertlhuD	QI'yaH! 'eH, yISolQo'!
Hamlet	Hu'tegh! 'eH, chav Data'rupbogh HI'ang.

Woul't weep? woul't fight? woul't fast? woul't tear thyself?
Woul't drink up eisel? eat a crocodile?
I'll do't.—Dost thou come here to whine?
To outface me with leaping in her grave?
Be buried quick with her, and so will I:
And, if thou prate of mountains, let them throw
Millions of acres on us, till our ground,
Singeing his pate against the burning zone,
Make Ossa like a wart! Nay, an thou'lt mouth,
I'll rant as well as thou.

Gertrude   This is mere madness:
And thus awhile the fit will work on him;
Anon, as patient as the female dove,
When that her golden couplets are disclos'd,
His silence will sit drooping.

Hamlet   Hear you, sir;
What is the reason that you use me thus?
I loved you ever: but it is no matter;
Let Hercules himself do what he may,
The cat will mew, and dog will have his day.

[Exit]

Claudius   I pray you, good Horatio, wait upon him.—

[Exit HORATIO]

[To LAERTES]

Strengthen your patience in our last night's speech:
We'll put the matter to the present push.—
Good Gertrude, set some watch over your son.—
This grave shall have a living monument;
An hour of quiet shortly shall we see;
Till then, in patience our proceeding be.

[Exeunt]

                   SCENE II   A hall in the castle.

[Enter HAMLET and HORATIO]

Hamlet   So much for this, sir: now shall you see the other;
You do remember all the circumstance?

Horatio   Remember it, my lord!

Hamlet   Sir, in my heart there was a kind of fighting
That would not let me sleep: methought I lay
Worse than the mutines in the bilboes. Rashly,
And prais'd be rashness for it,—let us know,
Our indiscretion sometimes serves us well,
When our deep plots do fail: and that should teach us
There's a divinity that shapes our ends,
Rough-hew them how we will.

Horatio   That is most certain.

Hamlet   Up from my cabin,
My sea-gown scarf'd about me, in the dark

SaQ'a'? Suv'a'? SopQo''a'? SIj'egh'a'?
rughtaS tlhutlh'a'? wa' mughato' Sop'a'?
vIta'rup je. naDev bIvIngrup'a' neH?
choqaDqang'a' neH, molDajDaq DaSupmo'?
bIyIntaHvIS DatlhejchoHmeH yImollu';
qatlhejbej. HuDmey DabuS'a' bIjaw'DI'?
maHDaq wa''uy' qell'qam jaDlu'jaj.
'ej woDDI' rIntaH, Hovmey quIDaq Dung
meQmoHjaj maH Dung HuD. 'ej qellu'DI',
'er ghIch neH rurjaj SISSoS'a'. ghuy'cha'!
mu' Doj Dalo'chugh, vaj jImly je jIH.

ghertlhuD   maw'ba'. 'ej yabDaj DantaHvIS QeHmISvam,
             reH ngaj neH poH. tugh Qa'be' tuvqu' rurchoH,
             bogh Qa'puqmeyDaj SuD 'e' tu'DI' 'oH—
             tugh ba'choH ghaH, 'ej 'av'egh tamtaHvIS.

Hamlet   yIja', qaH. qatlh bIDoch? reH qaparHa'pu'.
             'a ram. batlh mIwmaj raDchugh je veqlargh,
             vaj jaS jach Qogh, 'ej jajDaj tIvnIS targh!

             [mej]

tlhaw'DIyuS qatlhob, Horey'So QaQ. 'eH, ghaH yItlha'.

             [mej HOREY'SO]

             [LAYERTESvaD jatlh]

             bItul 'e' HoSmoHjaj wa'Hu' ram SoQmaj.
             SIbI' ghu' naQ wItI'. 'eH, ghertlhuD QaQ,
             puqlI'vaD mang tI'avmoH. molvamDaq
             nI'qu'jaj lom wIqawtaHmeH Hegh vanmaj.
             tugh qaS rep jot. 'a qaSpa', tuljaj Sanmaj.

             [mej chaH]

                 LUT 'AY'HOM CHA'. ta'qach'a' vaS.

             ['el HAMLET HOREY'SO je]

Hamlet   pItlh, qaH. DaH latlh yIbej. wanI'vetlh He
             Daqawchu' SoH, qar'a'?

Horey'So   vIqawbej, joH.

Hamlet   tIqwIjDaq Suvlaw' vay'. jIQong 'e' bot 'oH.
             jIH bItlaw' law', qammIr qama' bIt puS.
             ghu' vIqelQo'DI'—toH, rut lI' qelQo'ghach.
             vInaDbej, maHvaD QaplaHchu'mo' 'oH,
             lujtaHvIS nabmaj 'ong. vaj ghojlu'jaj:
             nemmaj raQbogh San'e' reH tu'lu'bej,
             bIH wIteyHa'taHvIS je.

Horey'So   DIch 'oH, joH.

Hamlet   raQpo'pa'vo' jIHu'. ngengpaH vItuQDI',
             jIqat'eghpu' neH. 'ej pa' Hurghqu'taHvIS,

Grop'd I to find out them: had my desire;
Finger'd their packet; and, in fine, withdrew
To mine own room again: making so bold,
My fears forgetting manners, to unseal
Their grand commission; where I found, Horatio,
O royal knavery! an exact command,—
Larded with many several sorts of reasons,
Importing Denmark's health and England's too,
With, ho! such bugs and goblins in my life,—
That, on the supervise, no leisure bated,
No, not to stay the grinding of the axe,
My head should be struck off.

Horatio	Is't possible?
Hamlet	Here's the commission: read it at more leisure.
	But wilt thou hear me how I did proceed?
Horatio	I beseech you.

Hamlet

Being thus be-netted round with villanies,—
Ere I could make a prologue to my brains,
They had begun the play,—I sat me down;
Devis'd a new commission; wrote it fair:
I once did hold it, as our statists do,
A baseness to write fair, and labour'd much
How to forget that learning; but, sir, now
It did me yeoman's service. Wilt thou know
The effect of what I wrote?

Horatio   Ay, good my lord.

Hamlet

An earnest conjuration from the king,—
As England was his faithful tributary;
As love between them like the palm might flourish;
As peace should stiff her wheaten garland wear
And stand a comma 'tween their amities;
And many such-like 'As'es of great charge,—
That, on the view and knowing of these contents,
Without debatement further, more or less,
He should the bearers put to sudden death,
Not shriving-time allow'd.

Horatio   How was this seal'd?

Hamlet

Why, even in that was heaven ordinant.
I had my father's signet in my purse,
Which was the model of that Danish seal:
Folded the writ up in form of the other;
Subscrib'd it; gave't the impression; plac'd it safely,
The changeling never known. Now, the next day
Was our sea-fight; and what to this was sequent
Thou know'st already.

Horatio

So Guildenstern and Rosencrantz go to't.

Hamlet

Why, man, they did make love to this employment;
They are not near my conscience; their defeat
Does by their own insinuation grow:

chaH'e' vISammeH Dat nejHa'll' ghopwIj.
Qap Qu'wIj. ta'nobchaj vInIH. 'ej rInDI',
pa'wIj vIghoSqa'. pa'Daq jaqmo' DujwIj,
DochHa'meH mIw vIllj, 'ej ghItlhchaj Dun
vIpoSmoHmeH jInglIchoH. 'ej Horey'So,
ghItlhDaq voDleH 'urmang vItu'. pa' ra'chu'—
nav 'IHmoHtaHvIS Sarbogh meqmey law';
'ej chepnIS Qo'noS wo' tera' DIvI' je,
lubuSqu'nISbogh chaH; 'ej ratlhchugh yInwIj,
vaj qaS maQmIghmey Dojqu', 'e' luDelDI'—
ra': ghItlhvetlh bejlu'DI', mImbe'nIS lenHom.
Qo', nom QIghpej rIHbe'nISlu' je jay'.
DaH Hamlet nach yIchev.

Horey'So	chay'! DuHneS'a'?
Hamlet	SuH, ra'bogh ghItlh yItlhap. tugh 'oH yIlaDchu'.
	'a ruchmeH mIw vI'oghpu'bogh yIQoy.
Horey'So	lu', joH.
Hamlet	jonmeH muDech mIghwI' mIqta'Hey 'ong.
	vaj yabwIjvaD vIlIlHpa', lut luDachoH.
	jIba'. 'ej ra'bogh ta'ghItlh chu' vI'ogh.
	vIghItlhlI'meH, pIqaDmey 'IH vIlo'—
	wa'ben, che'wI'pu' vuD vIghajtaH je:
	pIqaD 'IH SovDI' vay', naDHa'nISlu',
	toy'wI''a' Qu' neH 'oHmo'. chIch vIlIljqang.
	'a qaH, jIHvaD ne' matlh Qu' chavmoH laHvetlh.
	jabbI'IDwIj QIn pegh DaSovqang'a'?
Horey'So	HIja', joHwI'.
Hamlet	tera' ra' ta', 'ej bergh:
	"SumatlhlI'meH, rojmab boDIltaHvIS;
	'ej 'Iwmaj rurmej boqmaj, HoSqu'mo';
	'ej lettaHmeH nur Ha'quj tuQbogh roj;
	'ej not jup maHbogh nuQmeH tu'HomI'raH"—
	'ej DujDaj chIDmeH latlh "meH" law'qu' pongDI':
	"QInvam DabejDI' 'ej DaSovpu'DI',
	yIghoHchoHQo', 'ej Qu' yIchovchoHQo'.
	'a ghItlh qengwI'pu"e' SIbI' yImuH;
	'ej, HeSchaj DISmeH chaH, pagh poH yIchaw'."
Horey'So	chay' navvaD woQ Da'ol?
Hamlet	toH, SeHlI' SanwIj.
	Sengvam qay'Ha'moH je 'oH. tepwIjDaq
	vavwI' woQDegh vIghaj. Qo'noS Degh'e'
	Do' rurchu' 'oH, wej choHmoHpu'mo' ta'.
	vaj SoQmeH navwIj, latlh nav mIw vIlo'.
	vIql'. Degh ghItlh vI'uy. DaqDaq vIlan.
	'ej not choH 'ong luSov. toH, qaSDI' wa'leS,
	vID logh leng may'maj. tlha'pu'bogh wanI''e',
	SoHvaD vISovmoHpu'.
Horey'So	vaj rIntaH ghIlIDeSten; Hegh roSenQatlh je.
Hamlet	va, ghIghchaj ra'meH ta', lubochqangmoH.
	tIqwIjvo' Hop chaH. QIHchaj naQ luDuHmoH,
	Haqrupmo'. 'etlh QeH jIrmoHDI' 'ej DIjDI'

'Tis dangerous when the baser nature comes
Between the pass and fell incensed points
Of mighty opposites.

| Horatio | Why, what a king is this! |

Hamlet Does it not, think'st thee, stand me now upon,—
He that hath kill'd my king and whor'd my mother;
Popp'd in between the election and my hopes;
Thrown out his angle for my proper life,
And with such cozenage,—is't not perfect conscience
To quit him with this arm? and is't not to be damn'd,
To let this canker of our nature come
In further evil?

Horatio It must be shortly known to him from England
What is the issue of the business there.

Hamlet It will be short: the interim is mine;
And a man's life's no more than to say 'One.'
But I am very sorry, good Horatio,
That to Laertes I forgot myself;
For by the image of my cause I see
The portraiture of his: I'll court his favours;
But, sure, the bravery of his grief did put me
Into a towering passion.

Horatio   Peace! who comes here?

[Enter OSRIC]

Osric Your lordship is right welcome back to Denmark.

Hamlet I humbly thank you, sir.—Dost know this water-fly?

Horatio No, my good lord.

Hamlet Thy state is the more gracious; for 'tis a vice to
know him. He hath much land, and fertile: let a
beast be lord of beasts, and his crib shall stand at
the king's mess: 'tis a chough; but, as I say,
spacious in the possession of dirt.

Osric Sweet lord, if your lordship were at leisure, I
should impart a thing to you from his majesty.

Hamlet I will receive it, sir, with all diligence of
spirit. Put your bonnet to his right use; 'tis for the head.

Osric I thank your lordship, 'tis very hot.

Hamlet No, believe me, 'tis very cold; the wind is
northerly.

Osric It is indifferent cold, my lord, indeed.

Hamlet Methinks it is very sultry and hot for my
complexion.

Osric Exceedingly, my lord; it is very sultry,—as
'twere,—I cannot tell how.—But, my lord, his
majesty bade me signify to you that he has laid a
great wager on your head. Sir, this is the matter,—

Hamlet I beseech you, remember—

cha' ghol Doj, botlhDaq gho'qangchugh Qovpatlh,
vaj ghaHvaD Qob.

Horey'So	baQa', quvHa'bej ta'vam!
Hamlet	DaH ngaQ lojmIt. Qoch'a'? ta'wI' quv HoHpu'.

Hamlet DaH ngaQ lojmIt. Qoch'a'? ta'wI' quv HoHpu'.
SoSwI' ngaghHa'pu'. patlh vItulpu'bogh
nISpu', ta' chu' luwIvrupDI' yejquv.
'ej yInwIj baqrup, qabDaj 'angtaHQo'vIS,
muvoqqangmoHmo'. vaj tIq Say' vIghajbej,
chIch popDaj nobpu'DI', qar'a', 'etlh ro'vam.
'ej ghurmeH mIghbogh laHDaj, qo'maj ropvetlh
vISangchu'Qo'chugh, vaj jIwem, qar'a'.

Horey'So 'a tugh tera'vo' ghaHvaD pawnIS De'.
'ej Qu'Daj lujmoHbogh meq'e' tugh Sov.

Hamlet vaj "tugh" SeH ghaH. 'ach "wej" vISeHlI' jIH.
'ej "baH" neH jachmeH yapqu' wa' ghot yIn.
'a maqochwI', layerteSvaD jIberghmo',
jIQoSqu'. Qu'wIj nach vIbejchu'DI',
tugh Qu'Daj mIv vIleghchoHlaHlaw' je.
jup ghaH vIneHqu'bej. 'a mIymo', 'ItDI',
ghurqu' je nongtaHghachwIj.

Horey'So SuH. chol 'Iv?

['*el* '*oSrIq toy'wI*']

'oSrIq Qo'noSDaq SoHqa'taHneSghach wIlopjaj.

Hamlet qatlho'neS, qaH. [*Horey'SovaD*] pIpyuSvam Daghov'a'?

Horey'So ghobe', joHwI' QaQ.

Hamlet ghu'lIj chep law', ghu'wIj chep puS; qay'mo' ghu' ghaH
ghovlu'DI'. yoSmey tIn ghaj; lIng je bIH. Ha'DIbaHmey ghom
vu'wI'"a' Dachugh je wa' Ha'DIbaH'e' neH, vaj voDleH Sojpa'Daq
yaH ghaj 'oH, tugh net chaw'. Qa' ghaH, 'ach lam tIq ghaj 'e'
vIDellaH.

'oSrIq joH wIbHa', leSpoH DaghajneSchugh SoH quv, ta'vo' wa' Doch
SoHDaq jIja'nIS, HIchaw'jaj.

Hamlet vIHev, qaH, buSchu'rupvIS qa'wIj. mIvlIj yIlo'chu'; nachDaq
'oH DaqDaj'e'.

'oSrIq joH quv, qatlho'; tujqu'.

Hamlet ghobe', bIrqu' 'e' yIHar. chuch Sepvo' joqmoH SuS.

'oSrIq loQ bIrlaw'bej, joHwI'.

Hamlet 'ach vuD vIwuqmeH berghqu' 'ej tuj muDDotlhvam.

'oSrIq HIja'bej, joHwI'. berghqu'law'—qaSmeH 'e' mIw
vISovchu'laHbe' jIH 'ach. joHwI', mutlhob ta' batlh, SoHneS
vItlhojmoHnIS: tonSaw'lIjmo' mIymeH SuDpu' ta'. qaH,
fact of the matter 'oHna' De'vam'e'—

Hamlet yIqaw, qatlhob.

[*HAMLET moves him to put on his hat*]

Osric	Nay, in good faith; for mine ease, in good faith. Sir, here is newly come to court Laertes; believe me, an absolute gentleman, full of most excellent differences, of very soft society and great showing: indeed, to speak feelingly of him, he is the card or calendar of gentry, for you shall find in him the continent of what part a gentleman would see.
Hamlet	Sir, his definement suffers no perdition in you;— though, I know, to divide him inventorially would dizzy the arithmetic of memory, and yet but yaw neither, in respect of his quick sail. But, in the verity of extolment, I take him to be a soul of great article; and his infusion of such dearth and rareness, as, to make true diction of him, his semblable is his mirror; and who else would trace him, his umbrage, nothing more.
Osric	Your lordship speaks most infallibly of him.
Hamlet	The concernancy, sir? why do we wrap the gentleman in our more rawer breath?
Osric	Sir?
Horatio	Is't not possible to understand in another tongue? You will do't, sir, really.
Hamlet	What imports the nomination of this gentleman?
Osric	Of Laertes?
Horatio	His purse is empty already; all's golden words are spent.
Hamlet	Of him, sir.
Osric	I know you are not ignorant—
Hamlet	I would you did, sir; yet, in faith, if you did, it would not much approve me.—Well, sir.
Osric	You are not ignorant of what excellence Laertes is,—
Hamlet	I dare not confess that, lest I should compare with him in excellence; but to know a man well were to know himself.
Osric	I mean, sir, for his weapon; but in the imputation laid on him by them, in his meed he's unfellowed.
Hamlet	What's his weapon?
Osric	Rapier and dagger.
Hamlet	That's two of his weapons: but, well.
Osric	The king, sir, hath wagered with him six Barbary horses: against the which he has imponed, as I take it, six French rapiers and poniards, with their assigns, as girdle, hangers, and so: three of the carriages, in faith, are very dear to fancy, very

[*mIv tuQqa'meH ra' HAMLET*]

'oSrIq	Qo', joHwI'; pIvbejwIjvaD. qaH, Hu' puS naDev ta'juHDaq ghaHqa' layerteS'e'—HIHar, Suvchu'wI' pupqu' ghaH, DotlhmeyquvSarngaS, jup'a' Da 'ej po' qIp'egh nachDu'chaj tlhInganSuvwI' je ghaH. HIja', nong ghaHneSvaD *critique*'a'wIj qamuchmeH, SuvwI' mem, HIDjolevDaq joq wa'DIch ghaHchu'; toH, batlhDotlhmey law' ghajwI'meyvaD tIqDaj 'angqu' ghaH.
Hamlet	Delqu'ghachDaj mu'mey DapujmoHHa'be' SoH, 'ach batlhDotlhDaj Hochna' wIbuv 'e' wanI'qoq ta'meHchu' yapbejbe' bong vIt junlaw'wI' naDmey qu"e', yabmIw DIngtaHmoHmo' DotlhDu'HeyDaj. tlchHa'taHghachQIchwIj DaDI' teHna"e', ghaH vIqelchu'bej: qa'DajDaq quvmey law' lubuvlu'laH; povmo' qoj le'mo' DujDaj'e', naDDaj vItlu'taHvIS neH, vaj quvna'qu' wojDaj lu*tranSmI'*laH nom qabDaj gheghvo' qetqa'bogh 'otlh neH'e'. 'ej QIb neH'e' QeqHa' 'otlhbIQtIqvamDaq lIghwI', rurnIDwI' ghap.
'oSrIq	bIQaghHa'bejqu' SoHneS, ghaH DaDelchu'meH.
Hamlet	Hechghach'e', qaH? Suvwl'vam quvwojvItHey HoSghaj law'bogh, ghaH wIDechmeH mu'peQchemmaj'e' HoSghaj puSbogh, nuqmo' wIlo'taH?
'oSrIq	nuqjatlh?
Horey'So	Hol pIm Dayaj'eghmoHmeH bIQapbej'a'? yInID neH.
Hamlet	Suvwl'vam'e' DaqelmeH Qu' DughajmoH meq nuq?
'oSrIq	layerteS'e'?
Horey'So	HuchDaj natlh rIntaH. QIchDaj DIlmeH Hoch mu'DeQmeyDaj lo'pu'.
Hamlet	ghaH'e', qaH.
'oSrIq	bIghuHmeH DuSovmoHba' ngoD—
Hamlet	paghna' ngoD vISovba', qaH. 'ach wejpuH, 'e' Dajatlhpu'chugh, choDelmeH, vaj choquvmoHHa'ba'. taH, qaH.
'oSrIq	bIghuHmeH ngoD DaSov: pov layerteS—
Hamlet	'ach povba'mo' layerteS, 'utbe' ghuH, ghaH vI'ovQo'mo'. 'a gholHey pov ghovchugh, ghov'egh je povwI'.
'oSrIq	pov ghaH nuH ruQtaHvIS 'e' vIHechpu'. 'ach batlhDaj quvmoHbogh law'wI' qellu'DI', ghaH rurlu'chu'be'.
Hamlet	nuHDaj nuq?
'oSrIq	qutluch yan je.
Hamlet	vaj cha' nuH ruQ—'a ram.
'oSrIq	qaH, ghaHvaD jav toQDuj SuD ta', 'ej ta'vaD jav romuluSngan may'morgh veSjo' je DoQHa'qang ghaH, 'e' vIqawlaw'. bIH tlhej je luchchajvam: pu'DaH, begh, latlh je. 'ej *I'll be damned*, luHo'lu'meH 'umbej je wej Qanghachpat'e';

	responsive to the hilts, most delicate carriages, and of very liberal conceit.
Hamlet	What call you the carriages?
Horatio	I knew you must be edified by the margent ere you had done.
Osric	The carriages, sir, are the hangers.
Hamlet	The phrase would be more german to the matter, if we could carry cannon by our sides: I would it might be hangers till then. But, on: six Barbary horses against six French swords, their assigns, and three liberal-conceited carriages; that's the French bet against the Danish: Why is this 'imponed,' as you call it?
Osric	The king, sir, hath laid, that in a dozen passes between you and him, he shall not exceed you three hits: he hath laid on twelve for nine; and it would come to immediate trial, if your lordship would vouchsafe the answer.
Hamlet	How if I answer 'no'?
Osric	I mean, my lord, the opposition of your person in trial.
Hamlet	Sir, I will walk here in the hall: if it please his majesty, 'tis the breathing time of day with me: let the foils be brought, the gentleman willing, and the king hold his purpose, I will win for him an I can; if not, I will gain nothing but my shame and the odd hits.
Osric	Shall I re-deliver you e'en so?
Hamlet	To this effect, sir; after what flourish your nature will.
Osric	I commend my duty to your lordship.
Hamlet	Yours, yours.
	[*Exit OSRIC*]
	He does well to commend it himself; there are no tongues else for's turn.
Horatio	This lapwing runs away with the shell on his head.
Hamlet	He did comply with his dug, before he sucked it. Thus has he,—and many more of the same bevy, that I know the dressy age dotes on,—only got the tune of the time, and outward habit of encounter; a kind of yesty collection, which carries them through and through the most fond and winnowed opinions; and do but blow them to their trial, the bubbles are out.
	[*Enter a Lord*]
Lord	My lord, his majesty commended him to you by young Osric, who brings back to him that you attend him in the hall: he sends to know if your pleasure hold to play with Laertes, or that you will take longer time.
Hamlet	I am constant to my purpose; they follow the king's pleasure: if his fitness speaks, mine is ready; now

        nom beq toy'beH Qanghachpat lI'qu',
        'ej mIqta' 'IHchu' bIH.

Hamlet   nuq DapongmeH Qanghachpat Dajatlh?

Horey'So   mu' notlh DayajmeH 'ut bIngghItlh. 'e' vISovchoH rInpa' SoQDaj.

'oSrIq   begh 'oH Qanghachpat'e'.

Hamlet   chaq SoQvaD qar mu', yoDSut tuQlu'chugh je.
    'ach qarbe'mo' ghu'vam, begh 'oH. 'a taH! SuDmeI I,
    jav toQDuj 'ov jav romuluSngan may'morgh,
    luchchaj, wej Qanghachpat 'IHchu' je. tlhIngan jo
    'ov romuluSngan jo 'e' luSuD. qatlh Hochvam
    luDoQHa'qang—mu'lIj vIlo'meH jIvaq.

'oSrIq   wa'maHcha'logh SuQujchuqlI'taHvIS SoH ghaH je, wejlogh
    SoH DuqIppu'chugh ghaH, vaj SoHDaq *infliction*mey chelbe'
    ghaH, SuDmeH 'e' loy ta'. wa'maHcha'logh QujmeH ghaH Doq
    law', Hutlogh SuDmeH ta' Doq puS, 'ej SIbI' tob qoj Daj wanI',
    janglIj maghajmeH 'e' chochaw'chu'bejneSchugh.

Hamlet   'ej chay' qaS, "Qo'" vIjangchugh?

'oSrIq   joHwI', SuDwI'vaD tob qoj Daj wanI', "lu'" Dajangba'DI' 'e'
    vIHechpu'.

Hamlet   qaH, naDev vaSDaq jIyItchu'taH. berghbe'jaj ta' quv; DaH qaS
    qeqpoHwIj. toy'beHDI' nuH, SuvrupDI' Suvwl', 'ej reH may'
    tungbe'chugh ta', vaj ghaHvaD jIQap, laH vIghajchugh;
    vIghajbe'chugh vaj jISaHbe', 'ach jItuHchoHmeH 'ej loQ
    jIrIQmeH jIQap neH.

'oSrIq   De'lIjvam vIQaynIS'a'?

Hamlet   loQ yIQay, qaH—'IHmoHlaw'pu'DI' mu'taylIj.

'oSrIq   reH jIvum jItoy' je, joHwI' quv vIHeQmeH.

Hamlet   lu', lu'.

    [*mej 'oSRIq*]

    vummeH HeQDI', po' ghaH. jaS ghaHvaD HeQ pagh.

Horey'So   Haw' mughato' moH, nachDaq Soy'taHvIS pel'aQ.

Hamlet   SoS je'wI'Du' vanchu' ghaH, choppa'.
    vaj reH mu' Hach IIS neH ghaH, Sarvetlh latlhpu''e'
    je QatmoHtaHbogh bov qal. nughDaq
    QoD'eghtaHvIS, potlhpu' vuDmey tlhopDaq
    mu'tlheghmeyDaj bagh, 'ej SIghmeH luHlaH;
    'a chIch tlheghmeyDaj lupochHa'lu'DI' HuSHa'.

    [*'el yaS*]

yaS   joHwI', vaSDaq ta' loStaH Hamlet, ja' 'oSrIq
    Qup'e' batlh ngeHpu'bogh ta'. DaH layerteS
    DaQujqang pagh Quj DamImqang 'e'
    SovchoHmeH ngeHqa'neS ta'.

Hamlet   choHbe' mIw vIHechbogh; ta' wIv lob. mughomrupDI',
    jeywIj ra' jeyDaj, qaSDI' tupvam tupvetlh joq, laH

	or whensoever, provided I be so able as now.
Lord	The king and queen and all are coming down.
Hamlet	In happy time.
Lord	The queen desires you to use some gentle entertainment to Laertes before you fall to play.
Hamlet	She well instructs me.
	[*Exit Lord*]
Horatio	You will lose this wager, my lord.
Hamlet	I do not think so; since he went into France I have been in continual practise: I shall win at the odds. But thou wouldst not think how ill all's here about my heart: but it is no matter.
Horatio	Nay, good my lord,—
Hamlet	It is but foolery; but it is such a kind of gain-giving as would perhaps trouble a woman.
Horatio	If your mind dislike any thing, obey it: I will forestall their repair hither, and say you are not fit.
Hamlet	Not a whit, we defy augury: there's a special providence in the fall of a sparrow. If it be now, 'tis not to come; if it be not to come, it will be now; if it be not now, yet it will come, the readiness is all: since no man has aught of what he leaves, what is't to leave betimes?
	[*Enter KING CLAUDIUS, QUEEN GERTRUDE, LAERTES, Lords, OSRIC, and Attendants with foils, &c*]
Claudius	Come, Hamlet, come, and take this hand from me.
	[*KING CLAUDIUS puts LAERTES' hand into HAMLET's*]
Hamlet	Give me your pardon, sir: I've done you wrong: But pardon't as you are a gentleman. This presence knows, and you must needs have heard, How I am punish'd with sore distraction. What I have done, That might your nature, honour, and exception Roughly awake, I here proclaim was madness. Was't Hamlet wrong'd Laertes? Never Hamlet: If Hamlet from himself be ta'en away, And when he's not himself does wrong Laertes, Then Hamlet does it not, Hamlet denies it. Who does it, then? His madness: if't be so, Hamlet is of the faction that is wrong'd; His madness is poor Hamlet's enemy. Sir, in this audience, Let my disclaiming from a purpos'd evil Free me so far in your most generous thoughts That I have shot mine arrow o'er the house And hurt my brother.

	vIghajtaHvIS neH.
yaS	tugh paw ta' ta'be' Hoch je.
Hamlet	Do', maj.
yaS	batlh layerteS Davanchu', Quj botaghpa', neH ta'be'.
Hamlet	maHvaD 'oDchu' ghaH.
	[*mej yaS*]
Horey'So	Qujvam Daluj, joHwI'.
Hamlet	'e' vItem. romuluSDaq tlheDpu'DI' reH jIqeqtaH; muQaHmo' Quj pab wuqpu'bogh jIQap. jotHa'qu' tIqwIj ghu' 'e' DajuvlaHbe', 'ach ram.
Horey'So	ghobe', joHwI' QaQ—
Hamlet	Doghlu', 'ach chaq qoH ghIjlaH Qobqoqvam'e'.
Horey'So	Duj yIvoqtaH. naDev paw 'e' vImev 'ej chaHvaD ropqoqllj vIQIj.
Hamlet	va Qo' jay', maQmIgh vISaHQo'. leHII' San, pumDI' je Qa'. DaH qaSchugh, leS qaSbe'; leS qaSbe'chugh, DaH qaS; DaH qaSbe'chugh, leS qaS. reH Suvrup SuvwI'. leSmey'e' lonlu'bogh Sovmo' pagh nuv, qatlh ramHa' lonlu'meH wanI'? taHQo'.
	[*'el* TLHAW'DIYUS *TA', * GHERTLHUD *TA'BE',* LAYERTES, *jawpu',* *'oSRIQ, toy'wI'pu' je, 'etlhmey latlh je qengtaHvIS*]
tlhaw'DIyuS	Ha', Hamlet. Ha'. jIHvo' ghop'e' yItlhap.
	[HAMLET *ghopDaq* LAYERTES *ghop lan* TLHAW'DIYUS *TA'*]
Hamlet	bortaS yIqIIneS, qaH. qaQIH jIH rIntaH. 'ach QIH yIlIjneS, ghIt Darurrupmo'. ghu'vam IuSov yejquv. DaQoylaw'pu' je: muSengtaH maw'taHghachwIj. pe'vII qa'lI', batlhlIj, pe'vII bortaSIIj je lurIHbogh Hoch'e' vIta'bogh qaSmoH maw'taHghachwIj. DaH 'e' vImaq. layerteS QIHlaHpu''a' Hamlet? not. Hamletvo' yaHchugh Hamlet, 'ej layerteS QIHchugh ghaH, Hamletna' ghaHbe'taHvIS, vaj QIH ruchbe'pu' Hamlet. tembej Hamlet. toH ruch 'Iv? maw'taHghach. 'ej teHchugh ngoDvam, vaj noDqangwI'pu' ghomDaq jeS je Hamlet. Hamlet Do'Ha'vaD jagh Da maw'taHghachDaj. qaH, SaHtaHvIS yejquv, chIch chavvam mIgh vIruchpu' 'e' vItemmo', pung 'angbogh yablIjvaD jIchunqu'jaj. vaj juHDaj DungDaq pu' baHHa'chugh vay', 'ej bong loDnI'Daj rIQmoHchugh ghaH, vaj ghaH DIvjaj law', jIH DIvjaj puS.

Laertes   I am satisfied in nature,
Whose motive, in this case, should stir me most
To my revenge: but in my terms of honour
I stand aloof; and will no reconcilement
Till by some elder masters of known honour
I have a voice and precedent of peace
To keep my name ungor'd. But till that time
I do receive your offer'd love like love,
And will not wrong it.

Hamlet   I embrace it freely;
And will this brother's wager frankly play.—
Give us the foils; Come on.

Laertes   Come, one for me.

Hamlet   I'll be your foil, Laertes; in mine ignorance
Your skill shall, like a star i' the darkest night,
Stick fiery off indeed.

Laertes   You mock me, sir.

Hamlet   No, by this hand.

Claudius   Give them the foils, young Osric. Cousin Hamlet,
You know the wager?

Hamlet   Very well, my lord
Your grace hath laid the odds o' the weaker side.

Claudius   I do not fear it; I have seen you both:
But since he is better'd, we have therefore odds.

Laertes   This is too heavy, let me see another.

Hamlet   This likes me well. These foils have all a length?

               [*They prepare to play*]

Osric   Ay, my good lord.

Claudius   Set me the stoops of wine upon that table,—
If Hamlet give the first or second hit,
Or quit in answer of the third exchange,
Let all the battlements their ordnance fire;
The king shall drink to Hamlet's better breath;
And in the cup an union shall he throw,
Richer than that which four successive kings
In Denmark's crown have worn. Give me the cups;
And let the kettle to the trumpet speak,
The trumpet to the cannoneer without,
The cannons to the heavens, the heavens to earth,
'Now the king drinks to Hamlet.'—Come, begin:—
And you, the judges, bear a wary eye.

Hamlet   Come on, sir.

Laertes   Come, my lord.

               [*They play*]

Hamlet   One.

layerteS   yon tIqwIj.
'ej jIHvaD ghu'vammo' bortaS tungHa'nISqu'
tIq mo'. 'ach batlhwIj Dotlh vIqelnISmo',
SoHvo' jIHopnIS. boqmaj vItaghQo' je—
lambe'meH pongwIj batlh, vuDchaj, rojmab
nubwI'na' je lunobpa' batlh DIch qup.
'ach qaSpa' poHvetlh, batlh muSHa'ghach 'oSmeH,
muSHa'ghachlIj vIlaj, 'ej vInoDQo'.

Hamlet   vIneHqu': neHtaHghachlIj'e' vInaD.
'ej jIyuDHa', loDnI' HuchQujvam'e'
wIruchtaHvIS. Ha', maHvaD 'etlh tInob.
Ha', 'etlhmey.

layerteS   'etlh vItobnIS. wa' HInob.

Hamlet   chojeymeH, 'etlhlIj jey qa'ang, layerteS.
jItlhIbmo', ghI'boj Sech rur Hay'meH laHlIj:
povmo' tugh bochbej 'oH.

layerteS   chovaqlaw', qaH.

Hamlet   ghobe', qaH. ghop vI'IpmoH.

tlhaw'DIyuS   'eH, oSrIq, chaHvaD 'etlhHommey tInob.
Hamlet qorDu'ghot, SoHvaD jo vISuDpu'.
jo DaSov'a'?

Hamlet   HIja', vISovchu'neS.
lujwI' DaboQmeH jo DaSuDlaw'neS.

tlhaw'DIyuS   jIQoch. laHraj vIbejpu', qen SuSuvDI'.
'a Dub'egh ghaH. vaj SoHvaD Quj vImaSmoH.

layerteS   Qo'. 'ughqu' 'etlhvam. jIHvaD latlh yI'ang.

Hamlet   mubelmoH 'etlhvam. tIqtaHvIS rap'a' bIH?

               [*QujmeH qeq chaH*]

'oSrIq   HIja', joH QaQ.

tlhaw'DIyuS   raSvetlhDaq HIq HIvje' tIlan. peqIm:
Qapla' wa', cha' ghap Suqchugh Hamlet, qIpDI';
pagh wejDIch Suqchugh, jeyDaj cha'DIch noDDI'—
bachjaj Hoch may'morghmey. 'ej Hamlet vanmeH,
HIqvam tlhutlh ta'. HIvje'Daq qut vIchaghmoH.
tlho'qut tIn law'qu', Hoch qut'e' ben ngaSbogh
loS Qo'noS ta'pu' Qav mIv'a' tIn puS.
HIvje' tInob. chuS'ughvaD jachjaj DIr.
bachwI'vaD jachjaj je chuS'ugh. 'ej chalvaD
jachjaj je pu'beH. yuQvaD jachjaj chal:
"DaH Hamlet vanmeH tlhutlhlIl' ta'." peruch.
Ha'. 'ej noHwI'pu', HojlI'jaj mInDu'raj.

Hamlet   Ha', qaH.

layerteS   Ha', joH.

               [*Quj chaH*]

Hamlet   Qap!

Laertes	No.
Hamlet	Judgment.
Osric	A hit, a very palpable hit.
Laertes	Well;—again.
Claudius	Stay, give me drink.—Hamlet, this pearl is thine; Here's to thy health.—
	[*Trumpets sound, and cannon shot off within*]
	Give him the cup.
Hamlet	I'll play this bout first;—set it by awhile. Come.—
	[*They play*]
	Another hit; what say you?
Laertes	A touch, a touch, I do confess.
Claudius	Our son shall win.
Gertrude	He's fat, and scant of breath.— Here, Hamlet, take my napkin, rub thy brows; The queen carouses to thy fortune, Hamlet.
Hamlet	Good madam!
Claudius	Gertrude, do not drink.
Gertrude	I will, my lord; I pray you, pardon me.
Claudius	[*Aside*] It is the poison'd cup; it is too late.
Hamlet	I dare not drink yet, madam; by and by.
Gertrude	Come, let me wipe thy face.
Laertes	My lord, I'll hit him now.
Claudius	I do not think't.
Laertes	[*Aside*] And yet 'tis almost 'gainst my conscience.
Hamlet	Come, for the third, Laertes: you but dally; I pray you, pass with your best violence: I am afeard you make a wanton of me.
Laertes	Say you so? come on.
	[*They play*]
Osric	Nothing, neither way.
Laertes	Have at you now!
	[*LAERTES wounds HAMLET; then in scuffling, they change rapiers, and HAMLET wounds LAERTES*]
Claudius	Part them; they are incensed.
Hamlet	Nay, come, again.
	[*QUEEN GERTRUDE falls*]
Osric	Look to the queen there, ho!

layertcS	Qo'!
Hamlet	noH!
'oSrIq	maj. ghaH mupta'. ghaH mupbejta'.
layerteS	toH. SuH, maHay'qa' jay'.
tlhaw'DIyuS	wej. HIq HInob. SuH, Hamlet, qutllj 'oH. Qapla' yIghaj.

[*chuS chuS'ugh. 'emDaq bachlu'*]

ghaHvaD HIvje' yInob.

Hamlet	Qo', joH. 'ay' cha' vIrInmoHqang, jItlhutlhpa'. yIroQ. Ha'.

[*Qujqa' chaH*]

Qap! qamupqa'. nuq DaHar?

layerteS	choqIp. choqIp. jIchID.
tlhaw'DIyuS	tugh Qap puqma'.
ghertlhuD	va, ror 'ej tlhovchoH ghaH. Hamlet, Sut 'ay' yItlhap. SuH, Huy' yIQaDmoH. bIDo'meH tlhutlhII' je ta'be'nal, Hamlet.
Hamlet	majQa', joH.
tlhaw'DIyuS	ghertlhuD, yItlhutlhQo'.
ghertlhuD	jItlhutlh, joHwI'. Do' jIHvaD yInoDQo'.
tlhaw'DIyuS	[*pegh'egh*] tarwIj HIvje' 'oH. QI'yaH. paSbej Hoch.
Hamlet	jItlhutlhmeH jIngIlQo', joH. tugh vItlhutlh.
ghertlhuD	qabIIj vIQaDmoH; Ha'.
layerteS	joH, tugh vIqIpbej rIntaH.
tlhaw'DIyuS	'e' vIHon.
layerteS	[*pegh'egh*] 'a ghobwIj SujchoHlaw' wanI' wInabbogh.
Hamlet	layerteS, Ha'! may' wej wIruchrup jay'! bIHoblaw' neH. bIHIvtaHvIS yIralchoH. maHay'taHvIS, puq tlhIb jIH 'e' DaHarlaw'.
layerteS	qar'a'? Ha'.

[*Quj chaH*]

'oSrIq	Qapbe' cha' ghol.
layerteS	DaH ruv vISuq!

[*HAMLET rIQmoH LAYERTES. SoltaHvIS,*
'etlh mech chaH. LAYERTES rIQmoH HAMLET]

tlhaw'DIyuS	tIwav! tIwav! DaH QeHchoH.
Hamlet	Qo'! HIvqa'!

[*pum GHERTLHUD TA'BE'*]

'oSrIq	mev! 'eH, pa' ta'be' yIQorgh!

Horatio	They bleed on both sides.—How is it, my lord?
Osric	How is't, Laertes?
Laertes	Why, as a woodcock to mine own springe, Osric; I am justly kill'd with mine own treachery.
Hamlet	How does the queen?
Claudius	She swounds to see them bleed.
Gertrude	No, no, the drink, the drink,—O my dear Hamlet,— The drink, the drink!—I am poison'd.

               [*Dies*]

Hamlet	O villany!—Ho! let the door be lock'd: Treachery! Seek it out.

               [*LAERTES falls*]

Laertes	It is here, Hamlet: Hamlet, thou art slain; No medicine in the world can do thee good; In thee there is not half an hour of life; The treacherous instrument is in thy hand, Unbated and envenom'd: the foul practise Hath turn'd itself on me; lo, here I lie, Never to rise again: thy mother's poison'd: I can no more:—the king, the king's to blame.
Hamlet	The point envenom'd too!— Then, venom, to thy work.

               [*Stabs KING CLAUDIUS*]

All	Treason! treason!
Claudius	O, yet defend me, friends; I am but hurt.
Hamlet	Here, thou incestuous, murderous, damned Dane, Drink off this potion.—Is thy union here? Follow my mother.

               [*KING CLAUDIUS dies*]

Laertes	He is justly served; It is a poison temper'd by himself.— Exchange forgiveness with me, noble Hamlet: Mine and my father's death come not upon thee, Nor thine on me.

               [*Dies*]

Hamlet	Heaven make thee free of it! I follow thee.— I am dead, Horatio.—Wretched queen, adieu!— You that look pale and tremble at this chance, That are but mutes or audience to this act, Had I but time,—as this fell sergeant, death, Is strict in his arrest,—O, I could tell you—, But let it be.—Horatio, I am dead; Thou livest; report me and my cause aright To the unsatisfied.
Horatio	Never believe it: I am more an antique Roman than a Dane,—

Horey'So   cha' DopmeyDaq chagh 'Iw. DotIh nuq, joH QaQ?

'oSrIq   DotIh nuq, layerteS?

layerteS   qoHQa' vIDa, 'ej bong jIjon'eghpu'.
                   muHoH 'urmangwIj may.

Hamlet   ta'be' DotIh nuq?

tlhaw'DIyuS   vulchoHba', rIQmo' chaH.

ghertlhuD   Qo'. Qo'. HIq! HIq! va, Hamlet, tIqwIj puq!
                   HIq! HIq! muHoHpu' tar!

                   [*Hegh*]

Hamlet   Qu'vatlh! HeS mIghqu'! 'eH, lojmIt yIngaQmoH!
                   'urmang! 'eH, 'oH yISam! [pum layerteS]

                   [*pum LAYERTES*]

layerteS   naDev 'oH, Hamlet. Hamlet quv, DaHoHlu'.
                   DaH SoHvaD lo'laH 'u'vam naQ pagh Hergh.
                   bIyInmeH SoHvaD ratlh rep bIDHom neH.
                   bong ghopIIjDaq 'urmang chavwI' Daghaj.
                   jej 'etlh, 'ej tarDaq ngoHlu'. chegh nab mIgh,
                   'ej DaH mumuppu' 'oH. naDev jIQot,
                   'ej not jIHu'qa'bej. tar tlhutlh SoSII'.
                   pagh latlh vIja'laH. pIch ghaj ta'. ghaj ta'.

Hamlet   'etlhDaq tar lanlu' jay'!
                   vaj tar, DaH rInjaj Qu'lIj.

                   [*TLHAW'DIYUS TA' DuQ*]

'oSrIq, jawpu' je 'urmang! 'urmang!

tlhaw'DIyuS   HIHub, juppu'wI'. DaH jIrIQchoH neH.

Hamlet   'eH, wembogh, chotbogh Qo'noS pIn quvHa'.
                   tarvam yItlhutlhchu'. tlho'qoq DaSam'a'?
                   SoSwI' yItlha'.

                   [*Hegh TLHAW'DIYUS TA'*]

layerteS   majQa'. ruv Suqpu' ghaH.
                   tar nobta' ghaH. 'a DaH manoDchuqQo'jaj,
                   Hamlet. vavwI' HoH, HoHwIj je Hoch pIch
                   vIqII. 'ej HoHlIj pIch yIqIIneS je.

                   [*Hegh*]

Hamlet   DuchunmoHjaj yo' qIj! SIbI' qatlha'.
                   Horey'So, tugh jIHegh. ta'be' Do'Ha',
                   Qapla'. SuH, lotvam bejvIpbogh ghot'e',
                   SuH, lut DawI'pu' tam, 'IjwI'pu' joq:
                   ratlhchugh neH poH—va, moDlaw' qoptaHvIS
                   Sogh bergh, Heghqa'—vaj tugh Saja'laHbej—
                   'a ram. jIHegh, Horey'So. wej bIHegh.
                   jIHvaD yIja', 'ej batlhwIj Honchugh vay',
                   vaj chaHvaD 'oH yItl'.

Horey'So   Qo', vIta'Qo'.
                   tlhIngan jIHQo'. romuluSngan vIDarup.

Here's yet some liquor left.

Hamlet   As thou'rt a man,
Give me the cup; let go; by heaven, I'll have't.—
O good Horatio, what a wounded name,
Things standing thus unknown, shall live behind me!
If thou didst ever hold me in thy heart
Absent thee from felicity awhile,
And in this harsh world draw thy breath in pain,
To tell my story.—

[*March afar off, and shot within*]

What warlike noise is this?

Osric   Young Fortinbras, with conquest come from Poland,
To the ambassadors of England gives
This warlike volley.

Hamlet   O, I die, Horatio;
The potent poison quite o'er-crows my spirit:
I cannot live to hear the news from England;
But I do prophesy the election lights
On Fortinbras: he has my dying voice;
So tell him, with the occurrents, more and less,
Which have solicited.—The rest is silence.

[*Dies*]

Horatio   Now cracks a noble heart.—Good night, sweet prince;
And flights of angels sing thee to thy rest!
Why does the drum come hither?

[*March within*]

[*Enter FORTINBRAS, the English Ambassadors, and others*]

Fortinbras   Where is this sight?

Horatio   What is it ye would see?
If aught of woe or wonder, cease your search.

Fortinbras   This quarry cries on havoc.—O proud death,
What feast is toward in thine eternal cell,
That thou so many princes at a shot
So bloodily hast struck?

First Ambassador   The sight is dismal;
And our affairs from England come too late:
The ears are senseless that should give us hearing,
To tell him his commandment is fulfill'd,
That Rosencrantz and Guildenstern are dead:
Where should we have our thanks?

Horatio   Not from his mouth,
Had it the ability of life to thank you:
He never gave commandment for their death.
But since, so jump upon this bloody question,
You from the Polack wars, and you from England,
Are here arriv'd give order that these bodies
High on a stage be placed to the view;

            wej lojlaw' HIqvam.

Hamlet	Qu'vatlh, batlh Daghajchugh,

HIvje' HInob. ghop teq! baQa' vIjonbej.
Horey'So, ngoDmey teH luSovlu'be'chugh,
tugh rIQbej pongwIj batlh, jIHeghDI' rIntaH.
'eH, qaStaHvIS wa' tupHom, choparHa'chugh,
vaj loQ neH Do'taHghachvetlhvo' yIDach,
'ej 'u'vam webDaq lutwIj naQ Daja'meH,
'oy'lI'jaj tlhuHlIj, jup.

    [*Daq HopDaq chuS yItmeH QoQ, 'et 'emDaq baHlu'*]

                      qatlh chuS veS QoQ?

'oSrIq	qInSayavo' chegh charghbogh vortIbraS.

          tera'Duy vanmeH baH.

Hamlet	jIHegh, Horey'So.

'ej qa'wI' DungDaq mIytaH tarvetlh HoS.
tera'vo' De' vIQoylaHbe' jIyaHmo'.
'a cho'meH vortIbraS luwIv yejquv,
'e' pIH leSSovwIj. 'ej jIHeghtaHvIS,
cho'meH vIwIvmeH jIH jIjeS. vaj ghaHvaD
Hoch ngoD, Hoch ngoDHom je Daja'pu'DI',
'ej Hu' jIH mutungHa'—DaH tamchoH Hoch.

    [*Hegh*]

Horey'So	DaH ghor tIq quv. Qapla', joH quv. Qapla'.

blIeSmeH DaH DuDorjaj yo' qIj Dujmey!
SuH, qatlh naDev chol 'In?

    [*'emDaq chuS yItwI' QoQ*]

    [*'el VORTIBRAS, tera' Duypu', latlh je*]

vortIbraS	lotna' vIlegh jay'!
Horey'So	nuq Dalegh DaneH?

'ItmeH pagh yay'meH vay' Daleghqangchugh,
blInej vaj 'e' yImev.

vortIbraS	qaSpu' HoH'a',

'e' maq lomghomvam! va, blHemba', Hegh!
molvenglIjDaq yupma' DaqeqlawlI'mo',
joHpu'vam law' DamupmeH quq 'Iw lotlIj!

Duy wa'DIch	qaSbej Qugh'a'. DaHjaj naDev mapaSlaw',

tera'vo' De' wIqengDI'. De' wIja'DI',
luQoynIS teS. 'a DaH pagh De' lutu' blH.
vaj Qu"e' ra'ta'bogh voDleH wIchavmoH,
'ej Heghpu' roSenQatlh; Hegh ghIlDeSten je,
'e' QoylaHbe'. 'Ivvo' Qu' tlho' wISuq?

Horey'So	not nujDajvo' boSuqbej, 'e' yISov,

lItlho'meH ghaH wej yaHpu'chugh je yInDaj.
Hegh not 'e' ra'. 'a DaH naDev Supawmo',
rInDI' 'Iw may'vam qu'—tera'vo' tlhIH,
qInSaya noHmeyvo' SoH—DaH yIra':
lubejlu'meH muchDaqmey jenDaq lomvam
lulanlu'nIS. wej Sovbogh qo' nganpu'vaD

And let me speak to the yet unknowing world
How these things came about: so shall you hear
Of carnal, bloody, and unnatural acts;
Of accidental judgments, casual slaughters;
Of deaths put on by cunning and forc'd cause;
And, in this upshot, purposes mistook
Fall'n on the inventors' heads: all this can I
Truly deliver.

Fortinbras   Let us haste to hear it,
And call the noblest to the audience.
For me, with sorrow I embrace my fortune:
I have some rights of memory in this kingdom,
Which now to claim my vantage doth invite me.

Horatio   Of that I shall have also cause to speak,
And from his mouth whose voice will draw on more:
But let this same be presently perform'd,
Even while men's minds are wild: lest more mischance
On plots and errors, happen.

Fortinbras   Let four captains
Bear Hamlet like a soldier to the stage;
For he was likely, had he been put on,
To have prov'd most royally: and, for his passage,
The soldiers' music and the rites of war
Speak loudly for him.—
Take up the bodies.—such a sight as this
Becomes the field, but here shows much amiss.
Go, bid the soldiers shoot.

[*A dead march. Exeunt, bearing off the dead
bodies; after which a peal of ordnance is shot off*]

wanI'meyvam mcqna' vIDellaHchu'.
HeS'a', wem'a' je, 'Iw je ta'mey ral;
Qagh yoj je, HoH lunablu'be'bogh je;
Hegh'e' je raDpu'bogh Duj 'ong, meq ngeb je;
'ej, qaSmo' Hoch, 'oghwI'pu'chajvaD Qaw'bogh
Qu''e' ta'Ha'lu'bogh je, Hoch boQoylaH.
'ej Hoch vIjQIjlaHchu'.

vortIbraS	SIbI' DIQoy.

'ej 'IjmeH Hoch chuQun potlhwI' yIra'.
jIDo'choH batlh DaH 'e' vIlajqang jIH
jI'IQtaHvIS je. wo'vam Dun vIche'meH
DIb lulljbe'lu'bogh vIghajtaH jIH.
'ej wo' vIDoQmeH DaH mura'law' 'ebwIj.

Horey'So tugh ghu'vam De' vIja' je. De'vetlh'e'
jatlhmo' nuj potlh, vaj nujmey law'qu' jIjmoH.
'ach DaH wanI'mey naQ vIDelchoHchu',
qu'taHvIS ghot yabDu'. vaj tugh qaSbe'jaj
latlh lot. DaH yapbej QuSmey, Qaghmey je.

vortIbraS 'eH, muchDaq'a'Daq Hamlet quv luqeng
loS HoD. vaj batlh SuvwI''a'vaD peDa.
Hamlet joH toblu'chugh, vaj ta'na' mojlaw'.
'ej yo' qIj 'elmeH, ghaHvaD HoSchoHqu'
mang QoQ, veS tay je.
lommey tIwoH. vIq DaqDaq motlh 'Iwngengvam.
'a QI'yaH, naDev joch 'ej taQqu' Sengvam.
Ha'. baHmeH negh yIra'.

[*chuS lom vanbogh yItwI' QoQ'e'. mej chaH,
lommey qengtaHvIS. qaSpu'DI', vanmeH baHlu'*]

APPENDICES

Appendix I: Endnotes

Act I Scene I

Long live the king: *lit.* May the Empire endure! — the traditional Klingon expression of loyalty.

Not a mouse stirring: *lit.* not even a bug moved.

the Dane: *lit.* the master of Kronos. *Khamlet* is set in a time when the emperor's control over all regions in the empire was not yet consolidated. For that reason, the emperor is still regarded in the play primarily as ruler of Kronos, the Klingon Home World, and only nominally as ruler of the Klingon Empire; many of the outlying reaches of the empire were still under the control of the various Houses (such as the House of Duras and the House of Kinshaya), which retained a great deal of autonomy.

has this thing appeared again tonight? *lit.* did the apparent energy-being appear again tonight? At various points in this scene, a distinction is made between spirits or souls (**qa'**), which belong to the supernatural, and energy beings (**HoSDo'**), who would be a 'rational' explanation for the phenomena the watch are witnessing. Similarly, the pronoun used to refer to the spirit changes (as it does in the Terran version) from "they" (**bIH**) to "he" (**ghaH**), as the watch come to identify it with the King. Note that **HoSDo'** is always in the plural; Klingons (and most other humanoids) find it difficult to tell whether there are one or more energy beings in a room at any one time.

your ears, / that are so fortified against our story: *lit.* you seem to have prepared a force field for your ears, to stop our story from entering.

How now, Horatio! *lit.* What do you want, Horatio! "What do you want" is the traditional Klingon for "hello;" it is a short leap from there to a sarcastic "what's up?" or "what's the matter?"

when he the ambitious Norway combated: *lit.* when he duelled with the most insubordinate head of [the House of] Duras. The emperor's control over the empire was still lax enough, and his status as "first among equals" with the heads of the Houses was still low enough, that heads such as Vortibrash Senior could challenge him to a duel, and representatives of the House of Kinshaya could demand a succession ritual (**ja'chuq**) before the emperor's death, to unseat him.

sledded Polacks: *lit.* the Kinshaya in their armoured vehicles.

twice before: *lit.* now, three times (counting all appearances)

brazen cannon: *lit.* battle arrays.

whose sore task / does not divide the Sunday from the week: *lit.* their task is so urgent, that any break seems illegal for them.

all those his lands, / which he stood seiz'd of: as in the Terran version, there is a distinction between territory personally belonging to the head of a House or an emperor (the lands Khamlet Senior and Vortibrash Senior were prepared to gamble), and the territory belonging to the House itself, or the empire. These territories would not be affected by the wager.

of unimproved mettle hot and full: *lit.* because he is filled and heated up with an ensign's bravery, yet to be trained by time. It is unlikely that Vortibrash Junior actually was an ensign; Shex'pir is merely saying he has the bravado characteristic of brash young junior officers.

to some enterprise / that hath a stomach in't: *lit.* the youngster made their bile fierce (**HuH qu'moH**) for a gory quest [quest of bile (**HuH Qu'**)].

In the most high and palmy state of Rome, / a little ere the mightiest Julius fell: *lit.* In ancient times, in the honorable, prosperous empire of Romulus, a little before the truly great Yulyush fell. Yulyush is the legendary Romulan leader Yulyush Kayshar — held in high esteem by the Klingons for initiating the Klingon-Romulan detente. Another of Shex'pir's tragedies commemorates this leader.

Cock crows: *lit.* the dawn-voiced Kra. (A Klingon animal.)

'gainst that season comes, / wherein our Saviour's birth is celebrated: *lit.* when the season of Military Day [**QI'lop**, the main Klingon holiday] is coming, when we prepare to honor the soldiers of the Black Fleet [in which Klingon warriors are believed to fight on after death.]

Do you consent we shall acquaint him with it: *lit.* We will let him know of it. Any disagreement? (Or: Disagreed?) — and not, as in Federation Standard, "Agreed?" Klingon has 'disagree' as the basic verb (**Qoch**), and 'agree' as the derived verb (**Qochbe'**). There are, of course, clear implications to be drawn from this about the interaction between Klingon language and culture.

Act I Scene II

dropping eye. Some Terran commentators have taken the references to tears (**nIjDI'** "leaked," **mInbIQ** "eye-water," **bIQtIq'a'** "great river," **bIQHal** "fountain") as proving the Terran origin of the play (as is well known, Klingons do not have tear-ducts). However, there is an extensive history in Klingon theatre of references to tears. It is now believed this was a dramatic convention, originating from attempts by playwrights in some of the gorier schools of theatre to shock their audiences, by attributing this non-Klingon characteristic to their heroes. By Shex'pir's time, this had become a mere dramatic commonplace. The practice has proved so pervasive, it has worked its way into Klingon mythology (thus, Kahless is said to have filled the ocean with his tears when his brother cast his father's sword into the sea.)

impotent and bedrid: it is highly unlikely that the head of a Klingon House would endure such a state for long before suiciding in disgrace. Klaw'diyush is probably doing nothing more than scoring points against his political opponent.

out of his subject: any armies raised by a House, without the emperor's consent, and only from within the House's territory, would be interpreted as seditious.

to France: *lit.* to Romulus. Relations between the Klingons and the Romulans were still cordial at the time the play is set in.

my cousin Hamlet, and my son. / A little more than kin, and less than kind *lit.* Khamlet: my honored clansman (**qorDu''a'ghot** = extended-family member), and my son. / It's a tiny family (**qorDu'Hom**) [The family has shrunk after the death of the King, and Khamlet does not consider Klaw'diyush worthy of filling his shoes — or the numbers in the imperial family], and it seems the son is being scavenged at (**qorlu'**; Khamlet puns on the similarity between the words for 'family' and 'scavenge').

How is it that the clouds still hang on you? / Not so, my lord. I am too much in the sun: *lit.* Why have you preserved (**choq**) your black clothes for such a long time? / Not so, my lord. The son (**puqloD**) is not an elder (**quploD**). So I don't seem able to succeed (**cho'**) to any position at all. [Khamlet sarcastically attributes his failure to succeed to the throne to being under-age. Pretending to mishear Klaw'diyush as saying "why have you succeeded to black clothes," he answers "it seems I can't succeed to any rank at all."]

nighted colour: *lit.* your clothing, which seems made of a black hole.

'tis unmanly grief: *lit.* A warrior refuses to act like such a fool.

Wittenberg: *lit.* Vulcan. What a Klingon prince (and his loyal friend) should be doing going to university in Vulcan is never made clear, particularly as the characters still maintain the Klingons' enduring contempt for the Vulcans. There are, however, precedents for such exchanges, especially during the Klingon-Romulan detente. One would expect that a Vulcan-educated Klingon would make for broad comedy rather than tragedy. In fact (and all the major Klingon commentators are in agreement on this), it makes the tragedy even more poignant than the Terran version: while he retains a sense of Klingon honor, Khamlet is culturally dispossessed, given to rationalizing and talk instead of action — unlike Layertesh and Vortibrash, who he holds in such esteem throughout the play. His development through the play is seen as a voyage back to his true Klingon roots, until, at the conclusion of the play, he dies in honor.

or that the Everlasting had not fixed / His canon 'gainst self-slaughter: *lit.* If only the customs of warriors' honor, which refuse to allow a yet-to-be-dishonored warrior to kill himself, would allow it!

Hyperion to a Satyr: *lit.* If one considers the new king, he is no more than a tribble, and the king of yesteryear was the sun.

like Niobe, all tears: *lit.* Acting like a fountain, in that she was always crying.

Than I to Hercules: *lit.* then I resemble Kahless the Unforgettable too.

Elsinore: *lit.* Klin (the imperial district of Kronos).

Would I had met my dearest foe in heaven: *lit.* If I saw Fek'lhr while I was in Paradise.

If it assume my noble father's person: *lit.* If it has my noble father's eyes.

though all the earth o'erwhelm them: *lit.* Even if the galactic rim conceals them, for us not to find them.

Act I Scene III

as the winds give benefit: *lit.* whenever the Romulan Neutral Zone allows it (outbreaks of fighting over the Neutral Zone were notorious for interfering with communications, even during the Klingon-Romulan detente).

for he himself is subject to his birth: *lit.* even he, who makes others serve, must [himself] serve his great rank.

puff'd and reckless libertine: *lit.* a proud man, a great gambler, and a vessel out of control (Klingon proverbial expression for a undisciplined person.)

The wind sits in the shoulder of your sail: *lit.* your engines are being energized.

unsifted in such perilous circumstance: *lit.* you have not navigated many ships (Klingon proverbial expression for inexperience.)

Think yourself a baby... you'll tender me a fool: *lit.* Believe that you are a baby, because you kept on listening to these speeches (**SoQ**) while he was sabotaging you (**Sorgh**). Close (**SoQ**) your ears (**qogh**) to his speeches. And if you don't close your ears (or: belt) (**qogh**) — I am certainly offending the word, as I keep violently maneuvering it — then, as soon as your belt (**qogh**) falls (**pum**) [namely, when you have sex with him], I will be accused (**pum**) of being a true fool.

in honorable fashion. / Ay, 'fashion' you may call it: *lit.* His manner (procedure) was honorable. / Come on! It is merely his procedure (**mIw**) for bragging (**mIy**).

set your entreatments at a higher rate / than a command to parle: *lit.* and be doubtful that he is requesting two lovers [the two of you] merely to have a conversation, when he says "Grrrr" [the Klingon signal of sexual availability].

breathing like sanctified and pious bawds, the better to beguile: *lit.* and, in order to succeed at tempting, they act like human emissaries: they use big speeches, and so-called honor.

Act I Scene IV

and the swaggering upspring reels: *lit.* In running a great curse-warfare [a favorite pastime in Klingon bars], that great 'warrior' and his partners are most brave.

the kettle-drum and trumpet thus bray out/ the triumph of his pledge: *lit.* the 'heavy-noise' and the 'skin-drum' (Klingon musical instruments) proclaim the great victory of his throat.

Rhenish: *lit.* Romulan ale.

east and west: *lit.* On the sides of both the Neutral Zone and the galactic rim.

pith and marrow: *lit.* middle of the bone, and ships' engines.

or fortune's star: *lit.* or else their Fate is fed up with them.

his virtues else, be they as pure as grace: *lit.* even if all their honor is impressive enough that they could behave like Kahless.

the dram of evil...: *lit.* for the matter of true honor to be disgraced, merely the dirt beneath one's fingernails is evil enough for a discommendation to...

I do not set my life at a pin's fee: *lit.* A paperclip is more important to me than my life is.

Nemean lion's nerve: *lit.* Fek'lhr's muscles.

Act I Scene V

and duller shouldst thou be... wouldst thou not stir in this: *lit.* And even if, in refusing to accomplish anything, you might act like a Vulcan plant when it came to fighting [in a Klingon's eyes, as inert as a warrior could possibly get], you would still be ready to do your duty.

swift as quicksilver: *lit.* like the admiral's Bird of Prey.

unhouseled, disappointed, unaneled.. on my head: *lit.* No warrior stared at my eyes, or shouted beside my corpse. I was not prepared to enter the Black Fleet. My opportunities to repent were all gone. And, hell! While I still bore all my defects, he sent me off to be court-martialled by Fek'lhr.

Hillo, ho, ho, my lord! / Hillo, ho, ho, boy! Come, bird, come: *lit.* Come on! (**Ha'! Ha'!**) Come on, my lord! / Hahaha! A soldier must be laughing!

not I, my lord, by heaven. / Nor I, my lord: *lit.* The stars will speak before I do. / They will, lord. (Khorey'sho quotes one of the traditional Klingon secrecy proverbs.)

I will go pray: *lit.* I'm off to do calisthenics.

These are but wild and whirling words, my lord. / I am sorry they offend you, heartily: *lit.* These words are merely crazy (**maw'**) and weird, honored lord. / I am really sorry that they offended (**maw**) you, friend. Quite sorry.

Saint Patrick: *lit.* The chancellor of the Netherworld.

Hic et ubique: While Federation Standard is considered a language of learning by Klingons (with sometimes disastrous results, as with Oshrik), it is not associated with conjuring the dead, as Latin was in mediaeval Earth. Khamlet is probably being playfully disrespectful, using a non-Klingon language in the moment where it would be least appropriate (before the spirit of an ancestor.)

this is wondrous strange! / And therefore as a stranger give it welcome: *lit.* The situation is unlawful! (**Hat**) / So endure the temperature (**Hat**), and when it gets hot, don't build a fire by your own side (an old Klingon proverb, akin to the Terran "If you can't stand the heat, get out of the kitchen".)

so help you mercy: *lit.* so that you may enter the Black Fleet with honor.

so grace and mercy at your most need help you: *lit.* may you be lucky enough that someone cries out to the Black Fleet over your corpses.

and still your fingers on your lips, I pray: *lit.* And listen: no one can eavesdrop at any open door. (Another Klingon secrecy saying.)

Act II Scene I

Addicted so and so: *lit.* He kills these gagh (Klingon proverbial expression for counterproductive activities, gagh being serpent worms meant to be eaten alive.)

to youth and liberty: *lit.* to young men who have not yet fought (and whose maturity has thus not yet been established in battle.)

the taints of liberty: *lit.* the taints of a cadet who has yet to navigate a warrior's vessel (Klingon proverbial expression for inexperience.)

of general assault: *lit.* and he is willing to attack all things (**Doch Hoch**; a characteristically pedantic way of saying 'anything' (**Hoch**)).

as 'twere a thing a little soiled i' th' working: *lit.* one who would eat pipyus must break a few pipyus claws.

at tennis: *lit.* while competing at target practice.

your bait of falsehood takes this carp of truth: *lit.* your fake dumpling will obviously capture the Kra (Klingon animal) of truth.

and thus do we of wisdom and of reach / with windlasses and with assays of bias / by indirections find directions out: *lit.* And to sight (**puS**) targets (**DoS**) our phasers have to jump (**Sup**) and flood (**SoD**) the area. Because we are clever and perceptive enough, we claim our territory (**DoQ**) as soon as we maneuver our engines (**QoD**). (Anagram puns are not to all Klingons' liking, but they would certainly be pleasing to someone of Polonyush's temperament. As at least one Klingon commentator has noted, "Only Polonyush could come up with phasers jumping and flooding the area.").

It seems it is as proper to our age...: *lit.* When a person is old, they use a big scoop (Klingon proverbial expression for exaggerating) for their opinion; and while they are young, they carry a small scoop (Klingon proverbial expression for minimising) for their discipline.

Act II Scene II

brought up with him: *lit.* you have been together, while learning about honor [as all young Klingons must.]

to his youth and 'haviour: *lit.* because you are young and belligerent.

and here give up ourselves in the full bent: *lit.* and we are more willing to serve you, than is a phaser rifle about to fire.

Amen! *lit.* may fate allow it.

Give first admittance to th' ambassadors: *lit.* Let our ambassadors visit you, before I speak. The "our" illustrates how "instrumental" Polonyush is to the running of the state.

well, we shall sift him: *lit.* I'll even use a mind sifter.

the Polack: *lit.* The Kinshaya (a House which, unlike the Houses of Duras and Hamlet, was disgraced and weakened enough for its territory to be an open target — possibly as a result of their failed **ja'chuq** against Khamlet Senior, alluded to in I 1.)

since brevity is the soul of wit, / and tediousness the limbs and outward flourishes: *lit.* since sharpshooting in a speech acts as the soul's core to wisdom, and boring speeches act merely as the arms and saccharin of knowledge.

the cause of this effect... and the remainder thus: *lit.* And now we must discover what is starting to interfere (**nISchoH**) with his brain. Well, I should rather say "what is confusing (**mISmoH**) his brain." This interfering (**nISbogh**) confusion (**mIS**) must obviously have happened (**qaSnIS**), because something has 'adjusted' (**lIS**) [his brain].

have while she is mine: *lit.* I have (**ghaj**) her while I dominate (**ghatlh**) her — consistent with both Klingon notions of patriarchy, and the Klingon belief that domination is nine tenths of the law.

beautified. In the Terran, 'beautified' is merely affected; in the Klingon, **'IHchu'vaD** (perfectly beautiful) is also ungrammatical (the grammatical form is **'IHqu'vaD** "really beautiful"), prompting Polonyush's condemnation.

You are a fishmonger: *lit.* Do you recognize me, my lord? / Perfectly. Your species (**mut**) is Ferengi. / No, my lord. / Then I commend you for not being selfish (**mut**).

Let her not walk i' the sun: *lit.* [reading out of a book] "If a violent solar wind breeds baby worms in a targ's corpse, because high radiation can revive diminished life signs..." Do you have a daughter? / Yes, my lord. Keep her out of the raining region (**Sep**). Infant initiation calls for celebration, but because your daughter can breed (**Sep**), take my advice.

their faces are wrinkled: *lit.* the foreheads are smooth.

if, like a crab, you could go backwards: *lit.* you could join my young squadron, if you retreated like a cowardly cockroach.

As the indifferent children of the earth: *lit.* the satisfaction of bloodworms in the [blood-soaked] underground of yesterday's battle.

deal justly with me: *lit.* hurl the spear (Klingon slang for 'spell it out!')

What a piece of work is a man!: *lit.* A Klingon is an impressive specimen.

what lenten entertainment the players shall receive from you: *lit.* you'll meet the actors as if they were a bunch of human scientists.

when Roscius was an actor in Rome: *lit.* when the Romulans began occupying Remus...

O Jeptha, judge of Israel: *lit.* Now then, supreme court judge, old man Gowron! (A semi-legendary Klingon judge, and — at least so the official histories claim — distant ancestor of the current head of the Klingon High Council.)

It came to pass, as most like it was: *lit.* The water of the river grew red to him (Klingon proverbial expression for a momentous event.)

your voice...be not cracked within the ring: *lit.* your voice sings like a power generator; I should hope it hasn't been sabotaged!

We'll e'en to't: *lit.* We eat the fire skin (Klingon proverbial expression for hurrying.)

'twas caviare to the general: *lit.* [the citizens] are unwilling to eat todbaj legs on any occasion other than Military Day.

the rugged Pyrrhus... The Klingon original is old-fashioned, like its Terran counterpart, but is based on the old alliterative style. Here follows its literal translation:

Pay'rush of the black body hair seemed like a ball of antimatter...
Pay'rush of the black body hair's vigilant arms
seemed like midnight, for he intended to kill,
while lying in his fate's hull, there to prepare to make war.
The fanatic [Pay'rush] has now violently smeared the stabber's insignia
    onto his black, fierce body.
The leader [Pay'rush] is all red, from his face to his feet.
The blood of family and friends, pressed down
and slowly dried by the bonfire of the buildings,
has splattered all over him. So that bonfire seems to bring,
to the one ready to kill their ruler [Piray'am], the perilous shadow
of a criminal energy being. Bones and bile
are mixed up under his boot spikes, as he burns and hates.
His frenzied eyes are no different to a nova.
Suddenly Pay'rush, the hungry one from the Netherworld,
he who wishes to demolish, seeks out Piray'am,
the old great elder, in order to retaliate.

Soon he finds him.
That opponent [Piray'am] is clumsily striking at soldiers.
Because his hard betlekh disobeys his hand, it seems to idle
as soon as it falls. It seems insubordinate to its seizer's [Piray'am's]
    demanding.
Piray'am and Pay'rush start duelling, so that the dictator [Pay'rush] may
    fight dirtily.
Their battle is unfair. The dark one [Pay'rush] attacks.
His sword misses because he is enraged. But as the excited wind
of his vicious weapon stings him,
the tired great grandsire faints. The city too,
which can do no action, collapses, while a scavenging fire
surrounds its top. It seems to recognize that he will dominate.
As the city fell apart with great noise, it seemed to hypnotize
the ears of the deceiver [Pay'rush]. So the great dagger of his fist,
ready to accelerate onto the white head of the man of dignity,
seemed to refuse to drop, once raised. The implacable one
started to look like a dictator on a scanner. The immobile one was
    beginning not to enact
his anger and his duty.
But often, before the atmosphere becomes violent, the sky
seems to stop its protests. The expanding winds seem to refuse to make
    any sound.
The clouds seem heavy. The land, too, seems to be secretive,
for fear of dying. But soon enough the atmosphere
strikes its rays onto the countryside. It is not reported any differently
    than this.

After the one who charges [Pay'rush] had paused, too, wakening
    vengeance
made him set to work again. While the engineers who built
Kahless' charging shield of victory struck the metal,
they were aggressive enough. But his [Pay'rush's] sword of blood was as
    belligerent as possible,
when it fell onto Piray'am.
All Fate ever wishes to do is sabotage! May the council of the great spirits
round up its powers! May it render obsolete the rods
and the steppers of its great wheel! May they shoot the wheel's middle
out from the engine of Paradise! And when it is taken apart, may the
    Netherworld
swallow that machinery up!

Will someone capable of rescue find the wife of vengeance,
Khe'kuba of the great brows? Her boots absent,
the eye-water confusing her capacity of sight
seemed to threaten the shiny fires, flowing from her cheeks.
She kept vigil everywhere. A belt of crystals
had once appeared on her head. Today it is surrounded
by a cheap cloth. She had also traded her gown.
A mere piece of plastic had to accommodate her white belly,
which had been stretched and worn out to give birth to many warriors
    of honor,
when the abuse caused [her] alarm. This hostage [Khe'kuba] was to be
    pitied.
If anyone caught a glimpse of that panicked one [Khe'kuba], he should
    be belligerent.
"Distressing fate has devised treachery," is what
that person of reason would have to proclaim, in venomous speech.
If the council of the great spirits saw that woman —
when she had verified that Pay'rush's sword was wrecking
the bones of him that made her proud [Piray'am], so that the vulgar one
    [Pay'rush] could play games —
then, as the alarm of her voice, building up, told truth,
if the penalty of a mortal can make the great spirits take notice,
even the great lord of war would be moved to action, and the burning
    great eye of heaven
would have to become viscous.

with flaming top. The Klingon original (**DungDaj DechtaHvIS**) points to a
Sakrejian origin to this poem.

you were better have a bad epitaph than their ill report: *lit.* an illegal Death
Ritual is preferable to their discommendation. The remark is not so sarcastic in the
Klingon as in the English, especially considering the Homeworld's contemporary
outlook on the historical **SonchIy** (Leader's Death Rite).

tweaks me by the nose: *lit.* dammit, who shines my nose? An allusion to the
old Klingon mocking threat, **ghIchwIj DabochmoHchugh**, **ghIchlIj qanob**: If you
shine *my* nose, I'll *give* you your nose.

like John-a-dreams: *lit.* I resemble nothing more than a dreaming Vulcan.
(Possibly alluding to Khamlet's guilt over having stayed too long on Vulcan.)

pigeon-livered: *lit.* I must have the bile of a Betazoid.

Why, what an ass am I: *lit.* I would make the wind respect (me) (alluding to the saying "only a fool expects the wind to respect him").

must like a whore... a scullion! *lit.* I act as a mere Terran, because I lighten my heart into words; and I act like a bartender, babbling out curses — a barmaid! Another disapproving reference to curse-warfare. Some Klingon commentators have suggested that, being out of touch with Klingon culture for so long, Khamlet may carry a distorted idealization of that culture: most Klingons do not regard Klingon bar-culture, including curse-warfare, as inconsistent with the demands of being a warrior.

before mine uncle: *lit.* while my fat uncle is watching.

Act III Scene I

most like a gentleman: *lit.* Actually, he really did act like an honorable warrior.

it doth much content me: *lit.* the plates are full (Klingon proverbial expression for good news.)

sugar o'er / the devil himself. *lit.* We even take evasive actions against Fek'lhr.

To be, or not to be... Klingon does not have an equivalent of the verb "to be." (Although it seems personal pronouns are becoming grammaticalized into copulas, taking on verb suffixes, they cannot bear an existential meaning.) Therefore, the grammar of the Klingon original has been the subject of no little argument, with many scholars arguing for an archaic interpretation of **taH** ('continue' in contemporary High Klingon). The use of the third person as an impersonal is also highly deviant in Klingon literature. Apologists for the theory that Shex'pir originally wrote in Terran rather than Klingon have even gone so far as to claim that these four lines, or at least these three words (**taH pagh taHbe'**) were translated into Klingon by someone other than the person(s) who translated the remainder of the play. These wild theories need not detain us here. The literal translation of the 'disputed' passage is: "It [he?] either continues, or it [he?] doesn't continue. Now, I must consider this sentence [question?]. Is he honorable, when he endures the torpedoes and phasers of aggressive Fate in the brain? Or, when he takes weapons to fight a seeming ocean of trouble, and ends them by fighting them? He sleeps. He dies — he merely dies..."

when givers prove unkind: *lit.* When the giver betrays the receiver. So, I break up the alliance (i.e., our relationship).

My lord?: The Klingon **nuqjatlhneS** is an uneasy — and ungrammatical — mix of politeness (the honorific **—neS** suffix) and the no-nonsense directness of 'Clipped' Klingon (**nuqjatlh**: 'say what?') It speaks volumes about Ovelya's confusion at Khamlet's behaviour.

your honesty should admit no discourse to your beauty. / Could beauty, my lord, have better commerce than with honesty? *lit.* Then your status of being beautiful must be silent (**tam**), for the sake of your woman-honor (**be'batlhvaD**). My lord, can the status of being beautiful replace (**tam**) the tribute of woman-honor (**be'batlh van**)? What is happening here is obscure: it seems Khamlet has some traces of dialect Klingon, in which **D** and **n** sound alike (illustrated much more vividly by the clowns in the gravedigger scene). When he says to Ovelya "**be'batlhvaD**," she probably honestly hears him as saying **"be'batlh van,"** rather than trying to make a pun. Trying to make sense of Khamlet's sentence, she concludes he said: "Your beauty should replace the tribute that is your woman-honor;" in the following lines, Khamlet exploits this misinterpretation, by saying that indeed, "the power of the beautiful can change honor from its prior status into a dishonored prostitute."

nunnery: *lit.* squadron of the celibate. (The closest Klingon equivalent of a monastic order, these were bands of warriors — of either gender — who dedicated their lives to fighting, to the point of refusing to mate.)

O heavenly powers! *lit.* Power of Kahless.

the expectancy and rose of the fair state: *lit.* The fist and certain honor-to-be of the lucky empire.

suck'd the honey of his music vows: *lit.* I have eaten the chocolate of the music of his vows.

like sweet bells jangled: *lit.* like a bagpipe clumsily squeezed.

O woe is me, / to have seen what I have seen, see what I see! *lit.* Misfortune! He is surrendering to a sly disaster. (Klingons often think of illness as a cunning opponent, laying warriors low by trapping them, instead of confronting them with honor.) I have seen the entire genius (**wIgh naQ**) and I am now seeing an omen of evil (**maQmIgh**). Ovelya's attempt at a pun in Polonyush fashion is rather odd here, and she doesn't pull it off as successfully as her father.

to England: *lit.* To Earth. There is no documented instance where Terra paid tribute or ransom to the Klingon Empire; this is probably not a historical reference, although it has endeared the play to many young Klingons.

Act III Scene II

I had as lief the town crier spoke my lines: *lit.* I would prefer my words to be shot from a Federation battleship.

It out-herods Herod: *lit.* He [who does so] is more deserving to resemble Molor than Molor himself.

o'erstep not the modesty of nature: *lit.* in order to resemble the truthful universe, use your attitude control thrusters well.

neither having the accent of Christians...they imitated humanity so abominably: *lit.* they misresembled true Klingons while speaking, and they misresembled true Klingons, or true aliens, or true humanoids while moving; not to insult religion, but I would believe that their clumsy and noisy lives had been formed of dirt apparently misprocessed by incompetent partners of Black Fleet engineers, because [the actors] had so misresembled true people while acting.

if his occulted guilt / do not itself unkennel: *lit.* if his guilty instincts (**DuJ**, which also means "vessel, vehicle, spaceship"), which he has kept cloaked, refuses to appear outside the starbase.

as foul / as Vulcan's stithy: *lit.* as insubordinate as a Bajoran ensign.

of the chameleon's dish: *lit.* I'm like a bug, eating oaths dissolved in atmospheric gases. That couldn't replace a todbaj's meal.

It was a brute part of him to kill so capital a calf there: This is a reference to another of Shex'pir's plays, *yulyuS qaySar*. The pun is very intricate, *lit.* He [**yulyuS qaySar**] stood like a tree. In a district of conflict (**yol yoS**) a tree is a problem (**qay' Sor**).

here's metal more attractive: *lit.* I'm influenced by that very beautiful magnetism.

Do you think I meant country matters?: *lit.* Do you think I intend mating? / I think (**Qub**) nothing, sir. / That idea's good to lie on female legs. / What idea's that, sir? / You defend (**Hub**) nothing. The entire pun here is quite complex. Khamlet puns off Ovelya's line "**pagh vIQub**," ("I think nothing,") by facetiously misinterpreting it for "**pagh vIHub**," ("I defend nothing"). The Klingon word "**pagh**" means "nothing" or "zero," and in the native Klingon numeration system, the symbol for 0 (zero) is:

●

which would represent, for the sake of the pun, the sexual orifice to which Khamlet alludes. Thus: "I think (**Qub**) nothing," misheard as "I defend (**Hub**) nothing (zero/orifice)," i.e., I don't guard the orifice; I'm willing to mate.

let the devil wear black, for I'll have a suit of sables: *lit.* Fek'lhr deserts (**choS**) a happy fate. I'll take off my twilight (**choS**) clothes. Presumably, my mourning clothes of twilight color will be taken off, only to be replaced by those of night, darkening my mood.

he must build churches: *lit.* he must name planets.

the hobby-horse is forgot: *lit.* "Sherman steps on Koloth's name." A reference to a political scandal on Sherman's Planet, where the failed intelligence operation did more to bolster support and recognition for the planetary colonies than for the honor of Captain Koloth.

dumb show: A literal interpretation of the Klingon stage directions here would yield a description of the sadomasochistic interaction between the actors portraying the Emperor and Empress in the play, a not entirely uncommon theatrical technique in Shex'pir's time, often even exceeding the levels of violence that occur among Klingons under ordinary circumstances. It is thus literally: Enter acting Emperor and Empress. They act out their love for one another. They wound one another on the arms with their claws. She kneels to attack between his knees. He pulls her up and bites her neck. She picks him up and throws him to the ground. As soon as she sees that he went to sleep after having been pleased, she exits.

Be not you ashamed to show: *lit.* Will he explain what they were telling? / Yes, they had much to tell, while they were wounding one another. If you're willing to wound, then you'll learn. The one who explains (**QIj**) will recognize your body parts which wound (**QID**) and tell you [what they meant]. Here Ovelya and Khamlet refer to the play, discussed in the previous note. Although there seems to be a different connotation, the Federation translators' interpretation may not have been inappropriate, given the nature of Klingon romantic habits.

Wormwood! *lit.* An omen! (As the Player Queen's casual oath looks like a portent of Ghertlud's involvement in the death of Khamlet Senior.)

But what we do determine oft we break. *lit.* But to cancel our annoying plans, we often conduct diplomacy. (Given the traditional low regard for diplomacy amongst Klingons, this is tantamount to saying: "we equivocate.")

Grief joys, joy grieves, on slender accident. *lit.* The happy becomes depressed, and the depressed becomes happy, all because of nothing more than the dirt under their fingernails.

That even our loves should with our fortunes change; *lit.* our love must change, as soon as our long-lasting fate changes. (Their fate has been long-lasting in granting them their constant love.)

Nor earth to me give food, nor heaven light! / Sport and repose lock from me day and night! / To desperation turn my trust and hope! / An anchor's cheer in prison be my scope! *lit.* May I not obtain food from the earth! May my soul be dark! May my superior always take games and shore leave away from me! May I have only pet-food to look forward to in prison!

Let the galled jade wince; our withers are unwrung: *lit.* We law-abiders cannot be tortured by the mind sifter.

It would cost you a groaning to take off my edge: *lit.* you must give birth if you want to dull my knife. The word "knife" (**taj**), here used in dual metaphor, is presumably symbolic of wit and suggestive of the Klingon male anatomy.

Still better and worse / So you mis-take your husbands: *lit.* the conversation improves (**Dub**) and deteriorates (**Sab**). / A conversation volunteers (**Sap**) a strategy (**Dup**) to convince a woman to marry.

the croaking raven doth bellow for revenge: *lit.* when good revenge is served, the meal's very cold. A deliberate misquote of the famous Klingon proverb **bortaS bIr jablu'DI' reH QaQqu' nay'** ("When cold revenge is served, the meal's very good," i.e., "Revenge is a dish which is best served cold.").

mixture rank: *lit.* graveyard tea.

Gonzago's wife: *lit.* the queen. This absence of an explicit reference to the actor's character has all more impact against Klaw'diyush's conscience. His initial delay in reacting to the contents of the play is simply problematic.

For dost thou know... : *lit.* Brother, you should know this: they removed / Kahless from this empire on purpose. / The emperor was excellent; but he is now succeeded by, / and the empire now ruled by — a weakling. (The word which *would* have rhymed is **toDSaH** — a rather stronger version of "weakling").

your behavior hath struck her into amazement and admiration: *lit.* He makes me shocked (**yay'**) and amazed. / A mother does not have to be amazed at a son's victory (**yay**).

by these pickers and stealers: *lit.* by filling the bile of the enemy in my hands (from an old Klingon proverb). This foreshadowing, prompted by Roshenkh'ratz and Ghildeshten, illustrates that the bile will turn out to be their own, out of Khamlet's 'love' for them.

"while the grass grows": *lit.* "while the quadrotriticale is sufficient." The whole proverb is **yaptaHvIS loSpev, ghung yIH** ("While the quadrotriticale is sufficient, the tribble is hungry.").

why do you go about to recover the wind of me: *lit.* while I'm evading (**jun**) things by myself, why do you want to capture (**jon**) me into interrogation?

though you can fret me, you cannot play upon me: *lit.* you have the control panel (**SeHlaw**) to influence my frequency, but I won't allow you to apparently control (**SeHlaw'**) me.

Nero: *lit.* Molor (the cruel tyrant overthrown by Kahless the Unforgettable.)

Act III Scene III

like a gulf: *lit.* like a black hole.

never alone / did the king sigh, but with a general groan: *lit.* So the king never gripes alone. When someone important gets depressed, / the army must soon start complaining too, and the rough warrior must surrender.

arras: *lit.* large visual display (monitor).

'tis not so above: *lit.* But it seems no one can compromise with Fek'lhr.

Now might I do it pat: *lit.* the hoop is moving (Klingon proverbial expression for having to act before it is too late.)

and so 'a goes to heaven: *lit.* Let him fight in the Black Fleet. As in the Terran version, Khamlet realizes that what he has just said, intended to mean "let him die," may actually come true literally, as Klaw'diyush escapes punishment in the Netherworld.

'A took my father grossly... 'tis heavy with him: *lit.* When he surprised my father to kill him, my father was fat, and unready to fight. He could not obtain the opportunity to regret the crimes he had sinned in. And no warrior shouted over his corpse. How the soldiers of the Black Fleet accepted him when he arrived — it seems only they would know. But considering the kind of ethics we believe in, and how we guess the Black Fleet to be, the situation would quake (be perilous) for him.

And how his audit stands who knows save heaven: *lit.* Only the Black Fleet troops know the status of his travel permit.

in his rage; *lit.* when he is compassionate (an emotion much less appropriate to a candidate for the Black Fleet than rage).

a-swearing: *lit.* while conducting diplomacy. Again, this is something the Black Fleet would be far likelier to frown upon, although there was some ambivalence about diplomats in Klingon culture, and Ovelya actually praises Khamlet as a diplomat in III 2; presumably, diplomacy is a plausible explanation for his studying on Vulcan. Several Klingon commentators have pointed out that the differences in ethics and morality between the more idealistic Khamlets (Junior and Senior) Vortibrash Senior, Layertesh, and Khorey'sho, on the one hand, and the more pragmatic and political Klaw'diyush, Polonyush, and Vortibrash Junior, on the other clearly delineate changes in Klingon society.

Act III Scene IV

a glass / where you may see the inmost part of you: *lit.* In that scanner, you will be able to see the tendons (muscles) of your heart. (Ghertlud understandably takes this to be a threat against the integrity of her chest muscles.)

thou find'st to be too busy is some danger: *lit.* Now you find that knowing secret information can be unfortunate. (An old Klingon proverb.)

takes off the rose / From the fair forehead of an innocent love / And sets a blister there: *lit.* As it removes the rough bones from the innocent beautiful forehead of the beloved, the emblem of discommendation replaces them.

a rhapsody of words: *lit.* a Ferengi manuscript. (Ferengi literature is notorious for being of the same quality as their advertising.)

Hyperion's curls; the front of Jove himself: *lit.* The forehead of Kahless; the hair of Gorkon (not the Chancellor who initiated peace with the Federation, but one of his legendary forebearers.)

Here is your husband: *lit.* this specimen is now your husband.

nasty sty: *lit.* targs' toilet.

twentieth part the tithe: *lit.* half a half a percent (0.25%; the quantity in the Terran is 0.5%).

A king of shreds and patches: *lit.* he acts as nothing more than the "king" of Earth. (Klingons never made much sense of Terran representative democracy.)

I must be cruel, only to be kind: *lit.* I threaten (**buQ**) you, only to help (**boQ**) you.

pinch wanton... reechy kisses: *lit.* [Let him] strike your cheek to make you willing to mate. And, while he sloppily bites your lip...

whom I will trust as I will adders fang'd: *lit.* if I trust them, then I'll trust a Ferengi too.

to draw toward an end with you: *lit.* All Klingons hope to die on carrying out their duty (Modified Klingon proverb.)

Act IV Scene I

like some ore among a mineral of metals base: *lit.* he is like latinum amongst insignificant minerals.

with all our majesty and skill: *lit.* my authority must be as skillful as an eyebrow (old Klingon simile.)

As level as the cannon to his blank: *lit.* it is like a klevjax (spear thrown with a hook as an aid.)

Act IV Scene II

first mouthed, to be last swallowed: *lit.* now he sympathizes (**vup**), but later he will swallow (**ghup**).

the King is not with the body: A play on the verb form **tlhejta'be'** ("he has not accompanied [the corpse]."). Alternatively, **tlhej ta'be'** ("The Empress does accompany it.").

to be demanded of a sponge: *lit.* when the pneumatic hypo interrogates, how must the imperial son reply?

The King is a thing...Of nothing. Bring me to him: *lit.* the Emperor's spirit is an inanimate object. Bring me to it. Khamlet's insult is based on the reference of the spirit (**qa'**) with the pronoun (**'oH**) "it;" **qa'** is normally referred to in Klingon by the sentient pronoun (**ghaH**) "he/she."

Hide fox, and all after: *lit.* Your face looks like a collapsed star. A phrase used to initiate a game of Curse Warfare.

Act IV Scene III

diseases desperate grown... or not at all: *lit.* when the disease has grown significantly, and become toxic, then in order to cure it, the medicine must be toxic too. If it is not toxic, it will never cure it.

A certain convocation of politic worms are e'en at him: *lit.* bug troops which patrol the underground empire are occupying him.

Your worm is your only emperor for diet: *lit.* Only bug justice may dominate in a healthy empire.

Where is Polonius? / In heaven; send hither to see: if your messenger find him not there, seek him i' the other place yourself: *lit.* where is Polonyush? / In Paradise. Send something there to find him. If your probe doesn't find him there, then kill yourself (i.e., go to great lengths) to find him on your own. The phrase "**yIHoH'egh**" ("kill yourself") is being used figuratively. But if taken literally, Khamlet implies that since Polonyush is not to be found in Paradise, the Emperor should stop at nothing, even suicide, to find him in the only other obvious place. In Klingon ideology, suicide, or self-condemnation is an act whose result is expulsion into the Netherworld, the polar opposite of Paradise.

you shall nose him: *lit.* he will certainly strike your nostrils.

the bark is ready and the wind at help: *lit.* your shuttlecraft is ready to go, and the warp drive ready to accommodate you.

I see a cherub that sees them: *lit.* I access them via supernatural espionage.

Act IV Scene IV

should it be sold in fee: *lit.* even if a Ferengi was bartering for it on their behalf.

Yes, it is already garrisoned: *lit.* Not so. They have prepared a force field on it.

this straw: *lit.* the "issue" of this seeming paper-clip.

Makes mouths at the invisible event: *lit.* He shows his face to events he has not yet seen. The phrase 'I show my face' is the Klingon ritual challenge to a duel.

Even for an egg-shell: *lit.* Hell, just for a damned ponytail-holder!

quarrel in a straw: *lit.* he must be ready to fight even just because a glass has broken.

Act IV Scene V

though nothing sure, yet much unhappily: *lit.* they have no certainty (**DIch**), but they do have blame (**pIch**); and for that blame they act clumsily and, potentially, dangerously.

sandal shoon: *lit.* metal boots.

He is dead... : *lit.* He is dead and gone, sir [madam] / He is dead and gone. / The spirit now flees from his body. / He fights in the Black Fleet.

larded all with sweet flowers...: *lit:* he is surrounded by the insignia of a true warrior. / But no lip cried out next to his grave, / when Death irrevocably struck him.

God 'ild you: *lit.* may Kahless salute you.

They say the owl was a baker's daughter: *lit.* It is told that the daughter of the soldier of conflict became a pipius. An allusion to a story stemming from the era of the power struggle between Molor and Kahless.

God be at your table: *lit.* may Kahless promote you.

Tomorrow is Saint Valentine's day... : *lit.* Today is Lovers' Day. Hello! [What do you want?] / Listen: I'm coming to you while the morning is early. And I'm waiting by your window, / so that we may soon honorably love each other. / So the man got up, and stooped to the door. / He opened it before he put his clothes on. / The woman entered. The woman gained pleasure. And she threw away her maiden-honor. / It is known that the man soon abandoned the woman. / God damn! You betrayed me. Why do you punish me? / God damn! Have the decency [care enough] to be ashamed! / Young men are often prepared to deceive, in order to mate. / And they certainly have the blame. / The woman said: Before you mated with me, you verified to me / that you would never prevent me from marrying you. / True; but I confess: while I was promising you this, / you had not yet approached me to mate.

without an oath, I'll make an end on't: *lit.* I would not insult you, but pour the cold water into someone else's glass. Ovel'ya conflates two Klingon sayings, "pour the bloodwine into someone else's glass" ('tell someone who cares'), and "the glass contains water" ('you are utterly wrong').

will nothing stick our person to arraign: *lit.* and they are not afraid to take away the sash (Klingon proverbial expression for wounding one's pride.)

Laertes shall be king, Laertes King! *lit.* Layertesh, son of Polonyush, will become the king.

so giant-like: *lit.* so much like a space station.

profoundest pit: *lit.* a black hole.

Let come what comes: *lit.* The sword is in the water (Klingon proverbial expression, equivalent to "there is no turning back now.").

pelican: *lit.* Kahless' mother — who, like the pelican of mediaeval Terran legend, is said to have fed her child with her own blood.

O rose of May: *lit.* O Emblem that brings praise to the empire!

It is the false steward, that stole his master's daughter: *lit.* the corrupted ensign tempted the captain's daughter. This is another allusion to a story which describes how corruption and dishonor destroyed Mogh's army from within.

There is rosemary... And there is pansies: *lit.* I give you tea. It represents certainty. Please, have certainty, love. I also give you radan. It represents judgment... I give you deodorant, and gunpowder too. I give you blood, and I give myself some blood also. We could call it Warrior's Fuel of Military Day... I give you theragen. I was also going to give you topaline, but it dissolved when my father died.

And of all Christian souls, I pray God. God be wi' ye: *lit.* having all warriors' throats shout, I ask of Kahless. May you encounter Kahless.

Act IV Scene VI

God bless you sir. / Let him bless thee too. / He shall, sir, an't please him: *lit.* May Kahless strengthen you. / May he strengthen you too. / He certainly strengthens me, as long as the empire continues. One indication of the subtly colloquial style in which this soldier speaks is his use of the word "**taHvIS**" ("while it continues"). The standard would be "**taHtaHvIS.**" The colloquialism arises from the fact that the suffix **–vIS** ("while") is always used with the suffix **–taH** ("continuously"). But here the verb itself, "**taH**" ("continue") is identical to the mandatory **–taH** suffix, so the soldier hypercorrectly assumes that the verb "**taH**" can take its place.

pirate: *lit.* criminal merchant

Finding ourselves too slow of sail: *lit.* because our thrusters were insufficient to escape. The letter describes a battle in deep space. Terrorists and space pirates were indeed common around the Imperial–Federation Neutral Zone, and the passage through it was dangerous for unarmed vessels.

and in the grapple: *lit.* when the airlock connected

thieves of mercy: *lit.* honest rebels.

with as much speed as thou wouldest fly death: *lit.* engage the apparent warp drive of a Black Fleet command ship.

too light for the bore of the matter: *lit.* this slingshot is not enough to fire the ammunition of my information.

Act IV Scene VII

work like the spring that turneth wood to stone, convert his gyves to graces: *lit.* they behave as matter transtators [apparatus similar to Federation replicators]. As soon as they energize fetters, insignia of honor materialize.

so that my arrows... where I had aimed them: *lit.* So, as soon as my phaser had sighted him, its rays would have been too weak for the black hole of the noise [strength in voice] of the crowd. And they [the rays] would return to my phaser rifle, my marksmanship having failed.

Normandy: *lit.* Remus.

ride: the Klingon word **llgh** has been extended from its original meaning, and also refers to the acrobatic piloting so beloved of young Klingons like Layertesh — and, for that matter, of Romulans, probably under Klingon influence.

had witchcraft in't: *lit.* he seemed to control spirits.

He grew unto his seat: *lit.* He seemed to become the engine of that aggressive machinery [his fighter craft].

that I, in forgery of shapes and tricks, / come short of what he did: *lit.* So even if I turned into a human, in order to describe perfectly how he maneuvered and dodged, my task would fail.

But to the quick o' th' ulcer: *lit.* But let me stab the important part.

Act V Scene I

Is she to be buried in Christian burial that willfully seeks her own salvation: *lit.* is the funeral procedure to be honored if she searches for a shortcut into the Black Fleet?

The crowner: *lit.* the Presiding Death Officer (**Heghutlh'a'**) from a very peculiar dialect found mainly in the lower levels of the Klingon social strata. Such can be seen in their abbreviation of "**Hegh'utlh**" by "**Heghutlh**." The main characteristic of this dialect is hypernasalization, i.e., all **b** are spoken as **M** and all **D** as **N**. But the dialect also has many colloquialisms and localisms difficult to put into Terran terms.

se offendendo: *lit.* it certainly happened "In Self Offense," a slip for "In Self Defense," a legal term taken from Federation Standard, which has become the language of many upper level professions in Klingon society. Here the gravediggers have trouble with the language, since their families would not have been able to afford to send them to one of the exclusive Imperial military academies, where Federation Standard would be a requirement for cadets.

argal, she drowned herself wittingly: *lit.* "tlherevore," she flooded herself on purpose. The use of this corruption of "therefore" represents another instance of the gravediggers difficulty with Federation Standard.

will he, nill he: *lit.* Can either keep it or discard it—i.e. it does not matter.

Why, there thou say'st: *lit.* You sit in a chair—the Klingon proverbial expression for "it is obvious," to which the 'dirter' judiciously adds "obviously."

They hold up Adam's profession... Could he dig without arms? The pun here occurs later in the Klingon. Thus, *lit.* When the enemy contains (**Sev**) them, the Fleet's maneuvers (**tuH**) escape and re-dominate. / But they aren't ashamed (**tuH**) of their bandages (**Sev**).

ditchers: *lit.* "Dirters" (**lamwI'**) which is a slang term for those whose job is equivalent to that of a ditchdigger.

If thou answerest me not to the purpose, confess thyself / Go to: *lit.* I'll cause you to hear a second question, and if it connects to nonsense in your ears, then the night has no stars. / I am ready to light it up. This is a reference to the popular secrecy proverb "**Hov ghajbe'bogh ram rur pegh ghajbe'bogh jaj**" ("A day without secrets is like a night without stars.").

What is he that builds stronger than either the mason, the shipwright, or the carpenter / The gallows-maker: *lit.* which of these is the most useful? the engineer, the communications officer, or the technician? / A tribble merchant. He is useful to regulate the tribble population... / He buys (**je'**) hungry tribbles. If you don't feed (**je'**) an entity (**Nol**), you'll observe a funeral (**nol**). You can't trade (**mech**) tribbles for food. Therefore, you'll suffer (**Mech**) from a large tribble population. These dialectal puns are derived from the standard "**Dol**" and "**nol**" ("entity" and "funeral," respectively), as well as "**bech**" and "**mech**" ("trade" and "suffer," respectively), sounding virtually identical in the dialect.

tell me that and unyoke: *lit.* finish telling me and dock.

Cudgel thy brains no more about it: *lit.* Don't override your brain.

get thee to Yaughan. Fetch me a stoup of liquor: *lit.* Go to the ground inhabitant (**yavngan**). Tell him to boil some worm blood for me.

The hand of little employment hath the daintier sense: *lit.* To be very careful, his digging instincts take over control. / Absolutely correct. Clumsy ability substituted for instinct must be very careful.

How the knave jowls it to the ground, as if 'twere Cain's jawbone, that did the first murder: *lit.* damn, the idiot is so rude (**Doch**), when he causes the thing (**Doch**) to fall (**pum**), as if he were accusing (**pum**) the ruins of Molor.

This might be the pate of a politician, which this ass now o'erreaches; one that would circumvent God, might it not?: *lit.* perhaps it is the brain-holster [slang for "skull"] of a mastermind criminal that the puny fool now holds prisoner. Such a criminal might have evaded the High Council, isn't that so?

My Lady Worm's: *lit.* the hungry admiral of the cootie fleet is ready to chew on him.

chapless: *lit.* the chin collapses.

Here's fine revolution, if we had the trick to see't: *lit.* here it is observed that the phasers of fate aim differently, if we could observe fate's weapons which serve such good revenge. A reference to the proverb "Revenge is a dish which is best served cold."

sconce: *lit.* spine-helm, slang for "head."

Is this the fine of his fines...to have his fine pate full of fine dirt: *lit.* he searches (**nej**) for his authority to issue loans (**noj**), because he dreams (**naj**) that it leaked (**nIj**) from his mouth (**nuj**) into the dirt.

no more...than the length and width of a pair of indentures: *lit.* because he is harmless when his negotiating and bargaining words bite. It has been argued by some provincial Terran literary scholars whether "indentures" was intended as "contract" or "bridgework." The Klingon version makes this clear. In Klingon business relations, the oral verification of the transactor is highly preferable over the standard business record, contrary to Terran preferences. This is why many dealings between Terrans and Klingons end in failure. Cf., next note.

Is not parchment made of sheepskins? / Ay, my lord, and calveskins too. / They are sheeps and calves that seek out assurance in that: *lit.* Business is transacted using Terran computers, right? / Yes, sir, and Ferengi computers too. / The people who trust a business record to pay for something have the honor of Terrans and Ferengi.

I think it be thine indeed, for thou liest in it: *lit.* Who owns this grave? / I do, sir. / You certainly do, because it is a little refuge (**lulIghHom**) for you. / No, it's a hole (**NIS**). It can't give a ride (**lulIgh**) to bones (**Hom**). I own it but I do not sit (**Ma'**) in it. / You interfere (**nIS**) with me, because you refuse to confess (**DIS**) that it accommodates (**ma'**) you. You can't stand there, so you'll fall (**pum**). / Your accusation (**pum**) doesn't stand. You evade (**jun**) me but you're not innocent (**chun**).

How absolute the knave is. We must speak by the card or equivocation will undo us: *lit.* the silly idiot's interpretations go so parallel to the word. We must aim perfectly in hurling our speech (alluding to the expression 'to aim a spear' meaning 'to spell out'), otherwise our intermixing hailing frequency codes will disable our helms.

he galls his kibe: *lit.* he smears toenail dirt onto the ankle.

Upon what ground / Why, here in Denmark: *lit.* What is the reason (**meq**)? / I'm the only crew (**Meq**) in this graveyard here on Kronos.

will keep out water a great while: *lit.* for twelve days and twelve nights: a Klingon expression for a long time—though clearly not as long as the dirter should have invoked here.

whoreson fellow: *lit.* smooth forehead person. A term of abuse among Klingons, deriving from a popular insult employed often in the game of Curse Warfare, "**Hab SoSlI' Quch**" ("Your mother has a smooth forehead.").

A pestilence on him for a mad rogue: *lit.* may vicious bugs chew on him.

flagon of Rhenish: *lit.* pitcher of boiling worm wine.

those lips that I have kissed: *lit.* the chin which I have bitten.

let her paint an inch thick: *lit.* even if she underwent a thousand cosmetic surgeries.

Why may not the imagination trace the noble dust of Alexander till he find it stopping a bunghole: *lit.* couldn't the dreaming mind track down a little dirt from Kahless's wonderful corpse to find it plugging up a vatof liquor?

Imperious Caesar, dead and turned to clay: *lit.* As soon as Kahless turned into a corpse (**lom**), the emperor also turned into dirt (**lam**).

The corse they follow did with desperate hand /fordo it own life: *lit.* the hand of that corpse they follow seems to have been dishonored, because it cut off its own life, before a reason of honor made it necessary.

till the last trumpet: *lit.* before the Boss of the Netherworld (Fek'lhr) court-martialled her.

yet here she is allow'd her virgin rites: *lit.* but now it has been permitted that weapons are borne for her. (i.e., she has had an armed escort.)

to sing a requiem and such rest to her / as to peace-parted souls: *lit.* if we screamed over her eyes, and if she followed warriors who died violently, into the Black Fleet.

Pelion: *lit.* Snowmother, one of the tallest mountains on Kronos.

Olympus: *lit.* Great Spirit-Mountain, the tallest mountain on Kronos, and the focus of primitive Klingon spirit-worship.

Woo't drink up eisel? Eat a crocodile? *lit.* Will you drink an antimatter solution? Will you eat a mugato?

make Ossa like a wart: *lit.* Let the great Rainmother (another of Kronos' tallest mountains) resemble a mere Er's nose. (An Er is a Klingon animal.)

Act V Scene II

No, not to stay the grinding of the axe: *lit.* No. Let them not even quickly energize the agonizer.

like the palm: *lit.* So that our alliance may be as strong as blood, and so that the sash of dignity worn by peace may remain hard, and so that no trifle may ever annoy the friends that we have become.

and many such-like as's of great charge: *lit.* and, having named many other "in order to"'s (**-meH**; **meH** also means "ship bridge") to navigate his ship (metaphorically, his task).

stand me now upon: *lit.* The door is locked (cf. English "the die is cast").

Thrown out his angle for my proper life: *lit.* he was prepared to terminate my life while refusing to show his face. Allusion to the Klingon proverb "the Klingon who kills without showing his face has no honour."

It must be shortly known to him... / It will be short; the interim is mine: *lit.* He will soon know... / So, he has control of the "soon." But I have control of the "not yet" ("until then").

for by the image of my cause I see / the portraiture of his: *lit.* when I look carefully at the head of my quest, / it seems I can make out the helmet of his quest, too.

Your lordship is right welcome back to Denmark: *lit.* May we celebrate your Honor's again-being on Kronos. The young servant Oshrik here is the archetype of comic relief. His language, in addition to being laced with Federation buzzwords and catchphrases, is highly marked with unnecessary nominalizations, nonstandardized compounding, and heavily diluted sentences. This form is especially characteristic of the language spoken among a group of young, eager, upwardly-mobile Klingons, and commonly heard, it is said, in the officer's mess hall of the Imperial Academy. The portrayal of Oshrik's speech parodies the heavy influence of Federation Standard throughout the Klingon political spectrum. Here, however, fondness for the Federation Standard style has turned even this cadet's **tlhIngan Hol** into a vague, wordy, opaque corruption.

great showing: *lit.* he skillfully butts heads with Klingon warriors.

to speak feelingly of him: *lit.* passionately, in order to present you my great "critique" of him. As mentioned above, the markedly corrupted style is drenched with Federation vocabulary. Such, for the most part, may be likened to the prolific borrowings into English from the Latin-based languages during the late Renaissance, except that they were not nearly as extensive.

his definement suffers no perdition in you: *lit.* you do not unweaken his thorough description's words, but it is not definitely sufficient that we categorize all his honor-statuses with the fierce commendments of an accidental truth-avoider. Khamlet's appropriately affected rebuttal of Oshrik's round-about flattery of Layertesh only vaguely reflects the traditional "mess hall" dialect, but nonetheless serves to convey the proper contempt for such euphemism.

his umbrage, nothing more: *lit.* while his commendment is merely truth-told, his greatly definite honorableness's light can be "transmitted" by only the photons which run back from his rough face. And the mere shadow can be mis-aimed at by a rider on this photon river, or a resemble-attempter. In continuing the mockery of the corrupted form, Khamlet's facetious use of the common Federation verb "transmitted" is intensified by its accentuation: "**tranSmI'.**"

concernancy: "**Hechghach**" ("intendation"). The nominalization of "**Hech**" ("intend") is not only unnecessary, being better expressed as "**vIqelmeH chay' jIHech,**" but it is also ungrammatical. Ordinarily **–ghach** ("-tion, -ness") should follow a verbal infix (e.g., "**HechtaHghach**").

rapier and dagger: *lit.* Kutluch and sword.

he has imponed...six French rapiers and poniards: *lit.* the emperor gambles six Birds of Prey, and for him [Layertesh] is willing to dis-acquire six Romulan battle arrays and war machinery.

Three of the carriages, in faith, are very dear to fancy: *lit.* and "I'll be damned," three [of the] protection-systems are definitely qualified to be admired. The high esteem Klingons hold for their native curses — in fact, to the point that they consider it a "fine art" — seems to be of no significance. Doubly absurd is the fact that this remark does not even conform to the Federation ethical standard for swearing.

that's the French bet against the Danish: *lit.* they take the chance that the

Romulan resources compete with those of the Klingons. Likening the bet to the frequent arms races between the two adjacent empires effectively displays the distaste for the overgrown showmanship that Klaw'diyush and Layertesh are putting up.

he hath laid on twelve for nine: *lit.* [Layertesh] is more red to play twelve times than the emperor is to gamble nine times. The wordplay here on **SuD** "gamble/green" with **Doq** "red" probably assumes "more red" > "bloodier" > "suffers more," viz. Layertesh suffers more by playing than Klaw'diyush does by gambling.

with a shell on his head: *lit.* the ugly mugato flees, with a forehead shield teetering on his head.

as you are a gentleman: *lit.* as you are prepared to resemble an ax blade (the proverbial Klingon embodiment of honesty.)

I'll be your foil, Laertes: *lit.* I will show you the itinerary (**jey**) of your sword, for you to defeat (**jey**) me, Layertesh. (Presumably, "I will show you where to move your sword, to defeat me, through my incompetence in fencing.")

you do but dally: *lit.* you seem to be yawning (presumably: at my incompetence.)

like a star i' the darkest night, strike fiery off indeed: *lit.* bright as the Torch of G'boj: it is so excellent, it will shine. The Klingon for 'shine' also has the connotations of flattery, to which Layertesh takes offence.

I am more an antique Roman than a Dane: *lit.* I refuse to be a Klingon. I am prepared to act like a Romulan (whose rules on suicide were laxer than those for Klingons.)

and flights of angels sing thee to thy rest: *lit.* and may ships of the Black Fleet escort you to rest.

Appendix II: Notes on the Scansion of *Khamlet*

The verse of *Khamlet* — like that of the Terran version — is written in iambic pentameter, although the Klingon metre allows more freedom in movement of stresses than does the Terran metre. The basic pattern is five iambic feet (weak-strong), with an optional verse-final unstressed syllable. Thus:

$$\breve{}\,/\quad \breve{}\,/\quad \breve{}\,/\quad \breve{}\,/\quad \breve{}\,/$$

bIjatlh 'e' mev! peqIm! DaH cholqa' bIH!
Peace, break thee off; look, where it comes again!

$$\breve{}\,/\quad \breve{}\,/\quad \breve{}\,/\quad \breve{}\,/\quad \breve{}\,/\,\breve{}$$

'elbe'meH lutmaj, teS Surchem DarIHlaw'.
your ears / That are so fortified against our story

Strong syllables can be unstressed; in fact, it is very rare, in both English and Klingon pentameter, for all five strong syllables to be stressed. Thus:

$$\breve{}\,/\quad \breve{}\,/\quad \breve{}\,/\quad \breve{}\quad \breve{}\,/$$

vItlhejmoHpu'. vaj cholqa'chugh HoSDo'Hey,
Therefore I have entreated him along... That if again this apparition come

And, as in the Terran verse, the initial foot can be reversed into a trochee (strong-weak). Thus:

$$/\;\breve{}\quad \breve{}\,/\quad \breve{}\,/\quad \breve{}\,\breve{}\,/\,\breve{}$$

taH pagh taHbe'. DaH mu'tlheghvam vIqelnIS.
To be or not to be; that is the question.

Other feet in the verse can also be reversed; the most usual instance of this is for the two first feet to be reversed:

$$/\;\breve{}\,/\quad \breve{}\;\breve{}/\quad \breve{}\;\breve{}\;\breve{}\,/\,\breve{}$$

ta' vIqelmeH jI'IQba' 'ej jIvalba',
That we with wisest sorrow think on him

Furthermore, because of the monosyllabic nature of "**Quch**" Klingon, spondees (strong-strong feet) are more frequent in Klingon verse than in Terran:

$$\breve{}\,/\quad \breve{}\,/\quad \breve{}\,/\quad \breve{}\,/\;/\quad /\;\breve{}$$

wa' porgh lujeSchu'lI' qar'a' tIq, yab je.
The head is not more native to the heart

Readers who wish to declaim *Khamlet* correctly should be aware that the notes on stress in Okrand (2292), while accurate, are not always explicit. Therefore, the following brief guide may be of some help:

Nouns are stressed on the final syllable of the stem: **ghóp** *hand*, **puyjáq** *nova*, **bortáS** *revenge*. Any suffixes added on to the stem are not stressed: **puyjáqvam** *this nova*, **bortáSmey** *revenges*.

However, if any syllable in a noun, whether in the stem or in a suffix, ends in a glottal stop, it is stressed instead of the stem's final syllable. Thus: **bó'DIj** *court*, **ghopDú'** *hands*, **puyjaqvó'** *from the nova*. Adjacent syllables ending in glottal stops receive equal stress: **chú'wí'** *trigger*, although Klingon verse tends to stress the latter. Note that nouns derived from verbs are considered nouns: **vúm** *to work*, **vumwí'** *worker*, **vumtaHghách** *working*, **vumpú'ghach** *a bout of work*.

Verbs are likewise stressed on the final syllable of the stem: **Dál** *to be boring*, **ghIpDíj** *to court-martial*. Unlike with nouns, if the first suffix after the verb ends in a glottal stop, the suffix is *not* stressed. Thus the verb *she has been an alien* is **nóvpu'**, while the noun *aliens* is **novpú'**. If the suffix ending in a glottal stop is *other* than the first, then both it and the final syllable of the verb are stressed: **mughIpDíjchohDí'** *when she started court-martialling me*, **HóH'eghrupmó'** *because he was ready to suicide*.

Semantically important suffixes can end up stressed instead of the verb stem. In practice in Klingon metre (which systematises this tendency) negative and interrogative suffixes are *always* stressed: **jIDalbé'** *I am not boring*, **bImatlhHá'** *you are disloyal*, **luDelQó'** *they refuse to describe it*, **chol'á'** *is he coming?* Note that adjectival verbs are considered verbs: **'útlh mátlhqu'** *a truly loyal officer*. There are often cases where monosyllabic verbs and nouns are juxtaposed. In this text, adjectival verbs and subject nouns tend to be stressed more strongly, following an iambic pattern. Thus, **'utlh mátlh** *a loyal officer*, **matlh 'útlh** *the officer is loyal*.

Appendix III: Interplanetary Literature 759—The Klingon Bard

Starfleet Academy, Spring Semester, 2377

Even with the unprecedented degree of openness and exchange we currently enjoy with the Klingon Empire it is not difficult to find self-appointed authorities eager to deny what is as apparent as starlight or gravity, death or memory. They would have you believe that the phrase "Klingon literature" is an oxymoron of the highest order. Ignore these so-called authorities. *Hamlet* is a Klingon play, and this simple fact cannot be disputed. The sensibility, the conflict, the parallel complexities and simplicities, the very subject matter itself, all these scream out with the very nature of the Klingon heart and mind and soul.

If we are to believe the propaganda put forth by the Bureau of External Relations on Kronos, generations of Federation literary scholars from dozens of Terrestrial nations for centuries have generated libraries of criticism, commentary, and analysis on the plays of one William Shakespeare, a human. Innumerable companies of human actors have trod the boards and spoken the lines of these plays. Endless human school children have been required to memorize and present on command one or another soliloquy, like trained animals performing at an imperial festival.

You can disregard this viewpoint, but you do so at your own peril. Whether their claim is true or not, the Klingons certainly believe it. And it should be noted that the Federation's own leaders have not tried very hard to dissuade them. Rather they have allowed the allegation to remain relatively unchallenged, even as they continue the practice of teaching Shakespeare's life and work as part of Terran history. How then are you to juxtapose these conflicting points of view?

As students of this Academy, you must understand the magnitude of respect the Federation earns by its nonresponse. The Klingons have a word for it, **butlh**. We might translate this term as "guile," or perhaps more connotatively and colloquially as "chutzpah" (cf. *A Compendium of Colorful Federation Expressions*, Seqram, 2312). The Klingons appreciate guile. They praise it and almost revere it. The Federation's casual insistence that Shakespeare's plays are the product of a pre-Atomic Age Terran is so brass, so bold, so immense, as to overwhelm most Klingons. That, gentlebeings, is guile.

And yet, understanding the Klingon appreciation for guile, the question you need to ask is, ironically, whether they protest too much. Could their accusation of Federation duplicity actually be a blustery façade masking their own false literary construct? That would be guile indeed. A defensive Federation citizen might well turn the accusation around and suggest that the entire notion of Shakespeare as a Klingon is preposterous, that it is a Klingon lie, not one of Federation origin. Both sides have compiled vast collections of evidence, but such evidence is meaningless when the basic charge concerns just such fraudulent documentation. Stalemate? Perhaps not.

Elaborate and careful research performed by leading experts in the field of xenopsychology here at Starfleet Academy, at the Center for Inter-Alliance Study on Khitomer, and at the Progressive Institute of Organia, have yielded vital insights into Klingon philosophy and political science. These scholars note that such a prolonged campaign of deception, of elaborate intellectual ruses and literary machinations as would be necessary for this "Shakespearean ruse" is simply not the Klingon way. Indeed, upon final reflection the idea seems laughable, utterly inconceivable. The sheer and overwhelming passivity of such galactic disinformation would seem more apt to push the Klingon Empire to collective suicide rather than sustain such an effort. Irony again, when we consider the Klingon interpretation of *Hamlet* and the dire warning of the play's conclusion for their empire.

And now, a new question: should we consider the Klingon message of *Hamlet* as an instruction about our own Federation? What do we make of recent rumor and speculation concerning the existence of a clandestine agency operating within the heart of the Federation? If this "Section 31" exists, and is subject to no law and guided only by its own perception of what is right and good for the Federation, could centuries of Terran history be rewritten? Could the Federation's historical claim to Shakespeare be part of an elaborate ploy to confuse and deceive the Klingon people? Or more, is it an attempt to deny the natural majesty and complexity of Klingon culture, and to continue to ignorantly present a diverse alien empire as having a single face?

The malaise described by the Klingon *Hamlet* creates a grim and foreboding image, and one which we are not likely to solve any time soon. More than just dealing with a play of fiction, we find ourselves entrenched in meta-fiction. And the compelling question for us is not who is the author of the play, Klingon or human, but rather who is the author of the fiction surrounding the fiction and what is our role in it? To paraphrase Shakespeare, if all the galaxy's a stage, where is our entrance, and where, ultimately, our exit?

Appendix IV: Additional Vocabulary

The primary source for the Klingon in this work was of course Dr. Marc Okrand's *The Klingon Dictionary*. As more varied and detailed information regarding Klingon culture and linguistics came to light, Okrand released a second volume, *Klingon for the Galactic Traveler*. We have drawn on this latter book to produce this updated edition, as well as on other sources in which Okrand has published findings of his conversations and research with Maltz, his Klingon linguistic informant. Words taken from these additional sources are provided below as an aid to those Klingon scholars who might not otherwise be aware of their existence.

maQmIgh *dark omen, sign of evil coming* (n) [from **veS QonoS**, listed in *HolQeD*, Vol 1, No. 3]

naHjej *thistle* (n) [*KGT* p88]

nga'chuq *sex* (i.e., perform sex; always subject) [from **veS QonoS**, listed in *HolQeD*, Vol 1, No. 3. Note: it is unclear what part of speech this may be, though it is probably a verb and "always subject" probably refers to the concept that all involved parties collectively make the subject of this verb.]

ngIj *be rowdy, unruly* (n) [*KGT* p150]

qen *recently, a short time ago* (adv) [online newsgroup 2/3/99]

tatlh *return* (v), in the sense of returning a thing to its origin or source. [online newsgroup 7/19/99]

vIq *battle, combat* (abstract) (n) [*KGT* p47]

An ongoing list of canonical Klingon from secondary sources is maintained by Will Martin of the Klingon Language Institute, and is available at http://www.kli.org/kli/newwords.html on the KLI website.

Printed in the United States
By Bookmasters